MURDER ON THE HALF SHELF

Lorna Barrett

BERKLEY PRIME CRIME, NEW YORK

THE BERKLEY PUBLISHING GROUP
Published by the Penguin Group
Penguin Group (USA) Inc.
375 Hudson Street, New York, New York 10014, USA

USA | Canada | UK | Ireland | Australia | New Zealand | India | South Africa | China

Penguin Books Ltd., Registered Offices: 80 Strand, London WC2R 0RL, England
For more information about the Penguin Group, visit penguin.com.

MURDER ON THE HALF SHELF

A Berkley Prime Crime Book / published by arrangement with the author

Berkley Prime Crime Books are published by The Berkley Publishing Group.
BERKLEY® PRIME CRIME and the PRIME CRIME logo are trademarks
of Penguin Group (USA) Inc.

For information, address: The Berkley Publishing Group,
a division of Penguin Group (USA) Inc.,
375 Hudson Street, New York, New York 10014.

ISBN: 978-0-425-26273-3

PUBLISHING HISTORY
Berkley Prime Crime hardcover edition / July 2012
Berkley Prime Crime mass-market edition / July 2013

PRINTED IN THE UNITED STATES OF AMERICA

10 9 8 7 6 5 4 3 2 1

Cover illustration by Teresa Fasolino.
Cover design by Diana Kolsky.
Interior text design by Laura K. Corless.

ALWAYS LEARNING   **PEARSON**

continued . . .

"Fans of this series won't be disappointed. Ms. Barrett keeps the reader guessing as to whodunit, and I'm eagerly looking forward to visiting Stoneham again when the next book drops!" —*Fresh Fiction*

"A fast-paced, fun-filled, suspenseful read. There's plenty of action to keep you entertained, quirky characters to keep you laughing, and a mystery that keeps you guessing." —*Two Lips Reviews*

Chapter & Hearse

"Filled with action . . . Lorna Barrett has written a delightful amateur sleuth filled with red herrings and false leads that keep reader interest from the explosion till the explosive climax." —*Genre Go Round Reviews*

"There's misdirection, miscommunication, red herrings, and plot twists galore . . . If you've read other Booktown Mysteries, you're going to definitely enjoy this one. If you haven't read the other books in the series, don't worry, you'll come up to speed . . . Tightly plotted and paced to keep you turning the pages, this series is indeed getting better with each book." —*Gumshoe Review*

"There are many good things going on in this series, and they are starting to come together in this latest mystery . . . Well plotted and there are a few good suspects . . . Best of all, there is plenty of book talk sprinkled throughout and even a few of Angelica's recipes." —*The Mystery Reader*

Bookplate Special

"The third top-notch Booktown Mystery is a cleverly plotted cozy with everything a reader could want: mystery books, delicious food, and bad guys. With its bookstore setting and small-town charm, this series is bound to be a favorite for cozy readers." —*RT Book Reviews*

"Once again, Barrett has written an interesting, plausible murder mystery with an amateur sleuth that not only entertains but educates . . . Another excellent installment in this series."
—*Gumshoe Review*

"Barrett is skilled at making her characters flawed and fully believable. This book-based book is a perfect autumn read— right down to those smashed pumpkins—for mystery aficionados."
—*Richmond Times-Dispatch*

BOOKMARKED FOR DEATH

"Interesting characters, growing interrelationships . . . It's like visiting friends and having an adventure rolled into one book after another."
—*Gumshoe Review*

"Fans of Carolyn Hart and Denise Swanson rejoice! The latest [Booktown] gem . . . sparkles. This first-rate cozy artfully blends crime, cuisine, and even bookselling in a cheerful, witty, well-plotted puzzler."
—Julia Spencer-Fleming, Edgar® finalist and author of *One Was a Soldier*

MURDER IS BINDING

"Charming . . . The mix of books, cooking, and an engaging whodunit will leave cozy fans eager for the new installment."
—*Publishers Weekly*

"Move over, Cabot Cove. Lorna Barrett's new cozy creation, *Murder Is Binding*, has it all: wonderful old books, quirky characters, a clever mystery, and a cat named Miss Marple!"
—Roberta Isleib, author of *Asking for Murder*

For my wonderful aunts

Sonia and Michele

ACKNOWLEDGMENTS

Writing can be a lonely pursuit, but not when you have friends who are willing to share their expertise. Ellery Adams (also known as J.B. Stanley) acted as my first reader and gave me some terrific input. Not only is Hank Phillippi Ryan an award-winning author, she's an award-winning TV reporter and she has once again graciously helped with my description of TV stations and reporting. My pal Pat Remick always makes time to give me pointers on New Hampshire local color. Michelle Sampson, another source of local color, also "lent" me her beautiful Victorian house as the setting for the Sheer Comfort Inn.

It helps to have author friends to commiserate with, too. My thanks to my Cozy Chick blog pals, who are a constant source of support: Leann Sweeney, Ellery Adams, Deb Baker, Heather Webber, Kate Collins, and Maggie Sefton. Catch us at www.CozyChicksblog.com.

As always, I cannot forget my wonderful editor, Tom Colgan; his assistant, Amanda Ng; and my agent extraordinaire, Jessica Faust.

And thanks to all of you, my readers, for traveling with me on this amazing ride.

If you haven't already signed up for my periodic newsletter, I hope you'll visit my website to join: www.LornaBarrett.com. You can also find me on Facebook, Goodreads, and Twitter.

ONE

The overloaded luggage trolley bumped along the sidewalk, following Tricia Miles like an overgrown puppy. Ninety percent of the bags belonged to her sister, Angelica, whom Tricia trailed after. Head held high, marching along like a majorette, Angelica led the way to the Sheer Comfort Inn. When she stopped dead, Tricia nearly ran into her. "Tricia, you must keep up," she admonished.

Tricia steadied herself and the weight of the luggage nearly toppled the little metal trolley, taking her with it. "Tell me again why you've dragged me along on this little outing."

"My dear Tricia, for a little sister-to-sister bonding. It'll be just like camping," Angelica gushed, looking up at the lovely Victorian home before them and waving an arm to take it all in. The movement made her stumble on her three-inch heels, jostling the enormous suitcase, the corner of which dug into the back of Tricia's leg.

"Camping?" she nearly wailed. She'd brought only a small duffel with a nightshirt and a change of clothes, whereas Angelica had her big shocking pink Pierre Cardin suitcase, plus she had saddled Tricia with her overnight bag, a cosmetic bag, and a small cooler filled with snacks, while Angelica carried only her enormous purse.

The occasion?

A free overnight stay at Stoneham's newest (and to be honest, only) bed-and-breakfast inn. This was to be the B-and-B's trial run before the business opened to the public in a week's time. Angelica had won the prize at the last Chamber of Commerce meeting. She could have brought Bob Kelly, which might have been a much better idea than dragging Tricia along, but Angelica and Bob, head of the Chamber, had been on the outs more than the ins these last few months. Tricia wouldn't have been surprised to learn that Bob rigged the prize so that he and Angelica could spend a romantic evening in the cozy new inn. To say he'd been upset at Angelica's choice of roommate was putting it mildly. He'd even tried to bribe Tricia with a year's free Chamber membership to back out of the evening, but Tricia couldn't be bought—at least, not for such small stakes. And it rather pleased her to see Bob grovel, although at this particular moment she wished she had given in.

"I don't camp," Tricia asserted. She waved a hand at the lovely three-story Victorian home before them. "And you can hardly call staying the night at a place named *Sheer Comfort* roughing it."

"Well, I didn't know if they had hair dryers. And I had to bring my laptop. And since Bob said they serve sherry in the evenings, I needed to be able to change my clothes if the situation warranted it. In fact"—she pulled on the front of her waitress uniform, which showed through the opened buttons on her camel's-hair coat—"I can't wait to get out of these clothes."

"Why didn't you change at home? And you didn't have to bring four or five outfits. We're only going to be here one night."

"One never knows," Angelica said.

They turned to look at the house in front of them. A freshly painted white picket gate contrasted nicely against the privet that circled the patch of grass in front of the stately Victorian. The gingerbread accents on the porch and gable gave the appearance of an overgrown doll house. White wicker chairs and a love seat were decked out in chintz pillows, while the matching wicker tables looked like the perfect places to set silver trays with a couple of glasses and sweating pitchers of lemonade on a hot afternoon.

Those hot days were several months away. The sun was already sinking, and brass lamps glowed on either side of the brightly painted red door as Angelica opened the gate, scurried into the yard, and held it for Tricia, who hauled the luggage up the walk. "Give me a hand to lift this, will you, Ange?"

Angelica pouted, waving a hand with freshly lacquered nails at her. "I just gave myself a manicure—I don't want to ruin it."

She bustled up the steps while Tricia struggled to haul the trolley behind her.

Angelica grasped the door's brass knocker and tapped it as a winded Tricia tried to catch her breath. "Isn't the door open?" she asked.

"I didn't want to try it. After all, the inn isn't officially open. I wouldn't leave the door unlocked at dusk so just anyone could barge in."

"We're not just anyone. They're expecting us," Tricia pointed out.

"Hush!" Angelica warned as the thud of approaching footsteps sounded from within.

A moment later, the handle rattled and the door was thrown open. A middle-aged woman with shoulder-length blonde hair streaked with silver stood before them. She was thin, and dressed in a bulky lavender sweater, with polished black boots protruding under the sharp creases of her jeans. "Hello, I'm Pippa Comfort. You must be the Miles sisters."

Angelica giggled. "That makes us sound like a singing act, and I don't think Tricia can carry a tune."

Tricia was about to protest that she could, too, but thought better of it and forced a smile. Sometimes Angelica brought out the worst in her.

"Won't you come in," Pippa said with a welcoming wave of her hand, and stepped back to let them enter. Angelica sailed ahead. "Let me help you with that," Pippa said, and bent to give Tricia a hand to lift the luggage trolley up the final step and into the house.

As she straightened, Tricia caught a glimpse of a man standing down the hallway. He was dressed in a blue plaid flannel shirt, with a mop of graying brown hair, glasses, and a beard. But he made a hasty exit almost immediately.

"Oh, what a lovely place," Angelica said, her head swiveling to take in the attractive foyer.

Tricia's attention was drawn to the area as well. Polished white Carrara marble contrasted nicely with the darkened oak trim, which looked like it had never been painted. A bushy blooming Christmas cactus, which apparently didn't know the season, sat on an oak plant stand just inside the door, a lovely splash of color against the buff-colored walls. There didn't seem to be any kind of reception desk, and the three of them stood looking at each other for an awkward moment.

"It was so nice of you to offer the free accommodation," Tricia said at last.

"I'm pleased we could get a few people in for our final shakedown before opening next week."

"We're very pleased we won the raffle," Angelica gushed.

Pippa eyed Tricia. "Mr. Kelly had led me to believe *he* would be accompanying you this evening. I put you in the master suite."

Angelica laughed and waved a hand in dismissal. "Oh, that Bob. He's such a kidder."

Pippa seemed a tad annoyed that Bob wasn't going to be her guest. Had she been counting on him telling his out-of-the-area real estate clients to book rooms with the inn? She reached into her jeans pocket and pulled out a key. "The other guests are already here. We have some complimentary sherry out in the main parlor if you'd like to join us once you're settled in your room." She handed the key to Angelica.

"Thank you," she said. "Who else is here tonight?"

"Mary Fairchild and her husband, Luke. Chauncey Porter, and Clayton Ellington."

"Clayton Ellington!" Tricia repeated, surprised.

Pippa blinked. "Is there some reason he shouldn't be here?"

"No, I'm just surprised the owner of the Full Moon Nudist Camp and Resort would be here. I didn't even know he attended Chamber meetings."

"Maybe he's checking out the competition—for the clothed, that is," Angelica said with a smirk.

"Oh. I didn't realize . . ." Pippa said, looking annoyed for the second time in less than two minutes.

"About the luggage," Angelica said.

"Your suite is on the third floor. I'll go find my husband, Jon, to give you a hand. If you'll wait here." She took off down the hall.

"Thank you," Tricia said, grateful not to have to lug all Angelica's junk up two flights of stairs. Pippa's husband must have been the man she'd seen when they'd first arrived. Odd. There'd been something vaguely familiar about him. She shrugged it off.

"Nice place," Angelica said, and craned her neck to see what was in the room to their right. "Do you think Mary, her husband, and Chauncey are in there?"

"Go look," Tricia said, content to stand right where she was so that the top-heavy trolley didn't topple.

Angelica tightened her grip on the large purse that hung from her shoulder and charged forward. She stopped at the open, wide doorway, looked around, frowned, and turned back to join Tricia. "So far there's sherry glasses, but no one to drink out of them."

Dragging the trolley, Tricia moved to stand beside her sister and took in the room. The sofa was Victorian with a rust brocade, with matching chairs. A marble-topped table held a magnificent floral arrangement in pretty pinks and purples, like those found in the lobby of a high-end hotel. Too bad the space was much too small to properly accommodate it.

"The guests are probably in their rooms or out to dinner. Speaking of dinner, I haven't had any. And the inn only serves breakfast," Tricia said.

"I thought of that. I've brought a few goodies for later, but we could still get a bite to eat at the Brookview Inn."

"That's all the way across town. The Bookshelf Diner is open until ten."

Angelica frowned. "You know I don't like to patronize my competition."

"This is dinner, and your café only serves lunch," Tricia reminded her.

"We can go there. I have some marvelous cassoulet in the fridge. It'll only take a few minutes to reheat."

"But then we're going all the way back into the village anyway."

"May I remind you my café is only three doors down from the Bookshelf Diner."

"Okay, okay. But let's just dump our stuff and go right back out again."

Angelica looked down the hallway where Pippa had disappeared. "What's taking that bellboy so long?"

"He's not a bellboy, he's one of the owners," Tricia said, although she, too, was beginning to wonder where the man had disappeared.

Angelica frowned and cleared her throat. "Oh, let's not wait." She readjusted the purse on her shoulder and looked up the long staircase.

"Then you're going to have to carry some of this. I can't do it alone," Tricia told her.

Angelica removed Tricia's small duffel and her cosmetic case from the trolley, leaving Tricia to handle the biggest suitcase, and up the stairs she went.

Tricia was glad she was used to a two-flight hike several times a day, but at least there was a dumbwaiter at the back of her store, which meant she didn't have to lug heavy objects and risk her back—and her life—with them on the stairs. The Sheer Comfort Inn had no such facilities.

By the time Tricia arrived at the top floor, she was ready for a sit-down. She barely had time to notice the back stairs—probably left over from the days when houses like this employed servants—before she entered the only room on the top floor. She hadn't even had time to look around the suite before Angelica came out of the bathroom and closed the door behind her. "Oh Trish, there's a heavenly Jacuzzi tub in there, and look, here's a wet bar and glasses. We could bring a bottle of wine back and enjoy it here while I work tonight."

"You're going to work tonight?"

"I need to draft a list of changes for my web designer, and I do have a deadline looming for my next cookbook, you know."

Maybe that was another reason why Angelica hadn't wanted to bring Bob.

Tricia sighed. There wasn't even a TV for amusement, but then, as long as she had a book in her purse, she could be content anywhere.

Her stomach growled. She wanted to trudge down the stairs, drive back into the village, eat dinner, and then come all the way back to the inn like she wanted a tooth pulled. "Let's go. It was a long day. I'm looking forward to putting my feet up"—she saw a leather recliner by the window—"and taking it easy."

"Another bad day at Haven't Got a Clue?" Angelica asked.

Tricia said nothing. She didn't want to talk about it.

"Okay, let me change out of these clothes and we'll go," Angelica said. "There's just one tiny problem."

"Problem?" Tricia asked.

Angelica wagged a finger and beckoned Tricia to follow her into the bathroom.

Tricia followed, wondering what could be wrong with the necessary room. Angelica opened the door and a cheerful bark greeted the women. Sitting on the floor, looking as cute as a button, was Angelica's bichon frise, Sarge.

"Oh no," Tricia groaned. "Ange, the inn has a strict no-pets policy. Didn't you read the brochure Bob gave you?"

"Well, of course I did. But I can't leave Sarge all alone. He's not a cat, you know. He isn't litter box trained." Sarge barked once more, as though agreeing with that statement. Angelica bent to pick up the dog, straightened, and shoved him into Tricia's arms. "Now, you take Sarge out for a comfort walk while I get changed."

Tricia shook her head and tried to offer the dog back, but Angelica bustled over to her suitcase, placed it on the luggage stand, and unzipped it. "I've got to get changed. You take Sarge out."

"But they'll see me."

"Put him back in my purse. He's used to staying in there. And he won't make a peep."

"He's already barked."

"He was just glad to see me again. Now go on. Take him down the back stairs." She went back for her purse, took out a leash, and hooked it to Sarge's collar. "There, now he can't get away."

"What if he needs . . . you know. A litter bag."

"Oh, dear. I hadn't thought of that." Angelica went back

into the bathroom, found a little plastic pouch in a basket full of toiletries, and handed it to Tricia. "Here, use this."

"A shower cap? And then what am I supposed to do with Sarge's little bundle of . . . joy?"

"Put him back in my purse and find a garbage pail. They're sure to have at least one out back. Then come back up here and we'll leave."

"We are taking him *with* us, aren't we?"

"I thought I'd leave him in the bathroom. He'll be okay for an hour or so."

Tricia shook her head. "Uh-uh. Either he comes with us, or we're not leaving."

"Oh, all right. But that just means we have to sneak him back in again."

"*You* will sneak him back in. If anyone catches us, I'll disavow all knowledge of his existence."

Angelica sighed. "Have it your way. After your little walk, we'll meet at my car. I'll stop and tell Pippa we'll be back after we get a bite to eat."

"Don't take too long. You don't need to put on all new makeup if we're just going to Booked for Lunch."

"You are such a grouch," Angelica complained, then grabbed a sweater and slacks from her suitcase and stomped off for the bathroom, closing the door behind her.

Sarge looked after her with hurt eyes and whimpered. "You'll see your mama in just a few minutes," Tricia promised. "Now, back into the purse you go, little man. And don't you make a sound."

As Angelica had said, Sarge was used to being carried in a purse. His former owner had carried him around in the same fashion, and he wasn't the slightest bit upset to be hidden away. Maybe he looked at going into the purse as though it were some big doggy adventure. After all, he never knew where he'd end up once he was taken out again.

Tricia crept down the back stairs, looking around to make

sure the coast was clear and hoping she wouldn't run into anyone. But as she rounded the landing on the second floor, a voice called out to her. "Tricia, is that you?"

Mary Fairchild owned By Hook or By Book, the village's craft store. Tricia was used to seeing her sitting behind a counter, dressed in one of her store's aprons, with a knitting or crochet project before her. She so seldom saw Mary standing, let alone dressed in fashionable clothing, that for a moment she stopped in her tracks, stunned.

"I didn't know you'd be here," Mary said rather nervously. She seemed a little out of breath and her cheeks were pink. In her hands were two of the liqueur glasses that had sat on a tray in the living room not long before.

"Yes. Angelica won the night's stay and asked me to come with her."

Mary looked startled. "She didn't come with Bob?"

Was that going to be everyone's reaction?

"No. And everyone seems sad to see it's me she invited," she said, feeling a bit put out.

Mary laughed. "Don't be silly. It's just that . . . well, they say romance is rekindled at these little B-and-Bs. At least, that's what I'm hoping. When you've been married for half your life like Luke and me, romance can be hard to come by."

Romance was just as hard to come by when your so-called boyfriend was a cop, too, but Tricia didn't voice that opinion.

"Isn't this the most darling place? Have you done any exploring yet?" Mary asked, her eyes twinkling with mischief.

"I haven't had time. We came in through the front door and went right up to the master suite."

"I was just downstairs in the parlor, grabbing a couple of glasses of sherry." Mary eyed Tricia's coat and the large handbag hanging from her shoulder. "Looks like you're on your way out again."

Sarge moved around in the purse, reminding Tricia of her task. She forced yet another smile. "Yes, Angelica and I haven't had dinner. We're going out for a quick bite, and then we'll be back to enjoy all the inn's amenities."

"Then if I don't see you again this evening, I'll catch up with you in the morning. I can't wait to see what kind of breakfast they serve."

Breakfast? If Tricia didn't get out of there, she'd never even get her dinner. "Me, either," she said. "I'll see you later, Mary." And with that she wiggled her fingers in a wave and headed down the stairs once more.

Once at the bottom, Tricia gave a furtive look around. Luckily, no one was in the large spacious kitchen. From the looks of the gleaming stainless steel commercial appliances, granite countertops, and refinished hardwood floor, it had been recently remodeled. She hoped Angelica wouldn't come down the back stairs. She'd no doubt want to explore every inch of the room, which would delay their dinner even more.

Sarge gave an anguished yip from inside the purse, reminding Tricia that the little guy needed to make a pit stop before they could head for Booked for Lunch.

Tricia crossed the kitchen on tiptoes and found the door to the backyard unlocked. With special care, she opened the door and exited the inn, quietly closing the door behind her. A lamp on the northeast corner of the house bathed the yard in a harsh white light. After three steps down, she stood on the walk laid out in concrete pavers. She looked around, saw no one, and opened the top of Angelica's purse. Sarge's head popped up like a jack-in-the-box, and he gave an anguished bark.

"Yes, I know you've got to go," Tricia said, and removed the dog from the purse, setting him onto the grass. Tricia pressed the button to release the cord on the retractable leash. Sarge trotted over to the white picket fence, where he raised his left hind leg. Tricia sighed and looked away, grateful her cat, Miss Marple, could attend to her own lavatory needs.

Tricia glanced around the yard, noting how the branches

in the tall bare trees danced in the slight wind, and waited impatiently as Sarge started his sniffathon of the Comfort's backyard. The small patio promised many afternoons relaxing in the shade—perhaps with that sweating pitcher of lemonade she'd thought about earlier. The idea was certainly appealing. She'd spent most of her adult life living in an apartment. It would be nice to have a yard with trees and flowers . . . especially if someone else maintained it for her.

The lease on her mystery bookstore, Haven't Got a Clue, was soon to run out, and if she didn't find competent help soon to replace her former assistant, Ginny Wilson, she might as well close shop. Okay, that was an overreaction. Still, the past few months had seen a parade of men and women who just didn't fit in at the store.

She thought again about her digs above Haven't Got a Clue in the third-floor loft, where she'd lived for the past three years. She hadn't given any thought to trading it in for a real home, and she'd left it too late to start looking for a house should she lose her lease. So many of the homes in Stoneham were behemoths like the Sheer Comfort Inn—much too big for one person and a small cat. And she wasn't sure she could be happy in a tiny cottage like where her former employee currently lived.

A noise off in the darkened part of the yard startled her out of her daydream. It was Sarge, growling.

She extended her arm to reel in a couple of feet of Sarge's leash and tugged it, to signal the dog it was time to come back to her, but Sarge wouldn't budge.

"Sarge," she whispered.

The dog yipped and growled again.

She tugged harder on the leash and called again, but the dog only yipped louder. They'd be found out for sure if this continued.

Tricia walked across the yard to intercept the dog, who had his nose firmly planted between two of the pickets. "Sarge!"

The dog pulled his head back, looked up at Tricia, and barked—loudly!

"Shhh!"

She hit the button on the leash, reeling all but the last four feet in, and bent down and scooped him up. "Naughty dog! You must be quiet."

She put Sarge back into Angelica's purse, but before she turned back toward the house, she glanced over the fence and saw a mound of what looked like clothing on the other side. Taking out her keys, she pushed the little button on the fob and a little beam of light shot out. She dragged the beam over something purple—a bulky sweater—and it came to rest on a bloodied mass of tangled blonde-gray hair.

Pippa Comfort's hair.

TWO

 "Oh, no, not again!" Tricia said aloud to Sarge, who had started to whine. Tricia's heart pounded, and she fought to keep from hyperventilating.

She hurried to the gate several feet to her left, struggled to open it, and raced to where Pippa lay in the darkened grass. She set Angelica's purse down and fumbled to find a pulse along Pippa's neck, but of course there was none.

Pippa was definitely dead.

Tricia stood and swallowed. This was the fourth body she'd found in three years. After she'd found the first one on the floor of the Cookery, and then another person had died shortly afterward, a rumor had circulated through Stoneham that she was the village jinx. Now she wondered if that might not be true.

"It's for sure we'll get caught for bringing you here tonight," she told Sarge, who yipped in agreement. Then Tricia realized

14

how absurd the thought truly was. Nobody was going to get to stay at the inn for its shakedown run.

She took a couple of deep breaths to calm herself, reached for her cell phone, and punched in 911. "I'd like to report an accident."

Accident? A body bludgeoned to death was no accident. It couldn't have been ten minutes—fifteen at the most—since Tricia had spoken to the poor woman. And now she was dead. But Tricia didn't want to report that to the dispatcher. It would be much better for some official to make that determination.

She answered all the questions the dispatcher asked and stayed on the line until she heard the wail of sirens in the distance. Would it be the fire rescue squad or a member of the newly formed Stoneham Police Department who made it to the scene first?

Sarge had been trained to stay in the purse until retrieved. Tricia had almost forgotten about him until he let out another yip to remind her of his presence. She picked up Angelica's purse and retreated to stand beside the steps next to the house. The late March evening dampness seemed to be settling in her bones, and she shivered. She could feel the heat of Sarge's body through the purse and wished she had a coat similar to his, cursing herself for grabbing only a light jacket when she'd left home.

The handle above her rattled and the kitchen door opened. "Where have you been?" Angelica asked, clearly annoyed. "I've been back to the car twice now looking for you. Let's get going or it'll be midnight before we get anything to eat."

The sirens abruptly halted and within seconds a young officer dressed in a navy blue uniform rounded the corner of the house and skidded to a halt. "Where's the injured party, ma'am?" he asked, rather breathless.

Tricia pointed. "Behind the fence. I . . . think she might be dead."

"Oh, no," Angelica wailed. "We're not going to get to eat for hours now."

All the guests had been rounded up and separately questioned, but so far no one had been allowed to leave. They all sat in the front parlor in various states of boredom. After the first few minutes, the stilted, if polite, conversation had waned. As usual, Mary Fairchild had a bag of craftwork with her. She concentrated on crocheting a pink baby blanket while her husband held an e-reader, his eyes darting back and forth as he pursued his novel. He'd downloaded the book soon after they'd been told to sit there for an indefinite time period. Tricia tried to stifle a pang of jealousy. Her purse—and the paperback she was currently reading—was still up in the master suite.

It seemed that no one had seen Pippa leave the house. More telling, Jon Comfort was nowhere to be found. At least that gave the police someone other than Tricia to concentrate on as the chief suspect—for the time being. For some reason the local law enforcement community always seemed to want to blame her for every dead body that appeared in the village.

Tricia's gaze traveled around the room for at least the hundredth time. It was a nice room, with a white-painted fireplace surround with an oak mantel. A large oil painting of a working quarry graced the space above—no doubt an artist's interpretation of one of Stoneham's own. She would have rather seen a prettier landscape or a still life of flowers or fruit. The original floors looked to have been recently refinished, while an oriental carpet in rich hues blanketed the sitting area. Her gaze drifted to the large floral arrangement, seeing something underneath that she hadn't noticed before: a small embossed card with the words *Courtesy of Milford Nursery and Flowers.*

"I'm so hungry I could eat my foot," Angelica practically growled into Tricia's left ear. "I'm never going to get any work done tonight, either."

"And you'll be sleeping in your own bed tonight, too," Tricia added.

"That, too," Angelica muttered. "I was hoping to give that Jacuzzi tub a try. Now . . ." Her words trailed off as her stomach growled—loudly.

Everyone's head jerked up as a figure appeared in the doorway. At last, the chief of police, Grant Baker, was on the scene. Now finally Tricia and Angelica could leave. But instead of a welcoming smile, his expression was grim.

"Folks, thank you for your patience. I understand you've all got luggage in your rooms. One of my officers will accompany each of you as you return to your rooms to pack your things. Mr. and Mrs. Fairchild, why don't you go first."

The couple rose from the couch and headed for the stairs, with an officer dogging their heels.

"Sorry for the inconvenience," Baker said, and then turned. "Mr. Porter, you're next, and Mr. Ellington will follow."

"What about us?" Angelica asked.

Baker ignored her, glaring at Tricia. "Ms. Miles, if you don't mind, I'd like to speak with you privately."

Tricia felt her cheeks redden. Was she to be scolded like a naughty child?

"I haven't got time for this," Clayton Ellington said, and rose from his chair. "I've already been inconvenienced for the past two hours when I had nothing to tell your men. I'll send one of my employees over to pick up my belongings tomorrow morning. If you'll excuse me."

They all watched as he headed for the door. Baker didn't stop him, and instead he beckoned Tricia to follow him.

She trotted after him into the empty kitchen, which had recently been filled with officers and other officials, as evi-

denced by the dirt, leaves, and mud that covered what had
been an immaculate floor just hours before.

Baker turned to face her. "Tricia," he said with a shake of
his head, his voice weary.

"I did not kill Pippa Comfort."

"You found her," he as much as accused.

"I did not. Angelica's dog found her. I only reported it."

"It amounts to the same thing."

"It does not," Tricia cried, sounding incredibly defensive.
"I wouldn't have gone out back if Sarge hadn't needed a pee
break."

Baker sighed. "Tell me what you know."

Tricia crossed her arms over her sweater set. "I took Sarge
out of Angelica's purse and put him on the ground. He did
his business and then did what all dogs do—he started sniffing around until he found something interesting. Unfortunately, it was Pippa."

Baker shook his head.

The outside door rattled and opened, and the man in the
blue plaid shirt whom Tricia had seen earlier walked in, followed by one of the uniformed officers. "What's going on?
Why are the police here? What's happened?" he demanded,
saw Tricia standing by the counter, and then quickly looked
away.

Something about the man's voice hit Tricia like a shock
wave. A familiarity—a sound she never thought she'd hear
again. She stared at him, but he was looking at Baker, not her.

"Mr. Comfort. I'm very sorry to be the one to tell you, but
your wife was found murdered tonight," Baker said.

"Murdered," he repeated in disbelief. If he was acting, he
was doing a damn fine job of it.

Baker looked back at Tricia. "Will you excuse us, Ms.
Miles?"

She hated it when he called her that. But she nodded. However, as she went to turn away, she saw Comfort's profile and

despite the well-groomed beard, a memory from long ago surfaced—shattering in its intensity.

"Ms. Miles," Baker repeated, a bit more firmly.

Tricia ignored him, her heart pounding as recognition dawned. "Wait a minute. Your name's not Comfort," she told the man in the plaid shirt. "And you're supposed to be dead. Long dead."

THREE

 "Dead?" Chief Baker repeated.

Comfort raised his hands in a defensive pose and shook his head in denial. "You're mistaken, lady. My name is Jon Comfort."

"You can't hide behind that beard, Harry. I'd know your face anywhere. Why did you do that to me? How could you fake your death and put your family and friends through all that grief? How could you do that to your *fans*?" she demanded.

"Hold on," Baker said. It was his turn to raise his hand—if only as a gesture of disbelief. "Tricia, what are you talking about."

"This man," she pointed at Comfort, anger filling her voice, "is a fraud. His real name is Harrison Tyler, the author of *Death Beckons*, who supposedly drowned twenty years ago after a sailing accident near Martha's Vineyard."

"*Death Beckons*," Baker repeated. "Hey, I read that book. It was a best seller. A movie was made from it. And wasn't there a TV show in England based on it, too?"

Comfort's gaze was focused on the kitchen floor; beneath his full beard, his cheeks had gone a bright pink. "You said my wife is dead. I want to know what happened—who could have killed her."

"That's just what we want to ask you. Ms. Miles here told us that she saw you as she and her sister entered your inn. You hightailed it down the hall and disappeared. Within minutes, Ms. Miles found your wife murdered in the backyard."

"I told you, *I* didn't find her. My sister's *dog* found her," Tricia repeated.

"Whatever," Baker said, an irritated edge entering his voice. "Ms. Miles"—Tricia was really getting annoyed at him calling her that—"please stick around. I'd like to talk to you again when I'm finished with Mr. Comfort."

"Then I'm ordering a pizza. I'm starving," she said, then turned and exited the kitchen. The short walk from the kitchen to the parlor was not long enough for her ire to cool.

Angelica still sat on the couch, looking bored. But she glanced up at Tricia's arrival, studying her face. "Oh, dear—I can see you're in a mood."

"Wait 'til I tell you who I just saw—"

Angelica's blue eyes went wide in anticipation, but before she could ask, the Fairchilds came trundling down the stairs, suitcases in hand, with the officer bringing up the rear.

"Your turn, Chauncey," Mary said, and headed for the door. "See you later Tricia—Angelica."

Angelica waved good-bye, and Chauncey angled his bulk out of the chair he'd been occupying to follow the officer up the stairs.

Angelica moved her purse, making Sarge, who was still inside, give a stifled yip, and patted the couch cushion next to her. "Sit down and tell all."

Tricia flopped down and let out an exasperated breath. "Do you remember Harrison Tyler?"

"The one-hit wonder who wrote that big novel and then drowned in a boating accident?"

Tricia nodded. "That's the one. Well, he's standing in the kitchen—right this minute—pretending to be Jon Comfort, one of the owners of this inn!"

Angelica looked confused. "How does one pretend to own an inn?"

Tricia shot off the couch like she'd been set afire. She was about to lecture at length when she remembered that she and Angelica hadn't exactly been close during the years she'd been in college—or, in fact, for eighteen years afterward. It was as if her bones had lost their rigidity, and she sank back onto the couch again, feeling like a rag doll who'd been badly shaken.

She sighed. "Harrison Tyler and I were once . . . close."

"How close?" Angelica asked.

"Like sticky tape," Tricia admitted.

Angelica nodded sagely. "Ah."

"We'd been seeing each other for several months, and I'd been out with him on that boat four or five times before the accident. It broke my heart when the Coast Guard found that lovely sloop empty with the main mast broken and hanging in the water. Harry had gone sailing just before a hurricane struck the coast. And . . ." She didn't need to say any more.

Angelica looked toward the swinging door that held the kitchen at bay. "And you say this Jon Comfort is really Harrison Tyler?"

"I'd stake my life on it."

"Do you think his wife knew?"

Tricia shrugged. "Maybe. Maybe not."

"What are you going to do?"

For a moment Tricia wasn't sure what she wanted to do: hug the man or hit him. She was hurt and angry and—her stomach growled—hungry! "What *can* I do? I assume he'll deny it, but eventually they'll prove I'm right."

"Did he recognize you?"

"I'm sure of it. I'll bet that's why he disappeared the minute we walked through the front door. He wouldn't look at me in the kitchen, either. And why should he? I've blown his cover. But then, his wife being killed might've done that anyway. They always suspect the spouse first—and for very good reason."

"Bob gave the inn's managers the names of the raffle winners yesterday. He might've known since then that you were one of them. Maybe they argued about you."

"First of all, Bob didn't know I'd be coming with you. And why would they argue about me, anyway? I haven't seen Harry in twenty years."

"Some women are very jealous."

Yes, like you, Tricia somehow managed *not* to say. But then Angelica had had reason to be jealous. She always picked men with a wandering eye.

Angelica's purse began to wobble as a tiny whimper issued from it. "Poor Sarge. He needs a comfort stop. Do you think I'll get in trouble if I take him outside?"

"Who cares?"

"Well, I do. I mean—I don't want to be in trouble with the law."

"You'll be in trouble with Harry if Sarge pees—or worse— on his oriental rug."

"He's in my purse, which is waterproof," Angelica said, annoyed, and struggled back into her jacket. She grabbed the purse and headed for the front door. As soon as she was through it, Tricia was back on her feet and tiptoed to the swinging door that separated the parlor from the kitchen. She pressed her ear close to the crack around the door and listened, but all she heard was the low murmur of voices.

Frowning, she stepped away. All she needed was for Baker

to come flying through the door, knock her over, and catch her eavesdropping. She returned to her seat.

What else would Baker want to know about her former relationship with Harrison Tyler, and would he be asking out of professional or personal interest?

She waited. And waited. Finally Angelica returned, her pink cheeks attesting to the drop in temperature. "I don't care what the calendar says, it is not spring yet."

"Anything happening outside?"

"It looks like the medical examiner is about to take off. Good-bye, Pippa."

"Don't be so flip. She seemed like a nice person."

"Nice people get murdered all the time, but nobody here had a motive. Except, I would assume, for her husband."

"Harry? Why?"

"Jealousy. You watch. Chief Baker is going to be all over you when he's done with Mr. Comfort. He'll probably think you killed her to get back with your old boyfriend."

"I don't believe it. Sheriff Adams might have come up with that motive, but not Grant. And besides, I didn't even know Harry was in town until ten minutes ago."

"Ah, but as they're Chamber members, he could have known *you* were in town. They could have argued about you," she reiterated. "Now, bonk, she's dead."

"How does that implicate me?"

"If the cops don't come to that conclusion, the district attorney probably will. You need a lawyer. Yet again."

Tricia shook her head. "I do not need a lawyer. If Pippa knew about me and Harry, she sure didn't show it when we walked in."

"She *was* ticked you weren't Bob," Angelica reminded her.

"But was she *angry* at me? I don't think so. And if you want suspects, for all we know, maybe Pippa was having or once had an affair with Chauncey or Ellington."

Angelica laughed. "Chauncey? Not on your life. I mean,

maybe twenty years ago and a hundred pounds ago—*if* he had hair."

"Why not Ellington?"

Angelica bit her lower lip. "He's a possibility. He's not bad to look at, and he's rich." She pondered the thought.

Tricia shook her head. "Forget it. Let's leave this up to the local police force."

"Yes, their first murder—and once again, *you* were there."

"I'm starving. How about a pizza? I already told Grant I was going to order one."

"What about my leftovers at Booked for Lunch?" Angelica cried.

"I was going to have it delivered here."

"They already said we could go once an officer escorts us to get our luggage."

"Come on, you know Grant is going to want to talk to me about Harry."

"Well, *I* don't have to be part of that conversation," Angelica said crossly. She gathered up her purse, marched over to the door to the kitchen, and threw it open. "Chief Baker, I want to go home. Now!"

The chief's expression went from surprised to a scowl. "Then go."

Angelica let the door swing shut. "Tricia, you may bring my luggage home." Without waiting for a reply, Angelica stalked off to the front door, letting it slam behind her.

Chauncey Porter, who had apparently lost his police escort, stood at the bottom of the stairs. "Oh my," he said in a low voice. Tricia had completely forgotten he was in the house. How long had he been standing there, eavesdropping on their conversation? Had he heard what Angelica had said about him just minutes before?

Chauncey gripped the handle of his scuffed overnight bag tightly and hefted the book he'd been reading in the other. "I'd—I'd better be going home." He nodded to Tricia and hurried to the door, looking distinctly guilty. What did he have to hide?

Suddenly the thought struck her as ominous.

What if sweet Chauncey Porter wasn't quite so sweet after all?

Tricia shook her head and frowned. The fact that a violent death had just occurred encouraged her to think the worst of everyone. And Angelica had been right. When Jon Comfort was proven to be the long-lost best-selling author Harrison Tyler, suspicion was sure to fall on her.

Anger rolled through her for the years she had mourned the loss of her first lover, Harrison Tyler.

Now she could just kill him.

FOUR

The swinging door from the kitchen banged open and Chief Baker entered the living room with Harry Tyler right behind him. "Was that Mr. Porter leaving?" he asked.

"Yes, and I'd like to leave, too. If Mr. Comfort—or Tyler, or whatever he's calling himself today—will give me a hand with my luggage, I'll be off," Tricia said rather curtly.

"*I* will help you," Baker said.

"Fine with me," Comfort said, and stalked off for the kitchen once again.

Baker waited until the door swung shut before he spoke, his voice low, angry. "Why didn't you tell me about Tyler?" he demanded.

"Have you told me about every woman *you've* ever been with?" Tricia replied.

"Comfort or Tyler is a suspect in Pippa Comfort's death. And you could be considered an accomplice."

"How? I didn't even know he was alive until he marched into the inn's kitchen. You were there. You saw how surprised I was to see Harry Tyler return from the dead."

"Of course, but the district attorney might not believe it."

"That's ridiculous. I hadn't seen or heard from Harry since the day before he disappeared and was presumed dead over twenty years ago. I hadn't even thought of the man in years." Okay, that was bending the truth a little. She'd made a point of remembering Harry on his birthday, and on the anniversary of his so-called death, but after such a long period of time they were only wistful thoughts of what might have been. She'd mourned for him for a year or so, and then she'd dated other men and moved on with her life, eventually marrying Christopher Benson.

"It doesn't matter what I think," Baker said.

"Of course it does; *you're* the Stoneham chief of police. *You're* the one investigating this death."

"Yes, and I have to make sure that everyone who's a viable suspect gets treated exactly the same way. Including you."

"I did *not* kill Pippa Comfort!" Tricia said, a bit louder than necessary.

"And you didn't see anyone in that yard when you came out with the dog?"

"It was as quiet as a grave."

Baker actually winced at her word choice.

"Now, since you let Angelica leave in a huff, I've got to bring all her luggage home, and my sister does not travel light. And unless you or one of your men gives me a ride home, I've got to drag that luggage through the streets of Stoneham."

"I will give you a ride home."

"Thank you. The suite is this way." Tricia turned and started up the stairs with Baker hot on her heels.

"What were you doing here tonight, anyway?" he asked.

"Angelica won a raffle at the last Chamber of Commerce meeting. A night's stay at the inn. Pippa thought she'd be bringing Bob along. She was shocked to see it was me."

"Oh?" Baker asked suspiciously as they rounded the first landing.

"And don't read anything into that. Bob's a real estate agent. I'm sure she was hoping he'd tell prospective clients about the inn. Pippa gave us the master suite, which is why we're still climbing stairs." But by the time she'd said that, they had finished their ascent. Tricia rattled the door to the room and only then realized that Angelica still had the room key. "Oh, crap! Ange has the key."

"There's got to be a spare. I'll go down and ask Comfort for it. Do you want to come with me and see him again for yourself? Make sure he's the man you say he is?"

"After what he pulled, I have no desire to see or hear from Harry Tyler ever again. I'll wait here, thank you."

Baker frowned, noticed the back stairs, and took off.

Tricia leaned against the locked door and sighed. This was *not* how she'd envisioned her evening would go. A soak in the suite's Jacuzzi tub would be just the thing right now, too. Then again, she'd felt guilty leaving Miss Marple alone for the night. When she got home, she'd make up for her absence by filling the cat's bowl with kitty snacks.

She heard footsteps coming up the main staircase and seconds later saw Jon/Harry. He paused when he saw her standing there.

"What do you want?" Tricia asked.

"I live here."

"Not in this suite. Did Chief Baker ask you to come up with the key?"

"No, I—" He stopped, ran his tongue over dry lips, and didn't finish the sentence. He swallowed. "I thought you'd already be gone. I figured I should make sure the room was . . . inhabitable."

"You're still planning to open next week after what happened tonight?"

"I've got to make a living, if only to bury poor Pippa."

Poor Pippa indeed. Only he didn't sound all that sorrowful. Then again, maybe he was in shock. It hadn't even been an hour since he'd learned of his wife's death. Maybe he was in denial, and maybe Tricia was being too hard on him.

"I'm so sorry about Pippa. I only spoke to her for a minute or two, but . . . she seemed like a nice person."

"She was. Maybe too nice."

"Did she know about your past life—your other identity?"

Comfort hesitated. "We talked."

As evasive an answer as Tricia had ever heard, but at least he wasn't denying his former identity.

"Did you know I was in Stoneham?" she asked.

"Not until a couple of days ago when I saw the Chamber roster, and even then, I couldn't be sure it was you. And why in God's name did you have to show up here, anyway? Pippa was expecting Bob Kelly to accompany your sister."

Footsteps on the stairs made them both turn. An annoyed Baker topped the landing. "Here you are. I've been chasing all over the house looking for you. Do you have the passkey?"

Comfort took a ring from his pocket and offered it to Baker. "Which one opens this door?"

Comfort chose a key and handed it to the chief. "I'll be downstairs if you need me." He turned his attention back to Tricia. "Nice to meet you, Ms. Miles." He turned away and headed down the stairs.

Tricia's mouth dropped open in amazement, and for a moment she couldn't speak. "Don't tell me he denied being Harry Tyler when you questioned him before."

"He did," Baker confirmed. "And if he's lying about not knowing anything about his wife's death and then being Harrison Tyler, he'll be in even more trouble." He thrust the key into the lock and opened the door to the suite. "Let's not talk about this any more tonight. We'll get your luggage and get you home. I'm sure Miss Marple will be glad to have you back."

Baker ushered Tricia in. Thankfully, Angelica hadn't taken time to unpack. Tricia gathered up the white waitress uniform, stuffed it and the shoes into Angelica's suitcase, and zippered it shut. Grabbing her own duffel and the pink cosmetic case, she let Baker handle the enormous suitcase.

"Did you ever order that pizza?" Baker asked as Tricia preceded him out of the room. He turned off the light and closed the door, and they started down the main staircase.

"No. And it's probably too late now."

"I've got some leftover pizza at my place," he offered, and this time there was none of the irritation she'd heard in his tone during the previous hour. Still, after the evening she'd endured, she wasn't up to being interrogated, and she knew he'd only want to talk about the evening's events. He could do that tomorrow, during business hours. Right now all she wanted to do was jump into bed with a good book—not her sometime lover, full-time cop.

"No, thank you. Please, just drive me home. I have a feeling tomorrow is going to be another long day."

When they got to the bottom of the stairs they found no sign of Comfort. Exiting the entryway, they found that all but one of the police cruisers were gone. A young officer stood at the bottom of the porch steps. He nodded. "Chief. Ma'am."

"Give these keys back to Mr. Comfort, will you?"

"Sure thing, Chief."

"And stick around until the end of your shift, Rogers. Martinez will relieve you when he comes on duty."

"Yes, sir."

Baker took the lead, wrestling Angelica's suitcase through the door and out into the cold night air. Tricia followed him to his car. He hadn't bothered to arrive in his own police cruiser. Good. The last thing Tricia wanted was for any of her neighbors to see her arrive home in a cop car.

Baker stuffed the luggage in the back of his SUV and opened the door for Tricia to get in. Tricia had buckled herself in by the time he opened the driver's-side door and got inside. He started the engine.

"Well, aren't you going to say anything?" she asked.

"I don't know what to say right now. I have to be careful, Tricia. I'm the chief of police and I can't let our relationship get in the way of my investigation."

Tricia sighed. She hadn't seen or heard from him in three days. It was hardly what anyone would call an overly close relationship. But then he'd explained at least a thousand times how important it was to get the department up and running, and she knew from reading police procedurals that what he said was true. But why did his work always have to encroach on their time together?

"Well, aren't *you* going to say anything?" Baker demanded.

Tricia kept her eyes focused on the headlights' narrow beams, which cut through the darkness. "It seems to me that you've said it all."

They drove through the quiet streets of Stoneham, neither saying a word. And Tricia really didn't want to talk. It was late, they were both tired and hungry, and the timing wasn't right.

Baker paused on Main Street, did a U-turn, and pulled up in front of Haven't Got a Clue. Without uttering a word, they got out of the car and Baker retrieved the luggage from the back of his SUV. "I'll help you carry this into the store."

"Thanks. I figured I'd dump it in the Cookery. Otherwise I'm sure Angelica will make me carry it up two flights."

"Doesn't she have a dumbwaiter, too?"

"Yes, but that won't stop her from making me do it anyway."

Baker shook his head. "I'm glad I only had a brother." He followed her to the Cookery and waited as she separated the correct key from her ring, opened the door, punched in the security code on the pad on the wall, set the suitcase inside, then quickly reset the system and locked up again.

Baker walked her to her shop. "I know I don't deserve it, but can I have a kiss good night?"

"I don't just kiss anyone, you know."

"I've heard that." Her eyes widened with surprise, and he smiled. "Okay, I haven't heard that. But it got you going there for a second, didn't it?"

She wanted to be angry with him. Some part of her wanted to haul off and hit him.

Instead, she kissed him. And again. And then again . . .

FIVE

Despite their amicable parting, Tricia did not invite Chief Baker to accompany her inside her store. She really was too tired for that. Yet by the time she got upstairs, she found she was too restless to even contemplate sleep. Instead, Tricia dug through a box in the back of her closet to find an old photo album. Grabbing a glass of wine, she settled on her couch to study the pictures. After insisting on another helping of kitty snacks, Miss Marple deigned to join her.

The pictures dated from the time of her college graduation until just before she'd met Christopher. Included among those featured were three or four photos of Harrison Tyler—whom, at the time, she'd thought of as her first love. After seeing him again that evening, her emotions weren't quite that charitable.

The first photo was taken on the night they'd met at a dusty little bookshop in Soho. A small crowd had gathered to hear Harrison—"just call me Harry, darlin'"—speak about his phenomenal first novel, *Death Beckons*. The others had drifted away after a while, and the storekeeper was eager to close down for the night when Harry invited her out for a coffee. Giggling girlishly, she'd accepted.

It seemed like such a long time ago.

Tricia sipped her wine and thought about their last conversation. He'd made a phone call that, in retrospect, she should've realized had been his attempt at a last good-bye. And then of course she'd gone into mourning as soon as she'd heard about the boating accident.

It had taken her a long time to get over Harrison Tyler, and suddenly here he was again—back in her life, however reluctantly. And he was a fool if he thought he could keep his real identity a secret now that Pippa was dead.

Then again, he'd been a fool to fake his own death.

Tricia sipped her wine. Was she destined to love only fools who would never completely commit to her? It was a sad, sobering thought.

Miss Marple nudged her elbow, reminding her it was long past their bedtime. "Okay," Tricia said, setting the album aside and getting up from her seat. Miss Marple hopped down, too, and trotted off toward the bedroom.

Tricia reached for the lamp switch, giving the photo album one last look before she turned off the lights. She had a feeling she hadn't heard the last of Harry Tyler.

Sleep was hard to come by, but at last Tricia fell into a fitful slumber some time near dawn. She'd hit the snooze button three times by the time she was finally able to drag herself out of bed and start what might prove to be a very long day.

Tricia waited to make coffee until she and Miss Marple arrived at Haven't Got a Clue. She'd just hit the button on the coffeemaker when she heard a knock at the door. A glance at her watch told her the store wasn't due to open for another fifteen minutes, but there was also no reason not to let an eager customer in the door, either. But although the woman at the door had bought many books from Tricia, she wasn't there as a customer on that morning.

"Mary," Tricia said, letting her fellow shopkeeper in. "Shouldn't you be getting By Hook or By Book ready to open?"

"I should, but . . . I just need to talk. Do you have a minute?" she asked, sounding weary.

"Of course. I've just put the coffee on to brew. It'll be ready in less than five minutes."

"I could sure use a cup," Mary admitted, and headed for the reader's nook.

"What's wrong?" Tricia asked.

"Last night," Mary said, succinctly.

Tricia took the chair opposite her guest. "I know exactly how you feel."

"You're used to being involved in all kinds of murders. People like me are not."

Tricia wasn't quite sure how to respond to that. "I'm not involved in Mrs. Comfort's murder. It's just unfortunate that Angelica's dog happened to find her while I was taking him for a walk."

Mary waved a hand in annoyance. "You know what I mean. It was very upsetting to have to talk to the police. The way they looked at all of us, as if one of us were responsible for her death. We were *invited* guests."

"As raffle winners, I wouldn't exactly say we were invited. Tolerated. A means to an end—giving the innkeepers the opportunity to use us as guinea pigs for their shakedown before opening. But invited? No."

Mary sighed. "I suppose you're right. I feel traumatized by this whole ordeal. I've never known anyone who was murdered. I barely knew Mrs. Comfort. We only chatted for a couple of minutes after Luke and I arrived at the inn. No sooner had she shown us to our room when Chauncey Porter showed up and she excused herself." She tilted her head to one side and looked thoughtful. "That was weird."

"What do you mean—weird?" Tricia asked.

"I left our room to ask for more towels. As I rounded the landing, I heard Chauncey say something about her being out of uniform. I didn't get it. Then Mrs. Comfort gave him quite a dressing-down."

"What for?"

She shrugged. "But something about his remark distressed her. She stopped talking when I entered the room, asked me what I wanted, and then went to fetch me the towels."

Tricia considered her words. "Chauncey is such a sweetheart. I can't imagine him saying anything to upset someone. Did you tell Chief Baker this?"

"It completely slipped my mind until this morning when I started going over everything in my head. The more I thought about it, the more rattled I got. I even considered not opening my shop today—but then realized I'd probably just dwell on it all day, anyway. I need the distraction of customers coming and going or I'll have a nervous breakdown."

"How is Luke doing?"

"He's upset, too, of course, but he got up and went to work this morning just like usual. Men just don't feel things the same way as women."

That was an understatement.

The coffeemaker began to sputter, letting Tricia know it had finished brewing. "Let me get you that coffee," she said, and rose from her seat.

Mary followed, patiently watching as Tricia poured coffee into one of the shop's paper cups for her, and a china Haven't Got a Clue store mug for herself. Mary added sweetener and creamer to her own, mixing it with a spoon, and then took a scorching gulp. "Just what I needed."

The door handle rattled, and Mr. Everett entered the shop. "Good morning, Ms. Miles. Mrs. Fairchild—how nice of you to visit."

"Good morning," the women chorused.

"You're in early," Tricia said, as Mr. Everett headed for the back of the shop to hang up his jacket.

"I like to keep busy," he said. Mr. Everett had won the Powerball Lottery just over nine months before. Recently his wife, Grace, had opened an office across the street from Tricia's bookstore for the Everett Charitable Foundation. In fact, the foundation was located right above Angelica's café, Booked for Lunch.

Grace, who had never worked for a living and had only ever done volunteer work, had taken on the responsibility as though it were her life's mission. And, in fact, that was just what the job had become. She'd even found it necessary to hire an assistant to help her sort through all the requests for handouts. This had not pleased her husband of eighteen months, who preferred not to be separated from his wife for so many hours in the day. It had worked out for Tricia, however, because despite her best efforts, she hadn't yet found a suitable replacement for her former assistant, Ginny Wilson, who now managed the Happy Domestic shop across the street.

Mr. Everett's arrival had put a distinct end to Tricia and Mary's conversation. "I'd better get going," she said, and Tricia walked her to the door. "I hate to be a bother, but would you mind if I called you later—I mean, if I'm feeling all rattled again?"

"Certainly."

Mary rested a hand on Tricia's arm. "You are a dear. I'm sorry to be such a bundle of nerves, but like I said—this is all so new and strange for me."

"Don't give it a thought."

"Talk to you later. And thanks for the coffee," Mary said, and Tricia closed the door behind her.

"I see you've already made the coffee," Mr. Everett said as he tied on the green apron with the Haven't Got a Clue logo and his name emblazoned on it.

"Mary needed a little hand-holding this morning." She didn't want to go into why, but she knew it would eventually come up. "Feel free to help yourself."

Tricia retreated to the cash desk, where she counted out the money for the till. Miss Marple, who'd refrained from joining in the previous conversation, hopped up to her perch on the wall behind the register.

Mr. Everett approached the desk and stood there, waiting expectantly. Tricia looked up. "Is something up?"

"I understand there was another murder last night," Mr. Everett said, without making eye contact. "Is it true you found the body?" The unspoken word *again* seemed to echo off the tin ceiling.

First Mary, now Mr. Everett. She sighed. "I'm afraid so."

"It must be getting tiresome," Mr. Everett commented. "I mean, it's unfortunate that it always seems to be *you* who finds corpses around our fair village. And to think, we were once the safest village in all of New Hampshire."

Tricia held her breath. Was he going to voice that ridiculous *jinx* label that had dogged her since she'd found that first body in the Cookery two and a half years before?

Mr. Everett shook his head. "I'm so sorry, Ms. Miles. We both seem to have our share of problems today."

Problems?

"Is there something you'd like to talk about?" Tricia offered.

Mr. Everett shook his head, but the corners of his mouth drooped and for a moment she thought he might cry. But then he shook himself, stood just a little taller, turned, and headed for the beverage station to get a cup of coffee. "Are we to interview another candidate this morning?" Mr. Everett asked, as he measured out the creamer and placed it into his cup.

"I'm afraid so." Tricia frowned. "Mr. Everett, do you think our standards are too high? I mean, we've both been unhappy with the last three people I've hired."

Mr. Everett sighed. "It's definitely not just you, Ms. Miles. I, too, thought the last one might be different." He shook his head. "In this economy, people will say just about anything to get a job. But far too many of the candidates who've come through our door seemed more interested in texting than selling books."

"When Angelica had a hard time finding the right person to work at the Cookery, I blamed it entirely on her. But now I'm not so sure she was completely at fault—and I never thought I'd say that."

Mr. Everett nodded. "Don't worry, Ms. Miles. We'll find someone to permanently take Ginny's place. And soon. I'm sure of it."

Tricia wished she shared Mr. Everett's positive attitude.

The telephone rang, and Tricia hurried to answer it, at the same time dreading that it would be the latest job interviewee canceling at the last minute. "Haven't Got a Clue, this is Tricia. How may I—"

"Tricia? It's Grant Baker."

Not the person she wanted to speak to. "What can I do for you?" she said, trying to sound bright and cheerful.

"Will you come down to the station sometime this morning to file a statement about last night, or do you want me to send an officer over?" Why did he even ask? He knew she knew they were short staffed and really couldn't afford to tie up one of the uniforms with that kind of work.

"Of course I'll come over. But I'm interviewing another person for the assistant manager's job this morning. Would this afternoon be okay?"

"Sure."

"Have you learned anything new about the case since last night?"

"You know I can't talk to you about the murder investigation."

"Does that mean you can't talk to me at all?" Tricia asked.

"It makes things difficult," he admitted.

Yes, it certainly did.

"Let's give it a few days—see how things shake out."

"You mean until you rule me out as a possible suspect?" Tricia asked.

She heard him sigh. "Something like that."

There was no point in getting angry. In fact, she wasn't sure she *was* angry. She'd suspected this was coming, after all.

"Are you angry with me?" he asked.

She turned away, so that Mr. Everett wouldn't hear any more of the conversation, not that he would actively eavesdrop. And, in fact, he'd disappeared to commandeer the shop's lamb's-wool duster. "No. Resigned. When this is over, can we have an honest talk about where we're going as a couple?" Or, more to the point, where they were *not* going as a couple. *Couple?* The word wasn't even appropriate for the level of commitment he'd been willing or able to show.

Baker sighed again. "Why is it women always want to talk about that kind of stuff?"

"Because it's important to us. It should be important to you, too."

"I'm on the rebound," he admitted.

"So was I after my divorce. I'm not asking for a lifelong commitment, just something more than we've got now."

"You've been very patient with me."

That wasn't what she wanted to hear, but there was also no point in voicing that sentiment yet again, either.

"Before I hang up, is there else anything you want to tell me about what happened last night? *Anything*," he stressed.

"Do you think I'm keeping something from you?"

"No. I'm just doing my job."

"Well, in the inimitable words of Winston Churchill: carry on."

She waited for him to say good-bye, but instead, he simply hung up.

Tricia frowned as she put the receiver back into its cradle. Almost immediately, it began to ring again. Good. He'd probably accidentally cut short their call without the pleasantries. She didn't want to think it might have been deliberate.

She let it ring a third time before picking it up. "Grant?"

"It's Angelica. What are you doing for lunch today?"

It was Tricia's turn to sigh. "The same as I always do on a week day. Come over to Booked for Lunch for the tuna plate."

"I'm not going in today. Come over to my apartment. I'm testing a special recipe for the next cookbook and I need a guinea pig to try it."

It wasn't the grandest of invitations but about the only one Tricia was likely to get that day. "Appetizer, soup, salad, entrée, or dessert?"

"It's a surprise."

"Okay, I'll be there at noon. Can I bring anything?"

"A bottle of Riesling would be nice."

"No can do."

"Then anything alcoholic you can lay your hands on. I'm parched."

"It's ten fifteen in the morning."

"I've been up since four, and I went to bed late last night. And I want to hear everything that happened at the inn after I left last night, too."

"Well don't hold your breath, because there's not much to tell. I'll see you around noon." Tricia hung up—without saying good-bye. But then, she would be seeing Angelica in a couple of hours—not days.

Mr. Everett stood nearby, holding the morning mail. Tricia hadn't even heard the door open and the mailman arrive.

"You'd best look this over before our first customers arrive," he said, and handed the small pile to Tricia.

"Thank you."

"I'll just go back to my dusting," Mr. Everett said, and headed toward the back of the store once more.

Tricia sorted through the envelopes. Mostly bills, a few useless circulars, and a bubble envelope. Tricia's heart sank. It was too small to be one of the books she'd ordered. Her ex-husband had been making a habit of sending expensive gifts at the most inopportune time. Was this another one?

She glanced at the postmark and frowned. Nashua, New Hampshire. Christopher lived in Colorado. Her anxiety level dropped and she took out a letter opener to slit the package open. Inside was a white envelope. She slit that open, too, and a photograph fell out, landing on the top of the display case. Intrigued, Miss Marple jumped down from her perch to take a look.

Tricia turned the photo over. A Post-it note was attached. In block lettering it said: *We'll meet again.* Tricia peeled off the note and saw a picture of herself, taken some indeterminate time in the past at what looked like a sidewalk café. In it she wore a straw hat, sunglasses, and an outfit she didn't remember ever owning—and she was laughing.

"*Yow!*" Miss Marple said.

Tricia frowned. Who could have sent the picture? And why didn't she remember where it was taken, who had taken it, or the occasion? Was the note supposed to represent a threat or a wistful remembrance?

Mr. Everett appeared before her, dusting the sill around the display window. He looked over at her. "Is something wrong, Ms. Miles?"

Tricia shook her head and stowed the picture under the counter. Mr. Everett went back to his dusting.

But Tricia couldn't help but feel unnerved by the photo, and she wondered who could have sent it, and why?

SIX

As expected, the agency that was to send over the day's applicant to interview for Ginny's former job called to cancel. The candidate had apparently found a better-paying job. That worried Tricia. She was already offering two dollars over minimum wage. Maybe she'd have to raise the starting pay. But as the three previous contenders for the job had proven unsuccessful, she wasn't feeling overly generous. She'd get to that point *after* they'd stayed in the job for more than a couple of weeks.

After snagging a bottle of wine, Tricia grabbed her coat from the back and snuggled into the sleeves. "Mr. Everett, I'm leaving now."

Mr. Everett paused in his shelf straightening and hurried over to the cash desk.

"Are you sure you don't mind me taking an early lunch today?" she asked.

He shook his head. "Grace has a lunch meeting, so I'll be eating alone again today," he said rather wistfully. That had been happening a lot lately.

"I'm not going to the café, or else I'd promise to bring you back a sandwich. But Angelica always makes enough to feed an army when she's testing a recipe. I'm sure there'll be leftovers . . . I'm just not sure what kind of leftovers."

"I'll be fine. I brought a peanut butter and jelly sandwich."

Tricia tried not to shudder at the thought. Oh well . . . as long as he enjoyed them.

"I'll try to be back in an hour. But knowing Angelica, she'll probably try to get me to walk Sarge, too."

"That's why I prefer cats," Mr. Everett said. At that, Miss Marple lifted her sleepy head and blinked at them both. She'd been dozing in the front window, wound around a copy of the latest Tess Gerritsen book.

Tricia smiled. "See you in about an hour."

Tricia walked the ten feet to the Cookery and entered. Frannie Mae Armstrong, who managed the bookstore for Angelica, was with a customer. She waved a quick hello, and Tricia headed to the back stairs that lead to Angelica's loft apartment on the third floor.

The door was unlocked, so Tricia let herself in, hung up her coat, and followed the hall to the kitchen, which smelled heavenly.

"Anybody home?" she called.

"In the kitchen," Angelica hollered.

As usual, Angelica was standing over the kitchen island, making notes on what looked like manuscript pages. Sarge stood next to her and gave Tricia a chipper bark in greeting, the tip of his fluffy tail wagging merrily.

"What smells so good?" Tricia asked, and inhaled deeply.

"Sausage and vegetable strudel. It's a takeoff on a recipe I've made hundreds of times, only this is my pizza version. I hope you'll like it."

"I bet I will." She handed Angelica the bottle.

"Get out the plates and silverware, while I finish this."

"Yes, ma'am."

By the time Tricia had set the table, Angelica set her notes aside and took the strudel from the oven, transferring it onto a waiting platter. "It has to sit for a few minutes. Would you like a cup of coffee or a glass of wine to go with it?"

"With the way my day's going, I'll take the wine," Tricia said.

"Oh dear. That doesn't sound good. Tell me all about it," Angelica said, reaching for the glasses in the cupboard.

Tricia commandeered one of the island's stools. "Have you heard anything new about the murder last night?"

Angelica shook her head. "No, but I've already been interrogated by Frannie. She missed her calling. *She* should have been a police detective. How about you?"

"Luckily Frannie was busy with a customer when I came in, but I'm sure she'll try to catch me on the way out. I did have a quick conversation with Grant, though. *Quick* being the operative word. He says he can't talk to me—as a person—until this whole mess is sorted out. I'm supposed to go to the station to make a report sometime this afternoon."

"Me, too. But I didn't get a call from the chief himself," Angelica said wryly. "Have you heard from Harry yet today?" she added, with a sly lilt to her voice.

"Of course not. Why would I?"

"Well, if he was sweet on you once. And now he's suddenly available . . ."

"Oh, Ange, that's a terrible thing to say. His wife was just murdered."

Angelica shrugged and cracked the cap on the bottle of wine.

"Mary Fairchild came to see me this morning. She's terribly upset about the whole situation," Tricia said.

"Why not? Like the rest of us she got cheated out of a night in a lovely inn."

"That wasn't her complaint. She wanted some hand-holding. She seemed to think finding corpses doesn't bother me."

"Well, you *have* had more experience than the rest of us."

Tricia glowered at her sister. "I've been mulling all this over since last night. Do we know who recruited Pippa and Jon/Harry/whoever to Stoneham?" Tricia asked as she accepted a glass of wine from Angelica.

"What makes you think they were recruited? It's been obvious for some time that there's a lack of hotel space in the vicinity. Maybe they just did their homework. Or maybe they came to Milford's pumpkin festival and found nowhere quaint to stay in the area and thought, *Oh, this is an opportunity.* If I weren't overwhelmed with the Cookery, Booked for Lunch, and my writing career, I might have stepped up to the plate," Angelica admitted. There was something odd about the lilt in her voice.

"That's possible," Tricia agreed. "I understand they bought the place last fall and have been working on it for the past few months, but I'm not sure they actually own it."

"If you're so interested, why don't you talk to Jon Comfort?"

"Harry Tyler," Tricia corrected.

"Whatever. Maybe he's interested in selling now that he's lost his wife. I mean, he may need the money for his legal defense."

"Why would I want to talk to the man? He walked out on me."

Angelica waved a hand in dismissal. "That was over twenty years ago. You're not still carrying a torch for him, are you?"

"Of course not. But let's face it, it's the ultimate snub to walk out on your family, friends, *and* girlfriend, fake your death, and disappear into obscurity."

"Girlfriend or lover?" Angelica asked, ignoring the last part of Tricia's sentence.

"Both."

Angelica's smile was smug as she shook her head and tsked. "And Daddy always bragged how you were such a *good* girl."

Tricia gave her sister a sour look. "Let's get back to the subject at hand. Why was Pippa murdered?"

"I'd say it's up to the police to figure it out, but knowing you, you'll wrestle with it like a terrier with a rat." Sarge gave a solid yip in agreement. Angelica blew him two kisses and said, "Your mommy knows bichons are better. But I'm not sure your Auntie Tricia does."

"I'm no aunt to a dog."

"Well, of course you are."

"Do you consider yourself Miss Marple's aunt?"

"Definitely not. Dogs are man's best friend. Cats are . . . not."

"In case it escaped your attention, you are not a man."

"And glad of it," Angelica said.

Tricia sighed. Sometimes—okay, almost always—it was useless to argue with Angelica.

Angelica carried the strudel to the table, cutting it with a knife and placing slices on the waiting plates. She placed one before Tricia and took a seat opposite. They both cut pieces of the still-steaming strudel. Tricia blew on hers before taking a bite. She chewed and swallowed.

"Oh, this is decadent."

"Kind of like a pizza without the heavy crust, huh?" Angelica asked, pleased at Tricia's reaction.

Tricia ate another bite, then reached for her wineglass. "As if all these conversations weren't enough to spoil my morning, the mail brought something rather puzzling." She reached for her purse and withdrew the photograph. "Take a look."

Angelica leaned over to glance at the photo. "Nice shot of you. Who sent it?"

"I don't know. The postmark on the envelope was Nashua."

Angelica shrugged. "Who do you know in Nashua—besides customers and vendors, that is?"

"No one. It was taken quite a while ago. I don't remember where or when. And it came with a note that said, *We'll meet again*, and no signature."

Angelica studied Tricia's face. "You look kind of spooked."

Tricia shook her head. "It just bothers me that I don't remember anything about a day that someone seems to remember well. And why be so secretive about it?"

"Just to bug you? Do you think your Harry could have sent it?"

Tricia squinted at the picture. "Maybe."

"Ask him."

"Maybe," she said again, returning the picture to her purse before she turned back to her lunch and cut another piece of strudel.

"I am just swamped this afternoon," Angelica said, and grabbed her wineglass. I have so much to accomplish and could use a teensy favor from you before you go back to your shop."

Tricia had a feeling she knew what the request would be.

"It's almost time for Sarge's walkie-walk. Could you take him out while I type up this recipe?"

"I already told you, I'm supposed to go to the police station. I don't want to hold up Mr. Everett's lunch."

"Couldn't you combine the two? Pleeeeeease," she said with girlish pleading.

"I am *not* a dog walker," Tricia said with authority.

"Yes, but I've got three more recipes to test today, and if Sarge has to wait much longer his little eyes will turn yellow."

As if to back her up, Sarge whimpered piteously. Angelica had probably slipped him a command under the table to elicit the performance.

Tricia looked down at Sarge, who cocked his head and looked terribly sad. She took her last bite of strudel and stood. "Oh, all right. But this is the second time in less than twenty-four hours. The next time you come over to my place, I'll expect you to clean Miss Marple's litter box."

She grabbed Sarge's leash from the peg on the wall. The little dog began to dance around in circles, making it even more difficult to attach it to his collar. "Calm down. We're only going for a walk, not to Saks." She scooped up the dog and headed for the door.

"Thank you! See you in a few," Angelica called behind them.

Tricia put on her coat and started down the steps to the shop below. Usually Angelica just took Sarge out back to the alley for his comfort stops, but Tricia felt like she'd been cooped up long enough. The day was brisk but bright, and she decided to head toward the village park instead. She would combine the errands—unless the cops wouldn't let her enter their office with the dog. Then she'd have to come back another day to sign her statement. Or maybe Baker would be forced to come to Haven't Got a Clue and take her statement in person after all.

She carried Sarge through the Cookery and was stopped by several customers who wanted to admire the dog. Luckily Frannie was busy at the register—no time for an interrogation after all. "Sorry, ladies, but I'm afraid Sarge has a date with a fire hydrant. If you'll excuse us."

They gave Sarge one last pat on the head, and Tricia exited the store.

Once outside, Tricia set Sarge on the pavement, and he took off like a shot. Obviously he knew exactly where he was heading and even paused and sat at the curb to wait for the command to cross the street. "You really are a clever little boy," she told him, and Sarge wagged his tail as if to say, *Of course!*

Tricia guided Sarge across the street, and they headed for the village square. The granite gazebo with its copper roof, which had stood in ruins behind a rickety construction fence since August, was finally undergoing renovation. The business owners had sponsored a campaign to rebuild the structure, with the Board of Selectmen matching funds. It had taken a lot less time than anyone had imagined. Once it was rebuilt, maybe the sad incident that had caused its destruction could be forgotten—although certainly not the people who'd died as a result. Members of the Chamber of Commerce had already pledged to erect a plaque to be mounted on the gazebo itself.

Sarge moseyed up to his favorite hydrant, and Tricia looked the other way. After giving him a moment of privacy, she started off, intending to make a circuit of the park, and Sarge happily trotted along beside her.

As Tricia and Sarge neared the corner, Tricia saw a familiar figure heading toward Kelly Realty: Clayton Ellington. What could he possibly want with Bob Kelly?

Perhaps to discuss the fate of the Sheer Comfort Inn? Could Harry have put it up for sale already? What if it was Ellington who actually owned it? After a murder had taken place, he (or whoever owned it) might want to promptly dump the property. And honestly, would Jon/Harry want to live there after Pippa's death? And if Ellington didn't own the property, maybe this was the opportunity he'd been looking for to obtain it.

It was something to consider.

A gust of chilly wind ruffled Tricia's hair, and she decided not to include a trip to the police station on this errand after all. Instead, she and Sarge headed back toward the Cookery. She had just enough time to get the dog home before Mr. Everett's appointed lunch hour.

As she neared her store, she saw Amy Schram from Milford Nursery and Flowers pull up in her family's delivery van and park outside of the Have a Heart romance bookstore. Amy got out of the van and waved before she headed for the back of the vehicle and opened the door.

"Hi, Amy," Tricia called, and paused, watching as Amy withdrew a large plastic urn from the back of the van.

"Hey, Tricia. That doesn't look like Miss Marple," she said, and stooped to offer her hand for Sarge to sniff.

"Miss Marple doesn't like the cold. And she wouldn't stand still for a collar, let alone being walked on a leash." Sarge barked in agreement, and the women shared a laugh. "What's going on?"

Amy nodded at the gray planter with its faux patina of age, filled with fresh dirt. "New from the Chamber of Commerce and the Board of Selectmen. They thought it would be nice if every storefront had an urn filled with spring flowers."

"Shouldn't they have been planted last fall?" Tricia asked.

"We had a bunch of bulbs ready for just such an order behind our greenhouses. Once I've got all the urns in place, I'll dig them up and put them in the planters. They'll be very pretty in a couple of weeks—just in time for the tourists to return. Then after they're finished, I'll come by and put in some pansies once the threat of frost is gone."

"That sounds pretty ambitious."

"Anything to please the tourists. Happy tourists spend money. And we're sure glad for the business, too."

"Speaking of business, I saw a lovely arrangement at the Sheer Comfort Inn last night. Your family does such beautiful work."

"That was my mom's handiwork." Her smile of pride soon dimmed. "It's a shame about Mrs. Comfort being killed. I spoke with her when I made the delivery." She shuddered, and Tricia was sure it wasn't a result of the stiff breeze. "We were going to have a standing order to deliver flowers twice a week. Now . . . who knows?"

"Has Mr. Comfort already canceled the order?" Until the rest of the world knew Harry's story, Tricia thought it best to keep up the charade.

"Not yet. But if nothing else, the inn isn't likely to open as planned—if it opens at all. That's a shame, too. Stoneham could really use the extra accommodations." She turned back to the van and took out another planter.

"I won't keep you," Tricia said. "And I'll look forward to seeing my new planter."

"I should make it down to Haven't Got a Clue in another five or ten minutes. I'll wave at Miss Marple through the window."

Tricia smiled. "See you around, Amy."

Tricia started back down the pavement. She had just enough time to drop Sarge off and still get back to her shop by the stroke of one.

She halted before she got to the Cookery's door, picked up the dog, and, on impulse, gave him a quick kiss on the top of his head. "You're such a good boy. Don't tell Angelica, but I'd love to take you on a walk any time. You just ask."

Sarge yipped and licked her face. Tricia giggled and reached for the door handle, turned it, and stepped inside.

"I saw what you did!" said a commanding voice.

Caught!

SEVEN

 "Haw-haw!" Frannie said with glee, as Tricia shut the Cookery's door. She straightened and, with great dignity, placed Sarge on the carpet, where he promptly sat, looking up at her expectantly. "I don't know what you're talking about," she told Frannie, but she could feel the color rising up her neck to her cheeks.

"You kissed Angelica's dog—right on the head. Wait 'til Miss Marple smells that dog on you. She's going to be mighty upset."

"I only took Sarge for a walk to help Angelica out. It's not like I'm swearing off cats forever."

Frannie crossed her arms over her pink and white aloha shirt. "Uh-uh."

"Now, if you'll excuse me, I have to take Sarge upstairs," Tricia said, then tugged on the leash, and Sarge jumped to his feet and happily followed.

By the time Tricia returned to the kitchen, Angelica was

busy stirring something in a pot on the stove. She dipped the spoon out and held it out to Tricia. "Here, taste this."

"I really have to get back to my store. Mr. Everett is waiting," Tricia said, and quickly let Sarge off his leash, which she hung on a chair. "Gotta go!" she said, then hightailed it out of the kitchen, down the hall, and to the stairs that led back to the Cookery. She hoped she could escape without having to talk to Frannie again, but as there were no customers in the store, Frannie had lain in wait for her to exit the stairway and practically jumped out at her.

"Don't do that!" Tricia chided. "You could give someone a heart attack."

"Oh, sorry," Frannie apologized, but her eyes were alight with mischief. She was ready to dish some kind of gossip.

"I hear tell things aren't as they seem over at the Sheer Comfort Inn."

Tricia's eyes narrowed. "And who told you that? Angelica?"

Frannie shook her head. "She's too busy working on her new cookbook to stand around with the help these days. No, I got a call from a friend of a friend who said that Mr. Comfort isn't Mr. Comfort at all. And that you might have known him in the past."

Since Frannie considered Mary to be a friend, could the friend of a friend be Chauncey Porter? He'd been the only other person at the B-and-B the night before that Frannie might have known.

"I don't know what you're talking about," Tricia said, and headed for the exit.

"World-famous mystery author Harrison Tyler," Frannie said with a lilt in her voice.

That stopped Tricia dead. She turned back to face Frannie.

"Word is that you and he were as thick as thieves just before he disappeared and was presumed dead." Frannie shook her head. "You poor little thing. Tricia, next to me, you have got to be the world's unluckiest woman when it comes to love."

Tricia blinked, startled by that pronouncement. "Well, I—"

"Of course, Angelica has had her share of heartache, too," Frannie went on. "But no more than me. And I'm sure Chief Baker had to have had something to say about all this. Did you two have words? Are you a suspect? Did you know Mr. Tyler was here in Stoneham all along?"

"No, I didn't, and I—"

But before she could finish her sentence, Frannie continued. "I've gone and entered the twenty-first century. I've signed up for computer dating."

Tricia couldn't seem to stop blinking. Where was this conversation going, anyway? "You did?"

Frannie nodded. "Why not? I'm not meeting any men here in Stoneham. I don't mind driving to Portsmouth or Manchester— if the right fella comes along, that is."

"I—I never gave that a consideration."

"You should," Frannie said with authority. She leaned in and lowered her voice. "In case things don't work out for you with Mr. Tyler or the chief. I've already had three dates with three different guys."

"And none of them worked out," Tricia guessed.

"Hell no! I'm going to a Celtics game in Boston next week with one of them. And my second fella, Barney, is taking me out to dinner on Friday night. And then the third one wants me to go to a show with him." Frannie's grin widened. "I don't know when I've had so much fun."

For a moment, Tricia thought she might cry. But then she did a quick reassessment of her life and decided, *The hell with romance!* She had a career she loved, Angelica, and many friends. She'd had the princess wedding and things hadn't worked out. Her two rebound relationships had gone nowhere. But romantic interludes weren't all there was to life.

"I'm very happy for you, Frannie," she managed with a smile that she hoped looked genuine. She glanced at her watch. "I've

really got to be going. It's time for Mr. Everett's lunch break."
She started for the door.

"Just remember what I said about online dating. And don't
you worry one bit. I won't tell Angelica how you kissed her
dog, either."

Tricia didn't bother to wave good-bye. And she had no
doubt that the next time Angelica came down the steps into
her shop, Frannie would go and tell all, and in excruciating
detail. Frannie was often a great resource for gossip—except
when you were on the receiving end of it.

Mr. Everett's lunchtime came and went. He came down from
the second-floor break room looking sad and keeping himself
to himself, as her grandmother used to say. Since he wasn't
feeling talkative—except when it came to recommending
books to customers, of course—Tricia turned on some cheerful Celtic music and tried to concentrate on the paperwork
before her. Unfortunately, her conversation with Frannie kept
replaying on her mind. How long would it be before Angelica
called and taunted her?

Okay, Sarge was very cute. Tricia had entertained the idea
of adopting him herself before Angelica practically stole him
from the Milford Animal Hospital some eight months before.

But that wasn't really what was on her mind: Harrison
Tyler, aka Jon Comfort. She'd been so shocked—and more
angry—to see him that it hadn't really penetrated that his
disappearance just before his wife's death made him the prime
suspect in her murder.

Well, duh! As she'd told Angelica, the spouse is always the
first to become a person of interest in a murder investigation.

Part of her wanted to talk to him, commiserate with him.
The other part just flat-out wanted to kill him.

She looked around, wondering if any of the customers in
the store could read her mind.

The shop door opened, accompanied by the little bell that rang out cheerfully, and Harry Tyler himself walked in.

The part of Tricia that felt sorry for the rat quickly fizzled. "May I help you?" she asked tartly.

For a moment, Harry just stood there, taking in the bookshelves, the beverage station, and the photos of long-dead mystery authors framed on the hunter green walls. His gaze settled on one of them: his own. Tricia had almost forgotten she'd included his face among the no-longer-living legends.

While he was taking in the scenery, Tricia allowed herself to study Harry. He hadn't changed much. Just a few more lines around the eyes, and streaks of gray in his hair, which was longer, shaggier, too, although it seemed to fit him. His leather jacket was unzipped, and Tricia could see the contour of his muscles beneath a sky blue—and rather tight—sweater. Had he dressed to impress her?

Harry seemed to shake himself and shuffled over to the cash desk. "Hi."

"Hi," she said, and actually sounded civil. "What are you doing here? Did you come to see if I stock *Death Beckons?*"

He shook his head. "I was over at the Baker Funeral Home, making . . . arrangements."

"Surely the ME hasn't already released Pippa's—" She halted, unable to finish the sentence when she saw the stark look of anguish in his eyes. At one time she'd loved those eyes. Or at least she thought she had. It was so long ago . . . and yet, when she looked at him now, it might as well have been weeks—not years—since they were together. "I'm sorry, Harry."

He shrugged, as though he'd expected such a comment.

"When will you hold a service?" Tricia asked.

"I won't. At least not here. Pippa didn't know anyone here in Stoneham. I'm going to have her cremated and spread her ashes up north. That's where we lived for the past fifteen years."

Tricia nodded.

He ducked his head and looked sheepish. "I'm sorry we got off on the wrong foot last night."

"Have you admitted to Chief Baker who you really are?"

He sighed. "We haven't spoken today, but there's no hiding it now," he said, with a look toward the wall where his portrait hung. He turned back to face Tricia and offered a wan smile. "You're still a looker," he said.

Tricia stifled a laugh. "You used to be a lot more loquacious."

Harry nodded. "That I was."

"They declared you dead, you know."

He nodded and shoved his hands into his worn jeans pockets. "I don't have a problem with that."

"Well, I'm sure some branch of law enforcement will, if not the IRS, then social security."

Harry frowned, as though he hadn't given it that much—any?—thought until she'd brought it up. Was he suddenly a flight risk?

"So, the big question remains. Why did you fake your own death?" She'd been aching to ask that question since the previous evening.

Harry stuffed his hands into his pockets, hunching his shoulders. "You make it sound so . . . tawdry. I'd just had enough, okay?"

"Enough of what? The money? The adoration?"

"It was all too much. The press. The pressure to come up with another winner. My editor rejected the follow-up to *Death Beckons*. She hated it and told me to start over. Nearly two years' work down the drain. I couldn't write. Everything was falling apart. It just seemed easier to . . . walk away."

"So, your ego was bruised," Tricia said, unable to keep the bitterness out of her voice.

"I told you about that book. You knew it meant everything to me."

"More than your family? More than me?"

"Now whose ego is bruised?" Harry asked, sounding not the least contrite.

Tricia said nothing. She wasn't sure she could trust her voice not to give away how hurt she still was after all these years.

"So what did you do? Get lost in New York or L.A.?"

"I went to Idaho."

"Idaho? What for?"

"To think. To figure out what I wanted to do next. I found a guy who sold fake IDs. I became Jonathan Comfort. I worked on a farm for a while."

"Somehow I can't picture you hoeing potatoes," Tricia said.

He ignored her sarcastic remark and continued. "Eventually I made my way back east and got lost in Maine for a couple of years."

"You wanted to stay close to the sea?"

"Yeah, I worked a lobster boat for a couple of seasons and then ended up in Bretton Woods where I met Pippa. She worked in the bar at the big hotel there. I got a job as a groundskeeper. We got married a couple of years later." He looked up at her. "I take it you never married."

"Why, because my name is still Miles?" He nodded. "I was married for ten wonderful years, and then he dumped me."

"Why would anyone want to do that to you?"

"You could ask yourself that same question."

He shook his head. "I guess in my roundabout way I'm trying to say I'm sorry."

"You're about twenty years too late for that," Tricia said. And then, just as suddenly, she didn't care about the past. It was over. They'd both gone on with their lives, and, despite a few lows here and there, she wasn't too dissatisfied.

Most days.

"What will you do now—run away again?" she asked.

"I've thought about it. But . . . I've also thought about publishing more of my work."

"You mean online?"

His eyes narrowed. "You don't think I've still got what it takes to get published by a big New York house?"

"I was just asking. Because . . . I know a literary agent. He might be persuaded to take a look at your work."

Harry's eyes lit up. "You'd do that for me . . . after what I did all those years ago?"

"I would hope you're a different person now. And you're going to need income when the law catches up with you."

He looked downcast. "There is that, too. But I'm not totally without income. I've been teaching a writing course evenings at the Milford high school. I took the job so we'd have some money coming in while we got ready to open the inn."

"Are you published under the name Jon Comfort?"

"A few short stories," he admitted. "I've got a couple of novels in a trunk that are in pretty good shape, too. I just wasn't sure I could hack writing on a deadline ever again."

"The bane of the published author, at least those who want to stay that way," Tricia said offhandedly.

Harry scowled.

"The agent I'm thinking of doesn't normally handle mysteries—just the estate of Zoë Carter. But he's good. He's my sister's agent."

"Angelica is an author?"

She gave him points for remembering Angelica's name, not that he'd ever met her before. They'd been close but hadn't gotten to the point of meeting each other's families. "She writes cookbooks."

His smile was forced. "Pippa was the one who cooked in our house. I can only handle the barbecue."

"And I can barely boil water," Tricia admitted, and they both laughed. "I'll talk to Angelica about it and get back to you."

"Thanks. I'd appreciate that." Harry looked at the clock. "I'd better get going. Chief Baker awaits."

Tricia didn't envy him the upcoming conversation.

"Could you do me a favor, though?" He nodded over his shoulder. "Take down that picture. I don't deserve to be up there with all those real authors."

"You *are* a real author. You just lost sight of it."

He shrugged. "I guess I'll see you around, Tricia."

"I guess," she agreed.

He kind of hovered in front of her for a moment, and she thought he might lean forward and kiss her. But then he turned, headed for the door, and shut it behind him without looking back.

Tricia just stood there, staring at the empty doorway for a long moment before she heard a stifled, "Ahem."

She looked to her right to see Mr. Everett with a customer and wondered how long they'd been standing there. "Would you like to ring this up, Ms. Miles?"

Tricia smiled. "I'd be delighted."

The customer moved to stand before the cash desk, setting her books on the glass, and Mr. Everett turned away. "Could you bring out the stepladder, Mr. E? We're going to do a little switcheroo with the author photos."

He nodded. "As you wish, Ms. Miles."

Tricia rang up the sale, adding a couple of author bookmarks and the store's newsletter to the shopping bag. She'd take down Harry's portrait and shuffle the others forward, leaving a gap at the far end of the wall. She'd have to hit the stock photography websites to see if she could find something to fill in the empty space.

She'd miss seeing Harry's face looking down at her.

EIGHT

 Although it was almost April, Haven't Got a Clue's winter hours were still in effect and Mr. Everett was just zipping his jacket to leave for the day when the shop door opened. Thankfully, it wasn't a customer—Tricia hated to turn anyone away at the end of the day—it was only Angelica, dressed to the nines.

"My, don't you look pretty tonight," Mr. Everett said in greeting.

"Why thank you, kind sir," Angelica practically purred.

Mr. Everett nodded and headed for the door. "Good night, ladies. I'll see you in the morning, Ms. Miles."

"Good night," Tricia called after him.

"So, you and Bob are going out tonight? I was hoping we could have dinner together."

"Sorry, no can do," Angelica said brightly. "Michele Fowler and I are going out to dinner to discuss business."

Tricia and Angelica had met Michele the previous summer when she'd been the owner of an upscale art gallery. Thanks to the economy that refused to improve, that business had folded. But, as expected, Michele had rebounded.

"That woman could talk to whales under the ocean—and she has far more experience in the restaurant trade than you do. So what could you possibly have to talk about?" Tricia asked.

Angelica straightened her tan leather gloves, which perfectly complemented her camel's-hair coat. "She wants to pick my brain about how to best get along in such a small town."

"Like you're an expert?" Tricia asked. "You've lived here all of two and a half years."

"Which is plenty of time for me to have learned the ropes." She offered a conciliatory smile. "Why don't you come along with us—in fact, that's why I stopped by."

Tricia frowned. "What? And sit there all night just waiting for an opening to ask you to pass the pepper and salt? I'd never get a word in edgewise."

"Why, Tricia, I do believe you're jealous that Michele and I are friends," Angelica said with glee.

"Of course not." *That* was a bald-faced lie. Good thing she didn't have her hand on a stack of Bibles.

"Oh, yes you are. Every time I mention Michele's name, your eyes get all squinty and you seem to wince."

"I think she's a lovely person, and she's extremely lucky to have a friend like you."

Angelica positively preened. "Yes, she is—on both counts. We always have such fun when we're together. I haven't had a close girlfriend to confide in for ages."

"What am I, chopped liver?" Tricia asked.

"You're my sister. It's different," Angelica said with a dismissing wave of her hand.

Tricia couldn't help but feel hurt. During her entire childhood Angelica had shut Tricia out of her life. It had taken them forty years to become friends, and now this larger-than-life woman was spoiling the closeness they had shared for the past two-plus years.

Angelica seemed oblivious to her distress. "I was wondering, would you be a dear and let Sarge out this evening?" Ah, the *real* reason for her visit. "I hate to think of the poor little guy all alone with his tiny legs crossed. Better yet, I could bring him to your apartment and—"

"You know Sarge and Miss Marple don't get along. It's not fair for me to allow Sarge into the apartment to torment her."

"They'd get along fabulously if you'd only let them get acquainted," Angelica insisted.

Tricia held up a hand. "We're not going to talk about this again. But I *will* let Sarge out. I won't see an animal suffer because its mistress is negligent or cruel."

"I'm going out to dinner, not on a death march," Angelica said and glanced at the clock. "Oh, I'm late."

"Where are you meeting Michele?"

"I'm picking her up in Milford. Did you know she got an apartment there?"

"Yes, I seem to remember you telling me that before." About twenty times before.

"We're going to try a new family restaurant in Merrimack."

"That doesn't sound like your style."

"She's going to hire someone to work the grill at the Dog-Eared Page."

"It doesn't even open for another month."

"You can't leave these things until the last minute." She wiggled her fingers and started for the door.

"When will Sarge need to go out?" Tricia called after her.

"I let him out about an hour ago. He should be good until eight or nine. Although eight is better for my carpets. Ciao!" Angelica said, and pulled the door closed behind her.

A disgruntled *"Yow!"* sounded from behind the shelf on the wall where Miss Marple liked to perch. Other than that, the store was silent. Tricia was glad the clock on the wall didn't tick loudly; that would just reinforce her sense of loneliness.

"This is ridiculous. I *am* used to living alone," she said to herself, and Miss Marple jumped down on the sales counter to rub her head against Tricia's arm, as if to remind her she wasn't totally without company. Tricia scratched the top of Miss Marple's head, and the cat's purr went into overdrive.

Tricia locked up the day's receipts, tidied the store, and vacuumed, but all those tasks took only fifteen minutes. She still had the rest of the evening in front of her. She could watch TV or read but didn't feel the need to do either. It was nearing her own dinner hour, but she wasn't particularly hungry and wondered if a brisk walk would do her some good. As long as she as going, she figured she might as well take Sarge out, too.

Donning her coat and a Polar fleece hat, she grabbed her keys, shut off all but the security lights, and locked the door behind her. Three minutes later, she and an enthusiastic Sarge were on the sidewalk, striding toward the village park once again.

The lights were still on at the Patisserie as Tricia passed. She waved to Nikki Brimfield, who was swabbing out one of her big glass display cases, and gave a cheerful wave in return. That reminded Trisha that she needed to buy some cookies for her customers the next morning. Something else for her to-do list.

She stopped at the corner and, as before, Sarge promptly sat awaiting the command that it was safe to go. Since there was no traffic, Tricia tugged the leash and he sprang to his feet, eager to set off again.

They did a quick circuit around the park, but as the wind wasn't as strong as Tricia had anticipated, she decided to head on down one of the side streets. Sarge was quite happy to trot along by her side.

Minutes later Tricia found herself heading up Maple Avenue. She slowed her pace as she neared the Sheer Comfort Inn.

Unlike the last time she saw it, there were no welcoming lights in its mullioned windows. Even the sconces along the front door were dark so that the porch was bathed in shadows.

Tricia turned away. Was Harry in the back of the house somewhere, sitting all alone, brooding? Or was he in front of his computer writing? Or maybe he had lost himself in the pages of a book.

Why was she even thinking about him? It wasn't because she cared. Well, she did care. But she *didn't* care, too. Her feelings were all mixed up. She felt sorry for anyone in his position. But now she questioned her own motives for wandering in this direction.

She continued to walk down the pavement, into the shadow of the neighbor's hedges, which were in need of trimming. Sarge paused to give the base of the bushes a good sniff. Tricia tugged the leash, but Sarge had found something that had piqued his interest. The truth was, *any* smell piqued a dog's interest.

"Come on, Sarge, we'd better start for home," Tricia said, but the dog strained against the leash, trying to pull her forward. Had he found a dead bird or something equally smelly?

Tricia yanked her keys out of her pocket and pressed the button on the fob. A thin beam of light cut the darkness. She trained it on Sarge's head, then raked it along the base of the bushes. Tricia bent lower and could see something yellowish and metallic caught in the shrubbery. Her small flashlight's beam caught a rusty-colored substance along the bottom edge of the object and her stomach tightened. She yanked Sarge away from the bush and quickly crossed the street. Sarge reluctantly followed.

Tricia pulled her cell phone from her pocket and punched number four on her speed dial. It rang twice before a deep male voice answered, "Hello."

"Grant, it's Tricia. I'm on Maple Avenue a couple of houses

down from the Sheer Comfort Inn. I've found something I think you should see."

"Oh?"

"Yes. And . . . you might want to bring an evidence bag with you."

Tricia was frozen to the bone and night had fully fallen by the time Chief Baker's SUV arrived in front of the pretty Victorian home. She stood under a lamppost stamping her feet in an effort to keep the circulation going. Sarge sprang to his feet and started to bark as Baker exited the vehicle.

"Why is it always you?" Baker asked in exasperation as he joined Tricia on the sidewalk, holding a large flashlight in one hand.

She shrugged. "Just lucky, I guess. Come on, I'll show you what I've found." She led him and Sarge back to the hedges across the way. "Let me have your flashlight," she said, and he turned it on for her. It wasn't hard to find the object—Sarge had his nose right on it once again.

"Hold him back, will you?" Baker said, and took the flashlight from her, inspecting the object. "Is it a—"

"Brass candleholder," Tricia finished. "Pretty heavy, from the looks of it. It looked like there was some blood on it, too."

Baker squinted up at her. "Did you see another one like it in the inn the other night?"

"I wasn't paying that much attention. But I'll bet if you ask Angelica, she could give you an inventory of everything she saw in that house."

Baker straightened and looked her in the eye, his exasperation level escalating. "I'm glad you found it, but . . . I really wish *you* hadn't found it."

"Well, my fingerprints won't be on it, so that ought to clear me."

"Unless there are no fingerprints on it. That could mean

you wiped it down before discarding it. And what brought you out here tonight, anyway?"

"Angelica went out for the evening and asked me to walk her dog."

Baker scowled. "And the rest of it?"

"I don't know what you mean?"

"You just happened to be walking Angelica's dog—right past the house where a murder occurred the night before. A murder where *you* found the body. The body of your ex-lover's wife. And now you conveniently find what appears to be the murder weapon."

"Would you rather I hadn't reported it?"

He shook his head wearily. "No."

"Why don't we hope this *is* the murder weapon, and that it will lead you to the *real* killer, instead of all this supposition that I held some kind of grudge against a woman I'd known for less than fifteen minutes."

"You know perfectly well what the DA is going to think."

"And that should give you even more incentive to prove him wrong. That is, if you don't believe I'm capable of murder—unlike your ex-boss. Sheriff Adams was willing to railroad me to jail for a crime I didn't commit. Are you going to do the same?"

Before he could answer, a patrol car with lights flashing turned the corner and pulled up behind Baker's SUV. "Why don't you and Sarge wait in my car? At least you'll be out of the cold." Like all cops, he'd left the motor running.

Tricia reluctantly retreated to the car. She *was* freezing. She lifted Sarge, got in, and shut the door. Baker was already conversing with the officer, and they both went over to look at the candlestick.

Time dragged. After a while Sarge gave up watching the men across the road and curled into a ball on Tricia's lap and went to sleep. She wished she'd brought a book along.

Meanwhile, the Sheer Comfort Inn continued to stay dark.

If Baker or his officer had gone to check to see if the owner was at home, Tricia hadn't noticed. She'd been alternating looking out the window and watching the gas gauge plummet.

Eventually a Sheriff's Department cruiser showed up. Since Stoneham's newly reinstalled police department had no technical team, they still had to rely on the Sheriff's Department for some things.

After another five minutes of discussion, the deputy donned latex gloves and extracted the candlestick from the hedge. Baker finally returned to the SUV to check in with Tricia. She hit the button and rolled down the window.

"If you want to wait here in the car until we're done, I'll drive you home."

"How long is that going to take?" she asked.

He let out a weary breath. "Could be another hour."

"I think I'll walk." She lifted a groggy Sarge off her lap, opened the car door, and got out.

"I'll come over to your place later. Have you eaten?" Baker asked.

She shook her head.

"How about I bring a pizza?"

Tricia sighed. She had nothing else planned. "Sure. Why not?"

"You be careful walking home. You've got your cell phone, right?"

"That's how I called you in the first place," she reminded him. At least he was still concerned for her welfare.

"Oh, yeah." He looked like he wanted to say something else, and finally he just lunged ahead and gave her a quick kiss on the lips. The others had discreetly turned their backs on them.

"I'll see you in a while," Tricia said, and started off down the pavement once more. She looked back at the corner. Baker had rejoined the other officers, but he was watching her and gave a wave. She waved back and continued on her way.

After another circuit around the park, Tricia started back for the Cookery. She let herself in and took Sarge back to Angelica's loft. The lights were off. Angelica hadn't yet returned from her dinner with Michele Fowler.

Tricia had just locked the door to the Cookery when Baker pulled up and parked across the street from Haven't Got a Clue. Instead of a pizza box, he held a long paper bag with a sub sandwich inside. It was likely to be smothered in onions and hot peppers. Oh well.

He crossed the street.

"That was quick," Tricia said in greeting.

"Mr. Comfort hasn't yet returned home. I've left Rogers there to wait for him and have a call in to Judge Weaver for a warrant to search the inn."

"Looking for what? The matching candlestick?"

He nodded.

Tricia unlocked her own shop door and let herself in. Miss Marple rose and stretched on one of the readers' nook's comfy chairs. "Dinnertime!" Tricia called, and the cat jumped to the floor and headed for the back of the shop and the stairs leading to Tricia's third-floor loft.

Miss Marple bolted up the stairs and was impatiently waiting for Tricia to arrive and unlock the apartment door. Once inside, the cat went straight for her bowl. Tricia hung up her coat and hat and picked up the food and water bowls. She prepared the cat's meal while Baker hung his jacket over the back of one of the island's stools. He got plates out of the cupboard. "Glass of wine?" he asked. She nodded. He grabbed a glass, then retrieved the wine and a beer for himself from the fridge.

Miss Marple sat up pretty for her food, and then Tricia joined Baker at the island.

Baker unwrapped the sandwich, eased the smaller portion onto a plate, and handed it to Tricia.

"Since you've got his house staked out, I take it Harry is a viable suspect," she said, lifting the sesame roll to peek at the sandwich's contents.

"Everyone who was at the inn last night is a possible suspect, but we'll be looking especially hard at Mr. Comfort—or Tyler, or—whoever he is. We talked earlier today and he verified your story about his identity."

"Thanks for all your trust," Tricia said sarcastically. Why had he asked for oil instead of mayonnaise on the sandwich? "Do you think he's a flight risk?" she asked, removing the onions from the ham.

"Gut feeling?" Baker shook his head. "No."

"Are you ever wrong about these things?"

"Not lately. Why? Do you want him to stay here in Stoneham?"

For a moment Tricia wasn't sure how to answer, but she didn't have time to sort through her feelings just then. "I really don't care either way." *Lies, lies*, her conscience taunted.

Baker said nothing.

"I talked with Harry earlier today, too," Tricia admitted. "I need to put my hurt aside from so long ago. It doesn't matter anymore. And if there was anything concerning Harry Tyler that I loved, it was his writing. Hundreds of thousands of people have read *Death Beckons*. I think I can speak for them all when I say how much I've longed to read more of his work. His prose was luminous. His plotting flawless. His characterization superb."

"No mere mortal can compare with this paragon. Is that why your marriage failed? Could your ex hold a candle to Harrison Tyler?" he asked, and took an enormous bite of his sandwich—onions and all.

Tricia felt like she'd been slapped. "Grant—why would you say such a hurtful thing to me?"

He swallowed, then ran his tongue over his teeth to dislodge a piece of bread. "I'm sorry. It's just . . . maybe I'm a little jealous."

"Of Harry?" That was ludicrous. "I was twenty-two. I loved his book—his characters—probably much more than I ever cared for him."

"Would you have said that twenty years ago?"

Probably not, but if Baker might have to present her as a suspect in Pippa Comfort's death, she wasn't about to admit it.

She changed the subject. "On the walk home, I kept thinking about that candlestick. Why would someone dump it so close to the inn?"

"They wanted it found, probably to incriminate someone else."

"Exactly," Tricia agreed. "Now all we have to do is figure out who had the motive."

"Now all *I* have to do is figure out who had a motive. I don't want you to butt your nose into this. You're in enough trouble."

"How can I be in trouble when I haven't done anything wrong?"

"You have no eyewitness as to where you were between the time you spoke with Mary Fairchild and the body was found."

"It couldn't have been more than two or three minutes."

"Plenty of time for you to kill the poor woman, hide the candlestick in the hedge, and then very innocently call 911."

She was about to protest, but he held out a hand to stop her. "I'm not saying that's how it went down. I'm saying that's how it could be interpreted. I listened to the 911 call. You didn't say she was dead. Just that you wanted to report an accident. You knew she was dead, didn't you?"

"I suspected it," Tricia admitted, and that was all she was willing to admit without a lawyer present, and it was beginning to sound like she needed that lawyer. "You've known me for a year and a half. Do you seriously think I'm capable of killing anyone?"

"No. But I have to present all the evidence to the district attorney—"

"We've been over that ground before," Tricia said, interrupting him. She pushed her half of the sandwich away. Her appetite was long gone.

Baker stared at his food for a long time, then picked up the paper the sub had been wrapped in, folded it over his half, and put it back in the bag. "Until this case is solved, I think it best that we only speak to each other in an official capacity."

"Fine." Tricia said no more. She didn't trust herself to keep the growing anger out of her voice.

Baker shrugged back into his jacket, grabbed his sandwich, and headed for the door. Tricia followed. Miss Marple wanted to accompany them down to the shop, but Tricia nudged her back with her foot and followed Baker down the stairs and through the store. Baker unlocked the door, opened it, and paused. "I'm sorry, Tricia. This isn't how I'd like it to be, but it's as much for your protection as mine."

"Good night, Grant."

He hesitated, and for a moment she thought he might try to kiss her, but—he didn't. Instead, he turned and she shut the door behind him.

He'd been kind to her in the past, but no matter what, he'd never been able to commit to her—be it his ex-wife or his jobs that had kept them apart.

Fine.

As far as she was concerned, they were done. Kaput. Over.

She didn't look after him, just turned and headed back for the stairs to her loft and tried awfully damn hard not to cry.

NINE

No sooner had Tricia closed her apartment door than the phone in the kitchen began to ring. She was tempted to let it go to voice mail, but then decided if it was Baker calling from his cell phone in his car, she might just give him a piece of her mind anyway.

She grabbed the phone. "What other jolly news do you have to tell me?"

"Oh, Trish, you are psychic! How did you know I have good news to share?" said Angelica, her voice filled with excitement. "I was going to come right over and tell you but wondered when Sarge last went out."

Tricia looked at the clock. "About fifteen minutes ago."

"Oh good, then I'll be right up."

The line went dead, so Tricia hung up the phone.

True to her word, Angelica let herself into Haven't Got a

Clue and practically bounded up the stairs to the apartment within a minute of hanging up.

"I'm going to be on TV!" she squealed in delight, and actually jumped up and down a couple of times.

Miss Marple made a daring leap from the kitchen stool and hightailed it into the living room to escape the histrionics.

"What?" Tricia said.

But Angelica had already opened the fridge, rooting around until she found a bottle of Chardonnay. She grabbed a couple of glasses from the cabinet, removed the screw cap, and poured the wine.

She held up her glass. "Here's to my TV debut!" she said, and took a healthy swig.

"What TV debut?" Tricia repeated. "Take your coat off and tell me everything."

Angelica set her glass on the kitchen island and wiggled out of the sleeves of her coat. "At dinner tonight, Michele and I ran into the station manager and producer of *Good Morning, Portsmouth*."

"I never heard of it."

"Of course not. It's only been on the air since this morning. It's on the new start-up affiliate that just came to Portsmouth and began broadcasting today."

"If nobody knows the station is even on the air, how will that sell cookbooks?"

"Do you have to be such a stick in the mud?" Angelica snapped.

"I'm trying to be realistic."

"Can't you just be happy for me?" Angelica insisted.

Tricia sighed and sank onto one of the stools. "I *am* happy for you. In fact, I'm ecstatic. Tell me more."

Angelica's mood instantly returned to euphoric. "Well, it turns out this station manager, Bill Haskins, and Michele are old friends. She sold him a bunch of artwork for his condo in Tucker's Cove."

Tricia raised an eyebrow. She wouldn't have thought the manager of a start-up television station could afford to live in such a tony neighborhood. Or was that why he could afford to start up a new TV station in a city that had none?

Angelica settled herself on one of the island stools and took a more ladylike sip of her wine. "When Bill learned I was a nationally best-selling cookbook author, he immediately invited me to do a segment on the show Wednesday morning."

"That doesn't give you much time to prepare, does it? And what are you going to cook?"

"I have no idea. But it'll probably be a recipe from my first book—as the second one won't be out for another four months."

Angelica poked at the sandwich still on the island and picked out a piece of cheese, nibbling on it. It was then that Tricia saw a bit of ham on the edge of the island. Had Miss Marple helped herself to a little snack while Tricia let Baker out? Without a word she grabbed a napkin, scooped up the ham, and discreetly hid the evidence. Angelica didn't even notice.

"What are you going to wear?"

"I have no idea. I'll call Artemus tomorrow and see what he suggests."

It seemed to Tricia that Angelica bothered her literary agent, Artemus Hamilton, far too often with trivial questions. "Why don't you just Google it?"

"You know how Artie loves to hear from me," she said, then picked up the sandwich and took a bite.

Did Artie love hearing from her?

Angelica finished chewing and swallowed. "Besides, maybe he can send out a press release."

"Isn't that your job—not his?"

Angelica frowned. "I *am* one of his more successful clients. I'm sure he'll just ask his assistant to draft something."

"It's rather short notice—one day in advance."

"You worry too much," Angelica said, and drained her glass.

She got up from her seat, grabbed the wine bottle, and poured herself another. "And why are you so grumpy, anyway?"

Tricia offered her own glass to be topped up. "Oh, I don't know. The fact that Grant suspects me of Pippa Comfort's murder and said we can't see each other—let alone talk to each other unless it's about the case—until this whole situation is resolved."

"Why?"

Tricia took a fortifying swallow of wine before she related how she and Sarge had spent the evening.

"Oh dear," Angelica said, sobering. "Then I guess you won't be interested in buying advertising on Channel Nine. I mean, not if it looks like you'll actually be going to jail this time."

"I am *not* going to jail!"

"It doesn't sound too hopeful right now. Why did you take Sarge back to Maple Avenue, anyway? I told you he had an hour or more before he needed to go out. If you hadn't jumped the gun, someone else might have found that candleholder and you might not be looking at a stint at the New Hampshire State Prison for Women."

"I'm going to call Roger Livingston in the morning. Hopefully with his help—"

"You mean the help of one of his criminal attorney colleagues," Angelica interrupted.

"—I *will* clear my name," Tricia finished.

Angelica shrugged. "Let's get back to this TV show. This could be my big break—a one-way ticket to the Food Network."

Tricia sighed. How like Angelica to be more concerned with her own welfare. "Says who?"

"Me, of course."

"Only if you can get someone from the Food Network to watch the show."

"Hmm. That might be a bit hard. But I bet if I charm Bill,

he'll let me send a tape to an exec at the network." With that little detail worked out, Angelica took another big bite of the sandwich.

"Why are you eating my dinner?" Tricia asked. "You just got back from a restaurant."

Angelica chewed and swallowed. "Once I heard Bill was station manager, I was too nervous to eat. I'm starved. And where did you get this sandwich? It's delish."

"Grant brought it over . . . just before he told me we shouldn't see each other."

"Where's the rest of it?" Angelica said, and polished off the last bite.

"He took it with him."

Angelica swallowed. "Well, that wasn't very nice."

"It *was* his sandwich," Tricia pointed out.

"What else have you got to eat?"

"Not much."

Angelica went rummaging through one of the cabinets. "Let's see, saltines, brown sugar, an almost-full bag of chocolate chips. Where'd you get this stuff?"

"If you must know, I eat a lot of soup—which explains the crackers. As for the other, last Christmas I thought I might try my hand at baking again. I just never got around to it. I keep the chocolate chips in case of an emotional emergency. Actually, now that I think about it—now could be a chocolate emergency."

"If you've got real butter squirreled away, we've got candy."

"Candy?" Tricia repeated.

Angelica checked the freezer. "Oh, you do. Smart girl, giving up the processed crap that's disguised as butter." With that, Angelica found a saucepan, tossed in the butter, and turned the burner on low. "In about forty minutes, we'll have a delightful treat."

"I didn't know you were planning to stay that long."

Angelica glared at Tricia, then turned back for the stove.

"Line a cookie sheet with foil and spread out the crackers, will you. And turn on the oven to four hundred."

Tricia did as directed.

"Now," Angelica continued, "you've got to help me decide what to make for the TV show."

"Why don't you just make this recipe? It seems simple enough."

"I'm not even sure they've got a hot plate, let alone an oven. I'll call Bill in the morning to ask what I should bring."

Tricia could already smell the melting butter. Angelica measured the sugar and tossed it in, grabbing a wooden spoon from the utility crock to stir the mixture. "This recipe is so easy, even you could make it."

"You think?" Tricia said dutifully. The mix of ingredients didn't sound promising, but if Angelica said it would taste good, Tricia had to believe her. Then again, just about anything that was covered in chocolate had to be good.

"The recipe I use on the TV show has got to be simple," Angelica said. "Something I can have partially made, something I can cook in a skillet in a minute or so, and something with panache."

"Crepes flambé," Tricia suggested, expecting a scornful response. Instead, Angelica squealed with delight.

"Oh, Trish, that's perfect! Maybe you should help me pick out the recipes for the next couple of books. Too bad you don't actually eat much of anything besides iceberg lettuce and canned tuna."

"I do, too."

Angelica just shrugged and attended to her sugar-and-butter mixture, which was beginning to bubble. She inspected the tray covered with crackers, neatened up the rows, and then poured the hot mixture over the crackers. She placed it in the oven. "Now to let it bake for five minutes." She adjusted the stove's timer.

Angelica served herself the last of the wine and went looking for more. Sadly, that was the last of it. "You need to make a grocery run and restock your wine cellar."

"I've had a lot of help drinking the last few bottles," Tricia said, and drained her own glass. She sighed, allowing herself to pout. "I wouldn't have to drink so much if my life weren't such a mess."

"Cheer up," Angelica said without sympathy, "It can't get much worse." She bent to look into the oven to check on the crackers, which were madly frothing. The stove timer went off, so she grabbed a pot holder and removed the tray. "Hand me the chocolate chips, will you?"

Tricia did. Angelica sprinkled them over the crackers, then reached for a spatula. "When they're all nice and gooey, I'll spread the chocolate around. Oh dear. I forgot. They need to sit in the fridge for an hour or so before they can be eaten."

"So much for a quick treat," Tricia groused.

"Let them cool for a minute and eat one anyway. To err is human. To hang around waiting for perfection is just too damn long. You might want to apply that last little piece of advice to your love life, too."

"What do you mean?"

"I mean, you've been hanging around for nearly eighteen months waiting for Grant Baker to find time for you. It's time to move on, my girl."

"And we've talked about how slim the pickings are around here."

"Then broaden your horizons. Why not try a dating service?"

"Have you been talking to Frannie?" Tricia asked suspiciously.

"Only about her own love life—not yours, which is non-existent. You're not getting any younger."

"Neither are you. And if I'm not mistaken, you and Bob have been on the outs for quite some time, too."

"I'm busy with my careers. For the first time in my life, I

really haven't got time for romance, and I must say I don't miss it all that much. But I'm not swearing off men—just taking a much-needed hiatus. And the next man I commit to had better be monogamous. Or else."

Angelica poked at the cooling crackers, broke off a piece, and offered it to Tricia. She took a bite and her eyes widened with delight. She chewed and swallowed. "Whoa—who knew such innocent ingredients could taste so decadent."

Angelica laughed. "I'll make a cook out of you yet, darling Trish. And I've always found that the way to a man's heart *is* through his stomach. You might want to try that approach yourself."

Tricia broke off another piece of the candy and ate it. The stuff was seriously addictive, even if it did stick to her molars. Still, she hardly needed Angelica's advice when it came to men. And she remembered a conversation she'd had earlier that day.

"Were you serious when you said you were going to call your agent tomorrow?"

"Of course. Why?"

"I spoke to Harry this morning. He's still writing. And he's looking for a literary agent."

"He's not getting mine," Angelica snapped, and opened the fridge to make room for the baking tray. "Let him get his own agent. And why in the world would you want to help him, anyway, after he left you, his family, his publisher, *and* his agent in the lurch twenty years ago? What's to say he wouldn't go and do it again—especially with a murder rap hanging over his head?"

"He hasn't been charged with anything," Tricia pointed out.

"Yet," Angelica countered, and collected her jacket. "Grandma always said, 'A leopard doesn't change its spots.' Besides, you have enough men problems without adding *him* to the mix."

Tricia hated to admit Angelica was right. She ignored her. Anyway, Artemus owed her a favor, and she could call or e-mail him herself . . . but she wasn't quite sure she was ready to do that. Angelica was right about that, too. Had Harry changed, or was he likely to just cut and run again?

Harry Tyler was going to have to prove himself. And how long was that going to take, and how was Tricia to know he was worthy of her friendship, let alone anything deeper?

"Now, about this candy," Angelica said. "Leave it in the fridge for an hour. After it sets, you can break it up into pieces. It'll be something fabulous to offer Mr. Everett and your customers tomorrow."

"Thank you," Tricia said grudgingly.

Angelica pouted. "Trish, forget Harry. Forget Grant Baker. Concentrate on being the best shop owner Stoneham has ever seen."

"And be lonely for the rest of my life?"

Angelica shook her head. "I'm done talking *at* you, since it's obvious you have no intention of listening to my golden words of wisdom." She grabbed her coat and headed for the door to the stairway. "Think about what I've said, though. Good advice is seldom taken—and that's the only kind I have to give."

Tricia got up to follow her, but Angelica held up a hand to stop her. "I can see myself out—and lock up and reset the security system downstairs. See you tomorrow."

"Good night."

Angelica closed the door and, frowning, Tricia locked it behind her.

She absolutely hated it when Angelica was right.

TEN

Tricia's morning started as most mornings did. A run on the treadmill, a shower, getting dressed, feeding the cat, and drinking half a pot of coffee with a breakfast of black cherry yogurt. Only this morning Tricia extracted most of the candy Angelica had made the night before, put it on a plate, and took it down to the shop with her. It was too tempting to keep it all in the apartment. And as Angelica said, Mr. Everett and her customers would probably enjoy it.

Down in the shop, Miss Marple settled herself on a chair in the reader's nook while Tricia checked voice mail and found a message from the employment agency. They were sending over a new candidate at ten thirty and awaited a confirmation. She quickly returned the call. Would this person be the one to finally replace Ginny? All she could do was hope.

Tricia had just hit the button on the coffeemaker when Mr. Everett arrived for work several minutes early, still looking as sad as he had the day before. "Good morning," he greeted Tricia, but there was no heartiness in his voice.

Tricia waited until he'd donned his Haven't Got a Clue apron to approach him on what might be a sensitive subject. Mr. Everett wasn't usually one to wear his heart on his sleeve. That he was visibly unhappy meant something was definitely out of kilter. "Is something wrong?" she asked.

"It's hard to keep anything from you, Ms. Miles. Like the protagonists in many of your favorite mysteries, you would have made a fine detective."

"It doesn't take great sleuthing skill to see that you haven't been your usual chipper self of late. Is there something I can do to help?"

He looked thoughtful for a moment. "Perhaps you can. A man my age has outlived most of his friends," Mr. Everett admitted. "Except for Grace, I have no one else to confide in."

Oh dear. It didn't sound like an announcement of good news was on the way. "Why don't you tell me about it?" Tricia said in all sincerity.

His cheeks colored, and he wouldn't meet her gaze. "It's . . . my marriage to Grace."

Oh no! Trouble in paradise. They were the one couple she thought would never experience marital strife.

"You see, Grace is so preoccupied with running the charitable foundation, she has very little time for me any more."

Hmm. "Have you spoken to her about it?"

"On several occasions. She laughed it off."

"Oh, dear."

"I hate to put you in the middle of our marital discord, but . . . is there a possibility you could speak with Grace? She values your opinion."

"Oh, Mr. Everett. If it were on any other subject . . ." But then the old man's bottom lip began to tremble, and if there was one thing Tricia didn't think she could handle, it was Mr. Everett's tears. She sighed. "I'd be glad to."

His eyes widened but were still watery. "Thank you, Ms. Miles. She's in her office right now," he said, looking hopeful.

"Now?" she asked, her voice rising. That didn't give her much time to prepare something to say.

"If you wouldn't mind," he encouraged.

She sighed again. "Of course."

"I'll get your jacket," Mr. Everett volunteered, and headed for the back of the shop.

If she had to go out anyway, Tricia decided she'd combine the visit with a trip to the bank to deposit the previous day's receipts. Stuffing her blue bank pouch into her purse, she was ready to go after Mr. Everett helped her on with her jacket.

"Thank you, Ms. Miles. I really appreciate this."

"While I'm gone, help yourself to a piece of chocolate toffee. It's homemade." She indicated the plate sitting on the counter of the beverage station.

A look of panic came over Mr. Everett's face. "Did you make it?"

Tricia frowned. "Don't worry—it's safe to eat. Angelica made it last night."

Mr. Everett looked relieved, took a small piece of the candy, chewed, and brightened. "Your sister is a marvelous cook." Tricia could envision the thought balloon over his head that might've said, *Why can't you cook, too?*

"I'd better get going," Tricia said, then smiled wanly and headed out the door.

The air was brisk as she crossed the street, heading for Booked for Lunch. She peeked through the window, but all was dark in the dining room, although she could see a glint of light in the back where the kitchen was located. No doubt Tommy the cook was already preparing the day's soup.

Tricia stopped at the door that led to the building's other tenants on the second and third floors. The wall inside the small alcove held mailboxes and a short directory for the tenants. The Everett Charitable Foundation had offices on the second floor.

Tricia trudged up the stairs to the second floor, dreading the confrontation to come. She hadn't had a chance to visit the newly opened office, and if it weren't for the imminent conversation, she would have been looking forward to it. She opened the frosted glass door. Inside was a small carpeted area, a door leading to the inner sanctum, and a reception desk behind a half wall with a glass window that was closed. The atmosphere was reminiscent of a doctor's office, and not at all welcoming, which surprised her.

Tricia didn't recognize the woman who sat behind the window, sorting through an enormous pile of unopened mail. She had to be in her late forties or early fifties, clad in a vintage dress from the 1940s, with carrot-colored hair done up in a pompadour, heavy makeup, and a tattoo of a rose with a dagger through it on her left forearm. *Queen of the Roller Derby*, Tricia thought, and instantly felt ashamed for making such a quick value judgment.

The woman looked up at Tricia, and her face crumpled into a sneer. She reached to open the window. "Can I help you?" she said, her tone nasal and unwelcoming.

Trouble with a capital *T*. Tricia adopted what she hoped was a friendly smile. "My name is Tricia Miles. I'm a friend of Mrs. Harris-Everett's. Could you please tell her I'm here to see her?"

Carrot-top glared at Tricia for at least ten incredibly long seconds before answering, "No." She reached up and closed the window once again.

Aghast, Tricia stood there in disbelief. Then she shook herself and tapped on the glass with the knuckles of her right hand. "Excuse me."

Carrot-top ignored her and reached over to a small radio on the desk, turning up the volume on an oldies station.

Tricia rapped on the glass harder. Carrot-top continued to

ignore her and swung her chair around so that she could no longer see Tricia.

"Miss, miss!" Tricia insisted.

She reached over and opened the glass. "Excuse me, but I'm a friend of Mrs. Everett's. Her husband asked me to come here to speak with her."

Carrot-top finally stood and turned back to the window. "Yeah, right. If I had a buck for everybody who came in here or called with that story, I'd be a millionaire myself. Now beat it, before I call the cops."

"I'll have you know Chief Baker of the Stoneham Police Department is my . . . my boyfriend." Whoa! That was firing the heavy artillery, and not exactly true at the moment, either. Likewise, Carrot-top was not impressed.

"And Santa comes down my chimney on Christmas Eve," the woman replied.

Furious, Tricia turned for the door to the inner sanctum and grasped the handle. It was locked.

Carrot-top leaned across her desk and raised her voice. "I'm not kidding, lady. Get out of here or I'll come out there and bust your face myself."

Tricia's jaw dropped in shock. "Does Grace know you speak to visitors in that tone of voice and with such malice?"

Carrot-top smiled sweetly. "Who do you think told me to keep out the riffraff?"

Tricia just stood there, speechless.

"Shut your mouth, honey. Ain't no flies in here to catch."

Tricia did, and found herself puffing great breaths through her nose. She turned, very ladylike, and exited the office. However, the minute she closed the door behind her, she stuck out her tongue at it. It was stupid, it was childish, and it felt *good*.

Once outside, Tricia stood on the sidewalk and took a few moments to ground herself, glad she had the trip to the bank to help her decompress after her unpleasant encounter with old Carrot-top.

Before she had time to move, the door behind her opened again. She turned, wondering if Carrot-top was about to make good on her threat, but it was Amy Schram who nearly ran into her.

"Tricia! What are you doing blocking the door?"

"Sorry. I just came from the Everett Foundation." She found she didn't have the words to say any more about that unpleasant encounter. "What are you doing here?"

"I just rented the apartment on the third floor. It's my first place," she said, and beamed with pride. "What a relief to get out from under my mom and dad's thumb."

"You still work for them, though."

"Of course. But now I can come and go as I please without a lot of questions. I love my freedom."

Tricia well remembered her first apartment and the enjoyment she'd experienced while decorating—and entertaining whom she wanted when she wanted.

"Congratulations. I guess I'll be seeing a lot of you around the village."

Amy laughed. "You sure will. I'd better get back to work. Have to check on my bulbs." She gave a wave and took off down the sidewalk. It was then Tricia saw the Milford Florist and Nursery van parked near the Happy Domestic. She started off in the same direction, heading for the bank.

By the time she got back to Haven't Got a Clue, she found an impatient Mr. Everett waiting for her. "I'm sorry, Mr. Everett, but I wasn't able to get in to—"

But he cut her off before she could explain. "There's a person from the employment agency here to see you," he said, and nodded toward a thin woman of about fifty with windblown brown hair browsing among the books. She wore a buff-colored trench coat, hose, and black flats, and carried a leather briefcase.

"I'd better go introduce myself to her," she whispered, but first stowed her purse behind the cash desk. She took off her jacket and was about to stuff it under the counter when Mr. Everett reached for it.

"I'll hang it up," he said.

"Thank you."

Tricia made her way across the store. The woman looked up. "Hello. I'm Tricia Miles, owner of Haven't Got a Clue."

The woman offered her hand. "Linda Fugitt. I'm here about the assistant manager's job."

"Won't you sit down and we'll talk," Tricia said, with a wave of her hand toward the readers' nook. "Can I take your coat and get you a cup of coffee?"

"Oh no, I'm fine," the woman said.

They took adjacent seats in the nook and the woman pulled a résumé from her briefcase. "I haven't had retail experience in quite some time, but I learn fast and I'm good with people," she explained.

Tricia looked over the résumé, her stomach tightening. Linda Fugitt, whose last job was assistant director of the Anderson Foundation for the Arts in Manchester. With a master of science degree in nonprofit management, she was vastly overqualified for the position of assistant manager, and Tricia reluctantly told her so. "You'd have to work Saturdays as well."

"I'm more than willing to do so," Linda assured her.

Tricia couldn't keep from reading the title of assistant director over and over again.

"Ms. Miles, I'll be frank," Linda said. "I need this job. Since the economy tanked, charitable giving for the arts has taken a terrible tumble."

That was no exaggeration. For many years Tricia had worked for an NPO in Manhattan. She'd lost her job under similar circumstances.

"I've been unable to find any employment," Linda continued. "It's always the same story, too. I'm overqualified for every position I've interviewed for in the past six months. If you could just let me work for you for minimum wage for even a couple of months, if you're dissatisfied with me you could let me go, but at least then I could get a job with one of the other big-box retailers on the highway outside Milford."

Tricia looked down at the paper on her lap once more. Nicely typed, no misspellings or stray marks. It was a far cry from most of the recent applicants—most of whom hadn't even offered a résumé. She looked up and into Linda's hazel eyes and saw true desperation in them. "What do you know about vintage mysteries?"

Linda smiled. "Not much, I'm afraid. But contemporary mysteries and romantic suspense novels have always been my secret vice. I'm a big fan of Wendy Corsi Staub, Carla Neggers, and Karen Harper. But I'm a quick study and I can search Google with the best of them. I'm more than willing to learn. And I'd sure rather sell books than burgers and fries," she said eagerly.

Tricia looked down at the résumé. If she hoped to keep this employee from bolting to another minimum-wage job, she'd have to offer more than the competition. And maybe, just maybe, this one would stay longer than a couple of weeks.

"You aren't allergic to cats, are you?" Tricia asked.

Linda shook her head. "I have two of my own." Another good sign.

"How does two dollars over minimum wage strike you?"

Linda sighed with relief. "It sounds pretty darn good right now."

"When can you start?" Tricia asked.

"How about today?"

"Great." Tricia offered her hand, and they shook on it. "Now, how about that cup of coffee while you fill out the paperwork?"

"That sounds wonderful."

Tricia noticed that Mr. Everett had been waiting discreetly at the cash desk. He didn't look cheered. She motioned him to join them at the nook. "Mr. Everett, this is Linda Fugitt.

She's going to be joining us here at Haven't Got a Clue." At this news, he looked positively panicked.

"Oh. Well. Nice to meet you, Ms. Fugitt." His gaze darted to Tricia. "May I speak to you for a moment, Ms. Miles?"

Tricia stood and gave a cautious smile to her new employee. "Excuse me. I'll get the paperwork for you to fill out and be back in a minute." She motioned Mr. Everett to follow her to the cash desk.

"What's wrong?" she asked.

"It's just that—I've just realized having a full-time employee working here will cut my hours."

"I didn't think you wanted to continue to work nearly forty hours a week."

"That was before Grace made our charitable foundation her life's work. Speaking of which, what did she say when you spoke to her?"

"I'm sorry, Mr. Everett, but I couldn't get in to see Grace. Her receptionist wasn't at all welcoming and practically threw me out of the office. She seemed to think I was trying to run a scam by saying I knew Grace. I'm sure her attitude is not the impression either Grace or you want the public to receive when they visit your foundation."

"Good heavens," Mr. Everett said, taken aback. "I'll speak to Grace about it tonight when I get home. Or rather, later tonight—whenever *she* gets home."

He could speak to her about *that*, but not about the problems they were experiencing in their marriage?

"Too often these days, Grace has after-hours meetings," he continued. "She's trying to set up an endowment for the foundation so that after our lottery winnings are depleted, the good work can go on for many years to come."

"That's admirable."

"Yes, but time-consuming. At our ages, we don't have a lot of time left. I'd prefer we spend it with each other."

Tricia couldn't blame him for feeling that way. When Grant

Baker left the Sheriff's Department, Tricia thought she might see more of him, and on a regular basis. That hadn't happened, either. He didn't listen to his police scanner, as Russ Smith had done during their dates, but his cell phone was always nearby, and his dispatcher felt free to call him for the slightest reason. That he always took the calls had been a constant source of irritation. Of course, that would no longer be a problem if they weren't going to be seeing each other for the foreseeable future.

"I'd better get Linda to fill out the payroll information. After that, I'll give her a tour of the store and then the three of us can talk about how you both want to split your hours. Of course, I'd be very happy if you'd continue to work your full schedule until Linda feels comfortable being here." *And please let her feel comfortable and happy and not leave us!* she mentally amended.

Mr. Everett nodded. "I will not take advantage of the situation." He sighed. "Perhaps Ginny needs some part-time help at the Happy Domestic. I believe I'll give her a call during my lunch break."

"I'm sorry, Mr. Everett, but Linda seems like she could be a good fit, and we have been looking for someone for a long time now."

Again he nodded.

The door opened, and a customer entered. Mr. Everett perked up. "May I help you find something?" he asked, and Tricia left him to help the customer while she found the papers she needed and returned to the nook, where she found Miss Marple and Linda getting acquainted. The cat was sitting on Linda's lap, purring loudly. She looked up at Tricia's approach, her cheeks coloring.

"I couldn't help but overhear your conversation with Mr. Everett. Um . . . does he have a first name?"

Tricia laughed. "I'm sorry, it's William. I call him Mr. Everett, as do most of our regular customers, just out of respect."

"You did say the job was for forty hours, though—or did I misunderstand?"

"No, you're correct. It's just that . . ." She lowered her voice. "Mr. Everett is going through a rough patch just now and had hoped to maintain a full workload. I'm sure things will straighten out any time now."

Linda nodded and accepted the papers Tricia handed her.

"I should also mention that we host a Tuesday night book club," Tricia said. "It would be wonderful if you could join us now and then, but attendance certainly isn't mandatory—especially as it's outside your regular working hours."

"It sounds interesting. I already have plans for this evening, but perhaps I can attend a future meeting," Linda said, and bent to retrieve a pen from her purse.

The door opened once again, but instead of a customer it was Frannie Armstrong who entered the store. "Howdy, Mr. E. How goes it?" she called, her Texas twang quite pronounced. That often meant she had some good gossip to spill. But what was she doing at Haven't Got a Clue at midmorning when she should be running the till over at the Cookery? The fact that she wasn't wearing a coat gave Tricia a clue.

Frannie walked up to the nook. "Hey, Tricia. Angelica sent me over here to ask if you could give us some small bills. We had a couple of customers paying with cash who only had fifties and hundred-dollar bills."

"Sure thing," Tricia said, but before she started for her own register, she introduced Frannie and Linda.

"Pleased to meet you," Frannie said with a grin. "You're gonna love working for ole Tricia here. She's the best—well, next to my boss, of course. She and Tricia are sisters."

Linda gave a weak smile. "How nice."

"I'll get you that change," Tricia said, and Frannie gave Linda a nod and followed her to the register. She handed Tricia a hundred-dollar bill, and Tricia counted out the equivalent in twenties, tens, fives, and ones.

"So what's new?" Tricia asked, giving Frannie an open invitation to spill her guts.

Frannie leaned in closer and lowered her voice. "The rumor mill is alive and well this morning," she confided. "There's another suspect in the Comfort murder case."

Tricia's eyes widened. "Really?"

Frannie nodded. "I've heard tell that Miz Pippa Comfort once had a relationship with that Ellington fella who owns the Full Moon Nudist Camp and Resort. In fact, they got together when she was a Playboy bunny."

"A Playboy bunny?" That had to be years ago. The last club shut down back in the late 1980s . . . although, hadn't it been resurrected in Las Vegas some time ago? Tricia wasn't quite sure. "Where did you hear all this?" she asked.

"I have a friend who works at the nudist camp. I won't name names," Frannie said with pursed lips, "but she had a relationship with Ellington—*had* being the operative word. When the relationship soured, she threatened a sexual harassment lawsuit. She kept her job and got a big fat raise, and now the two of them pretend that nothing ever happened."

"So what did she say?" Tricia asked, since it was apparent that Frannie was dying to finish her story.

"What she told me was all pillow talk. They'd spoken about ex-lovers, and how many women do you know with the name of Pippa, anyway?"

None, Tricia admitted to herself.

"Anyway, it seems Mr. Ellington had contacted Miz Pippa and told her that Stoneham was in need of hotel rooms."

"Why would he do that?"

"After her bunny days, Miz Pippa went to Cornell University and got a degree in hotel management. I guess she spent the past five years as an assistant manager at the Mount Washington Hotel and Resort until the opportunity arose for her to manage the Sheer Comfort Inn."

Tricia knew of the Mount Washington Hotel by its reputation and was dutifully impressed. Had Pippa become tired of working for a large hotel chain and found the thought of managing a much smaller operation more appealing?

"Did Ellington have a stake in the inn?" she asked.

Frannie shook her head. "Not that my friend said. But she also said that, despite the name, the Comforts didn't own the inn. They just ran it for someone else." So, maybe Ellington *did* want to buy the property. And Kelly Realty was the most likely agency to list the property.

And could the current owner of the property be Nigela Ricita Associates? If so, had its local representative, Antonio Barbero, spoken to Ellington to arrange such a deal? Tricia wondered if she ought to pay a visit to the Happy Domestic to see what Ginny knew about the situation. After all, she was engaged to Antonio. Then again, Tricia hoped to see her at the book club that night. Good old Ginny continued to patronize the gathering even after moving on with her career. If nothing else, it gave her and Tricia a chance to catch up on things while the rest of the group discussed the chosen book.

"Will you be at the meeting tonight?" Tricia asked.

"I wouldn't miss it for the world. We're going to decide our next few reads, and I've already got my list typed up." Her tone was almost a challenge, and Tricia couldn't think why she would speak that way.

"I'd better get back to the Cookery. See you later." Frannie gave a wave good-bye and left the store.

Tricia stared at the closed door for a long time. She heard a *brrrpt!* from behind her and turned to find Miss Marple regarding her from her perch on the shelf behind the cash desk. "Yes, it does seem like a bad omen."

Again Miss Marple said *"Brrrpt!"* and seemed to nod toward the display case. Tricia looked over to see a small stack of mail on the counter. It must have arrived while she was out. She shuffled through the circulars and found a square envelope addressed to her in care of the bookstore. The address was printed as though by a computer, but there was no return address and the postmark was smudged. She grabbed the letter opener from the mug of pens on the desk and slit it, withdrawing a piece of copy paper that had been placed around something else. Unfolding the paper, she discovered a stained cocktail napkin. Embossed in gold was the name of what she assumed to be a bar: the Elbow Room.

The Elbow Room? The name held no significance for her.

She sighed, frowning. First the photo, now this. Someone was playing with her, and she didn't like it.

Not one bit.

Was she supposed to be intrigued, upset, or frightened by this second mysterious offering in the mail?

At that moment the only emotion she could muster was annoyance.

Paperwork in hand, Linda approached the cash desk. "I think I've filled everything in properly. Would you like to go over it and then give me the grand tour of the store? I'm eager to get started."

Tricia shoved the envelope and its contents under the cash desk, forced a smile, and accepted the paperwork, giving it a brief glance. "Everything seems in order. Let's get another cup of coffee and I'll explain how we operate here at Haven't Got a Clue."

She managed to give the tour sounding cheerful and enthused, despite the growing disquiet within her.

ELEVEN

 No sooner had Tricia said good night to Linda and turned the sign on the door from OPEN to CLOSED than the members of the Tuesday Night Book Club began to arrive at Haven't Got a Clue. The first in was Julia Overline, clutching her copy of the current discussion book, Ross MacDonald's *The Goodbye Look*. She greeted Tricia with a cheery hello and was almost immediately followed by the newest member of the group, Donna Mitchell.

Donna was a wiry wisp of a woman in her late forties and probably never married. At least she didn't wear a wedding band. She looked like something that had been washed a few times too many, gray and tired—except for the lascivious gleam that often entered the woman's eyes. She liked to discuss the sex scenes (or lack thereof) in the mysteries the group read. Tricia didn't much like the woman and thought she might be a better fit with the village's romance bookstore's book club, but she didn't like to discourage anyone from joining her mystery group—especially if they bought the reading selections from her inventory.

"Won't you ladies help yourself to coffee while we wait for the rest of the group to arrive?" Tricia suggested.

"Thanks," Julia said, dropping her book on the readers' nook's table and heading for the beverage station. "Can I get you both some?"

"I'll take mine black with sugar," Donna said, but Tricia shook her head. She'd had more than enough coffee that day and was looking forward to closing the door on the book group and heading back to her loft for a much-deserved glass of wine—then remembered she had none.

Within minutes Mary Fairchild, Frannie Armstrong, and Nikki Brimfield had closed their businesses and were in attendance. As they all had to close businesses, they were often as much as fifteen minutes late for the meeting, and everyone liked to catch up on news and local gossip for another ten or fifteen minutes before Tricia could start the evening's discussion. Among the missing were Grace and Mr. Everett. Grace could be counted on to keep the group focused, but since she'd opened the new office for the Everett Charitable Foundation, she hadn't been able to attend one meeting. And now even her husband was scarce, determined to spend with her whatever time she could spare him.

Tricia drifted around the store, setting out the folding chairs, straightening stock, and eavesdropping on the various conversations. She thought the voices sounded a little lower this evening and, dare she even think it, a bit conspiratorial? She shook the thought away and was about to interrupt and begin the evening's discussion when the door to Haven't Got a Clue opened yet again, this time admitting a harried-looking Ginny Wilson.

Tricia crossed the store to meet her. "Hey, stranger," she called with real pleasure. "Glad you could make it."

"I heard through the grapevine that you've got another new hire?" Ginny said with a giggle, and shrugged out of her jacket.

"I'll bet the grapevine had a Poirot mustache and kindly blue eyes, too."

"As a matter of fact, he did. Mr. Everett called and asked if I could use some part-time help at the Happy Domestic."

"And you said," Tricia prompted.

"Yes. I lucked into a niche market here in Stoneham. The locals seem to support the Happy Domestic far better than they do the rest of the booksellers, thanks to all the cutesy knickknacks and such that I stock. Business has been good and will probably pick up once the tourists come back next month. But I'm hoping things will even out with Grace and she and Mr. Everett will get to spend more time together."

"Me, too. As for my new hire . . . why don't we go to lunch in a day or so and I'll let you know how Linda is working out. That'll give her time to shine."

Ginny cocked her head and met Tricia's gaze. "You think she's the one?"

"She could be."

"Well, now that I'll have Mr. Everett covering for me, I think a lunch break now and then away from the store would be heaven."

"Ahem!" Frannie cleared her throat, diverting their attention to her. "Hi, Ginny. Um, Tricia—shouldn't we get started?"

"By all means." Tricia directed Ginny to one of the open chairs and took a seat next to her. She preferred to sit rather than stand over the group. She found it made the conversations more open and intimate. "I'm glad you all could make it tonight. Before we get started on our current read, let's recap what we agreed on at our last meeting."

"I'd rather talk about what's happening here in Stoneham," Donna said, her eyes wide and trained on Tricia. "A real-life murder and *you* found the body."

On second thought, maybe she should stand. Tricia wasn't keen on opening up her own personal life to the group—especially on the topic of Pippa Comfort's death.

"My sister's dog found the body," she clarified. "And I've been asked by the Stoneham Police Department not to talk about the crime." That last part wasn't exactly true, but she hoped it would shut down that topic of conversation. Donna frowned and looked away.

"Mary was also at the inn the night it happened," Frannie pointed out. "Did you see anything suspicious before the killing?"

Mary's mouth dropped open, and she quickly turned to Tricia as though looking for backup. Tricia could only shrug.

Mary's cheeks colored. "I was in my room for quite some time before Mrs. Comfort was found dead."

That wasn't quite true.

"Did your room overlook the backyard where the poor woman died?" Frannie pressed.

Eyes widening, Mary suddenly looked frightened. "I didn't see anything. If I had, I'd have told the police—not all of you."

Frannie shrugged. "Sorry, Mare. I didn't mean to ruffle your feathers. But you have to admit, it's scary and exciting all at the same time."

"Scary is right, and I really don't want to talk about it," Mary said, her voice shaking and her cheeks going pinker.

"And I think we should respect Mary's wishes," Tricia seconded, glad to put the subject behind them. "Now, we agreed we'd select the three books we'd like to read before we take a break for the summer. We decided we'd tackle one classic and two contemporary mysteries and narrowed it down to three authors and six titles. They are: *No Love Lost* or *The Tiger in the Smoke* by Margery Allingham; Patricia Cornwell's *The Scarpetta Factor* or *Port Mortuary*, and *Fade Away* or *Back Spin* by Harlan Coban." Tricia had already read every one of them, but the nominations had been a group decision. "Shall we vote by a show of hands?"

Julia raised her hand, but not to vote. "I'd like to add one more title to the mix. Harrison Tyler's *Death Beckons*."

"Oh darn," Frannie cried, "that was going to be my suggestion." She eyed Tricia with glee. "Especially since we now know the author lives right here in town and that Tricia is his ex-lover."

Tricia winced at that descriptor, true though it might be.

"What was he like in bed?" Donna asked, leaning in for the juicy details.

Tricia cleared her throat. "We won't be going there," she said with authority. At least Donna had the good grace to look embarrassed.

"Were you starstruck when you met Mr. Tyler?" Frannie asked. "And how did you meet him?"

Everyone's eyes were now focused on her face. Tricia felt heat move from her neck to her cheeks. They weren't going to let this go. Perhaps if she answered the most innocent of their questions, they'd leave it at that. She sighed. "I was fresh out of college, and a voracious mystery reader. Mr. Tyler gave a talk at a bookstore near where I worked. We had coffee afterward and ended up closing down the café."

"Sounds romantic," Julia said wistfully.

It had been.

"That was a long time ago. I'd much rather talk about our next book selection," Tricia said firmly.

"Let's vote on *Death Beckons*. All in favor?" Frannie said.

Everyone except Ginny voted for the book.

"Terrific," Frannie said, sounding satisfied.

"Have any of you ever read the book?" Tricia asked.

"When it first came out, but that was a long time ago," Julia admitted.

"I haven't read it," Frannie said. "And I'd especially like to get your take on it when we discuss it," she said, again staring right at Tricia.

Ginny, who had been silent during the whole conversation,

lifted a hand to gain the group's attention. "I think we ought to consider Tricia's feelings on this. Perhaps she wouldn't like to lead the discussion on this particular book."

"I could do it," Donna volunteered. That was a first. If the monthly book held no sex scenes, she was usually content to sit back, drink the shop's free coffee, and nibble on the complimentary cookies.

"I agree with Ginny," Nikki said. "We haven't considered Tricia's feelings."

"But the book is back on the *New York Times* best sellers list," Donna insisted.

That wasn't true. While the book had never gone out of print, it would be weeks before it could possibly show up on any of the major book lists. And Tricia hadn't even considered ordering additional copies. If memory served, she had one or two used paperbacks in the bargain section.

Right now all she wanted was to put this whole mess behind her. That wasn't going to be possible if the group insisted on reading it. And maybe she should just let Donna lead the discussion. The group could meet at the store and she could stay behind the cash desk and catch up on her paperwork.

"*Death Beckons* it is," Tricia said without enthusiasm. "Now how about the other titles?"

Thankfully, Tricia was able to keep the remainder of the meeting focused on the discussion of *The Goodbye Look*, although Donna seemed bored by the conversation and kept staring off into space. She wasn't fond of older mysteries, which made Tricia wonder why she remained part of the group.

The meeting was winding down and Tricia was picking up empty coffee cups and crumpled napkins when Nikki pulled her aside. "Have you got a minute to talk?"

"Sure. What's up?" Tricia said, and deposited the papers into the wastebasket.

Nikki pursed her lips and looked embarrassed. "This probably isn't the best time to mention this, but I didn't want you to hear it from somewhere else," she said, and lowered her voice even more when she spoke again. "Russ and I are moving in together."

Tricia blinked, startled. She and Russ had gone out together for about a year before he'd unceremoniously dumped her—and not even for another woman but a job opportunity that never materialized. Then he'd wanted her back—something she was not keen on. "Oh, well. Congratulations," she offered.

"In fact." Nikki held out her hand. "We're engaged."

Tricia moved from startled to shocked. "Oh." Her mind whirled. Russ. Happy. Even more mind-boggling: Russ and the word *engaged* in the same sentence. Engaged meant commitment, something he wasn't willing to do for Tricia. But then, he definitely wasn't what Tricia wanted in a life partner, anyway. And since that was the case, why was she so surprised—upset?—by the news?

Nikki laughed. "Is that all you can say?"

Tricia managed to paste a smile on her lips. "Congratulations—I mean, best wishes. To say I'm surprised is . . ." Somehow she couldn't finish the sentence.

"To be quite honest, I was positively shocked when Russ got down on one knee and offered me the ring—it was so romantic. I've been through one bad marriage. If anyone had told me two years ago I would even contemplate going through it all again, I'd have spit in his eye. But now . . ." She again offered up her finger so Tricia could inspect the ring. It was a small solitaire, probably three-quarters of a carat. Tricia's engagement ring from Christopher had been two carats and in bright sunshine could blind small animals. He'd actually wanted to buy a ring with a bigger stone, but she thought they looked gaudy and unappealing.

"It's lovely," she said, and gave Nikki a genuine smile. "Have you set a date?"

Nikki shook her head. "It all depends on finding a place for the reception. The Brookview is all booked. We thought about the Sheer Comfort Inn, but now it looks like they won't be opening at all."

Tricia's gaze dipped, and Nikki's hand flew to cover her mouth. "I'm so sorry. I shouldn't have mentioned that. It must have been just awful for you to find Mrs. Comfort."

More upsetting than finding Mrs. Comfort was learning about Mr. So-Called-Comfort, but Tricia didn't voice that. "I really don't like to talk about it, and I wish the group hadn't pressed me for details."

"I'm sorry. I didn't think it was a good idea, either. Shame on Frannie for being so pushy."

After Frannie had been the object of the same treatment, she'd backed off for several months. But now she was back to her old habits.

"I think I'll remind them not to bring it up when we start discussing *Death Beckons*."

"I'd appreciate that."

Nikki nodded and headed back to the group gathered around the reader's nook.

Ginny shrugged back into her jacket and joined Tricia at the cash desk. She looked around the place. "I sure miss working here sometimes. I didn't realize how easy I had it."

"I'm sure you've exceeded your new employer's expectations with everything you've done at the Happy Domestic."

Ginny giggled. "I got another raise last week. According to the books, or what there was of them, sales have tripled since I took over. Ms. Ricita is very pleased with me. At least I think so. I was hoping I'd have had a chance to meet her by now. Antonio is always making excuses for her not visiting Stoneham."

"Will she be coming to your wedding this summer?"

"She's on the invitation list, and Antonio promised she'd make it." Ginny's gaze dipped, and her expression sobered.

"I'm so sorry for all this Harrison Tyler crap. I see his picture is missing from the wall."

"He asked me to take it down."

"Well, I won't ask you any of the details. But if you need to talk to someone, you know I'm discreet."

"I appreciate it. And I would like to go to lunch with you sometime soon."

Ginny laughed. "No time like the present to arrange it."

They made a date to meet during the next week before Ginny waved to the group and headed out the door. Her departure was a catalyst for everyone else to round up their books, coats, and purses.

"Oh, oh!" Frannie said, waving her copy of *The Goodbye Look* in the air. "Don't forget to watch my boss on TV tomorrow morning. *Good Morning, Portsmouth* on that new Channel Nine. She's promised a big surprise."

"Can't, gotta work," Nikki said, and Mary agreed.

"DVR it. That's what I'm going to do," Frannie said as they all headed toward the exit.

The others followed her out the door, with only Mary holding back. "Do you mind if I wait a few minutes? Luke said he didn't want me to walk home alone. He picked me up after closing yesterday. He says he'll keep doing it until they catch whoever killed Mrs. Comfort."

"He's a sweet husband."

Mary laughed. "I think I'll keep him."

A car pulled up to the curb and honked its horn. "Oh, there he is now," Mary said. "See you later."

Tricia waited behind the door until Mary got in the car, and then both she and Luke waved and he gave the horn another honk in farewell before the car took off north down Main Street.

The meeting hadn't taken as long as usual, and it was only seven thirty when Tricia went to turn the deadbolt on the door. She moved to lower the blinds on the big display window and noticed Michele Fowler standing on the sidewalk in front of By Hook or By Book, staring at the building across the street. Was she admiring her handiwork? Angelica had said she'd been hired to manage the latest Nigela Ricita Associates investment—the Dog-Eared Page.

Maybe it was because she felt picked on by the readers' group—or maybe it was just plain guilt—but Tricia realized that Angelica was right on yet another count. There was absolutely no reason for her to be jealous of her sister's friendship with Michele.

On impulse, Tricia grabbed her jacket and keys and locked the shop door behind her. Huddling into her collar, she walked up to Michele. "Hey, how's it going?"

Michele turned, her eyes lighting up and her smile widening. "Hello, Tricia." Tricia loved to hear that English accent. Michele swept a hand in front of her to take in the front of the new building. "I felt the urge to just stand here for a few minutes and admire my new baby from afar. Isn't it smashing?"

Tricia eyed the building's new façade, not at all like its previous incarnation. That was because it had been built to mimic the building it replaced as it originally looked when it was first erected back in 1896. Carved into the granite lintel were the words *Stoneham Hose Co. No. 1*. The bar sign hadn't yet been hung. What were they waiting for—the liquor license?

"I'm curious. How did you get the job?"

Michele looked confused. "Sorry?"

"To manage the Dog-Eared Page?" Tricia clarified.

"I interviewed, of course."

"Yes, but how did you find out about the opening?"

"I didn't. Antonio Barbero paid me a visit at the gallery last fall and asked me what my future plans were. He'd heard I was about to close it and said he wanted to talk to me about the possibility of managing the pub when it opened."

"Did he say how he heard about you?"

"Of course. Angelica told him."

"She did? I didn't know she ever spoke to him."

"Well, I believe it was actually Antonio's girlfriend who told him about me, but she had heard about me through Angelica. Isn't networking divine?"

"Yes, it is."

"When did you officially start work?" Tricia asked, wondering if she'd missed her calling and should've been a reporter, or perhaps a prosecutor, although Michele didn't seem to mind the mini interrogation.

"I've been working for the firm since November. There are a lot of decisions to make when opening an establishment such as this, and I've pretty much been given a free hand to do what I please."

"A free hand?" That sounded like it could be expensive—for NR Associates.

"Mostly with the decoration of the pub," Michele clarified. "And of course everything is approved at the corporate level."

"Have you ever met Ms. Ricita?"

"No, but Antonio says it won't be long. He hinted she might come to Stoneham for the pub's opening. Wouldn't that be brilliant?"

"Yes. Brilliant." But Tricia was more interested in hearing about the pub, and pleased that Michele either didn't know or didn't care about her finding Pippa Comfort's body. "Now that Ginny manages the Happy Domestic, I don't get to see her, or even talk to her as often as I'd like. I see Antonio even less."

"And the local gossip machine isn't keeping you informed? Well, we'll have to do something about that, won't we?" she said with a laugh. "Come on over, and I'll pour you a drink."

"Now?" Tricia asked.

"The bar's fully stocked. I'd like your opinion on what we've accomplished so far. Angelica says you have a real eye for detail."

Did she? For some silly reason, that pleased Tricia.

"I'd love to," Tricia said, and the two of them crossed the empty street. Michele withdrew a ring of keys from her jacket, picked out the appropriate one, and opened the door. She took a few steps in, threw some light switches, and the inside of the pub practically glowed.

For months Tricia had seen trucks pull up to the site and disgorge their loads, most of them giving no clue as to what they'd delivered. What lay inside the building absolutely delighted her. The tin ceiling had been painted with glossy black paint many times over, softening the tilelike design so that it looked at least a century old. The massive oak bar stood against the south wall, its brass foot rail shining brightly. A large mirror behind the back bar was bright with lighted Victorian stained-glass panels framing each side.

Five or six booths lined the north wall, while ten or more stools stood before the bar, and a smattering of small tables filled the rest of the space. Along the back wall was a small stage, indicating live music would be in the offing.

"Oh, it's lovely. Is this what you were used to back in England?"

Michele shook her head, shrugged out of her coat, and tossed it on the bar. "Not really. But this is what Americans expect from a British pub, and I'm happy to give it to them. Sit down," she encouraged, and Tricia obligingly settled on one of the bar stools.

"What'll you have?"

"I don't suppose you have any cream sherry?"

"I certainly do," Michele said, and turned for the mass of bottles lining the back bar. She selected one, found a delicate stemmed glass, and poured.

"Will you get in trouble for inviting me in before the official opening?" Tricia asked.

"Not at all." She handed Tricia the glass and then stooped to fill a glass with ice, poured a generous Gordon's gin for herself, and topped it with tonic from the well trigger. "No lime, I'm afraid. No point in cutting fruit garnishes until we're actually open." She held her glass up in a toast. "Here's to the Dog-Eared Page, and long may I be employed." She laughed and took a hearty sip.

Tricia sipped from her own glass. She hadn't had sherry in a long time and had forgotten how much she used to enjoy it. In fact, it was Harry who'd first introduced her to the stuff. They'd had a picnic at sunset on his boat. Nestled under a blanket, watching the sky for the first star to appear, they'd shared French bread stuffed with chicken salad, a little Brie, some grapes, and tiny glasses of sherry. And after that . . .

"You look like you've just traveled a fair distance . . . maybe back in time?" Michele suggested.

Tricia smiled. "Is it that obvious?"

Michele shrugged. "A good barkeep can almost read minds. We listen well, too."

"I do have a lot on my mind," Tricia admitted. "This most recent murder, my new employee. Angelica's TV debut tomorrow . . ."

"I'd say that's a full plate," Michele agreed, and downed another swig of gin. "Angelica tells me you're a pretty good detective."

Tricia frowned. She'd thought she could avoid talking about Pippa Comfort's murder. "Not really."

Again Michele shrugged. "You've sniffed out a couple of killers in the past couple of years. Who's at the top of your list of potential murderers this time around?"

Tricia shook her head and scowled. "I know almost all of the players. I can't imagine any of them being responsible."

"I understand they're all Chamber of Commerce members. I've yet to meet any. Angelica thought I should get my boss to pony up the funds to join. I probably will. I have lots of ideas and no one to dump them on."

"Ideas?" Tricia asked.

"To make Stoneham more enticing to visitors."

"I'm open to anything you have to suggest," she said, grateful for the change of subject.

"I understand there's been a rash of murders during the last couple of years."

This was getting into uncomfortable territory again. Tricia moved her gaze to the bar top.

"I was thinking, if there were any unsolved murders from a century or so ago, perhaps the local historical society could have a ghost walk at Halloween. I haven't had a chance to check them out, but it is a lovely and dear cemetery."

Lovely and dear? Tricia had never thought of a cemetery in those terms.

"Back home, our cemeteries are centuries older, and those with tombstones that survived are difficult to read. Hell, even if we couldn't find an unsolved murder, I'm sure there must be lots of fascinating genealogy associated with the vicinity that could be played up."

"I never gave it much thought," Tricia admitted.

"It would also be great if the Chamber could entice some kind of light industry to set up shop in the area. They also need to do more to get the locals interested in patronizing the shops and businesses in the area."

"Not only should you join the Chamber—maybe you should run for president. They'll be holding an election later this year."

"Isn't Bob Kelly the head of the Chamber?"

Tricia nodded. "And has been for at least a decade. It was great that he brought in all the booksellers, but I'm afraid it was also selfishness on his part. He owns most of Main Street. It might be time for some fresh blood. I'll bet you could give him a run for his money."

"You're getting ahead of yourself, girl. I haven't yet joined the organization."

"Wishful thinking," Tricia admitted, and took another sip of her sherry. Her gaze slid to the clock on the wall. "Good grief, is that the time? My cat is probably pacing the floor waiting for me. Her dinner is already an hour late."

"My life has been ruled by dogs—but I'm between them right now. When my life settles down again, I'm sure one will find me. In the meantime, I'll just go to Angelica's for a little puppy love. Isn't Sarge adorable?"

"Yes, he is." Tricia donned her coat once more. "Thanks for the drink—and the conversation."

"Any time. And I'm not kidding. Once we open, we're going to depend on the locals to keep us in business. You're one of them."

Tricia laughed. "I'll do my best. Just make sure you have plenty of wine in the cellar."

"Already stocked," Michele admitted, and walked Tricia to the door. "I guess I'll see you around."

"You sure will."

The door closed on Tricia's back, and she glanced across the street to Haven't Got a Clue. Standing in the doorway, back to the street, stood a solitary figure. Now that Russ had given up stalking her, there was only one person she could think of who might be hanging around waiting for her . . . and she wasn't eager to talk to him.

TWELVE

Despite the fact Tricia was pretty sure she knew who lurked around her doorstep, she wasn't about to take chances. Taking out her keys, she held them so that three of them poked out between the fingers of her right hand. After all, there was a murderer hanging around the village, and what if her visitor was indeed that person?

She started across the street. Halfway there she called out, "Can I help you?"

The figure turned. Sure enough, it *was* Harry Tyler.

"Help? You tell me."

Harry was likely the prime suspect in his wife's death, but for some reason Tricia didn't fear him at all. She singled out the key to her door, opened it, and let him in. An alert Miss Marple, who sat on one of the chairs in the readers' nook, reprimanded Tricia with a sharp "*Yow!*" for being late in serving her dinner.

Tricia ignored the cat for the moment. She was more interested in what Harry had to say. "My Tuesday Night Book Club
has voted to read *Death Beckons*."

"Ah, new sales. Too bad I no longer get those hefty royalty
checks. They'd sure come in handy right now."

As Tricia turned to face him, Miss Marple jumped down
from the chair, bounded across the room, and rubbed her head
against Tricia's black slacks, leaving a trail of gray hairs in her
wake. "How would you use the money?" *To run away—again?*

"I hired a lawyer this afternoon. I didn't kill Pippa—but I
wouldn't be the first husband railroaded to jail just so some
DA could add a successful prosecution to his résumé. I've
written that scenario myself."

Tricia bypassed that topic of conversation. "Who gets the
money?" she asked, folding her arms across her peach sweater
set.

"For *Death Beckons*?" Harry asked. Tricia nodded. "My sister. I'm sure she won't be at all happy to learn I've resurfaced."

"Do you intend to make a claim for the money?" she asked,
and ignored Miss Marple, who cried piteously at her heels.

"I don't have the wherewithal to fight her for it—and she
won't give up that gravy train without a battle. She's the one
who had me declared legally dead, after all."

No love lost there. "Why did you leave your estate to her?"

He shrugged. "She was the only family I had."

The silence lagged. Only Miss Marple's hopeful purring
broke the quiet.

"Would you like some coffee? I think there's still a cup or
two left in the pot," Tricia said. No way was she going to invite
him up to her loft—despite Miss Marple's attempts to hurry
her along.

He shrugged. "Sure."

"Sit down in the reader's nook. I'll give my cat a treat and
then bring it right over."

Miss Marple knew the word *treat*, and also that Tricia kept a bag of them behind the beverage station. She trotted in Tricia's wake and sat at attention until Tricia produced the snack. Tricia filled a small bowl, giving the cat more than she usually would—just in case this conversation should become prolonged.

Although it had been twenty years, Tricia remembered to doctor Harry's coffee with creamer and two teaspoons of sugar. She handed him the Haven't Got a Clue paper cup. He took a sip and smiled.

"Strong and sweet. Just how I like it." The pleasure in his smile warmed her. But when she thought about it, her satisfaction turned to discomfort. After so many years, had he remembered anything she liked?

"To what do I owe the pleasure of your company?" Tricia asked, and seated herself.

Harry's smile was lukewarm. "I hope you won't judge me as despicable if I tell you I'm lonely."

An overwhelming sense of momentary excitement quite suddenly turned to regret. "I think that's to be expected after losing your wife so suddenly. How long were the two of you together?"

"Fifteen years."

Oh yes, he'd said that earlier. No wonder he was lonely. And yet . . . he didn't seem to be wearing his heart on his sleeve, either.

"I was wondering," he continued, "if you'd like to go out with me some time? Just for dinner," he amended. "I know you've got the store to take care of during the day. But it might be fun to catch up over a nice bottle of Bordeaux."

Tricia blinked in surprise. "Your wife just died. Aren't you worried how it would look if you were to be seen with another woman so soon after losing her?"

"We were together for a long time, but these last couple of

years our relationship was pretty much platonic. In fact, it was more of a business relationship," he corrected. "I've already told the police the same thing."

Tricia's mind was spinning. If Baker already thought she might have some kind of motive for killing Pippa, being seen in public with Harry was sure to reinforce that misconception. "I'm very sorry for your loss, Harry, but even if circumstances were different—you walked out on me once before. Why would I want to take a chance you'd do it again?"

He seemed to mull that over for a few moments. "Maybe because we have unfinished business."

"Harry, you're the prime suspect in Pippa's murder. Getting involved wouldn't be advisable—for either of us."

His lips settled into a thin line. "You're sweet on that cop, Chief Baker, aren't you?"

"As a matter of fact, I am. He's a decent human being. More than decent," she added, thinking of how Baker had stood by his ex-wife during her recent illness.

He nodded and sipped his coffee. "You can't blame a man for trying." He gave her a shy smile. "By any chance did you happen to talk to your sister about her literary agent?"

Small fingers of annoyance tapped a relentless tattoo in rhythm with her quick pulse, and whatever interest she might still have had in the man instantly evaporated. Despite their shared history, his invitation to dinner had been a sham. He just wanted her help to revive his long-dead literary career.

"Sorry. I haven't had time," she apologized without much feeling. "My shop keeps me pretty busy during working hours, and tonight was our book club, so I haven't had a chance to mention it to her." That was more polite than telling him Angelica had refused.

"Do you think you could carve out a few minutes tomorrow to contact him or her yourself?"

Tricia let out a long, almost imperceptible breath. The look in his eyes was definitely avaricious.

"I'll see what I can do," she halfheartedly promised.

He smiled again. "Thanks." He reached for her hand. "I really am sorry about what happened all those years ago. It was a stupid mistake to walk out on everything, and I've spent years regretting it."

But not making things right, Tricia thought.

"When this gets out . . . I'd like to have a few friends in my court. I'm hoping I can count on you."

Tricia smiled but made no comment. Instead she looked at the clock. "It's been a long day. I hope you don't mind if I—"

"My apologies. I shouldn't have come here so late. I just thought I might catch you and . . . well, talk."

She nodded, wishing he would go away. He leaned in for a kiss and she turned her cheek to one side. He couldn't miss that blatant form of rejection . . . could he?

He pulled back. "I'll call you."

"I'm in the book," she said, and walked him to the door.

"Good night, Tricia."

"Good night." She closed the door on him. "And good riddance," she said under her breath. She lowered the blind on the door and stepped over to the big display window. She looked to the north, expecting to see him heading toward the municipal parking lot, but there was no sign of him. She looked southward and didn't see him. Maybe his car was parked along the street. She waited for a full minute, but none of the cars pulled away from the curb.

Frowning, Tricia closed the blinds. Maybe he had cut through the passage between the Patisserie and the Have a Heart bookshop, to go through the alley. Although that was the wrong direction to take as a shortcut back to Maple Avenue.

Miss Marple said "*Yow!*" reminding Tricia that a snack was fine, but it didn't replace a fine dinner bowl of Friskies tuna.

"All right, all right," she reassured the cat, and turned off all but the security lights before heading for the back of the shop and the stairs leading to her apartment, with Miss Marple scampering off ahead of her.

She thought again of how Harry had disappeared, melting into the shadows on Main Street. But then hadn't he proved to be very good at disappearing? *A leopard doesn't change its spots*, her grandmother had always said. That saying still rang true for Harry Tyler.

THIRTEEN

 After another restless night, Tricia began to think of sleep as a hobby she sometimes made time for. She was up bright and early Wednesday morning and had finished reading the paper, slogged through her four miles on the treadmill, and showered, and still she arrived at Haven't Got a Clue more than an hour before opening.

She'd already started the coffee and was about to open the store's blinds when she heard the sound of a car trunk slam. She peeked out the side of the big display window to see Angelica standing on the sidewalk, sorting through her key ring. She hightailed it to the door to intercept her sister before she could get in her car.

"Are you off already?" Tricia asked.

Angelica nodded. "I just loaded my ingredients, mixing bowls, frying pan, and a hot plate. Are you going to watch the show? It starts at ten."

"I meant to ask Mr. Everett or Linda to come in early so I could make sure I wouldn't miss it," Tricia said, hugging herself. It was cold!

"Who's Linda?"

"My new assistant. She used to work for an NPO."

"Just like you. You can compare notes between customers."

"I suppose."

Angelica glanced at her watch and frowned. "I'll have to meet her later. I need to get going. I'm not exactly sure where the station is located and want to leave myself plenty of time in case I get lost."

"You need a GPS."

"I have one," she said, "but sometimes we don't agree."

"Come to the store when you're done and I'll take you to lunch."

"Where?"

"Where else? Booked for Lunch."

Angelica frowned and stood there staring at Tricia for long seconds.

"What's wrong?"

"Aren't you going to wish me good luck?"

"Break a leg," Tricia wished, in true show biz parlance.

Angelica's frown deepened. "I already did that once—and it was no fun."

"You broke your ankle, not your leg."

"Close enough. Gotta go!" She gave a quick wave and got into her car. Tricia watched as it pulled away from the curb and headed for the highway. When she turned to go back into her store, she saw Mary Fairchild coming up the sidewalk, making a beeline for her.

"Good morning," she called, but as Mary approached she feared this encounter would be anything but good. Mary's face was drawn with lines of worry.

"Hi, Tricia. Have you got a few minutes?"

Yes, she definitely looked like she needed yet more hand-holding.

"Sure. Let's get inside my shop. I'm freezing," she said, and led the way. "Coffee?"

"Yes, please," Mary said, and followed Tricia to the beverage station.

"What brings you out so early? Your store doesn't even open for another ninety minutes," Tricia said, then picked up the coffeepot and poured them both a cup.

"I'm an absolute nervous wreck thinking about a murderer lurking here in Stoneham," Mary said, tagging along behind her. "I don't understand how you can remain so calm."

"Chances are whoever killed Pippa Comfort won't want to draw attention to himself by committing any other crimes," Tricia reassured her.

"Luke has gone off to work, and I can't bear to be at home all alone worrying about a crazed killer running around. You're close to Chief Baker—is he any closer to catching the killer?"

Tricia took a sip of coffee and shook her head. When did Mary think she'd had time to learn anything new since the book club meeting the night before?

"Do you think it was her husband?" Mary asked, adding creamer to her coffee.

Tricia chose her words carefully. "I knew Harry Tyler a long time ago, but I don't think he's capable of murder."

"Did you think he was capable of walking out on his life, his career, and his family and friends? And," she added in a low voice, "you?"

Tricia sighed. "Never."

"Then he's probably the most viable suspect. He said he wasn't at the inn at the time of his wife's death—but was that the truth? And he practically ran away when he saw you arrive."

"He said he didn't want me to recognize him."

"Do you think it's true?"

"I do. Or I did," she said thoughtfully. Now that he was pressing her to talk to Angelica's agent, she wasn't quite so sure.

"You've been through all this before," Mary said once again. "Isn't there anything we can do to speed up the police investigation? I just want this person caught so I can go back to my life and not worry who might be lurking in the shadows or plotting another death. I'm scared," she admitted.

"I know," Tricia said. She wasn't sure what else she could say that Mary would find reassuring.

"I saw Angelica taking off. Is she going to the TV station already?" Mary asked.

"Yes."

"What's this big surprise Frannie said she concocted?"

"It's not a surprise, it's just a flashy recipe. Crepes flambé."

Mary scowled. "As far as I'm concerned, pancakes are pancakes no matter how thin they are. And they're no good without good old New Hampshire maple syrup." She followed Tricia back to the cash desk and watched as she counted out the money for the till.

"It has to be that Harry Tyler who did it," Mary said, sounding more sure of herself.

Tricia closed the cash drawer and wished Mary would drop the subject.

"What about Clay Ellington? A man who runs a nudist camp is probably capable of anything."

"Why do you say that?" Tricia asked.

"It's immoral—everybody running around in the buff. This time of year, they'll all catch their death from pneumonia."

"I think they do most of their running around inside the resort at this time of year. It's supposed to have a spa, an indoor Olympic-sized pool, a restaurant—the works," Tricia said.

"Have you been there?"

She shook her head. "Who has the time—or the inclination?" she said, and laughed.

Mary didn't find her statement funny.

Tricia sighed. "I don't know the man. And the killer doesn't have to be one of the inn's guests, either. If Pippa was killed where she was found, someone probably lured her outside."

"That girl from the Milford florist was just leaving the inn as Luke and I arrived."

"Yes, so she told me."

"Then you've spoken to her?"

"On Monday morning when she delivered the urns for the spring flowers outside all the bookshops."

Mary looked thoughtful. "Do you think she's strong enough to bludgeon someone to death?"

"Mary," Tricia chided. "She's a sweet girl. I'm sure she wouldn't be mixed up in a murder. And what would be her motive?"

Mary shrugged. "I'm just speculating."

Tricia left the cash desk to retrieve her coffee at the beverage station.

Mary followed her like a puppy.

"Have you spoken to Chauncey since Monday?" Tricia asked.

Mary shook her head. "I wasn't sure what to say. You're chummy with him," she pushed.

"I wouldn't exactly say *chummy*," Tricia said. "We've spoken at Chamber functions, but that's about all."

Again Mary shrugged. "Oh." She sipped her coffee, looking thoughtful.

Tricia glanced at the clock on the wall. It was still more than an hour before the store was to open. She liked Mary, but she needed to get some work done, too.

Mary noticed where her gaze had strayed and took the hint. "I'd better be going. You must have lots to do. I know I do."

"It is going to be a busy day," Tricia agreed.

Mary raised her cup in salute. "Thanks for the coffee. Call me if you hear anything about the investigation."

"Of course," Tricia said, but she wasn't sure she would.

Mary headed for the door and gave a wave before she left the store.

Tricia exhaled a breath, took a fortifying gulp of coffee, and headed for the back of the store to grab the vacuum. She really did have a lot to accomplish before the store opened.

By the time Mr. Everett arrived, ten minutes early, Tricia had vacuumed the store and written out checks for the mail. She was especially pleased to see him, as she wanted to make sure she was in front of her television when *Good Morning, Portsmouth* went on the air at ten o'clock. However, once again his expression was hangdog, and he hung up his coat and put on his apron with the enthusiasm of a condemned man. Miss Marple seemed to notice as well and jumped down from her perch behind the register.

"Is everything all right?" Tricia asked.

"It's . . . Grace." He sounded like a condemned man, too. He allowed Miss Marple to nuzzle his hand. "Would you have time to speak with her today? I mentioned the problem you had yesterday when you came to visit her. She was very apologetic and assured me she'd speak with her assistant."

Did he even know the assistant's name?

"Angelica is going to be on TV in a little while. As soon as the show is over, I'd be glad to go visit Grace."

His expression lightened. "Thank you."

The door opened, and Linda entered the store. "Good morning," she called.

"Ready for another day of retail?" Tricia asked.

"Very much," she said, taking off her coat and heading for the pegs at the back of the store. When she returned, wearing a Haven't Got a Clue apron, Mr. Everett spoke again.

"Ms. Miles's sister is going to be on television any moment now."

"How nice," she said, and then frowned. "How come?"

"She's a best-selling cookbook author. She's going to do a

demonstration," Mr. Everett explained. "In addition, she's a very successful businesswoman. She owns the Cookery cookbook store next door, and the café across the street. They make very nice soups," he added.

"I guess I have a lot to learn about Stoneham—and its residents."

Tricia closed her checkbook and stowed it under the counter. "I'd better get upstairs."

"May I get you a cup of coffee, Ms. Fugitt?" Mr. Everett asked.

"Please, call me Linda."

Tricia left them to it and scooted up the stairs to her apartment with Miss Marple in hot pursuit. Tricia headed straight for the TV, ignoring the cat's loud yowls for a treat.

Tricia found the remote and turned on the set, switching it to Channel 9. It occurred to her that she should have asked Angelica exactly what time her cooking segment was scheduled to air. It could be a very long hour and she hated to leave Linda and Mr. Everett alone too long, even though she knew Mr. E could handle just about any emergency. And why hadn't she just added DVR to her cable package? Probably because she rarely watched TV and hadn't envisioned Angelica being asked to do a televised demonstration.

The show's host was exchanging banter with another man on the set, who stood before a weather backdrop. A look out her window told Tricia the day was clear and bright. She gazed around the room. She should have brought her bills up with her. Maybe she could dust the room or straighten the bookshelves while she waited. Or she could sit there and laze . . . read a book in the middle of the day with no one watching over her shoulder—except Miss Marple, who had jumped onto the back of the couch.

A commercial came on, and Tricia left the room to check out the contents of her refrigerator. She'd forgotten to eat breakfast. Miss Marple reminded her that cat snacks could be eaten at any point in the day, but Tricia resisted the temptation to give her more.

By the time Tricia got back to the living room, with a peach yogurt in hand, the commercial had ended and the program's host stood holding a copy of Angelica's book, *Easy-Does-It Cooking*. The shot widened to include Angelica standing behind a boxy counter covered with cooking utensils and ingredients, and looking surprisingly composed.

So far Tricia wasn't impressed with the show's production values. The set was pretty basic. Dull gray drapes hung as a backdrop. Angelica wore a white blouse with the Cookery's sunflower yellow apron over it. As the host spoke to her, her eyes kept darting to the top of the screen. Tricia leaned forward and squinted, noticing the edge of the boom microphone popping in and out of view. But Angelica was a trooper. Even that distraction couldn't keep her from being a master saleswoman and cook.

"I understand you've got three great careers going," the host continued.

"That's right, John, and I'm so happy to be here today to show your viewers just how easy it can be for them to make a simple, tasty dish and still amaze their guests with a little bit of showmanship."

"What are you making for us today?"

"Crepes flambé. My sister suggested it," she said, and beamed with pride.

"Give me a plug for the store," Tricia told the TV, but Angelica continued with her patter.

"With all due respect to Julia Child, most people are intimidated by French recipes. But crepes are so easy to make and you can enjoy them for a light breakfast, lunch, or dinner." And to demonstrate, Angelica began to dump her ingredients into a bowl, giving the instructions and measurements as she went along.

She did make it look easy. So easy, in fact, that Tricia considered trying the recipe herself. But did she even own a whisk? Angelica stocked all kinds of cooking utensils in her store. Tricia could pick up one later that day.

"Now we're ready to cook the crepes," Angelica said, pouring batter into the shallow skillet.

Again Tricia marveled at how relaxed Angelica seemed in front of the camera. She often bragged that she was destined to be the next Paula Deen cooking queen. Could she actually be right?

Again the boom microphone intruded into the frame, dipping a little too low. Angelica's smile never wavered as she swatted at it as though it were a fly.

"Sorry about that," John the host said, sounding embarrassed. "Our crew is new and we're still working through some of the bugs."

Angelica's smile tightened, but she continued with her instruction without missing a beat. But no matter how poised she remained, the broadcast was beginning to look like an amateur-night production.

"And now for the crowning touch." Using a small butane torch, Angelica lit the alcohol and shook the skillet, allowing the flames to leap in dramatic fashion. The camera moved in closer, as did the boom microphone, which dipped into the frame, and this time it actually crashed into Angelica's forehead, causing her to stumble.

Tricia watched in horror as the flaming syrup flew through the air in a blue arc and splashed against the drapery backdrop. Then—*whoosh!*—it seemed as if the entire set was awash in flames.

FOURTEEN

 Tricia launched off the couch like a rocket. "What happened—what happened!" she hollered at the TV set. She heard screams and hollering as the camera flew sideways and then the picture disappeared, replaced by electronic snow.

Angelica!

Mouth agape, she stared at the screen for long moments, unsure what to do. She couldn't call the station—they were so new, would they even be listed? Besides, if the whole place was on fire, there'd be nobody at the switchboard. Should *she* call 911? She didn't even know the address of the place. Surely someone at the scene would do that—and more likely the place was full of sprinklers and everyone was wet and scrambling for the nearest exit. But if the lights had gone out, Angelica wouldn't know where to go. She had been closest to the fire.

The TV's static was nearly as aggravating as the sound of

nails on a chalkboard. Tricia stabbed the remote's mute button and began to pace the confines of her living room. What should she do? What *could* she do? Then it hit her—call Grant. He had connections—he might be able to find out something. Even if they were on the outs, surely he wouldn't ignore her desperation.

She grabbed her phone and stabbed in his personal cell phone number. It rang and rang and rang.

"Hello."

"Oh, thank God you answered."

"Tricia?"

"Grant, Angelica was just doing a cooking demonstration at the new TV station in Portsmouth when the whole place erupted in flames. You've got to do something. You've got to find out if Angelica is all right!"

"Calm down, calm down!"

Tricia took a breath to do just that and realized she was crying.

"Grant, she's my sister and I don't know if she's still alive. Please, *please* call somebody in Portsmouth—the cops, the fire department, *someone*—and find out if she's okay?"

"You said it was a TV station—I didn't know they had one."

"It's new. It just went on the air on Monday. I don't know the call letters or anything else about it."

"Okay, okay. I'll find out what I can and get back to you— keep your cell phone with you."

The line went dead.

Miss Marple sauntered up to Tricia and rubbed against her legs, looking up at her with sympathetic eyes, and gave a quiet, sympathetic "*Yow.*"

"Thank you," Tricia said, and sniffed. She picked up the cat and dried her tears in Miss Marple's fur. "She'll be okay," she told the cat over and over again. "She'll be okay. We have to believe that."

Putting the cat down, she went to the kitchen and stared at the counter, wondering if she should make herself a cup of coffee. Coffee was available at the beverage station downstairs in her shop, she reminded herself, but she wasn't sure she could tell Mr. Everett and Linda what she'd just witnessed on television. Not without bursting into tears, that is.

She found herself opening the fridge, but there was no bottle of comforting wine, just a few pieces of the leftover saltine candy Angelica had made on Monday night. Tricia withdrew the container and shut the fridge door. She leaned against the counter, opened the container, and ate a piece of the sticky candy, finding its sweetness somehow comforting. Unlike Angelica, she had never eaten for comfort, but at this exact moment she saw the appeal. Before she could stop herself, she'd eaten every last piece. She put the empty container in the sink.

By this time, her hands had stopped shaking and what she wanted most was a breath of fresh air. She decided to go collect Sarge—for surely Angelica would not have brought the dog with her to the television station—and take him for a walk. Sarge loved Angelica—he was a connection to her, however silly that sounded under the circumstances. By walking him she'd be doing something constructive, and if she needed a cuddle, Sarge was sure to oblige. She retrieved her cell phone from the charger and started down the stairs to Haven't Got a Clue.

Tricia collected her coat from the peg in the back of the shop and headed for the front door. Mr. Everett intercepted her midway.

"How did your sister's cooking demonstration go?" he asked eagerly.

Tricia swallowed. "She set the house on fire," she managed, her voice cracking.

"Oh, it went well then," Linda said, not bothering to look up from the pile of books she was shelving.

"Are you all right, Ms. Miles?" Mr. Everett asked, concerned.

"I've—I've got a lot on my mind," she admitted. "I feel the need to get some air, to clear my head, if you wouldn't mind watching the store for a few minutes longer."

"Not at all. Perhaps you could make a slight detour to our foundation's headquarters and visit Grace as well?" Mr. Everett asked politely.

Tricia blinked, forgetting for the moment why she would want to do that—and then she remembered her promise to Mr. Everett and the upsetting encounter with Grace's receptionist the day before. While she had promised she would again try to speak to Grace on his behalf, was now the right time?

Maybe. If she went to the Cookery, Frannie was likely to interrogate her about the cooking demonstration.

"Great idea," Tricia agreed. "I'll go visit Grace now."

"Thank you, Ms. Miles."

Tricia retrieved her keys from under the cash desk and hurriedly left the store. There wasn't much in the way of traffic and she scooted across the road, holding on to her cell phone for dear life. How long would it take Baker to learn what had happened?

Tricia stepped into the building's entryway and trudged up the stairs to the Everett Foundation's office once again, idly wondering what Amy Schram's third-floor apartment looked like.

Tricia's stomach tensed as she reached for the foundation's door handle. She would not let Carrot-top rile her. This time Grace was expecting her.

She entered the anteroom once again. Carrot-top, who was once again dressed like an extra from an old B movie, was on the phone. Instead of interrupting her call, she simply glowered as she waved Tricia into the office's inner sanctum, and it was all Tricia could do not to poke her tongue out at the woman.

Tricia eased the cheap hollow-core door closed behind her and ventured down the hall, past a small conference room, to a door at the end that was ajar. She rapped her knuckles against it.

"Grace? It's Tricia." Somehow she'd managed to keep her voice steady, although she still wasn't exactly sure what she was going to say.

"Come in, come in."

As Tricia pushed open the door, Grace rose from behind the old mahogany desk, which had been polished until it shone. Behind her were sparkling clean windows that overlooked Main Street. A large portrait of Grace and Mr. Everett hung on the west wall, and photographic prints of Stoneham at the beginning of the twentieth century decorated the other walls.

To the right of Grace's desk were a computer with a flat screen monitor and a printer. To the left stood a new, tall wooden file cabinet that had been stained to match the desk. Twin chairs, upholstered in a neutral gray fabric, sat before Grace's desk. In all it was a small, comfortable, yet efficient office.

Grace had changed, at least in appearance, since the last time Tricia had seen her—before she'd moved the Everett Charitable Foundation from her home office to the new digs here on Stoneham's Main Street. Gone were the shirtwaist dresses. Grace was now attired in a tailored navy skirt, white blouse, and jacket. She still wore more than the requisite amount of jewelry but had toned it down a notch. It wouldn't look good for the chief administrator of a charity to be dripping in diamonds and pearls.

"Tricia, it's so good of you to come. Welcome to my home away from home."

That didn't sound good. Perhaps Mr. Everett had a right to feel slighted.

"I'm so sorry you couldn't get by my gatekeeper yesterday," Grace said with a chuckle, and offered Tricia a chair.

Tricia took her seat. "It was disconcerting not to be able to speak with you yesterday. You were so close, and yet your receptionist was emphatic that you not be disturbed." That was putting it mildly.

Grace waved a hand in dismissal. "Oh, don't mind Pixie. She has a few rough edges, but she's got a heart of gold."

A *few* rough edges? The woman could've doubled as a jagged-cut splintering board. And that name sure didn't go with the plump, overage woman with a severe fashion handicap and an abrasive personality. "Wherever did you find her?"

"From one of our requests for help. She needed a job. I interviewed her for the position, and we worked out a mutual agreement."

"You didn't answer my question," Tricia pressed.

Grace sighed. "It's true that Pixie is on parole, but she was a nonviolent offender and her crimes were not white-collar crimes, so have no fear. She won't try to embezzle the charity."

"That wasn't what I was thinking," Tricia admitted.

Grace lowered her voice. "She's an ex–lady of the evening."

A prostitute? In Stoneham? That was the last thing Tricia expected to hear. And wasn't Pixie a little long in the tooth to be practicing the world's oldest profession?

"The foundation is proud to help give Pixie a fresh start," Grace continued. Her smile wavered a little. "I just wish she weren't quite so zealous when it comes to interacting with the public. I'm so sorry she was rude to you, Tricia. I have spoken with her and it won't happen again." Grace leaned forward and folded her hands on top of the desk's blotter. "Now, what was it you wanted to see me about, dear?"

For the briefest of moments, Tricia considering a histrionic recitation of what she'd seen on her television only minutes before, and leaping from her chair and demanding a comforting hug from her friend. The Grace of old would have done so without hesitation. Tricia wasn't so sure she'd receive that treatment from the businesswoman in front of her. And even though she'd had a day to prepare, she still wasn't sure how to approach the subject. Perhaps forging ahead was the best way.

"Mr. Everett asked me to speak to you about a rather sensitive subject."

Grace looked puzzled and gave a nervous laugh. "William asked you to speak to me? I didn't think there was anything he couldn't tell me himself."

"I would've thought so, too. And I must say, I feel very uncomfortable playing go-between." She looked into Grace's blue eyes and saw the sudden worry there. "I think your dear husband is jealous."

"William? Jealous?"

"Of the amount of time you spend here at the foundation's office. He's very proud of you and the way you've stepped up to take care of the charity, but . . . I'm afraid he feels you might be putting in too much time here."

"The work is important and needs to be done," Grace said quietly but firmly.

"I agree, and so does your husband. But . . . he misses you."

"He could have told me that himself without mentioning it to one of our friends."

"I believe he's tried."

Grace pursed her lips. Tricia had never before seen her friend angry, but her current expression distinctly reflected that emotion. Tricia decided she'd said enough on the subject. Whatever else needed to be said, the couple could say to one another without her further intervention.

Luckily the phone rang. Under other circumstances, Tricia doubted Grace would have interrupted their conversation to answer it. This time, she did.

"Grace Harris-Everett." She listened for a few moments, her frown deepening. Finally, "Just a moment." She looked over at Tricia. "I'm sorry, but I really need to take this call. Was there anything else you wanted to say?"

Tricia rose from her chair. "I'll talk to you later, Grace. Thanks for seeing me. I'll let myself out." She backed out of the room and closed the door.

Pixie had leaned over the partial wall that overlooked the hall from Grace's office. "That was a short conversation," she said with a sneer in her voice.

Tricia didn't want to get into an argument with her and simply opened the door to the anteroom and left the office.

Once outside, she stood on the sidewalk for a long time, just breathing in the chill fresh air, wondering if she'd just lost a friend.

FIFTEEN

 Frannie was with a customer when Tricia entered the Cookery. She gave a quick wave and headed for the stairs. As she unlocked the apartment door, she heard a sharp yip. Sure enough, Sarge was bouncing up and down like a yo-yo on a string, ecstatic to see her. She picked up the little dog and kissed the top of his head. "Do you want to go for a walk with your Aunt Tricia?"

Good heavens! Just three days earlier she'd admonished Angelica for calling her that.

Sarge wiggled in her arms, trying to stretch up far enough to lick her face.

"Your mama's in trouble," she said, "but I'm here to take care of you until—" The breath caught in her throat and she had to swallow. "Until she comes home."

Sarge whined a little and she retrieved his leash, closed and locked the apartment door, and headed down the stairs.

Frannie was at the register, cashing out her customer, and Tricia gave a wave. "We'll be back," she called, and headed out the door. Out on the sidewalk, she set Sarge down and checked her cell phone. She hadn't missed any calls. She put it back in her pocket and set off for the park, with Sarge jauntily walking beside her.

She passed several people, who gave a nod of acknowledgment, but she was grateful not to meet anyone she knew. All she could think about was Angelica—and at that moment she didn't even care if Grace was angry with her.

The small village park was empty on this cold April morning, and Tricia allowed Sarge to sniff at the squirrel tracks that were invisible to her. She sat on the forest green bench and brooded. What if Angelica had died? She'd named Tricia the executor of her estate. Had she designated her to receive the proceeds from her cookbooks? What was the status of her latest manuscript? Would she be able to access Angelica's computer should her editor need it? What would she do about the Cookery and Booked for Lunch?

Sarge barked, glaring at her as if admonishing her for such morbid thoughts.

"You're right. I'm just so upset, I don't know what tangents my mind is liable to wander off on."

The retractable leash let Sarge sniff a twenty-four-foot radius from the bench, and he must have covered every inch twice by the time Tricia realized she was nearly frozen to the bone. They had probably been in the park a good half hour by the time she stood and started back for Haven't Got a Clue. She decided she would keep Sarge with her until she heard—either way—about Angelica's fate. Miss Marple wasn't going to be happy about that, but she could stay on her perch out of the dog's way. She'd reward her handsomely with cookies after she closed the shop for the day.

As Tricia neared Haven't Got a Clue, she saw Chief Baker's SUV pull up to the curb. She squinted to see who was with him in the car and did a double take before dashing up the sidewalk to intercept, with Sarge's little legs struggling to keep up with her. The SUV's passenger door opened and Angelica got out.

Tricia rushed up to her soot-smudged sister, throwing her arms around her and pulling her into a crushing embrace. "Good grief, I thought I'd lost you," she said, taking in the stench of smoke that permeated Angelica's hair.

Angelica pulled back. "I'm pleased you're glad I'm still among the living, but didn't Mr. Everett tell you I'd phoned?"

"I've been out of the store for over an hour. I was expecting a call from Grant."

Sarge bounced up and down as though on a trampoline. Angelica scooped him up and kissed the top of his head. "Did your Auntie Tricia take my little man for a walkie-walk?"

"Yes, and he's been as good as gold. Why didn't Grant call? He promised me he would," Tricia said, feeling hurt.

"I'd told him I'd already called your store. Can we go inside? I'm freezing to death." But instead of slamming the car door, she turned to speak to Baker. "Thank you so much for the ride home, Grant. I don't know what I would've done if you hadn't shown up and rescued me."

Tricia stuffed her ungloved hands into her coat pockets, realizing they were as cold as ice, and she, too, spoke to Baker. "Thank you, Grant. I didn't expect you to go off to Portsmouth to collect Angelica, but I'm very grateful you did."

"All part of my job," he said with a wry smile and gave a small salute. "Now, if you'll excuse me, ladies, I've got a village to take care of."

Angelica shut the car door and they both waved as the SUV took off for the police station.

Tricia threw her arm around Angelica's shoulder and bustled her into Haven't Got a Clue. "Come and sit down and have a cup of coffee with me—it'll warm us both up."

She led Angelica to the readers' nook. Mr. Everett and

Linda approached, both looking concerned. "Is everything all right?" Mr. Everett asked. Angelica was a disheveled sight, after all.

A low growl came from the perch behind the register. Angelica turned to glare at Miss Marple, who'd noticed Sarge's entrance—although he didn't seem to notice her.

"I'm fine now, Mr. Everett, but I nearly burned to death during my cooking demonstration this morning."

Mr. Everett looked aghast. He turned accusing eyes on Tricia. "But you said nothing . . ."

"I didn't want to worry you."

"Can I get you some coffee?" Linda offered, looking stricken.

"Yes, please—for all of us, and then Angelica can tell us all what happened."

Linda nodded and took off.

Angelica took a seat and set Sarge on the floor. His sniffer went into overdrive as he must have caught Miss Marple's scent.

"Ange, are you really okay?" Tricia asked, resting a hand on Angelica's sooty sleeve.

"Yes. But as soon as I drink my coffee I must go home and shower. I don't think I can stand this burnt smell much longer."

In less than a minute, Linda returned with a tray filled with cups, sugar, and creamer and set it on the nook's table.

Angelica looked up at her. "I don't believe we've been introduced."

"I'm sorry," Tricia said. "Angelica, this is Linda Fugitt, my new assistant manager. Linda, this is my sister, Angelica Miles."

"I'm so sorry to meet you under these circumstances," Linda said.

Angelica reached for a cup. "No sorrier than me," she said and doctored her coffee. "What a nightmare. I lost my coat and worse—my purse! It had my car keys, my cell phone—all my credit cards. It'll take days—weeks—to pull my life back together again."

"Thank goodness Sarge wasn't in it," Tricia said.

"There is that," Angelica admitted, and reached down to pet the dog, who was more interested in sniffing the upholstery.

"Now sit back and tell us what happened," Tricia implored.

"Weren't you watching the show?" Angelica asked, hurt.

"Yes, and I've been panicked ever since. I called Grant as soon as the station went off the air."

"Yes, he told me." Angelica took a gulp of coffee. "Got any cookies?"

"I'll get them," Mr. Everett volunteered, and took off for the beverage station.

"Ange," Tricia said, her voice a warning. "All I saw was you lurch and the crepes flambé went flying into the set, which erupted into flames. Then the screen went blank."

Mr. Everett arrived with the cookies, and Angelica choose one of Nikki Brimfield's famous jellied thumbprints. "I had everything under control. It was going well, except for that uncoordinated oaf with the boom microphone. I mean, what did they need that for? I was already wired up, which wasn't all that comfortable, either, let me tell you."

"Go on," Tricia urged her.

"Well, he kept swooping over us with that thing, and that last time he swung the thing toward me, he hit me in the head with it. Maybe I should get checked out to see if I have a concussion—there might be a lawsuit in this. Anyway, he nearly knocked me off my feet. The pan of flaming syrup went flying and then—*whoosh!* Suddenly we were surrounded by flames." She paused to take a bite of cookie. "Mmm. These are heavenly."

"Then what, then what?" Tricia said. She'd seen all that for herself.

"The lights went off and the sprinkler system came on, and

we stumbled for the exit and stood out in the parking lot, soaking wet and freezing. Thank goodness there was a fire station just around the corner. They took us all there, wrapped us in blankets, and not too long after, Chief Baker showed up to take me home. Let me tell you, Trish, I was never so happy to see a familiar face in all my life. It was so nice of him to come get me—especially with the two of you being on the outs and all."

"Oh dear," Mr. Everett said, turning his concern on Tricia now.

"Let's leave that subject for another time," Tricia said, and took one of the cups, fortifying herself with a large gulp of coffee.

Angelica drained her own cup, set it down, and then stood "Well, Sarge and I had better get home. Trish, can you drive me to get my car later this afternoon?"

"Of course."

"And can I borrow your keys so I can get back into my apartment?"

"Hang on." Tricia retrieved the ring from her coat pocket and extracted the keys for the Cookery and the apartment.

"Now to hope I can find my extra set of car keys," Angelica said, and started for the door. "I suppose I've got to go through all this again with Frannie now. Oh well. At least I'm here to tell the tale."

"Call me when you're ready to go," Tricia said.

"Better yet, just come and fetch me in half an hour. It'll give me an excuse to cut my story short and get moving. I still have a lot of things to accomplish today."

Tricia nodded. "Will do."

Angelica waved as she strode through the door. After she'd gone, Mr. Everett turned to Tricia. "I wish you'd let me know you were worried about your sister. I would have never asked you to speak to Grace with that hanging over you."

"I only wish our conversation had gone better. Speaking to her may have made things worse for you."

He nodded solemnly. "I knew that was a possibility. What did she say?"

"In not so many words? To mind my own business."

Mr. Everett looked appalled.

"It's okay," Tricia assured him. "We'll get through this." She wanted to say that she and Grace had been friends a long time, but that wasn't true. They'd met only two and a half years before. Still, they had a bond that Tricia had thought was strong enough to weather such ripples in a friendship. Only time would tell.

The bell over the door jangled and a couple of customers entered. The phone rang, too. "I'll get the phone," Tricia said. "You and Linda handle the customers."

Mr. Everett nodded.

Tricia stepped over to the cash desk and picked up the old Art Deco phone's receiver. "Haven't Got a—"

"Tricia, it's Angelica. Rescue me! Bob just heard about the fiasco at the TV station and is threatening to come over. I don't want to talk to him right now—maybe never."

"I thought you were going to take a shower."

"It'll be the fastest one on record. Come over, will you?" she pleaded.

"I'll be there in a few minutes." She hung up the phone and looked toward her customers. Linda was listening to Mr. Everett as he spoke with the women, taking in everything he said like an attentive student. So far she seemed to be doing well and had quickly picked up the routine. Tricia mentally crossed her fingers that she had finally found a worthy replacement for Ginny.

She snagged her purse and bypassed the knot of people clustered around the side shelves. As she headed back for the shop's entrance, she paused to let Linda know where she was going.

"We'll be fine," Linda assured her, sounding much more confident than she'd been the day before.

The clouds had begun to gather. Tricia left the shop and bent her head to avoid the worst of the wind, hurrying to the Cookery. Frannie was alone in the store and looked up at her arrival, putting an *Easy-Does-It Cooking* bookmark between the pages of a book before closing its cover. As expected, it was a copy of *Death Beckons*.

"Where's Angelica? She just called to ask me to take her to get her car."

"That was quick," Frannie said. "Your sister went up the stairs less than ten minutes ago."

"Did she tell you what happened at the TV station?"

Frannie nodded. "The short version. She promised me all the details later. What a terrible experience. And the station just went on the air, too. I was looking forward to seeing more local newscasts instead of what's going on in Boston or Manchester." She shook her head. "Did you see the broadcast?"

Tricia nodded. "It was terrible, but it happened so fast . . ."

"I DVR'd it, so I can't wait to get home and see it for myself. I'm just glad Angelica is okay."

"Me, too."

"I saw Chief Baker drop Angelica off in front of your store. That sure was nice of him—and to pick her up in his own car instead of using the village's cruiser, too. That'll win him points with everybody. I'm sure villagers who voted against reinstating the police force would have kicked up an awful stink if one of our officers used an official vehicle for personal use."

Would they ever, Tricia agreed, but not aloud. "Is anything else going on in town?" she asked, if only to change the subject.

"Still no word on an arrest in Pippa Comfort's death, if that's what you mean. Goodness knows there're plenty of suspects."

"Who's at the top of your list?" Tricia asked, trying not to sound too eager.

Frannie's eyes narrowed. "Chauncey Porter."

"Chauncey? What possible motive could he have for killing Pippa?"

"Don't you remember—Jim Roth and Chauncey were great pals. That's why I asked him to give the eulogy at Jim's funeral gathering last year." And what a fiasco that was, but Tricia didn't bring that up.

"I don't see what that has to do with that poor woman's death."

"Chauncey recognized Miz Comfort from a spread in Playboy magazine."

"But that was years ago, Tricia said.

"Jim told me that Chauncey has quite a collection of pornographic magazines and videos, which he has cataloged on his store's computer. He told Jim they were all e-rot-ic art, but if you ask me, it's just plain smut."

Chauncey Porter into porn? Well, it kind of made sense. He wasn't the most attractive male on the planet. He was overweight and balding, and . . . no longer young. Perhaps he'd settled on a life of voyeurism rather than pursuing any kind of relationship with a living, breathing woman. Your heart didn't get broken if you never risked loving someone, but oh what an empty life he must lead. Then again, maybe the love of his life had died or deserted him and it just seemed easier to fantasize than risk being hurt again.

"What are you thinking?" Frannie asked.

"Even if what you said is true—why would Chauncey kill her?"

"Maybe he was jealous. Mr. Comfort had a Playboy bunny all his own. Let's face it, Chauncey never would."

"Don't you think that's reaching for a motive?"

Frannie shrugged. "I haven't been reading mysteries as long as you have, but I have to admit, I look at strangers and wonder, *Have you committed a crime? Are you capable of committing a crime?* I guess reading mysteries has made me a little paranoid."

Tricia could second that statement.

Thankfully, Angelica burst through the door at the back of the shop marked PRIVATE. Her damp hair hung in ringlets, and she wore slacks, boots, a puffy pink jacket, and a matching purse. This time, she held Sarge like a football under one arm. "Let's go!" she called, and headed for the back door. "I'm not sure when we'll be back, Frannie, and we're hightailing it out the back door. Could you reset the alarm after we're gone? And please don't tell Bob Kelly where we're heading."

"Sure thing," Frannie said, and scrambled from around the sales counter to follow Tricia and Angelica to the rear exit.

The door closed behind them and Tricia struggled to keep up with Angelica, who'd already trundled down the steep concrete steps to the alley. "Hurry up, Tricia," she said, and began to jog.

"Ange, wait!" Tricia called, but when Angelica was motivated, nothing could stop her. That is, until she came to the end of the line of buildings where the alley ran into the Stoneham Municipal Parking Lot. She crept up to the edge of the building and looked around it, quickly retreated, and pressed her back to the brick wall. "It's Bob!" she squealed, and quickly put Sarge in her purse.

Tricia caught up and poked her head around the side of the Patisserie. Sure enough, coming down the west side of Main Street was Bob Kelly, clad in his beige raincoat and sans a hat, looking like a man with a mission. And as Angelica said—he did not look pleased.

Angelica grabbed Tricia by the sleeve, hauling her back behind the building. "Don't let him see you!"

"Why are we hiding from Bob? I'm sure he only wants to express his concern over what happened to you at the TV station," Tricia said, not that she really believed it.

"I don't think so," Angelica said. "He's definitely angry with me."

"Why?"

"It's complicated," she said with a shake of her head.

"Your whole relationship with Bob has been complicated," Tricia pointed out.

"Yes, well . . . I think he found out something I'm involved in."

Tricia scrutinized her sister's face. Not only did Angelica sound guilty, she actually looked sneaky.

"I think you'd better tell me what's going on."

Angelica frowned and Sarge popped his head out of her purse, giving a cheerful bark.

"Shhh!" Angelica hissed and pushed the little curly head back into the bag.

"Ange," Tricia scolded.

Angelica sighed. "Bob's angry with me for making a certain real estate investment here in town."

Tricia's eyes widened. "Oh?"

"It's not really a big deal, and it's really nobody's business but my own, but . . . I kind of own a share in the Sheer Comfort Inn."

SIXTEEN

"I don't think I heard you right," Tricia said, feeling a bit betrayed herself. She had thought that Angelica told her everything. "What's going on?"

"I'm a silent partner in the Sheer Comfort Inn."

"Why didn't you tell me? And more importantly, why did you let me think the Comforts owned it?"

"I can't be a silent partner if I go around blabbing about it, now can I?"

"How much of a stake do you have in the inn and who's your partner?"

"Partners," Angelica admitted. "It's a very long story and I'm freezing. See if Bob has passed by and then we can get in your car and drive away."

"You can't avoid him forever," Tricia said.

"All I care about is avoiding him right now." She pushed Tricia to the edge of the building.

There was no sign of Bob. "The coast is clear. Let's move," Tricia said, and the two women threaded their way through the cars until they came to Tricia's Lexus. She pushed the button on her key fob and the doors unlocked. Angelica opened the door, stuck her big purse on the floor, and jumped inside. Tricia followed suit, quickly buckling herself in.

"Let's go!" Angelica urged, and Tricia started the car.

She pulled out of the lot and looked to the left before pulling onto Main Street. Sure enough, Bob Kelly was jogging toward them.

"Get us out of here," Angelica shouted. Sarge barked his encouragement from the depths of her purse, and Tricia hit the gas. The car leapt out into the street with the wheels spinning.

Tricia looked into her rearview mirror to see Bob standing on the sidewalk, shaking his fist at them.

"I can't believe what I've just done," Tricia said, gripping the wheel.

"You got me out of a tight spot."

"But you can't avoid Bob forever."

"I may have to enlist your on-and-off boyfriend to play interference for me."

"Why is Bob so angry, anyway? I'm the one who should be angry. I'm really hurt you didn't tell me about this."

"I'm sorry. Actually, I should have asked if you'd like to invest. Don't you think it would be fun to run an inn?"

"No, I don't. And I thought you were a silent partner."

Angelica sighed. "Otherwise they might be pet friendly and I wouldn't have had to sneak Sarge in on Sunday. And it would've been fun if I'd been consulted about the amenities."

"Did you look at the inn before you purchased it?"

Angelica shook her head. "No, which is why I was so interested to see how it looked on Sunday night."

"Why is Bob angry?"

"Because he wanted in on the action and was bumped from the deal when I came on board."

"Why would he be bumped?"

"I kind of made it part of the deal. They were looking for a bigger share of money, and . . . I came up with it. It's as simple as that."

"You still haven't told me who your partners are."

"I thought you might get angry."

"Why would I be angry?"

"Because I'm in cahoots with Nigela Ricita Associates."

Yes, that would've made Tricia angry.

"How did you find out about the deal?"

"Antonio Barbero." Of course, Ginny's fiancé. "Apparently NR Associates is stretched thin and cash starved, what with all the other investments they've already made in Stoneham. I guess because I already have a store and a café, they decided to ask me if I wanted a share in the business."

"Did you hire the Comforts to run the inn?"

She shook her head. "Antonio found them networking with Clayton Ellington through the Chamber of Commerce." Angelica's voice dropped to a simper. "Are you mad at me?"

"Not mad, just shocked you'd join forces with a firm that you've spoken out against in the past. You're the one who said they were trying to take over the village."

Angelica shrugged. "They offered me an opportunity I couldn't refuse."

"And that was?" Tricia prompted.

"The chance to get back at Bob."

"Because he cheated on you?" This didn't make sense.

"I trusted him. I trusted him and he was no better than my four scumbag ex-husbands. That bimbo he dallied with couldn't hold a candle to me. Even you have to admit that," she challenged.

Angelica was right on that account. "But how did Bob find out about you being co-owner?"

"Real estate transactions are public records," Angelica explained. "The deed was only amended yesterday. Being in the real estate business, Bob's got contacts who feed him information."

"So you knew he'd eventually find out." She tore her eyes from the road to risk a quick glance at her sister, who looked very smug.

"Umm . . . maybe."

"Have you told Grant Baker about this?"

"Why is that relative?"

"Because someone died there on Monday night."

"Why is that the fault of the owners?"

"Because she was your employee?"

"Oh. I guess you're right. Okay, I'll give him a call when I get home. Or maybe tomorrow. Oh dear. I guess we should do something like send flowers or something. When's the funeral?"

"Harry's having her ashes tossed on a mountain. That'll save you on a Teleflora order. Of course, if the law decides to go after Harry, he might need money to mount his legal defense and sue you."

"What for?"

"I don't know. That's what lawyers do—sit around and think of ways to sue people."

Angelica sighed and a pout crossed her lips, erasing her smug expression. "We'd better think of who else might have killed Pippa Comfort."

"Frannie thinks it was Chauncey Porter."

"What?"

"That was my reaction, too," Tricia said, and braked for a red light. "Apparently Pippa was once a Playboy bunny and Chauncey's hobby is porn."

"Porn?" Angelica repeated, aghast. "Chauncey Porter is into porn? I would've never thought it—he's always been such a gentleman."

"You think that's bad—Grace Harris-Everett's new receptionist is a former prostitute."

Angelica's jaw dropped. "A prostitute—in Stoneham?" She shook her head. "What is this world coming to?"

"Mary Fairchild told me that Chauncey spoke to Pippa when he first arrived at the inn on Sunday night. He told her she looked different out of uniform. I'm assuming he meant her Playboy bunny outfit."

"Why, that lecherous old fool!" Angelica cried.

"According to Mary, it really upset her. Apparently Pippa thought she'd put those days behind her a long time ago."

"Was she afraid he'd tell other people about her past? Not that being a bunny is the same as being a stripper or a pole dancer. At least they wear a costume that covers up more than it actually shows."

"It's not the kind of news you want potential customers to know—not if you're trying to convey a sense of wholesome family values."

"Isn't the whole idea of going to a romantic inn to have fabulous sex?" Angelica asked.

"Oh, yeah? Then why did you invite *me* to be your guest at the inn and not Bob?"

Angelica leveled a piercing gaze at Tricia. "You know very well that we have had our ups and downs since last year when he cheated on me. We're in a down period right now."

Apparently they'd been in a down period for a full nine months. Bob had to really be a glutton for punishment to hang on this long hoping for a reconciliation.

"But even if Chauncey is into porn, that doesn't make him a murderer. What possible motive could he have for killing Pippa?" Angelica asked.

"There she was, an object of his desire—"

"Some twenty years later," Angelica said pointedly.

"Maybe he figured if he couldn't have her, why should anyone else?"

"That sounds more like Frannie's reasoning than your own."

Caught! "I'm just trying to think of all the possible suspects."

"And the most obvious one is her husband. Or just because you had a relationship with Jon Comfort—"

"Harry Tyler," Tricia corrected for what seemed like the hundredth time.

"—you don't want to see him guilty. Am I right, or am I right?"

"Wrong!"

Angelica heaved a dramatic sigh. "Go on. Who else is on your suspect list?"

"What's wrong with Clayton Ellington? He was one of Pippa's former lovers. If he recommended her to Antonio, maybe he wanted her to be close at hand."

"If he went to all that trouble, why would he want to kill her?"

"I haven't figured out a motive yet."

"And what if he has none?"

"It seems suspicious to me that he'd call up an old lover after twenty years and say, 'Hey, I've got a line on a job for you. Come live in the same small town as me and my wife.'"

"All the more reason why he wouldn't kill her. Murdering an ex-lover is not the way to keep your marriage intact."

"Some people don't think ahead."

"You do if you're a successful businessman."

"And successful people with money often get rid of problems."

"How was Pippa a problem?"

"I haven't—"

"—figured that out yet," Angelica finished for her. "I've already heard that explanation once in this conversation. And why are you still ignoring the fact that her husband might have done it?"

"I'm not ignoring it. I just don't have any idea *why* Harry would do it. He said they weren't close, but if he wanted to leave her, he didn't have to accompany her here to open the inn."

"Divorce is expensive," Angelica pointed out. "I know. I've been through four of them." She waggled her right index finger close to Tricia's face. "You just don't *want* him to be guilty of murder. You still *care* for him."

"I do not!" Tricia protested.

"Oh, yes you do. Admit it, things haven't been going well with you and Chief Baker. Before that, Russ dumped you. And before that, Christopher. But now there's the possibility that you and Jon Comfort—"

"Harry Tyler!"

"—could get back together again."

"You're living in fantasyland."

Angelica's eyes blazed, and Tricia figured she had better put an end to the argument before they both said something they'd regret. "This is where I could use a GPS," Tricia said. "How about telling me where to go?"

"Do you realize the opening you just gave me?" Angelica said with just a touch of malice.

Tricia frowned. "I could let you out here."

"Turn left at the next light," Angelica directed with lips pursed.

Except for directions, they rode the rest of the way without speaking, which was okay with Tricia. Even Sarge remained quiet at the bottom of Angelica's big purse.

After dropping Angelica off at the parking lot, Tricia waited to make sure she and Sarge got into the car and started the engine before she took off. She felt guilty for spending so little time in the store since Linda had started, even though she knew she was in Mr. Everett's knowledgeable hands. But there was one more stop she wanted to make before she returned to Haven't Got a Clue.

Tricia stepped on the gas and headed for home, making a stop at a doughnut joint to buy a half a dozen greasy fried cakes. After all, in some respects, cops and journalists weren't all that different.

Tricia had to summon up some courage to enter the *Stoneham Weekly News*. She and the paper's owner, Russ Smith, had had a stormy relationship. They'd started out as adversaries, migrated into lovers, and then had an acrimonious parting. It was only when Russ had started dating Nikki Brimfield that Tricia felt she could again speak to him in a friendly manner. Thanks to past events, she didn't think she'd ever again feel completely comfortable around him.

Patty Perkins, who seemed to do a little of everything around the paper's office—from answering phones to writing advertising copy—sat at the reception desk behind a computer, pecking away at her keyboard. She looked up as the buzzer sounded when Tricia opened the door.

"Hey, Tricia. Long time no see."

Tricia clutched the white bakery bag and braved a smile. "I've been busy. How about you?"

"Still employed," she said, nodding toward the door to Russ's office. "You wanna see the boss?"

"If he's in."

"Russ!" she called. "Tricia's here to see you."

Seconds later, Russ shambled into the doorway. His hair always seemed to need a trim, and his glasses were perpetually sliding down his long thin nose. A plaid shirt—in shades of red today—and wrinkled jeans seemed to be his standard uniform. "To what do I owe the pleasure?" he asked Tricia, smiling.

"I just stopped by to say congratulations on your engagement and to bring you a little present to celebrate the event." She held up the grease-stained bag.

Russ's head dipped and his cheeks colored in embarrassment. He had to push his glasses back up his nose to keep them from falling off. "Nikki mentioned that she'd told you."

"It's wonderful news. You've got yourself one fine lady—and all the goodies you can eat, I'll bet."

"That turned out to be quite the unexpected perk," he admitted, and his eyes slid over to the counter that stood against the wall, housing a coffeemaker and a plate of Nikki's thumbprint jam cookies. "I'll probably have to start going to the gym in Milford if she keeps feeding me like she has. Cakes, cookies, breads." He patted his stomach, which was straining against his belt more than it had when the two of them had been a couple. But then Tricia had rarely—if ever—cooked for him. Still, she knew Russ's preferences for bad fast food would not be usurped by Nikki's decadent desserts.

"Come on in and sit down," he said, ushering her into his office. "Can I take your jacket?" Russ glanced at the coat rack that stood in the corner and held his own bomber jacket.

"I can't stay long," Tricia said, then handed him the bag of fried cakes and took one of the chairs in front of his desk. "Have you made any headway on a venue for the wedding reception?"

Russ took the faux leather chair behind his desk, opened the bag, and took out one of the doughnuts. "Not yet. We're not in any great hurry."

No, she doubted *he* was. Especially if Nikki was going to move in with him ahead of the ceremony. But she wasn't going to mention that. His commitment difficulties with her were ancient news. She really *did* want to see the two of them happy. She got a glimpse of pure bliss when he bit into the doughnut, betting he hadn't had anything as common as a fried cake in months.

"I get the feeling your good wishes aren't the only reason for your visit," he said, and brushed a stray crumb from his mouth. "Whenever a crime happens in Stoneham, you'll always find a way to be involved."

"Just the luck of the draw that I always seem to be present when someone is killed around here."

"Maybe you *are* the village jinx," he said, and seemed to enjoy it when she winced at the phrase. "And now you've come to me to see what I know about the investigation. What's the matter, your cop boyfriend won't talk to you about it?"

"That's exactly it. Because I knew Pippa Comfort's husband some twenty years ago, he seems to think that makes me a viable suspect. He thinks there might be some kind of conflict of interest if we see or talk to each other in the interim."

He laughed. "I'll bet that didn't go over well with you."

"You got that right. Still, I'm rather surprised *you* haven't come to see me to pump me for information about Harry Tyler's resurrection."

Russ shrugged, took another bite of doughnut, chewed, and swallowed. "I edit a piddly weekly rag. It's not a blip on anybody's radar."

Tricia scrutinized his smug face, and understanding dawned. "You've already spoken to Harry Tyler, otherwise you would've been over to see me pretty darn quick."

He took another bite, swallowed, and grinned. "You got it."

"Did he give you an exclusive?"

Russ shook his head. "Not exactly. But I brokered a deal for him for a cut of the money."

She should've seen that coming. "Who did you sell the story to?"

"*People* magazine."

It figured. She had nothing to trade and had wasted four dollars and change for the fried cakes. He wasn't likely to give her any information now.

"I can read your mind," he said in a low voice. "I always could."

"I don't think so."

He gave another slight shrug. "Okay, I could read your mind maybe seventy-five percent of the time, then."

That was a definite possibility.

"So, who are your suspects in Pippa Comfort's death?" he asked, and wiped the sides of his mouth with his thumb and index finger.

"Harry Tyler, of course. He's bound to get the most scrutiny, too."

"With you coming in second?"

Tricia hated to acknowledge it, but he was probably right, too.

"Chauncey Porter and Pippa had words not long before her death," she said, to divert him from that subject. Russ straightened ever so slightly, his eyes widening in real interest. Aha! He hadn't heard *that* nugget of information. "Did you know that years ago Pippa was a Playboy bunny?"

"I did hear that in passing," he admitted.

"Chauncey recognized her as soon as he laid eyes on her. It seems he has quite a *Playboy* magazine collection." Okay, that was a guess. If he was into porn he probably started off with *Playboy* and worked his way to the harder stuff. "He made a flip remark about Pippa's change of uniform and she gave him a thorough dressing-down."

"And you witnessed it?"

Tricia shook her head. "Mary Fairchild did." She could almost see him make a mental note to call Mary the minute Tricia left his office. And he'd probably take a walk down the street to visit Chauncey at his store, the Armchair Tourist.

"Anyone else?" he asked.

"They say Clayton Ellington suggested Pippa take the job as manager of the inn. Was he doing a favor for an old friend, or did he have other motivations?"

"More than one?" Russ asked.

It was Tricia's turn to shrug. "And other people visited the inn the day Pippa died."

"Besides you and Angelica?"

"Amy Schram from Milford Nursery and Flowers, for one. There may have been other deliveries that day, too."

Russ shook his head. "I might believe that if the murder happened on Saturday. But on a Sunday? I don't think so."

"I've told you my suspects; who's on your list?"

"What makes you think I have a list?"

"Russ, you always have a list."

A sly smile crept onto his lips. "I do."

"And?" she prompted.

"*People* deal or no, Tyler's the most likely suspect. As far as I know, he hasn't got a firm alibi for when his wife was murdered, and he didn't return home for an hour or more after the cops showed up."

"I know. I was there." It did look bad for Harry, but somehow . . . Tricia couldn't believe he'd kill his wife. Or was it that she didn't *want* to believe Harry was capable of killing her—or anyone. But how trustworthy was a man who faked his death and walked away from his family and friends—and his life—because he was under stress? Were Harry and Pippa stressed simply because of the challenges inherent in opening a new business—even if it didn't belong to them?

Russ ducked his head and waved a hand in front of Tricia. "Hey, what are you thinking?"

"Nothing," she said with a shake of her head. "Do you plan on talking to anyone else about the murder?"

Russ shrugged. "Probably not. It's a pretty boring case."

"A former Playmate of the Month being bludgeoned to death is boring?" What did a victim have to do or be to warrant a little interest from the media these days?

"She wasn't a Playmate," Russ went on. "She was a Playboy bunny and was featured in a story about the New York club. The pictures weren't the least bit provocative."

"Then you've seen them?"

He sheepishly nodded. "They came up on a Google search."

If the pictures weren't memorable, why had Chauncey remembered them after so many years?

Russ reached for the bakery bag, rolled the top down, and

stowed it in his desk drawer, leaving no obvious evidence of her visit.

"Harry Tyler's new in town. How could he know to come to you with his story?" Tricia asked.

"I may have given him a call," Russ admitted.

"And you just happen to have an in with *People* magazine?"

"I wasn't always just some hack at a weekly rag, you know. I've got contacts—big contacts."

"So you've said," Tricia said, unimpressed.

That was the thing. Russ had always had an ego that seemed to eclipse his journalistic talent. What had she ever seen in the man? But then she had a talent for choosing the wrong guy. There were plenty of wonderful men in the world who made great lovers, great husbands, and great dads. Why did she attract men who were just the opposite?

She stood. "Thanks for your time, Russ. I wish you and Nikki all the happiness in the world."

"Thanks. And thanks for the great fried cakes, too. And I'm sorry, old girl, you just weren't the one." His smile was crooked.

Old girl?

Somehow Tricia held on to her temper. "Good-bye, Russ."

She turned and left his office—and hoped she'd never have to speak to him again.

SEVENTEEN

It was well past two o'clock when Tricia returned to Haven't Got a Clue. Linda's smile was tight when she greeted her new boss.

"What's the matter?" Tricia asked.

Linda's gaze darted to Mr. Everett, who seemed to be assaulting the books in the biography section with his lamb's-wool duster.

"I think you'd better go talk to him. He came back from lunch quite upset. I tried to draw him out to find out what was wrong, but I'm afraid it'll take time before he considers me a friend, and I think he could use one right now."

Tricia nodded. "Thanks. I'll speak with him now." She gave Linda a smile. "It'll be okay," she said, but had little faith in her words.

She approached Mr. Everett, who looked up from his task. "Welcome back, Ms. Miles." His words were correct but held no warmth.

"Is something wrong, Mr. Everett? You look like you've lost your best friend."

"I'm afraid that's exactly what has happened." He sighed and his mouth drooped. "The situation is dire, Ms. Miles. I'm afraid my actions have done irreparable damage to my marriage."

"Irreparable?" Tricia echoed, horrified—and just as frightened about what he might say next.

"I met Grace for lunch and we had a terrible exchange of words."

"Oh, Mr. Everett, I'm so sorry. I had no idea my speaking to her would cause you so much trouble."

He shook his head. "It's my fault. I asked you to do so. If I had had the courage to talk to her myself, all of this might have been avoided."

Tricia bit her lip, her stomach tensing. "Is there anything I can do to help?"

He shook his head sadly. "I'm sure it will all work out," he said without conviction. "Grace and I have weathered worse storms when we lost our first spouses. I just never anticipated how winning that damn lottery could cause us so much trouble."

It was the first time Tricia had ever heard Mr. Everett curse, which proved how upset he really was.

Tricia heard the phone ring, and Linda answered it. She rested a hand on Mr. Everett's. "I'm so sorry." She couldn't think of anything else to say.

"Tricia—phone call," Linda said, holding out the receiver.

Tricia hurried to the cash desk, "Tricia Miles, can I help you?"

"It's Grant. You were supposed to record a statement about the Comfort murder on Monday. This is now Wednesday."

"I was on my way to the station and got sidetracked. I can be there in five minutes."

"I'll time you," he said, but there was no humor in his voice.

She hung up the phone. "I've got to run yet another errand," she told Linda. "I'm sorry to keep leaving you to fend for yourself."

"Don't worry about it. That *is* why you hired me," Linda said. "Mr. Everett and I can manage."

Tricia nodded, happy she hadn't taken her coat off. "I'll try to be back within the hour," she said, and out the door she went.

Chief Baker wasn't waiting for her when she arrived at the station, but his administrative assistant was. And it took just about an hour before she took Tricia's statement, let her read through it for mistakes, and then had Tricia sign it. By the time she headed back to Haven't Got a Clue it was after three o'clock, and not only did Tricia feel like she'd gotten nothing accomplished that day, but she felt terribly frazzled, wondering what else could go wrong.

She found out upon entering the store when a distraught Linda met her at the door.

"I'm terribly worried about Mr. Everett. He came over all flushed a while ago and started to sweat. I wanted to call his wife or an ambulance, but he wouldn't let me."

Ambulance?

Tricia hurried over to the old man sitting in the reader's nook. "Mr. Everett, are you okay?" The flush Linda had spoken of had left his sweating face, but he looked pale and Tricia could see he was having trouble breathing.

"I'm fine," he said in between short gasping breaths.

"I don't think you are. I'm going to call 911."

He held up a hand to stop her. "Please don't. I'll feel better in a few moments. I just needed to sit down for a few minutes."

If he was having a heart attack, they couldn't afford to wait a few minutes.

"I'm sorry, but this is one time I'll have to overrule your wishes," she said, and hurried to the old Art Deco phone on the cash desk. Dialing the nine and waiting for it to cycle back seemed to take forever, and Tricia cursed herself for having such an ancient phone. But it looked pretty, and since she sold vintage books, she felt it added to the ambience of her store—but now it was just a relic that was holding up help for her dear friend. Finally a dispatcher came on the line.

"The EMTs will be there in no time. Do you want to hang on until they come?"

"No. I'd better call his wife," Tricia said, and ended the call. She didn't want to wait for the incredibly slow phone to make the connection, so she took her cell phone from her coat pocket and punched in the number.

"Everett Charity Foundation. This is Pixie. How can I help you?"

"Hi. This is Tricia Miles—" But before she could say anymore, Tricia heard a click in her ear and then nothing. "Hello? Hello?"

She dialed again. "Everett Charity Foundation."

"Pixie, this is Tricia Miles. I must speak to Grace immediately, it's an em—"

"Sorry, bitch. You got around me this morning, but you're not getting through to the boss now. I don't care what your excuse is. You crossed me. I got in trouble. Now you're dead to me. Good-bye."

Again the line went dead.

Tricia dialed again, but this time Pixie didn't pick up. She probably had caller ID.

The sound of sirens broke the relative quiet of Main Street and a fire rescue truck pulled up across the street. Tricia hurried to the door to open it for them just as an ambulance pulled up in front of Haven't Got a Clue. The EMTs tumbled out of the van and collected their gear. Tricia held the door open for them to enter, and Linda waved them to the reader's nook.

Tricia stood back as the EMTs asked Mr. Everett a series of questions, which he answered. He was starting to look scared—as scared as Tricia felt.

He'll be okay, he'll be okay, she kept repeating to herself.

"Were you able to get hold of his wife?" Linda whispered.

Tricia shook her head. "She's right across the street. I should go over there right now and holler through the door." At Linda's puzzled look, she explained about Pixie.

One of the EMTs joined them. "We're going to transport him to St. Joseph Hospital in Milford—just to be on the safe side."

"I'll try to find his wife and follow in my own car."

The EMT nodded and headed out the door.

"I'm going across the street to get Grace. I'll be right back," Tricia told Linda, and headed out the door. The EMT was removing a gurney from the back of the ambulance as Tricia left the store. She looked up and saw Pixie looking down at the street, probably alerted by the flashing lights. When she saw Tricia looking at her, she turned away.

Tricia frowned and hurried across the street. She entered the building and practically ran up the stairs to the second-floor office, but when she reached for the door, she found it locked.

"Pixie, open up! I must speak to Grace."

Suddenly she heard a blast of music shake the walls and door.

"Open up!" she demanded, but the decibels only cranked higher.

Giving the door one good kick, she turned and hurried back down the stairs. She made it to the street just as they were loading Mr. Everett into the back of the ambulance. She hurried to catch up and the EMTs paused to let her speak to him.

"I haven't found Grace yet, but I'll keep trying."

"Will you come with me?" he asked, sounding frightened. He reached for her hand, and she captured it. "Yes. I'll grab my purse and I'll follow the ambulance. I'll see you there."

The EMTs gently removed his hand from hers, loaded him in, and closed the doors.

Tricia hurried back to Haven't Got a Clue.

"I've got to go with him," she told Linda.

"What do we do about the store?"

"Can you lock up at closing?"

"Yes, of course. You can count on me."

Tricia went behind the register and grabbed her purse. Tucked in the inside pocket was the key she had once given to Ginny. She handed it to Linda. "I don't know when I'll be back. Could you give Miss Marple some cat snacks before you leave? There's a bag under the counter at the beverage station."

"Of course. Now go. Mr. Everett needs you," she said, giving Tricia a hopeful smile.

And out the door Tricia flew, just as the ambulance took off. She looked up at the windows of the Everett Charitable Foundation, but this time she did not see Pixie. And though she couldn't hear the booming music, she could almost swear she heard the sound of mocking laughter.

EIGHTEEN

It was long past dark by the time Tricia let herself into Haven't Got a Clue and instantly heard a plaintive *brrrpt!* Miss Marple loped across the darkened store to meet her. The cat twined between Tricia's legs, scolding her for nondelivery of her dinner. According to the clock on the wall, Miss Marple should have been fed two hours before.

"I'm sorry, my pet, but you wouldn't have wanted me to leave Mr. Everett alone at the hospital until I was sure he'd be okay, would you?"

Miss Marple gave an understanding *"Yow."*

Tricia picked up the cat and started toward the stairs to her loft apartment. She could always use the lint brush to remove any lingering cat hairs. But she stopped when she heard the sound of angry pounding on the store's front door. She turned. "What the heck?"

Miss Marple reminded her that she was very, very hungry

with a strident "*Yow*," but Tricia put the cat down and warily approached the door—after all, there was a murderer on the loose in Stoneham. But as she peeked through the slats in the blind, she saw that it was Grace Harris-Everett who stood behind the door.

Tricia quickly unlocked the door and opened it. "Grace, what on earth are you doing he—"

"Where is William?" she demanded and pushed her way into the store.

"I tried to call you numerous times. I left instructions with my new assistant manager, Linda, to try to get in touch with you, too."

"About what?" Grace snapped.

"Grace, Mr. Everett is at St. Joseph Hospital in Milford. He was pale and sweaty and couldn't catch his breath. I thought he might be having a heart attack, so I called 911. I tried to call you even before the ambulance arrived—"

"Ambulance!" Grace cried, terrified.

"But Pixie hung up on me. I called back and she told me off—called me a bitch who'd crossed her because I'd gotten in to see you today."

"I don't care about any of that—please!—tell me what's happened to my husband."

"He's okay—stable. The doctors don't think he suffered a heart attack—"

"Good Lord," Grace cried, and for a moment Tricia thought she might faint. She grabbed the woman's arm to steady her and led her to a chair in the readers' nook.

Grace fell into her seat, hunched over, and began to sob, while Tricia stood over her fighting her own tears. "He'll be okay, Grace. But he'd really like to have you by his side. He thinks—" She paused, unsure how to continue. "He's feeling a little unloved right now. He feels you've become obsessed with the charity to the extent that you've forgotten about your life together."

If anything, Grace just cried harder.

"I know you want to give Pixie a chance, but she's so protective of you she kept both Linda and me from communicating with you when you were needed most."

Grace struggled to compose herself. "She needed a second chance."

"And she probably deserves it. But her gifts might not include dealing with the public. I know there are people out there who will try to abuse you and the charity, but being civil has to be a prerequisite and I'm afraid right now Pixie doesn't seem capable."

"I'll fire her tomorrow," Grace said with yet another sob.

"That's not what I'm suggesting. Why not train her to learn the difference between scammers and those who are sincere in their need—as well as those who can benefit the charity? You've got a big heart, Grace. Use this experience as a teaching moment for Pixie. Maybe this is something the charity can do for others, too. Not just job training, but life training for people who never had the opportunity to learn those skills."

Grace nodded. "You're right, Tricia. I truly wanted to help Pixie make a better life for herself. But it frightens me that she took it upon herself to insulate me when William needed me most."

"Mr. Everett was asleep when I left, but I know he'd feel so much better if he awoke to find you holding his hand. I'd be glad to drive you to the hospital."

"Oh, yes, please," Grace said and stood. "Can you ever forgive me for being such an old fool?"

"Grace, your generosity is legendary. I think you just lost sight of who you love the most and how the opportunity to indulge that generosity came to you."

Grace shook her head sadly. "William is more important to me than anything else on this earth. And you're right. I did lose sight of that. It will never happen again." She let out a long sigh, and her eyes again were heavy with tears. "Please—

please take me to the hospital. I don't think I could safely drive there by myself."

"Of course," Tricia said, and gratefully accepted the hug Grace offered.

"*Yow!*" Miss Marple interrupted and Grace pulled back from the embrace to laugh. Although weak, Tricia could tell it was heartfelt.

"Just give me a couple of minutes to feed my cat, and then we'll be on our way. I'm afraid she's quite overdue."

"Of course," Grace said.

Tricia headed to the back of the shop and the stairs to her loft with Miss Marple galloping behind her. True to her word, Tricia returned to the store a few minutes later and found a much more graceful Grace waiting for her. "Let's go," she said, and started for the door. But then she paused. "Oh dear. If I drive you to the hospital, you'll be stranded."

"Oh, that's right," Grace agreed.

"Hold on," Tricia said, and retrieved the cell phone from her pocket. She punched in the code for Angelica's loft landline.

"What's up, Trish?" Angelica answered.

"I need a favor . . ."

Half an hour later, Tricia stood behind the hospital's double doors, staring through the glass to the driveway. Angelica's car pulled up and Tricia exited the building and hopped into the passenger seat.

"Grace told me to thank you and give you a give hug," Tricia said.

Angelica didn't answer but took her foot off the brake and let the car roll forward, heading toward the exit. She sniffed a few times, and Sarge, who was in the backseat on one of his travel beds, whimpered.

"What's wrong?" Tricia asked, concerned. "When I spoke to you last, you sounded so chipper."

"Oh, Trish—the absolute worst thing in the world has happened," Angelica said, and Tricia could hear the tears in her voice.

"Worse than burning down a TV station?"

"Yes! Somebody uploaded a video of my cooking demonstration to the Internet. The whole fiasco is on YouTube! I'm publicly humiliated. There's already been more than five thousand views since it went up at lunchtime." She looked both ways, then pulled into traffic.

"Five thousand," Tricia echoed.

"And the comments . . . they're just terrible. They make fun of me. What I'm wearing. My cooking technique."

"Are all the comments bad?"

"Well . . . not all of them. But enough to make sure no other bookstore, radio, or TV station will ever again host me."

"I think you're being far too hard on yourself," Tricia said, not sure if that was the truth. After all, what did she know about these things?

"Oh, and look who's talking. Your world fell apart and you were humiliated when Christopher left you, and from what appears to be no fault of your own."

Appears to be? Tricia fumed, astounded by Angelica's assessment. "What has all this got to do with that video?"

"It's just that . . . my life was finally straightening out. I was a successful businesswoman. I was going to be the next Paula Deen, and now . . . now my writing career is over. People will be afraid to eat at Booked for Lunch for fear the place will erupt in flames. And—"

"Calm down. This is not the end of your world."

"So you say."

It was definitely time for a change of subject. "Did Bob ever track you down this afternoon?"

"What? No. But he left me plenty of voice mails. He's absolutely livid that I bought into the Sheer Comfort Inn."

"Is that why you sounded so chipper when I called earlier?"

That brought half a smile to Angelica's face. "Maybe. But honestly, between Bob and that video, tomorrow I'm calling my providers to have all my phone numbers changed."

"Has anyone called to talk about the video?"

"Not yet, but it's inevitable. I checked my e-mail just before I left, and I'd reached the maximum my inbox could hold. They've all got subject lines that say *Fire* or something similar."

"Are they all bad?"

"Who knows? I'm going to delete them all—sight unseen."

Tricia frowned. "Is that wise?"

"It's self-preservation."

Angelica pulled into her usual spot in the municipal parking lot and cut the engine.

"Do you want to come up to my place for a glass of wine and unwind before you have to face your computer?" Tricia asked.

Angelica sighed dramatically and shook her head. "Thank you, but no. Miss Marple doesn't like Sarge, and I don't want his little ego to be crushed. I've suffered enough of that today for both of us." It was just as well. Tricia had forgotten that she hadn't replenished her wine cellar.

They got out of the car, with Angelica retrieving her dog from the backseat. She clipped Sarge's leash onto his collar and set the dog on the ground, and then the three of them headed for the sidewalk along Main Street.

"Shouldn't you take Sarge to the park before you turn in for the night?" Tricia asked.

"I'll take him out in the alley after we get inside."

"Don't you ever feel vulnerable doing that? It's not well lit."

"Vulnerable? Here in Stoneham? Never," Angelica declared.

The streetlamps shed scant light on this gloomy evening. No moonlight brightened the night sky, which seemed even devoid of stars. Their footsteps echoed faintly as they walked past the Patisserie.

As they approached the Have a Heart bookshop, a figure

jumped out of the space between it and the bakery. Startled, Tricia grabbed Angelica's arm as Sarge exploded into shrieks of frenzied barks, tugging at the leash with the ferocity of a pit bull.

"Call off that animal," said a male voice they instantly recognized.

Tricia's anxiety immediately evaporated. "Bob, what do you think you're doing, trying to scare us like that?"

"I want answers—and not from you, Tricia. Go home."

"And leave my sister alone with an angry man? No way!" she declared.

"I have Sarge to protect me," Angelica yelled over Sarge's barking.

"Shut up!" Bob hollered.

Again Sarge lunged at him, but Angelica held him back. "What is your problem, Bob?" she demanded.

"You! You betrayed me."

"Oh, and you think sleeping with that little tramp wasn't a betrayal to me?" she countered.

"I told you, I'm not even sure I *did* sleep with her. I was drunk."

"And that's supposed to reassure me?" Angelica cried.

Tricia wished she were elsewhere—but she wasn't about to leave her sister alone on a dark street with this nutcase. Besides, Sarge's barking was beginning to get to her, too.

As though Angelica could read her mind, she tugged on the dog's leash and said, "Shush." The barking stopped.

"Just tell me why?" Bob said, and Tricia was sure his voice cracked on the last word.

"I presume you mean about me investing in the inn."

He nodded.

"Because it seemed like a good venture. Stoneham needs places visitors can stay. You've been more concerned with collecting rent on your own properties. That's good for you, but the booksellers and restaurants need income to survive. Stoneham needs more development—more than you're willing to promote."

"But I was in on the deal—until you cut me out."

Angelica merely shrugged.

Bob scowled. "I suppose next you'll tell me you're going to challenge me for president of the Chamber of Commerce."

"To tell you the truth, I haven't ruled it out," Angelica declared.

Bob laughed uproariously, and Tricia fought the urge to kick him.

"There's no way the booksellers and other merchants would vote you in against me."

"Oh no?" Angelica asked.

Did Bob hear the menace in her voice? Tricia stifled a laugh. Boy, was he in trouble now.

"I *own* this village," Bob continued. "You have as much chance of taking my Chamber job as I have of becoming the next Miss America."

"Oh, I don't know, Bob, I think you'd look sweet in a rhinestone tiara," Tricia said.

He turned an evil glare at her. "Shut up."

"Don't you talk to my sister like that," Angelica cried.

"I'll do what I please," Bob asserted, "and you can't do anything about it."

"Oh no?" Angelica asked with more than a hint of threat in her voice.

Bob's chest seemed to puff out. "Yeah."

Angelica's mouth twisted into a devilish smile. "Sarge—attack!"

The tiny dog lunged at Bob as Angelica hit the release on his retractable leash, and was instantly attached to Bob's left pants leg.

"Get him off, get him off me!" he cried, shaking his leg to try to dislodge the dog, but Sarge was a growling ball of fur tugging at the fabric.

Tricia laughed. Of course, she was instantly sorry—but she'd felt the same as Sarge on more than one occasion.

"Bad dog," Angelica said, jerking the leash back, but there was no remorse in her voice. Sarge would probably get a pâté treat once Angelica got him back home. She hauled in the leash and picked up the still-barking dog.

This time it was Tricia who ordered Bob to "Go home."

Bob's lower lip trembled as he rubbed at his calf, but apart from a tear in the fabric, there was no dark bloodstain marring the light-colored material. For a moment, Tricia thought he might burst into tears.

"Please, Bob—just go home," she said softly.

Without a word, Bob shoved past them and soon disappeared into the gloom between the streetlights.

The sisters looked after him for a long minute. Sarge's sharp barks winnowed into grunts as Angelica petted him and murmured "Good boy" into his ear. Eventually, she set him back down on the ground. "Well, that was unexpected," she said.

"Hardly. You had to know Bob would eventually catch up with you. This is a tiny village, after all."

"Yes, but who knew it would be so satisfying?" Angelica said smugly.

"You've just made an enemy of your landlord. Bob isn't going to let you forget it. He owns the buildings where you live and work."

"And I've got six months left on the lease for the Cookery and eighteen on Booked for Lunch."

"What if he won't renew them?"

Angelica shrugged. "I might have to move. I wouldn't like that," she admitted. "I like living next door to you, but—I'd adjust."

Tricia had been appalled when Angelica had bought the Cookery's assets and signed a three-year lease for the building. Now she couldn't imagine her sister living even a block away from her. "What about me?" she asked as they paused in front of the Cookery.

"You'd adjust, too." Angelica fumbled for her keys and sighed. "I may not have any business left if interest in that damn video doesn't die down."

"Then that nonsense you told Bob about taking his job at the Chamber was all bluff and bluster?"

"Oh, no. I was serious about that. I am a woman scorned." She looked down at Sarge, who looked back adoringly. Smiling, she picked him up again, planting a kiss on his head. "Wasn't my little man brave to stand up to that bully Bob?"

"I didn't see any blood on his pants, but if Sarge broke the skin, odds are you're looking at a lawsuit."

"You're my witness. Bob ordered you to leave. I felt threatened. You don't deny that, do you?"

"No," Tricia answered, unsure if that was the honest truth. "And I'd feel better if I accompanied you to the alley for Sarge's comfort stop, just in case Bob shows up again."

"It's okay with me," Angelica said, and opened the Cookery's door. They entered the store and Angelica turned on the lights and led the way to the back entrance. She disabled the security system on the back entrance and opened the door. Tricia followed her down the concrete steps to the alley and paused, thinking she'd heard some odd, unidentifiable noise.

Across the one-lane asphalt drive was a weedy strip of grass. Sarge knew why he was there and quickly finished his business. "Come, come!" Angelica called, but the dog's ears pricked up, and he gave one sharp bark before he bolted. He ran until the leash pulled taut, jerking him to a halt, and he barked his displeasure.

Tricia squinted to try to identify what the dog was interested in. A mound of something littered the alley.

"What is that?" Angelica asked.

"I don't know," Tricia said, "but I could swear it moved." The women looked at one another and by unspoken agreement headed in the direction of the mound. Sarge bounded forward as soon as he realized the leash had gone slack and was soon upon the darkened hump, excitedly sniffing his prize.

"Good grief," Tricia said, and picked up her pace. "I think it's a person."

"A person?" Angelica asked, and struggled to keep up with her sister.

Tricia bent down and reached for what she thought was a shoulder. It was a struggle to pull the body over. She gasped in recognition.

"Oh dear! It's Chauncey Porter!"

NINETEEN

Although Tricia had touched too many dead bodies—including Pippa Comfort's just three days before—she steeled herself to see if she could find a pulse along Chauncey's neck. A giddy thrill ran through her as she felt the blood coursing through the carotid artery under his right ear. She looked up into Angelica's worried face. "He's alive," she said, and then looked down again, noting a small patch of blood on the asphalt.

"Chauncey—Chauncey! Can you hear me?"

The portly gent's eyes roved under his closed lids before he opened them. His hand jerked up to probe the back of his head. "Somebody hit me," he gasped, then winced and seemed to deflate, falling back on the cold hard road surface.

"Call 911," Tricia told Angelica as Chauncey's hand groped to catch hers.

"No!" he cried. "Please don't."

"But we have to report this," Tricia told the older man.

"No, don't. I won't speak to the cops," he cried, and tried to rise, but his bulk made it too difficult and he lay back again, panting.

"What are you doing here in the alley?" Angelica asked.

"I'm trying to lose weight. For the last few weeks I've been walking the streets and alleys of Stoneham at night. So far I've lost ten pounds. My goal is sixty."

A lofty goal, and one Tricia hoped he would make.

"You'd better press this against the back of your head. It's bleeding a little," she said, extracting a wad of clean but crumpled tissues from her pocket. "Do you know who hit you?"

Chauncey pressed the tissues to his head and winced. "No," he said, but Tricia wasn't sure she believed him.

Angelica retracted Sarge's leash before she grabbed Chauncey's left arm while Tricia took his right, and the women struggled to pull the hefty man to his feet. Chauncey staggered, righted himself, and then let them steady him.

"Thank you for helping me, ladies. I'll be on my way now." He lurched, and it was only because they both held on to him that he didn't fall.

"Are you sure you don't want us to call an ambulance?" Tricia asked.

Chauncey nodded and winced. "If you could just help me back to my store, I'd appreciate it."

Tricia looked to Angelica, who nodded. "Can do," Tricia said, and with Sarge leading the way, they started down the alley.

By the time they hit the cross street that connected with Main Street, Chauncey seemed to have regained his sense of balance. They crossed to the west side of Main, passed the Dog-Eared Page, and stopped at the door to the Armchair Tourist.

Chauncey fumbled in his coat pocket for his keys. His hand shook when he tried to insert the key in the lock, so Tricia did it for him. She opened the door and held it for him to enter, and then she, Angelica, and Sarge followed.

"You needn't worry about me. I'm fine now."

"You don't look fine," Tricia said, noting his pale complexion. "You could have a concussion. I'd feel better if you'd let us stay for a few minutes—just to make sure you're okay."

"I could use something hot to drink—a cup of cocoa or something," Angelica said. "I could dash over to Booked for Lunch and make some for all of us."

"That won't be necessary. I have a hot pot in the back and plenty of packets of hot chocolate. I'd given them up since starting my diet, but I think I could use one right now."

"Great," Angelica said, and handed Sarge's leash to Tricia. "I'll go make us some. Be right back." She bustled to the back storeroom. Sarge gave a plaintive whine, then settled down on the floor with his head resting on his paws, his gaze riveted on the door left ajar to the back room.

Chauncey lurched to the stool behind his cash desk and took a seat. Then he struggled out of his jacket, setting it on the ledge behind him. From the back of the store Tricia heard the sound of running water and the clanking of cups, but other than that, the store was silent. Chauncey's gaze was focused on the top of the display case that acted as his sales counter. He didn't seem to want to look her in the eye. If he knew who assaulted him, he didn't want to talk about it. Would he talk about what happened at the inn on Sunday night?

"It hasn't been a very good week, has it?" Tricia asked, breaking the ice.

Chauncey shook his head. Was there anything sadder than a lonely old fat man?

A not-so-old thin single woman with a mystery bookstore might give him a run for his money, she decided.

"I understand you and Mrs. Comfort had words before she was killed."

That got his attention. His head snapped up, and for a moment Tricia wasn't sure if he was angry or might cry.

"What happened?" she asked gently.

Chauncey's cheeks grew red. "It was nothing, really. As usual, I made an ass of myself in front of a pretty woman. I'm sure it won't be the last time."

"I understand you recognized her from another time."

He frowned, his eyes narrowing. "I'll bet Mary Fairchild is spreading it all over town. I'm surprised no one has asked me about it before now."

Again Tricia asked, "What happened?"

"I . . . I'm ashamed to admit it, but . . . I was awed by Mrs. Comfort's former celebrity. I'm afraid I made a rather crude joke. I don't normally say such things to women." The additional color in his cheeks testified to that.

"What was her reaction?" Tricia asked, keeping her tone level and nonjudgmental.

"She was offended. She told me it would be a very long night indeed if she had to put up with the likes of me."

But it wasn't a long night for her. Within an hour or so, Pippa Comfort was dead.

"How did you remember her face from a magazine that was published so long ago?"

Chauncey looked up. "Magazine?"

"Yes. I understand she was a Playboy bunny and a model."

"A bunny, yes. A model? I don't think so. She used to wait tables at the Playboy Club in New York. I was a member. She was always nice to me. She was my favorite. I used to give her big tips, but I think she was embarrassed that I remembered her after all these years."

That didn't mesh with what Frannie said.

Tricia decided to push him, but how without letting him know it was Frannie who'd outed him as a collector of pornographic material?

"Umm . . . I understand that there was great cachet in being a member of the Playboy Club and having that coveted key."

Chauncey smiled. "That there was. The heyday was back in the sixties when I was a brash young man from Youngstown, Ohio, living in a cold-water, fourth-floor walk-up. I had two indulgences: my yearly subscription to *Playboy* magazine and my membership at the Playboy Club. I could barely afford either." He sighed wistfully. "I loved the short stories in the magazine and became a fan of some of the greats. Jean Shepherd, Roald Dahl, Shel Silverstein, and even Stephen King sold to *Playboy* in the golden days of the magazine. Ah, yes, those were the days." He laughed. "My copies were well thumbed, but I think I enjoyed the editorial content as much as, if not more than, the pictures."

Which again did not agree with Jim Roth's—or was it Frannie's?—spin on the story.

"Do you still have the magazines?" Tricia asked.

"A few of the rare ones encased in inert plastic. I really should try to sell them. I might even make a month's rent if I did. That could keep Bob Kelly off my back for a couple of weeks."

"Has he been hounding you?" Tricia asked.

"Only when I'm more than a day behind in the rent."

Angelica entered the room with a makeshift tray made from the lid of a paper carton and containing three mugs. Sarge looked up hopefully, but when no treat was forthcoming, he settled back down again.

"Here we go," Angelica said, and doled out a thick restaurant china mug to each of them. "Did I hear Bob Kelly's name mentioned?" she asked, her tone neutral.

Chauncey blew on his steaming cocoa before nodding.

Angelica frowned. "Your back room is awfully cramped, Chauncey. There's even a cot back there. One would almost think you've moved in."

Again Chauncey's face colored in embarrassment. "I had a

choice. Give up my apartment or give up my store. I guess you can tell where things landed."

"Are things really that bad?" Angelica asked.

Chauncey shrugged. "I couldn't very well sign a new lease on my apartment if my income is going to continue to be so erratic."

Tricia sipped her cocoa and wished she could say or do something to ease the poor man's problems. For what it was worth, she didn't think he was capable of killing anyone, but would the law think that way? He had deep financial problems and had had words with the dead woman not long before she was found dead. Would Grant Baker try to make something of it?

Why did he have to go incommunicado right now? And was he plotting to toss her in jail at any moment?

"You know," Angelica said, breaking the quiet. "What you need to do is diversify your product line."

Again Chauncey shrugged. "I sell travel books—and mostly used ones at that."

"Couldn't you sell things travelers need? Like plug converters, so people going to England can plug in their shavers and other electrical items. Or compact pillows and travel blankets. Maybe foreign language software. Luggage tags."

Chauncey frowned. "All that takes money. I'm cash starved."

"That is a problem," Angelica agreed.

"Can you hang on until the tourists start coming back? It's only a month or so," Tricia added.

"That's why I moved into the back room. If things don't turn around, I figure I've got maybe three, maybe four months until I have to close down and declare bankruptcy."

They sat there for a long time sipping their hot chocolate and not talking. It was Angelica who finally set her mug down on the counter. "Well, sorry to break up this happy meeting, but Sarge and I really need to call it a night." At the sound of his name, the dog jumped to his feet, his tail wagging with joy.

Oh to be a dog and to be so happy, Tricia thought, her frown deepening. "Are you sure you're going to be all right?" she asked Chauncey.

He nodded and smiled, apparently grateful that she cared enough to ask.

Angelica placed a hand on his shoulder. "Things will get better. I have a feeling about these things."

"I hope you're right."

"I'm not often wrong," Angelica said with a wry smile. She straightened and took Sarge's leash from her sister. "Come along, Tricia."

Tricia followed obediently.

The door closed behind them with the sound of the deadbolt clicking.

As usual, the streets of Stoneham were deserted at that time of night. At first the quiet—or as Tricia had initially described it, virtual deadness—had proved disturbing after the perpetual hustle and bustle of Manhattan. Now the nighttime quiet gave Tricia a sense of peace and contentment.

Most of the time.

"He's going to lose his business," Tricia said idly as she, Angelica, and Sarge crossed the street.

"There ought to be low-cost loans available for the business people here in Stoneham. The Chamber of Commerce ought to be talking to the Bank of Stoneham to arrange such things."

"That isn't likely to happen with Bob in charge," Tricia said. They paused in front of Haven't Got a Clue. "Were you serious when you said you might run for president of the Chamber?" she asked again.

"Deadly serious," Angelica said. As though to second her declaration, Sarge gave a sharp yip in agreement.

"Frannie painted Chauncey as some kind of porn fiend, but that's not the impression I got talking to him tonight," Tricia said.

Angelica shook her head. "Frannie's a terrific store manager, and I love her for it, but she's a terrible gossip. I don't think she means to hurt people with her opinions, but she often speaks before thinking. I trust your assessment of Chauncey, and I'd like to help him stay in business if I could. I just don't think I have the means. I'm stretched pretty thin right now, what with my investment in the inn, and the fact that I may lose most if not all of it thanks to Pippa Comfort's death."

Pride in her sister swelled within Tricia. She had underestimated Angelica's capacity for generosity. Tricia reached out and patted her sister's arm. "Maybe we'll think of something. I just hope Bob doesn't find out Chauncey's living in the back room of his store. I'm sure there's some ordinance against that."

"Probably for good reason, but not if your choice is being homeless," Angelica agreed. She frowned. "I suppose I should take Sarge back out in the alley."

"Oh my goodness! Did we ever lock up before we took Chauncey back to his place?"

"Oh no!" Angelica wailed, and the women hurried over to the Cookery. Angelica fumbled with her keys and finally managed to get the front door unlocked. They ran to the back of the store. Sure enough, the back door was wide open, but it didn't look like anyone had entered the store. Still, Sarge began sniffing the carpet that led to the stairwell that led to Angelica's apartment, and started barking.

Tricia tried the handle. It wasn't locked. She turned a worried gaze toward Angelica. "What if somebody's up there?"

"We could just go look," Angelica said, and started up the stairs, but Tricia grabbed her by the sleeve. "No! Somebody attacked Chauncey. Somebody killed Pippa Comfort. What if that person is now hiding in—or ransacking—your apartment?"

Angelica cocked her head to listen, but Sarge was making too much noise. "Hush!" Instantly the barking ceased. They both listened intently, while Sarge stood there panting and wagging his tail. "I don't hear anything."

"We should call 911."

"And what if there's nobody up there?"

"Then we'll look like a couple of scared women—which we are. Better safe than sorry, I always say."

"You've never said that," Angelica complained. She let out a huffy breath. "I'd say you were crazy if Sarge hadn't kicked up a fuss, but since he has . . ."

Tricia retrieved her cell phone from her pocket and quickly punched in the number. The dispatcher answered almost immediately. "Are you calling again?" the voice demanded.

"I beg your pardon?"

"First you called Sunday night to report an accident that turned out to be a murder, and then you called this afternoon for an ambulance."

"Yes, and the reason I'm calling now is so that someone can come and check out the Cookery to make sure that the murderer who's still running around doesn't kill us, too!"

"We'll send someone right over. Do you want to remain on the phone?"

"That won't be necessary," Tricia said, and ended the call. "Gosh, she's snippy. You'd think a 911 operator would be a little more professional. I've a mind to tell Grant . . ." But then she remembered she and Baker weren't exactly on friendly terms at that moment.

"Chauncey didn't want us to mention he'd been mugged. Should we report it anyway?"

"No," Tricia said. "That would be a breach of confidence."

"Well, they're going to wonder why we wandered off and left the door open for a good half hour."

Hmm.

They moved to the front of the store to wait, and Tricia wondered if they should arm themselves with marble rolling pins from one of the display racks. Before she had time to act on that thought, the blue flashing lights of a Stoneham police cruiser pulled up in front of the Cookery. The beefy officer got out of his car, resting a hand on the butt of his gun and the

top of his nightstick before he approached the store. Angelica
handed the leash to Tricia once again and met him at the door.
As soon as she opened it, Sarge started barking once again.

"Hush!" Angelica said, and the dog immediately quieted.
"Hello," she greeted the officer.

"So you think you've got a prowler on the premises?"

"Maybe. We kind of . . . took the dog for a walk and left
the back door open," Angelica said with a titter. "We were
gone about half an hour . . ."

"We thought we should err on the side of caution, especially
since you haven't arrested whoever killed Pippa Comfort on
Sunday night," Tricia finished.

"Have you searched the ground floor?" Officer Martinez
asked.

"There aren't many places down here one could hide," Angelica said, her eyes roving to the washroom in the back.

"I'll take a look. You ladies wait here."

They nodded and retreated to stand by the big display
window.

After looking around the store and checking out the washroom, the officer headed up the stairs.

Twin beams of light sliced the darkness on Main Street,
and Tricia recognized the SUV that pulled up on the opposite
side of the street. "Oh no," she groaned.

Angelica turned to look. "Is that . . . ?"

Tricia grimaced. "It's Grant, all right. We're in big trouble
now."

TWENTY

 "Tricia!"

How could one spoken word convey so many different implications? Exasperation seemed dominant. Disapproval seemed to be second on the list. And at a far third might—*might*—be actual concern.

"What are you doing here?" Tricia asked Chief Baker, and frowned.

"When I heard the address on my scanner, I naturally grabbed my coat and jumped in my car to find out what was happening. Are you okay?"

So, he *did* still care.

"Yes, we're both okay," Angelica answered, perturbed, and Sarge issued a low growl, baring his teeth.

"Don't mind Sarge," Tricia said, indicating the dog. "He's very protective of Angelica."

Sarge gave another growl to make sure Baker understood who was top dog.

Baker ignored him. "So, what's going on?"

Tricia told him—leaving out all mention of their encounter with Chauncey Porter and feeling guilty for doing so. But her gut feeling was that Chauncey was innocent of Pippa Comfort's death. Still, he might be a target of whoever killed her. And the most likely suspect was still Harry Tyler. Even if he hadn't killed his wife, she might have told him how Chauncey had recognized her, conveying her anger, and even though she was now dead, Harry might still have punished Chauncey for bringing up a sore—or shameful—subject to Pippa.

Oh yeah? something inside her taunted. Harry had told her he and Pippa weren't even close anymore. Would he really care to avenge her reputation now that she was dead?

He might. If it helped restore his.

Baker waved a hand in front of Tricia's face to gain her wandering attention. "What are you thinking about?" he asked suspiciously.

Tricia shook herself. "Oh, nothing important."

Baker looked skeptical. "Sure." Only he dragged the word out for at least four seconds. He turned his attention to Angelica. "Are you in the habit of taking your dog for a walk and leaving the door wide open?"

Angelica faced him, offended. "No."

"Then why tonight?"

"Sarge caught the scent of something and dragged us along."

Well, she hadn't lied, but neither did she admit the truth.

"Uh-huh," Baker uttered, and still looked unconvinced.

The uniformed officer came back downstairs. "All clear," he called and then, at the sight of his boss standing in the middle of the shop, came to a halt and straightened. "Chief. What are you doing here?"

"Just following up. Go get the big flashlight out of your

cruiser. Ms. Miles here"—he indicated Angelica—"says her dog was interested in something in the alley. I'd like to take a look."

"Sure thing."

The young officer left the store in a hurry.

Angelica sighed. "I need a drink—preferably alcoholic— and hopefully incredibly strong, thanks to the day I've had."

"We're not quite through here," Baker said.

Angelica sighed. "I can see why you installed comfortable upholstered chairs in your store, Tricia. I could sure go for one right now."

"What do you hope to find in the alley?" Tricia asked Baker.

"Hopefully, nothing."

"Yes, me, too," Angelica said, "because upstairs there's a gin and tonic with my name on it."

The officer returned, and he and Baker went out the back door.

"Oh no!" Tricia hissed. "What if they find the blood?"

Angelica looked at her as if she had lost her mind. "What blood?"

"Chauncey's head was bleeding. There was a patch of blood on the asphalt."

"Oh. That blood." Angelica bit her lip and shrugged. "It's dark. They'll never see it."

"I hope you're right."

But they did see it.

Not five minutes later Baker came back into the store, his expression grim. "I don't mean to alarm you ladies, but we found a patch of blood out in the alley. That's probably what your little dog was interested in."

"Ooh, you're good," Angelica said under her breath.

Baker looked pleased.

Tricia rolled her eyes.

"I'm having a tech come by and take a sample. You'll probably see flashing lights in the alley for the next hour or so. I didn't want you to worry about it."

"Worry about a possible mugging or something?" Angelica said, and Tricia shot daggers at her.

"Why would you say a mugging?" Baker asked, again suspicious.

Angelica shrugged. "Do you suspect something worse?"

"I don't know what to suspect," Baker said, and scrutinized the women. "Is there something you're not telling me?"

"I told you what's on my mind. A nice tall drink. Now, Chief, I'll take my dog out for one last pee and then I'm going to bed." She turned toward her sister. "Tricia, you've got a long day ahead of you, too. It's time you went to bed." She glared at Baker. "And apparently alone."

She picked up Sarge and headed for the back door.

"I'm sorry, Grant. Angelica really has had a tough day."

"Yes." He moved to stand in Tricia's personal space, something she'd been longing for for days, only now she wished he hadn't. "Tricia, if something is going on in this village that I should know about, for heaven's sake—tell me!"

"If I could, I would." Talk about being vague.

He studied her face, and she willed him to kiss her, but instead he turned aside. "Come on. I'll walk you to your front door."

That was the best offer she'd received in a week, and she accepted with resignation.

Baker waited until she'd let herself in before he turned to leave. No good-night kiss, just a terse "See you," and he headed back down the sidewalk, presumably to take the shortcut to the alley next to the Patisserie and join up with his officers.

Miss Marple made a solitary—and hungry—welcoming committee. She eagerly followed as Tricia climbed the steps to her loft apartment. She fed the cat and, being bone tired, got ready for bed.

Despite the fatigue that weighed down on her, Tricia thought it unlikely she'd be able to fall asleep. Instead of immediately retreating into a book, she turned off the bedroom light and raised the blind on the window.

Stoneham's streets were deadly quiet, but after such a tumultuous day Tricia drank in the tranquility. Chief Baker's SUV still sat outside Haven't Got a Clue, but within a minute or two Tricia saw him walk back down the street to claim it. He looked up at her window, but because of the darkness did not see her watching him. He turned away and climbed into the vehicle. Moments later, the headlights came on and the SUV slowly pulled away from the curb.

"Good night, Grant," Tricia said with a pang of regret.

Miss Marple jumped up on the windowsill with a sympathetic "Yow!" She nuzzled her head into Tricia's hand and purred loudly.

Tricia was about to turn away from the window when movement on the sidewalk across the street caught her attention.

Someone—a man—walked briskly up the west side of Main Street, heading north. Tricia recognized the gait—and the set of the shoulders—even though the street was bathed in partial shadow.

Harry Tyler.

And what was he doing in this part of the village at this time of night?

Not surprisingly, Tricia slept late and the morning came far too early. First thing, Tricia called the hospital and found that Mr. Everett had already been released. Okay, the day was starting out with something good, but she didn't expect to see him at work that day, and she hadn't had time to do any of the after-hours tasks, nor had she had time to train Linda to do them. That put something else on the to-do list.

After a quick shower and even quicker breakfast, Tricia hurried down the stairs to Haven't Got a Clue. Miss Marple followed in her wake, always eager to start the workday.

Considering Linda had only observed one closing, the store

appeared neat. The mail had been opened and was paper-clipped in stacks on the counter, which Linda had labeled with Post-it notes. Ads and circulars—probable recycles—bills, and . . . a pastel, multicolored silk scarf. Clipped to it was a printed note that had obviously been cut from a larger sheet of copy paper. It read: *Remember when you wore this?*

Tricia felt heat rise up her neck to burn her cheeks. No, she didn't remember ever wearing the scarf. Who was sending her this junk in the mail? First the picture, then the cocktail napkin—now this. Could someone have gotten her mixed up with another person? That didn't seem likely. The picture had definitely been Tricia.

She looked below the cash desk to the wastebasket, but it was empty. She searched under the counter, but there was no sign of the envelopes the mail had come in, nor the packaging for the scarf.

But something else was missing, too.

The blue bank pouch that should have been under the counter was also missing.

Tricia straightened too quickly and hit her head on the edge of the counter. Stars flashed before her eyes as she touched the top of her head and winced.

"*Yow!*" Miss Marple offered in sympathy, but Tricia had no time to converse with the cat. She opened the register and her heart sank. There wasn't a cent in it. No checks, no credit card slips. Nothing. Even the loose change had been removed.

She glanced at the clock. Ten minutes until opening. She had a few questions for Linda when she arrived. But first things first. She headed to the back of the store and brought out the vacuum cleaner, hoping to finish the carpet before the day's first customers arrived.

She did that and got the coffee started, too. By the time she poured herself a cup, it was ten ten.

No customers. No Linda.

She checked the store's voice mail but found no messages.

Tricia had a bad feeling about this.

After a quick search, she came up with the paperwork Linda had filled in two days before. Scanning the page, she found Linda's telephone number and dialed. After one ring, a recorded message said: "You have reached a number that has been disconnected or is out of service. Please check the number and try again."

As suggested, she tried again—and got the same message.

Tricia's stomach tightened as she set the heavy receiver back in its cradle.

The door opened and a customer came in. Tricia braved a smile. "Hi, welcome to Haven't Got a Clue. I'm Tricia. Please let me know if you need any help."

"Thanks," the woman said, and shuffled off to peruse the shelves.

Sensing something was wrong, Miss Marple jumped up on the sales counter and said, "*Brrrpt!*" Tricia petted the cat. "We're going to believe the best about Linda."

But ten minutes later, as her customer tried to pay for her purchase in cash, Tricia had no money to make change. She apologized and accepted a check instead. She smiled and gave a wave as her customer let herself out and then sighed. What should she do? Close the store so she could go to the bank and get some change? Borrow some money from Frannie next door?

Call the police?

The phone rang—could it be Linda with a perfectly good explanation as to why she was late and the store's receipts were missing?

Tricia grabbed the receiver. "Haven't Got a Clue—"

But it wasn't Linda on the other end of the line.

"Trish! The worst—the absolute worst thing has happened."

"Calm down, calm down," Tricia told Angelica.

"I can't calm down. That stupid video of me on TV yesterday has gone viral. Now I'm not only the laughingstock of all of New England, but I'm the laughingstock of all of North America—maybe even the world!"

"You're exaggerating," Tricia chided her.

"No I'm not," Angelica howled, verging on tears. "The comments are horrible! Everyone's acting like it was *my* fault that the TV station burned down. If that stupid boom guy hadn't hit me in the head with his phalliclike microphone, I'd be on my way to being—"

"The next Paula Deen—yeah, yeah, I know."

"You could be at least a little sympathetic," Angelica wailed.

"I'm sorry, Ange, but I've got problems of my own. Remember how I rarely let Ginny close for me?"

"What's that got to do with—"

"With Mr. Everett heading to the hospital yesterday, I left the keys to my store with Linda and told her to lock up at the regular time. Well, she did. And this morning she hasn't come in and the money from the till is gone."

"She stole from you—on her second day on the job?"

"I so want to give her the benefit of the doubt. I mean, she's not that late, just—" She glanced at the clock. "By twenty minutes."

"Maybe she had car trouble," Angelica offered.

"I tried calling her at home. The number's been disconnected."

"Oh dear. Your day is starting just as crappy as mine," Angelica said, sounding not quite so paranoid.

"At least one good thing has happened. Mr. Everett was discharged from the hospital and is, presumably, home."

"Oh good." Angelica sighed. "Thank you for mentioning that. I'm afraid I have gotten all caught up in myself this morning. I need to keep reminding myself that I have a good life, a good sister, two thriving businesses, and many fine friends."

"Can't you make lemonade out of lemons with the video situation?"

"What do you mean?"

"I'm sure I've heard you say there's no such thing as bad publicity. Call your agent and brainstorm this."

"Oh, Trish. You're right. I'm going to do that right now. Thanks. And you should call Grant and ask his advice about Linda."

"I don't want to do that just yet. I'll give her until lunchtime and then . . ." *I will be a complete fink and turn her in.*

"It's business, dear. You hardly know this woman."

"But I *wanted* to trust her."

"I know. Do you need some cash to get started for the day?"

"Yes, please."

"I'll send Frannie right over. And while she's gone I'll call my agent. Do you still want me to mention Harry Tyler to him?"

"No way."

Angelica giggled. "Your wish is my command. Look, I'd better go. Talk to you later, and thank you for making me feel better. Ta-ta for now."

Tricia put the phone down and stared at it, feeling foolish. Of all the candidates she'd interviewed and hired since Ginny had left, Linda had been the most promising. She'd been frank about her financial situation. Was that why the bank pouch was missing? But there couldn't have been more than a couple of hundred dollars in the till. Was it worth going to jail for that?

That was the logic a former employee at the Happy Domestic had gone with. Only in her case she got probation—and found a friend in Grace Harris, who found her a job.

Angelica was right. She really should call the police. But she would wait at least until Linda was an hour late for work. She could at least give her that much benefit of a doubt.

The shop's door opened and Frannie breezed into Haven't Got a Clue, clutching a number ten envelope that jingled with change as she walked. "Hi, Tricia. Angelica said you needed some money. What happened—someone rob you?" she said, and laughed.

Tricia stared blankly at her.

The mirth vanished from Frannie's face. "I was only kidding." She handed over the envelope and watched as Tricia counted out the money and settled it into the register tray. She seemed to be waiting for an explanation, but Tricia didn't feel inclined to give one.

Frannie leaned her elbows on the top of the glass display case, resting her head in her hands. "I hear Mr. Everett is out of the hospital. That was a close call, wasn't it?"

"Too close for comfort," Tricia agreed. "He was better when I saw him last evening. I'm hoping he'll be back to work in a few days."

"That'll be nice," Frannie agreed. She didn't seem in a hurry to get back to work at the Cookery. "Have you heard anything new on the Pippa Comfort murder investigation?"

"No," Tricia said, counting the pennies into the far right section of the coin tray.

"Everyone's so tight-lipped about this murder," Frannie complained. "Makes me wonder what's going on."

"What could possibly be going on?" Tricia asked.

Frannie shrugged her shoulders. "I dunno. Maybe it wouldn't be good for the village if the murderer was revealed."

"What do you mean?"

"Well, say it was somebody from Nigela Ricita Associates."

"There's only one person in Stoneham who works for them."

"Two," Frannie corrected. "You're forgetting that woman who's going to run the Dog-Eared Page."

"You think Michele Fowler killed Pippa Comfort?" Tricia asked in disbelief.

"I didn't say that. I was just wondering. Of course, what if it's that charming young man of Ginny's?"

"That's just as terrible a thing to suggest. And what motive would either have for killing Pippa, anyway?"

Again Frannie shrugged. "I don't know. Maybe they decided the inn wasn't a good investment for their development company. Maybe they wanted to get out of the deal."

"That's ridiculous. Nigela Ricita Associates might be moving fast to accumulate properties here in Stoneham, but everything they've done has benefited the village." Tricia realized she was defending the company—something she hadn't done before. Maybe because Angelica was now involved, and she didn't want gossip to taint her sister's reputation—especially when it came from Angelica's own employee. Of course, there was a good chance Frannie didn't know Angelica had a share in the inn. But that knowledge was sure to become commonplace in the not-too-distant future. Still, if Angelica wanted Frannie to know about it, she could tell her herself.

"Who else is on your list of suspects?"

"I should be asking you that question," Frannie said. "After all, it was you who found the body."

"I haven't given it any thought," Tricia said.

"It's gotta be a man, and the motive had to be jealousy. That leaves three suspects: the victim's husband, Chauncey Porter, and Clayton Ellington. They all knew her—and more than one if not all of them—biblically, if you catch my drift."

Tricia glanced up at the clock. "Oh, look at the time. I'm sure Angelica must need you back at the Cookery, and I have an important phone call I have to make."

"You don't have to chase me out. I was just about to leave," Frannie said, not so graciously.

"I'm sorry. I didn't mean it to come out that way. I'm just so preoccupied, what with being here on my own this morning." Oops. That wasn't a good revelation. But Frannie didn't seem to pick up on it, and she let it drop.

"Okay. I'll be seeing you, Tricia. Have a good day."

"You, too." Tricia said, and made to pick up the phone. She started to dial, but when the door closed on Frannie's back, she put the receiver back down. She had always liked Frannie, but these past few days she found herself hard-pressed to re-member why.

Eleven o'clock finally came and went and still Tricia had not heard from Linda. It was with a heavy heart that she picked up the phone for real and dialed the direct number for the Stoneham police instead of 911. This wasn't an emergency, after all.

"Our officers are all tied up right now"—*dealing with* real *crime*, the dispatcher's voice seemed to hint—"but we'll send somebody over in the next couple of hours to take a report."

"That'll be fine. Thank you," Tricia said and hung up the phone.

Therefore, she was surprised when ten minutes later Grant Baker's familiar SUV pulled up outside Haven't Got a Clue.

"Will there ever be a day when you don't find yourself mixed up in some kind of trouble?" Baker asked upon entering the store.

"Good morning to you, too. Isn't a shop owner *supposed* to call the police when she's been robbed?"

"Robbed of what?"

"Yesterday's receipts."

"And how much was that?"

"I'm not quite sure. Now that you mention it, I forgot to run the receipts from the register."

Baker sighed. Heavily. "Do you keep calling the police just to see me?"

"My, don't you have an inflated ego."

"And just who robbed you?"

"My new hire. Her name is Linda Fugitt. At least that's what she said her name was."

"How long has she worked for you?"

Tricia felt a blush creep up her neck to stain her cheeks. "A day and a half."

"And did she break in?"

"No. I . . . left her here in charge of the store."

"You left a person you barely know in your store with an open register?"

"I thought Mr. Everett had had a heart attack. I couldn't get hold of his wife. I had to go to the hospital until I was sure he was okay."

"And you left this woman alone in the store?"

Tricia hung her head, feeling like a scolded child. "Yes."

"Did she fill out any paperwork?"

"I tried the number she wrote on her application, but it's been disconnected."

Boy, did *that* sound bad.

"And you left a near-perfect stranger—with a bad phone number—alone in your store with an open register."

"Will you stop saying that? At the time it seemed a perfectly sensible thing to do."

Baker did not look convinced. "All right. I'll write up a report and we'll try to see if we can track this Fugitt woman down. If that's her real name. Of course you realize the Stoneham police are very busy right now."

"Yes. You've got a murder to solve. Quite frankly, I'm surprised the dispatcher sent you yet again."

"I heard the address on the scanner and I—"

"Took it upon yourself to investigate? Are you sure you don't keep showing up here just to see me?"

It was Baker's turn to blush.

The door rattled and the little bell chimed as a breathless Linda burst into the store.

"Oh, Tricia, I'm so sorry I'm late, but my car wouldn't start and my phone is out of order and I had to cancel my cell phone after my unemployment ran out and you can't find a pay phone anywhere these days, and I figured you'd be worried since I didn't know what to do with the money from the register, which I took home with me, and I knew you'd need change this morning and—" She finally ran out of breath as she opened her purse and took out the missing bank pouch. As she went to hand it to Tricia, she suddenly seemed to recognize that it was a uniformed policeman who stood in front of the register.

"Oh, I'm sorry. Is everything okay? Did something else happen since I closed last night?"

"Um . . . no," Tricia said. She indicated Baker. "The chief and I are friends. He just dropped by to say hello. Didn't you, Grant?" she said, her eyes imploring him to agree.

"Yes. Hello, Tricia," Baker said in a clipped tone. "Well, I guess I'd better be off."

"So soon?" Linda asked, and unbuttoned her coat.

"I've got an investigation to get back to." He nodded at Tricia. "I'll be seeing you." It almost sounded like a threat.

Tricia watched him go as Linda headed toward the back of the store to hang up her coat. The SUV was pulling away from the curb when Linda returned, tying on a Haven't Got a Clue apron.

"How's Mr. Everett?" she asked.

Tricia busied herself at the cash desk, neatening a stack of unruly bookmarks. "I haven't heard from him or Grace yet today, but he was released from the hospital early this morning."

"Oh, good. I've been so worried. He really is a dear sweet man."

"Thank you for opening the mail yesterday . . ."

"You're welcome."

"—but I really do prefer to do it myself."

Linda looked unsure of herself. "Oh. Okay. My secretary used to do that for me and it seemed one less burden I had to tackle on any given day."

"I do wish you'd left a note saying you'd taken the bank pouch," Tricia said, finding it hard to keep the strain from her voice.

"But I did. It's right—"

She looked at the shelf behind the register where Miss Marple lay curled up in a ball. "Oh. It's not there. I put a Post-it note on Miss Marple's shelf, thinking you'd see it right away. It must have fallen down."

Tricia cast about and saw a square sheet of yellow paper on the floor in the corner. She bent to pick it up. Sure enough in tight script it said: *I wasn't sure what to do with the money. I've taken the bank pouch home. Will try to get in early tomorrow. Linda.*

Tricia's heart sank. She looked up at Linda and opened her mouth to speak, but couldn't find the words so she closed it again.

Understanding dawned. "Oh, Tricia, I hope you didn't think—"

"I'm sorry, Linda. I didn't know *what* to think."

"That's why the cop was here. To take your statement that you'd been robbed."

Tricia wasn't sure how to interpret Linda's words—her tone was so neutral.

"It must have been awful for you to think your new employee was . . ." Linda stopped, as though unable to say the word.

"A thief? I'm the one who should feel bad. I didn't trust you, and I apologize."

Linda shook her head and waved a hand to dismiss the notion. "No. It's perfectly understandable under the circumstances." She looked up at Miss Marple, who was pretending to be asleep. Her eyes were shut, but her pricked ears betrayed that she'd been listening to the whole conversation. "You're a naughty cat," Linda scolded.

"*Brrrpt!*" Miss Marple replied, and still didn't bother to open her eyes.

"I don't know what to say," Tricia said.

"Why don't you say, 'Linda, how would you like to learn to do inventory?' I think that might be a good start. Mr.

Everett was telling me how Ginny took care of that for you, and that you've had to do it all yourself since she's been gone."

Tricia managed a smile. "Thank you for—"

"Let's not talk about it any more. But would you mind if we talked about inventory over a cup of coffee? After the morning I've put in, I'm pretty stressed. And I'll bet you are, too. Here, let me get you a cup. You like it with just creamer, right?" And off she headed for the beverage station.

It was then that Tricia was sure she'd found a permanent replacement for Ginny.

Linda did learn fast. She'd mentioned that Google and Wikipedia had become her new best friends and had spent the previous evening doing research on vintage mystery authors. She was helping a customer, and holding her own in a discussion of Agatha Christie versus Dorothy L. Sayers, when the phone rang. Tricia picked up the receiver.

"Haven't Got a Clue. This is Tricia. How may I help you?"

"Ms. Miles?" It was Mr. Everett!

"Oh, Mr. Everett, I'm so pleased you called. How are you feeling?"

"Much better today. In fact, I'd like to come back to work this afternoon. If it's all right with you, that is."

"Oh, so soon? Shouldn't you rest?"

"The doctors told me I had an anxiety attack—nothing more serious. I am back in the pink and eager to get back to work. Grace has already gone into the office for the day and I find it quite lonely being here by myself."

"Then by all means come back to work. Linda and I will be waiting for your return."

"Do you think she's working out?" he asked hopefully.

"Yes, I do." And she wasn't going to mention her fears of earlier in the day—to anyone.

"That's very good," he said, but he didn't sound enthusiastic. She'd mention to him that Ginny at the Happy Domestic was looking forward to sharing his work time with Tricia. It was a win-win situation for all, really.

"Is everything all right between you and Grace?" Tricia asked, feeling terribly nosy.

"We had a long talk. I believe things will be different from now on. Better."

"That's wonderful."

"I shall report for work at my usual time," Mr. Everett said, regaining control of the conversation. He didn't like to talk about personal things, after all.

"Very good. I'll see you then. Good-bye."

"Good-bye."

As Tricia hung up the phone, she decided she should get some of Mr. Everett's favorite thumbprint cookies as a welcome-back gesture. And she'd buy an extra dozen or so to make sure that he could take some home to enjoy later, too. She liberated a twenty-dollar bill from the till and approached her new assistant.

"Linda, I'm heading over to the Patisserie for some cookies. I'll be back in a few minutes."

"Sure thing," Linda said, and went back to her conversation with the customer.

Since it wasn't a long walk and it was a sunny day, Tricia left Haven't Got a Clue without a coat and hurried down the sidewalk. Now if only Nikki still had the cookies on hand. Mr. Everett was particularly fond of the thumbprints with raspberry jam but would happily accept any other kind.

She'd timed it right and there were no other customers in the bakery when she arrived. Charging in, she called a cheerful hello but was greeted by a stony-faced Nikki. "Can I help you?" she said coldly.

For a moment Tricia wasn't sure who Nikki was speaking to, and she looked behind her to see if she'd missed seeing someone else in the bakery's small waiting area. But as she'd already noted, there was no one else around. "Um . . . have you got any thumbprint cookies today? Mr. Everett is coming back to work after his scare yesterday and they're his favorites."

"Yes," Nikki said. "How many did you want?"

"How many do you have?"

"Four dozen."

"I'll take them all. Whatever my customers don't eat, Mr. Everett can take home. I assume they freeze well."

"Yes, they do." Nikki turned away and filled a bakery box with the cookies. She closed and tied the box with thin white string and rang up the sale.

Tricia gave her the twenty and then accepted the change. "Is anything wrong, Nikki? You don't seem especially happy this morning."

"Then I'll cut to the quick. I don't appreciate you visiting Russ at his office. You two are no longer together, as if I had to even say it."

Tricia blinked. "But we're still—" She gulped. "Friends." Okay, that was pushing it.

"It's *me* he chose, not you. I think you should just back off."

"I assure you we didn't talk about anything personal," Tricia said, finding it hard to believe Nikki could possibly be jealous of her recent conversation with Russ.

"Stay away from my man," Nikki said bluntly.

"Believe me, I have no romantic interest in Russ. Remember, *he* dumped *me*."

"He still talks about you—way too much."

"I can't help what he says," Tricia replied, feeling defensive. "I only went to his office to ask him what he knew about Pippa Comfort's murder."

"Why is it whenever somebody dies here in Stoneham, you're always involved? You really are the village jinx."

Not *that* again!

"Nikki, how can you say such hurtful things? We're friends."

"Not anymore. I'm sorry, Tricia, but I really don't want you to patronize my store."

"But Mr. Everett loves your cookies. All my customers do."

"Then if you wish to continue to offer my products, you can send Mr. Everett in to get them."

"Nikki—" Tricia began, feeling incredibly hurt.

"It goes without saying that I will no longer be a member of the Tuesday Night Book Club. And you are definitely *not* invited to our wedding."

Tricia felt hot tears fill her eyes. What had Russ told Nikki after their brief meeting the day before? Had he boasted to her that Tricia still needed him for information? Had the louse lied and said that she'd made a play for him? The doors to his office had been open. Patty Perkins had probably heard their entire conversation and could vouch that nothing untoward had gone on between them. But somehow Tricia doubted that Nikki would believe her—or Patty.

There were other, deeper ties that Tricia had believed bound her and Nikki together as friends. Had Nikki decided that was worth nothing, too?

Tricia's lower lip trembled, but somehow she managed to speak. "I'm sorry you feel that way, Nikki. I've tried to be a good friend to you. How could you even think I'd betray . . ."

"Please leave," Nikki said, her face rigid with disdain.

Tricia's fingers clenched the bakery box and her throat constricted. It was just as well; she couldn't think of anything to say to sway Nikki's resolve.

She turned and left the Patisserie, perhaps for the very last time.

TWENTY-ONE

"So, *did* you hit on Russ?" Angelica asked, looking at Tricia over the top of her sunglasses. Despite the fact they were inside Booked for Lunch, sitting in the back booth, Angelica insisted on wearing the glasses and a headscarf. She said she wanted to keep a low profile.

"Of course not," Tricia answered, and poked at the lettuce on her tuna plate. "You know I'm involved with Grant. Well, sort of. After he figures out who killed Pippa Comfort, we'll be back together again," she said confidently.

"Are you sure you *want* him back?" Angelica asked. "After all, he considers you a suspect in Pippa's death."

"It was me who found her," Tricia said reasonably. "Well, Sarge and me. And I did have a relationship with Harry—albeit twenty years before. Of course he has to officially consider me a suspect." She pushed the plate away. After her altercation with Nikki, she didn't have much of an appetite.

Angelica shook her head sadly. "How long have you two been chums? Eighteen months and he still doesn't know you well enough to realize you could never hurt—let alone kill—someone?"

Tricia's eyes widened. She hadn't thought of the situation in quite those terms.

Angelica sighed. "What is it about us that we accept bad behavior from men and excuse them for it?"

"Not all men are rats. Daddy never cheated on Mother."

"That we know of," Angelica countered.

"Mr. Everett would never cheat on Grace."

"No, but he'd prefer to find her at home making him a casserole instead of managing the charity they set up with his lottery winnings."

"He's just worried she'll overdo it. He's also from a generation where the man went to work and the woman kept the home fires burning."

"Nonsense," Angelica said. "Women have always worked. It's just that they were ashamed to admit the family might need money—that one salary wasn't cutting it back in the good old June Cleaver days."

"Grace never had to work, but I think she's enjoying it now."

"Hey, is that you, Angelica?" a mocking voice called out. "Gonna burn down any buildings today? The fire exit is over here, folks!"

Everybody in the café had turned to look at the man dressed in overalls, a plaid shirt, a brown Carhartt jacket, and tall black rubber boots. Then their gazes followed his to lock on Angelica. She turned in her seat to glare at the fool. "I will not dignify that question, Sully. And if you're not careful, I will never bring my car to your service station for an oil change ever again—and you will *not* get free seconds on the coffee the next time you come in."

The idiot actually looked hurt. "Aw, I was just joking. Everybody could see it wasn't your fault the TV station burned to the ground. But boy, the expression on your face." And he laughed.

Big mistake.

Without another word, Angelica pointed to the door, shooting daggers at the guy. He realized his gaffe and seemed to shrink under her unforgiving stare. Meek as a mouse, he shuffled toward the door.

Everybody else in the café found somewhere else to look.

Angelica turned back to Tricia. "Now, where were we?"

Tricia leaned in and whispered. "I can see now why you're wearing the sunglasses. Have you been getting this kind of treatment all day?"

Angelica nodded, stirring her by-now cold soup with a spoon. "E-mails, phone calls, catcalls on the street. You name it. I'm the brunt of everyone's jokes. I've even heard that your being a jinx has rubbed off on me."

Tricia cringed.

"Don't worry, I don't take that seriously."

Tricia didn't want to pursue that subject. "How did the conversation go with your agent?"

Angelica shrugged. "He was more interested in Harry Tyler than talking about my problems."

"I thought you weren't going to mention Harry."

"*I* didn't. *He* did. Haven't you been reading the *Nashua Telegraph*? It's a big deal that your ex-boyfriend has surfaced."

"I must've missed the three-inch headline announcing it."

"Anyway, Artie asked me for Harry's number. I didn't know if you wanted to tell him yourself or if I should just give him a call and give him the number."

Tricia thought it over. She didn't particularly want to speak to Pippa's husband again, but she had a few nagging questions in the back of her mind. "Sure, I'll give him the message."

"Fine. I'll give you Artie's number before you go back to work."

"I'm puzzled about something," Tricia said. Angelica lifted

her head enough to look over the top of her shades. "I was looking out my bedroom window last night, watching Grant take off in his SUV—"

"Pining for him, were you?" Angelica asked.

"No. But I must have been lost in thought because I was staring out the window when . . . I swear I saw Harry walking north on Main Street."

"Where did he come from?"

"That's just it, I don't know. He wasn't there—and then he was."

"He's not a ghost. He can't just appear and then disappear into thin air."

"I thought it was strange he was walking the streets of Stoneham so late."

"Well, Chauncey was walking late. Maybe Harry was trying to get in some exercise, too."

"He hardly needs it. He's got abs like a washboard."

Angelica pulled her sunglasses off. "And *when* did you see those?" She waggled her eyebrows knowingly.

"Under his shirt. He came to visit me on Monday. And get your mind out of the gutter, please. If you'd been more observant, you would've noticed, too."

"When? I've never met the man."

"You almost did—the night of the murder. I saw him for a brief second before he pulled his vanishing act." Angelica shrugged. "You know, I've been thinking a lot about that night. We must've seen something."

"What?" Angelica asked.

Tricia shook her head. "Something so insignificant that it meant nothing to us."

Angelica sighed. "We were inside the front door for all of two minutes before we went up to the suite, and then you and Sarge were only there a couple of minutes before you took him out and found Pippa's body."

"That's true," Tricia said.

"We didn't even run into any of the guests."

"I did."

Angelica frowned. "When?"

"When Sarge and I went down the back stairs to the kitchen. I saw Mary Fairchild on the landing."

"What was she doing?"

Tricia thought about it. "Nothing. She was just standing there, holding a couple of glasses of sherry, when I rounded the stairs."

"Do you think that's significant?"

Tricia shrugged. "Maybe. But probably not. I mean—this is Mary we're talking about."

"I barely know her," Angelica admitted. "We've only spoken a few times at the Chamber of Commerce breakfast meetings."

"She's been a member of the Tuesday Night Book Club for a few months now. And now that Nikki isn't going to be there, we need all the warm bodies we can get. And speaking of Nikki once again, what am I going to do about the cookies?"

"What cookies?"

"The ones I serve in my store. I've always bought them from the Patisserie. Nikki said she might allow someone else to buy them—presumably Mr. Everett or Linda—but what if she changes her mind? My customers love them, and so does Mr. Everett."

"You *could* learn to bake."

"So far my baking escapades haven't been all that successful," Tricia reminded her.

"That's because you haven't really tried. I have a wonderful recipe in my upcoming cookbook and I'm willing to walk you though making it."

Tricia nodded, resigned. "And this time I'll try to take the lesson more seriously. Baking's not difficult—"

"If you can follow simple directions, anyone can bake or cook," Angelica said for about the millionth time.

"Yes, ma'am." Tricia glanced at her watch.

Tricia saw movement outside the big display window outside. Grant Baker stood there, peering in. He saw her, gave a wave, and moved on down the street—presumably for the Bookshelf Diner.

"You just lost a customer."

"You mean Sully?" She shook her head. "He'll be back. I have to berate him for something at least twice a week. I think he enjoys it."

"No, Grant Baker was just outside. When he saw me, he waved and headed north down the street."

"Oh crap! I just started to get the locals in here, and now you're chasing them away."

"Just Grant—so far no one else," Tricia said tartly.

"Sorry," Angelica said sincerely. "I didn't mean it."

"I know."

"You miss him, don't you?"

Tricia nodded. "But as long as he suspects I might have had something to do with Pippa Comfort's death . . ."

"Then do something about it."

"Like what?"

"You've never been shy before when it came to asking questions about a murder here in Stoneham. Go forth and confront your suspects."

"That could get me killed."

"Only if you're in the proximity of a large, heavy brass candleholder."

"I've already spoken with Harry and Chauncey."

"Then go talk to Clayton Ellington."

"Under what pretext?"

"I suppose pure nosiness isn't a good excuse."

"No."

The two women were quiet for a few minutes, neither of them touching their lunches while the café bustled around them once again. Finally, Angelica spoke. "You know, you could ask Ellington how he managed to win the raffle for the free night at the inn when he wasn't even at the last Chamber meeting."

"He wasn't?"

Angelica shook her head. "In fact, I don't know as I've *ever* seen him attend a Chamber meeting, and I haven't missed one in the past six months. You ought to make more of an effort to go—then you wouldn't have to keep asking me and everyone else what went on and who dished what dirt."

"So what happens with these raffles?" Tricia asked, ignoring the dig.

"Everyone present puts a business card in a fishbowl and then Bob pulls out however many to give away the prizes. If you're not there, you can't win. But Ellington *did* win."

"Why didn't you tell me this before now?"

"I hadn't given it any thought *until* now."

"Do you think Bob rigged the drawing?"

"Of course. Why else was everyone so surprised when I showed up at the inn with you and not Bob? He made it rather obvious that he expected to rekindle our long-dead relationship that night. As if!"

"Then what about the other winners? Do you suppose they had a reason to be at the inn, too?"

Angelica shook her head. "What motive could Chauncey or Mary have to be there?"

"Chauncey once had the hots for Pippa. He said he used to tip her well when she was a Playboy bunny. Maybe he hoped she'd remember him and . . . well . . . reciprocate in kind."

"The way he looks now? I'll bet he wasn't attractive on his best day ever. Besides, Pippa was married—"

"Unhappily so, according to Harry," Tricia countered.

"And she pitched a fit when Chauncey made a crack about her less-than-sexy attire," Angelica finished.

"Yes, but let's say he had unreasonable expectations. The fact that she got angry with him, and in front of a witness— it could have driven him to kill the thing he loved most."

"I suppose. And what reason could Mary have had to kill Pippa?"

"I have no idea. But she does seem overly interested in the whole situation."

"The same could be said of you. At first glance, it would appear you've got a reason to see the woman dead. Can you prove you haven't seen Harry in twenty years?"

"Probably not—but they can't prove I did, either."

Angelica took off her sunglasses. "Then that leaves one more suspect—Clayton Ellington. Go talk to him and find out what dirty tricks he's playing."

"Who says he's playing any dirty tricks? For all we know Bob could be behind this."

"You could be right. But to get to Bob you'll have to talk to Ellington first," Angelica declared.

Tricia nodded. "Did anything seem out of the ordinary when Bob announced the winners?"

"Not that I remember. It was a pretty standard meeting. Eggs, bacon, croissants, and jam. Bob went around the room and collected everyone's business cards for the drawing, and while the waitresses were busing the tables, he pulled the four winners. He pulled my name last. It was a huge surprise."

I'll bet.

Tricia wasn't eager to embrace the idea. Instead, she glanced at her watch. "Look at the time. Mr. Everett will be arriving at Haven't Got a Clue any moment now. I'd better scoot." She grabbed her coat from the seat beside her and got up. "Will you have time in the next few days to walk me through that cookie recipe?"

"I'll have plenty of time—especially if I'm still in hiding," Angelica said, and slipped her sunglasses back on.

Tricia wrestled into the sleeves of her coat. "See you later, then." She headed for the door.

She wasn't sure what bothered her more—trying to find an

excuse to see Ellington, or having to go to the Full Moon Nudist Camp and Resort to track him down.

"Please, Ms. Miles, don't make a fuss. I assure you I'm all right," Mr. Everett said, sounding a little frustrated after Tricia not only made him take a seat at the readers' nook but brought him several of the thumbprint cookies and a cup of coffee, placing them on the big square coffee table.

"I'm sure you are," she said, "but please let me spoil you for at least a couple of minutes."

Mr. Everett's cheeks turned a bright shade of pink. "Oh, very well."

Miss Marple seemed equally pleased to have Mr. Everett back and jumped on his lap, purring loudly and nuzzling his chin. "My dear Miss Marple, I missed you, too," he said, and petted the cat.

Linda joined them. "I'm so glad you're back, Mr. Everett. There's a lot I need to learn about Haven't Got a Clue, and I've enjoyed our talks so far."

"As have I," Mr. Everett admitted.

The door rattled and the bell rang, and Grace entered Haven't Got a Clue with her sheepish-looking receptionist, Pixie, in tow. If Pixie was in costume once again, her long gray raincoat hid it. "Hello, Tricia," Grace said, and stepped over to the reader's nook. "And you must be Linda," she said, offering her hand.

"This is my wife, Grace Harris-Everett," Mr. Everett said, introducing them.

Linda and Grace shook hands. "So glad to meet you. You've got a keeper here," she said, and nodded toward Mr. Everett, whose pink cheeks went a shade darker.

"I like to think so. But when I think of how close I came to losing him last night . . ." She let the sentence trail off, and then cleared her throat and glanced at Pixie, who had so far not made eye contact with any of them. "This is my reception-ist, Pixie Poe."

Tricia raised an eyebrow at the last name. Linda and Mr. Everett nodded, since Pixie did not move forward to shake their hands. "I believe Pixie has something to say to you, Tricia."

Tricia was glad all eyes were now on Pixie instead of her, for like Mr. Everett she felt her cheeks grow hot with embarrassment.

"I . . . I apol—" That was as far as Pixie got before her face crumpled—but not with shame. It was anger that made her eyes suddenly blaze. "No! I will not apologize to this bitch!" she cried, and glared at Grace, whose jaw had dropped open in shock. "She crossed me!" Pixie swiveled her gaze to glower at Tricia. "Because you tattled on me to Mrs. H-E, I got a real dressing-down. You disrespected me and I will *not* back down. I don't care if I lose this job, lose my parole, and go back to the joint—I will not apologize to the likes of you." She paused long enough to take them all in. "In fact, go to hell—all of you!" she shouted, then turned and stormed out of the store.

Miss Marple hissed at her retreating back, and Mr. Everett began to pet the cat at warp speed in hopes of placating her.

Grace stood rooted, her mouth still agape. "I—I don't know what to say, Tricia. I am so very sorry."

Tricia didn't dare speak, so deep was her shock.

Linda stepped forward and placed a comforting hand on both Tricia's and Grace's arms. "Why don't we all have a nice warming cup of coffee and a couple of cookies to make us feel better?"

No one said a word.

Linda guided Grace to one of the nook's empty chairs. "Please sit. I'll bring you a cup. How do you like it?"

"Black, please," Grace murmured, still in shock.

Linda nodded and left the three of them alone.

Grace shook her head. "When I spoke to Pixie, I thought

she understood . . . I tried to make her realize how her treatment of you was inappropriate. I honestly thought she accepted that her behavior was inappropriate. I told her she'd have to apologize to you, and then all would be forgiven—and she agreed to do so."

"Grace, I know you wanted to help that woman," Mr. Everett began, "but perhaps her social skills just aren't adequate for the job."

That was the truth.

"But if she doesn't have a job, there's a good chance she might go back to prison," Grace cried, her voice filled with despair.

Tricia bit her lip, guilt weighing her down. All she had wanted to do was help Mr. Everett and Grace through a rough patch. That she was the catalyst of all this trouble made her feel terrible, but she honestly didn't know what she could have done differently.

As though sensing her distress, Grace reached out to touch Tricia's hand. "It's not your fault, dear. I'm completely responsible for all of this. If I hadn't paid more attention to the job than to William, all this could have been avoided. And I so wanted to help the poor woman. I should go and try to find her." She made to stand, but Mr. Everett reached out to stop her.

"I must put my foot down, dear. Ms. Miles is our friend. We owe her for changing our lives for the better—and even for bringing us together. Your—our—loyalty must be to her, not this lowlife stranger."

Grace bristled at his description of her former assistant but said nothing.

Linda arrived with a tray filled with cups and a small plate of cookies. "Just what kind of business do you run, Grace?"

"A charitable foundation."

That sparked Linda's attention.

"I don't know how I'll manage without Pixie. I guess I'll

call Libby Hirt at the Food Shelf and Job Bank to see if she has any other candidates with office experience."

Linda bit her lip as she passed out the cups of coffee.

Tricia said nothing. She wasn't about to suggest that Linda apply for the job. She had experience at a nonprofit, but Grace wasn't looking for a person of Linda's caliber. She needed someone to answer phones and lick envelopes, which was far below Linda's skill and qualifications.

And working retail isn't? a small voice inside Tricia asked.

The four of them sipped their coffee, although Tricia was fairly certain none of them really tasted it. It was only when a customer entered the store that both Linda and Mr. Everett sprang from their chairs—which sent Miss Marple flying to the floor—to see if they could help that the mini pity party broke up. Grace also stood, and Tricia followed.

"I really must be going," Grace said.

"Yes, and I have an errand to run as well," Tricia said.

"I'll see you soon," Grace said, and reached for Tricia's hand. "I am sorry about all of this. And even sorrier about Pixie. I had such high hopes for her. She was my first test case—and my first failure. I shall have to reevaluate the validity of the whole Everett Charitable Foundation."

"Please don't give it up because of this one incident. You've already made an impact for good—I'm sure this is just a temporary setback."

Grace's smile was faint. "I'm sure you're right." But she didn't sound convinced. "Good-bye, Tricia."

Tricia leaned forward and gave Grace a quick kiss on the cheek.

She watched as Grace said good-bye to her husband and Linda. Pixie sure had blown her chance to make amends. Which reminded Tricia of her own dilemma. In order to get back with Grant, she had to clear her name. Angelica was right. Her first step should be to talk to Clayton Ellington.

She headed for the back of the store to retrieve her coat.

With both Linda and Mr. Everett to watch over Haven't Got a Clue, she knew she could leave her store without worrying.

As the door closed behind her, she worried more about what she'd say to Ellington when she arrived at the Full Moon Nudist Camp and Resort, and wondered if she'd be terribly overdressed.

TWENTY-TWO

Tricia admitted to having more than a few butterflies as she turned into the drive. A FULL MOON NUDIST CAMP AND RESORT sign resplendent in hunter green and gold leaf greeted her. She drove slowly up the long driveway and parked her car outside the reception building. Somehow she expected a bigger parking lot. Instead of a sea of asphalt, there was only a small pond of tarmac surrounding the cottagelike building. Painted white with black trim, the squat building with a red tile roof could have passed for a Hollywood bungalow from the 1920s.

Tricia stepped out of the car, feeling self-conscious. What was she going to say to the receptionist? Worse, where was she going to look?

She opened the plate glass door, and a blast of hot air hit her. *They probably need to keep it set high to keep warm*, she thought, and approached the pony wall that separated the inner sanctum from a rather luxurious waiting room filled with tapestry-upholstered chairs. A woman holding a spreadsheet leaned over the receptionist, and they conversed in low tones for a moment before noticing her presence. Tricia hadn't been sure what she expected when she walked into the reception area, but finding the staff fully clothed was a little startling.

The woman with the spreadsheet whispered, "We'll finish this later," and disappeared inside one of the offices.

"Hello, may I help you?" the receptionist politely asked Tricia. Not only did she look smart, she was everything Pixie was not when it came to presenting a positive image. A placard on the half-wall's shelf read *Sarah*. Was this the woman Frannie had spoken of, the one who'd had the affair with Ellington?

"Um, you ladies are dressed. I thought this was a nudist camp," Tricia said.

"It *is* only fifty-three degrees outside. Do you want us to freeze?" Sarah asked, then laughed. "I'm sorry. This office is just like any other. You have to actually go inside the resort if you want to be a part of the lifestyle."

"Oh. Um, I was hoping to speak with Mr. Ellington."

"His office is in this building. Do you have an appointment?" Sarah asked, and consulted her computer screen.

"No. I'm a member of the Stoneham Chamber of Commerce and—"

"Your name?"

"Tricia Miles. I own Haven't Got a Clue, the mystery bookstore in the village."

"And do you have a clue?"

Tricia forced a smile. If she had a dollar for every time she heard that line . . . "Yes."

Sarah rose from her chair. "I'll tell him you're here."

The woman whom Tricia had seen a few minutes before looked out of her office and eyed her, then disappeared again. What was with that? Maybe they didn't get a lot of visitors in the late winter and anyone visiting the office was fair game for gawking.

Sarah returned to her post. "Mr. Ellington has a few minutes free before another appointment. You can go in now. Please follow me." She led the way back to Ellington's office, then shut the door behind her.

Sumptuous. That was the word that immediately came to mind as Tricia looked at the furnishings and paintings. No doubt about it, a nudist resort had to be a gold mine. Black leather chairs and couch, deep-pile carpet, expensive window treatments, and original artwork—nudes, of course.

Ellington hung up his phone and stood. "Ms. Miles—I wondered how soon it would be before you visited me."

Tricia blinked. "I'm sorry."

"Your reputation precedes you."

And it was probably Bob Kelly who'd warned him she might pay him a visit.

Ellington gestured for her to take one of the chairs in front of his polished cherry desk. "Now, what was it you wanted to ask me about Pippa Comfort's murder?"

"Did you do it?"

It was Ellington's turn to blink. "That's not very funny."

"It wasn't meant to be."

He shook his head. "I had no motive to kill the lady."

"But you had been friends many years ago."

"That's true." Ellington sighed, and his gaze drifted to his left as though a melancholy memory had overtaken him.

Tricia wasn't sure how much of his time Ellington would give her, so she figured it was time to test her budding theory. "Why did you bribe Bob Kelly for a night at the Sheer Comfort Inn?"

That shook him out of his reverie. "Who says I bribed anyone?"

"Bob, for one." Okay, that was really fudging things, but how was she going to get people to level with her by telling the truth, the whole truth, and nothing but the truth?

Ellington glowered. Tricia could almost read the thought balloon over his head. *The slimy little bastard.*

"Mr. Ellington, everyone knows"—*except me apparently*—"that Chamber members have to be at the meetings to win the monthly raffles. You weren't in attendance the day the winners of the night's stay at the inn were drawn. There's only one way you could have won, and that was if Bob announced your name instead of the card he actually pulled. He isn't known to be particularly generous."

Ellington sighed, defeat making the lines around his eyes more pronounced. "I wanted to see the inn—to see what Pippa had done with it."

"Why couldn't you just visit?"

"Because her husband is the jealous type."

Tricia's eyes widened in disbelief. "Jealous?" she asked. That wasn't the way Harry had described their relationship. He'd said it was essentially platonic.

He nodded. "Pippa refused to come and see me at the resort, and she wouldn't let me visit her at her inn. All I wanted was an opportunity to talk to an old friend." He shook his head. "But I figured if I won the raffle, her husband couldn't complain."

"He knew you were old friends?" Tricia asked.

"Who do you think got her the job?"

That verified what Frannie had said.

"If that's the case, I would think she'd be eager to see you—to thank you. Or—" Here came a real leap in logic. "Was she afraid you two might pick up where you left off years ago?"

"I didn't think so, and neither did Pippa. But I'm afraid my wife thought so." Had she caught Ellington with his co-worker? If so, she had reason to distrust her husband.

"Why didn't you bring your wife with you when you went to the inn?"

"As it happens, she's out of town."

"If she's the jealous type, wouldn't it look suspicious for you to go to the inn to see an old girlfriend—stay the night—without her?"

Ellington frowned. "I'm sorry, Ms. Miles, but you're getting awfully personal. I allowed you to come in here thinking I might persuade you to stop asking questions, and instead, you've crossed the line."

"I apologize. But we are talking about a murder that's taken place in Stoneham. In a tourist destination like this, it behooves all of us to cooperate with the police and see that the murderer is quickly found so that our visitors will once again feel safe."

"I agree. But I don't know what else I can contribute to the investigation."

Of course he did—the fact that he'd bribed Bob to give him the free pass to visit the inn. But she wasn't about to press the issue. If he was the guilty party, he might just come after her. It was time to leave with discretion.

Tricia stood. "Thank you for speaking with me, Mr. Ellington."

"My pleasure," he said, but it was obvious he was simply being polite—although that was as far as it went. He didn't stand to see her out.

"I'll see myself out," she said, and turned.

"Why did you come here to talk to me?" Ellington asked, causing Tricia to turn. "You'd be better off talking to Bob Kelly. He's the one with all the answers."

Perhaps he was right. But she and Bob weren't exactly on speaking terms.

She'd have to fix that and quick . . . unless there was another way, and there was only one person who could make that happen.

Now to persuade Angelica to help.

It was almost five when Tricia returned to Haven't Got a Clue. Since it was the slow season, she wasn't surprised to find the store devoid of customers and Linda and Mr. Everett seated in the reader's nook exchanging a laugh.

"Looks like I've missed some fun," she said.

"We were just talking," Linda said, and moved to stand, but Tricia waved her back into her seat. She turned back to Mr. Everett. "And she wanted to return the book after she'd dropped it in the bathtub?"

Mr. Everett nodded. "She complained that the pages had swelled to such an extent that it wouldn't sit well on her bookshelf."

"And you accepted the return?"

"Ms. Miles okayed it in the name of good customer service," he replied.

"It paid off in the long run," Tricia said as she took off her coat, carefully folded it, and laid it over her left arm. "She came back a couple of weeks later and bought more than two hundred dollars' worth of merchandise."

Linda shook her head. "I guess I have a lot to learn about the book business."

"And we shall be pleased to teach you," Mr. Everett said.

"Have you had many customers since I left?" Tricia asked.

"Two or three," Linda said.

Tricia frowned. It really didn't pay for her to have two people on the sales floor when she had a distinct shortage of paying customers coming through the door.

As though reading her mind, Mr. Everett spoke up. "If it's all right with you, Ms. Miles, starting tomorrow I shall go back to the hours I kept before Ginny left us." He looked at Linda and beamed. "I know between the two of you that Haven't Got a Clue will be in good hands when I'm absent."

"Thank you for the vote of confidence," Tricia said with a grin. Mr. Everett always took everything so seriously.

"And fear not," he said, joining her in a smile, "tomorrow I will be working at the Happy Domestic for several hours. It will be good to spend time with Ginny again on a regular basis."

"Oh. With Pixie gone, I thought you might decide to spend some time with Grace at the charitable foundation."

Mr. Everett's smile evaporated, and he shook his head. "When I owned my own store I discouraged family members from working together. It made for added tension, which wasn't good for employee morale—or the morale of the related employees, either."

"But surely she needs someone right away to keep the work from piling up."

"I'm afraid she needs more than just a receptionist. She should have hired someone with far more experience who can take a greater role in helping her run the foundation." And with that, his gaze shifted to Linda, who stared fixedly at the floor.

I will not offer up Linda—I won't. I need her, Tricia thought, and instantly felt guilty.

Linda said nothing.

"I'd better hang up my coat," Tricia said.

"And I should get mine," Mr. Everett said, and rose from his chair.

Tricia waved him to stay put. "I'll get it." As she walked to the back of the store, she could feel both pairs of eyes on her. Rats! She'd taken a chance hiring Linda, and although it had been only a couple of days, she seemed to fit in well so far. The idea of going through the whole interview process again did more than depress Tricia.

She returned to the readers' nook with Mr. Everett's coat. "I guess we'll see you on Saturday, then."

"That you will," he said as he slid his arms into the sleeves. They watched in silence as he zippered the coat. "Good night, ladies," he said, and headed for the door. He paused, then looked over to where Miss Marple lay on her perch behind the register. "And good night to you, too, Miss Marple."

Miss Marple gave a languid *"Yow!"*

After the door had closed behind him, Tricia tried not to

look at her new assistant manager. The quiet was nerve racking.

The shrill sound of the telephone was just the distraction Tricia was looking for, and she hurried to answer it. "Haven't Got a Clue. This is Tricia. How may I—"

"Oh, Tricia! The best thing in the world has happened," came Angelica's voice through the receiver. "You'll never guess—you'll never guess."

"No, I won't—so tell me!"

"I just got a call from my editor. Thanks to that YouTube video, there's been a tremendous interest in my book. Sales for *Easy-Does-It Cooking* have skyrocketed. The publisher has ordered a ten-thousand-copy reprint. With those kind of numbers, there's a chance it could hit the *New York Times* best sellers list!"

Tricia doubted that, but she chose to sound enthusiastic. "That's terrific." And perfect timing, too. If Angelica was in a good mood, she might be more receptive to helping Tricia get into Bob Kelly's office to check the pockets of his suit coat.

"I'm going to celebrate tonight with champagne and lobster," Angelica gushed. "I'd love it if you'd join me."

"I'd be very happy to. Can I bring anything?"

"Just a smile and the will to celebrate."

"Sounds like heaven. I'll be over after I close the store and feed Miss Marple."

"Great. See you then!"

Tricia hung up the phone and looked up to see Linda tidying the beverage station, her expression somber. She could tell the last hour of business was going to be awkward.

Why couldn't Pixie have just apologized to her instead of exploding in a rage and quitting her job? Why did Linda just happen to have a degree and experience in the field of nonprofit organizations just when Grace needed such an employee to work at the Everett Charitable Foundation?

And why couldn't Tricia ever get a break?

TWENTY-THREE

Angelica wasn't kidding when she said she wanted to celebrate. As Tricia made her way up the stairs to Angelica's loft, she could smell the heavenly aroma of roasting garlic. She hung up her jacket and headed down the hall that led to Angelica's kitchen and found the table set with candles, Angelica's good china, sterling silverware, and Waterford crystal. A silver champagne bucket was filled with ice with a bottle just waiting for its cork to pop. Earlier in the day Tricia had felt overdressed. Now she felt underdressed.

"Everything looks lovely, Ange."

"When I'm in the mood to celebrate, I celebrate."

The phone rang.

"Dinner won't be ready for another twenty minutes. Would you like a glass of Chardonnay before we open the good stuff?" Angelica asked.

The phone rang again.

"Why not?" Tricia said, and she reached for the cabinet that held the everyday glassware.

The phone kept ringing.

"Aren't you going to answer that?" Tricia asked.

"No! It's probably Bob. He's been leaving messages on my landline, my cell, and at the store and café all day long," Angelica said, and pulled out a wooden cutting board. "I *don't* want to talk to him."

That didn't bode well for the success of Tricia's admittedly harebrained plan.

Finally the ringing stopped.

Tricia poured the wine and handed Angelica a glass. "I've been waiting all day for this," she said, taking a sip. She pouted before speaking again. "Seems like there's trouble all over Stoneham."

Tricia recognized trouble, too—in the tone of her sister's voice. She had something to say that Tricia knew she wasn't going to like.

"Didn't you say Grace's receptionist was named Pixie?"

Tricia nodded warily.

"I had a long conversation with a customer who said her name was Pixie. A hard-looking woman with orange hair."

"That's Pixie the horrible," Tricia said, and sipped her wine. She had a feeling she should have poured herself something stronger.

"She had more than a few rough edges, but I wouldn't say *horrible*," Angelica said.

Tricia decided not to comment on that last remark.

"She came in to Booked for Lunch and sat at the counter. Bev was on a break so I served her. She ordered a double chocolate milkshake to drown her sorrows."

"Oh, was she actually sorrowful?" Tricia asked.

"She said she'd just quit her job and that she'd be in trouble with her parole officer because of it."

"I can't say I'd shed any tears if Pixie was tossed back in the clink."

"I don't suppose you would. But I'll bet you didn't know that she's a walking encyclopedia of trivia—and one of her specialties is vintage mysteries."

Tricia gave her sister a sour look. "I'll bet."

"No, honestly. I tested her with a few questions. She really does seem to know her stuff. Apparently she had a lot of time to read during her stretch in the State Prison for Women. It seems the books in their library are kind of old."

"And why am I supposed to care?" Tricia asked.

Angelica shrugged. "I was thinking . . . wouldn't it make a lot more sense for Linda to work for Grace and Pixie to work for you?"

Tricia's eyes bugged. "You've got to be kidding! I wouldn't even let that woman walk through the door of Haven't Got a Clue, let alone work there. And did I not tell you she called me a bitch?"

"She was a little upset," Angelica said.

Tricia scowled. "Why have you taken on this woman's cause?" she asked suspiciously.

"I'd just hate for her to have to go back to jail. I mean, how much work is there for an overage hooker here in Stoneham?"

"None at all, I should hope."

"And let's face it, Linda is way overqualified to be selling books. Didn't you say she worked at a nonprofit agency? Grace is running a nonprofit. Don't you think it would be a much better fit for her, too? You wanted Ginny to get ahead in her business career. Why not Linda?"

"Why do you care about *any* of this?"

"Who says I care? I'm just making conversation."

Tricia thought about it. Logistically, what Angelica proposed made a lot of sense. But emotionally she didn't think either she or Pixie could overcome the bad blood between them.

"There's no way Pixie could ever take orders from me. And I would never put up with the kind of behavior she displayed while working for Grace. Besides, with her negative attitude she'd drive my customers away." She shook her head. "I couldn't even consider her. Besides, I'm looking for someone who could assume the duties of an assistant manager. Someone I could trust to make decisions when I'm out of the store. I wouldn't trust Pixie to clean the washroom, let alone handle the money in the till."

Angelica shrugged. "You're probably right. I just thought that Linda's talents are probably being wasted while Pixie's aren't being utilized." She shook her right index finger in front of Tricia's nose. "But mark my words, as soon as Linda can find a job more commensurate with her talents, she'll be jumping ship and you'll be back to looking for a replacement in no time flat."

Again Tricia scowled. She'd known that from the instant she'd hired Linda. "Did you mention your great idea to Pixie?" she asked.

"Of course not. But I do think she regretted her actions the minute she walked out of your store. She really doesn't want to go back to jail. And, of course, Grace and Linda would have to be brought on board."

"What brought on all this altruism?" Tricia asked.

"I want to see people fulfilled in their working life—like you and me."

Tricia gave Angelica an assessing stare. Her sister had changed during the past couple of years. She wasn't as self-centered. And while she still drove Tricia crazy on a regular basis, Angelica's personality had definitely softened since she'd come to live in Stoneham, as evidenced by this situation and her compassion for Chauncey Porter.

"You know," Angelica continued, "I'd be willing to play mediator for you. And if Linda does leave to work for Grace and it doesn't work out with Pixie, I'll help you find a perfect assistant manager. I promise." She held her fingers up in a Girl Scout salute.

"I don't know." Tricia mulled it over, sure she'd end up on the losing end of the deal, but she liked Linda. And it was true she would be better suited working with Grace to guide the Everett Charitable Foundation. With her experience, she could help Grace avoid all kinds of pitfalls and perhaps take over a lot of the work, leaving Grace free to spend more time with her husband. Neither of them was getting any younger—Linda *could* be the answer to all their problems if Tricia was willing to accept Angelica's proposed compromise.

Yet the very thought of working with Pixie was totally repugnant. If she hadn't been willing to apologize to Tricia to save her job at the foundation, she wasn't likely to do so for a job that probably paid less and with less desirable hours, too.

If she had to let Linda leave, then she darn well would make Angelica live up to her promise to help her find an acceptable replacement.

It wasn't quite a win-win situation, but it might work in the long run. And if Tricia could appease Angelica with this, it might be time to ask for a few concessions for herself.

"Okay," she said at last. "But Pixie would have to apologize not only to me, but to Grace *and* Mr. Everett."

"Let's not get ahead of ourselves," Angelica cautioned. "First let me talk to all parties. If everyone agrees, we'll meet and talk—maybe even tomorrow. What do you say?"

"I guess."

Angelica smiled and nodded, looking self-satisfied. "Leave everything to me."

"Good. Now can we talk about something else?"

"Pick a subject," Angelica offered, and turned her attention to the baguette that sat on her counter.

"I could use your help on something else. You see, I followed your advice"—Angelica practically beamed at that admission—"and I paid a visit to Clayton Ellington this afternoon."

"And?" Angelica said, her eyes widening and her voice rising, eager to hear all the dirt.

"He hinted that I should talk to Bob, and that I shouldn't

expect him to talk to the police about his part in the rigged
raffle drawing. I'm still trying to decide if I should call Grant.
I don't have any proof, except for your word."

"I should think that would be enough. I'm a very honest
person," Angelica said, sounding hurt.

"Yes, you are. But how much can we trust Ellington or Bob
to tell the truth?"

Angelica shrugged. The smile had definitely dimmed. She
withdrew a bread knife from the block on the counter and
began slicing the baguette.

"Which reminds me, did anything else out of the ordinary
happen at that Chamber meeting?" Tricia asked.

Angelica looked thoughtful. "Bob was so eager to talk to
me about my winning the raffle that he practically chased me
out of the function room. He caught the sleeve of his jacket
on one of the French door handles and tore it as we were leaving. You know, that's one thing we desperately need and don't
have here in Stoneham—a tailor."

"He must've gotten the jacket fixed by now. I mean, it *is*
the only jacket he owns."

"Don't be silly. He's got half a dozen of them. He keeps
them in his office in case he spills something on the lapel. I
don't suppose he's had time to find someone to repair it. It's
not like he needs it done fast."

Was it possible Bob had stuffed the real winning business
cards in the pocket of his torn jacket and that it still hung in
his office? If Tricia could prove that Bob had rigged the draw,
it might lead the Stoneham police to Pippa Comfort's murderer.

Or could it be just a wild-goose chase? She'd never know
if she didn't pursue it. She studied her sister as she piled the
bread on a plate. Angelica continued to smile. A smile that
could light a room better than a hundred-watt bulb. A smile
that mirrored her contentment and her success, and, for just
a few hours, could banish all the heartache she'd ever endured.

And Tricia knew she'd have to burst that bubble of content-ment if she was to find out what she needed to know.

"As I was saying before we went off on a tangent," Tricia began.

"You said you needed my help," Angelica repeated, sound-ing smug—as though she had all the answers. She grabbed a couple of pot holders, opened the oven, and took out a small ceramic pot.

"I need to put Pippa's death behind me so that Grant and I can get back to . . . whatever it is we have going."

Angelica lifted the lid, revealing the roasted garlic. "You know I'll do my best," she promised.

"I want you to lure Bob out of his office so I can check his sport coat pockets."

"Except that," Angelica declared, all the sweetness and light now absent from her tone.

"Oh come on, I'm giving you what you want with the Pixie situation. Why can't you help me with this?"

"I'm just trying to help the poor, bedraggled woman. It's really for your benefit—not mine."

"If you're going to play Mother Teresa helping the down-trodden, you have to expect to get your hands dirty."

Angelica ignored the remark and called to Sarge, who'd been resting in his small bed. "Come here, boy. I'll give you a treat."

Tricia moved to stand by the kitchen window that over-looked Main Street, most of which was bathed in darkness. The lights were on in Amy Schram's apartment, and at the Dog-Eared Page once again. Was Michele Fowler entertaining another of the booksellers? Once the bar was opened it was hoped the tourists might actually stay in the village past the dinner hour, making the last couple of hours the booksellers were open more profitable. Of course, it was also hoped the bar would build a small local clientele as well. It might be fun to have somewhere to go in the evenings and relax with a glass of wine while a spirited game of darts was played, or hear a musician or singer perform on the tiny stage.

She glanced up the street and saw a solitary figure walking along the sidewalk. She thought she recognized the man as he walked past Booked for Lunch but then halted at the door that led to the Everett Foundation. He disappeared behind it.

Tricia frowned and turned away from the window.

"So, are you going to help me with Bob?"

"Help you how?" Angelica asked, and turned up the heat on a big pot of water.

Good, the fact that she even asked meant Tricia might be able to wear her down.

"You've got to lure Bob away from his office so I can check his sport coat pockets."

"But I don't want to even look at him, let alone talk to him," Angelica said, and shuddered, as though Bob might have cooties.

"Please. *Pretty please*," Tricia pleaded.

Angelica sighed. "You're almost as bad as Bob when you prey on my better nature."

Tricia tried to emulate Sarge's sad puppy-dog eyes.

Angelica sighed once again. "What do you want me to do?"

"Just lure him out of his office so I can get in there and check his jacket pockets for those business cards from the raffle."

"First of all, he's got a part-time secretary. You can't snoop around his office if Bonnie is sitting at her desk typing up sales copy. Second, if she isn't on duty, Bob's paranoid—he keeps that place locked up tighter than Fort Knox even if he's just ducking next door to the Chamber headquarters."

"Can't you tell him you'll only talk to him out on the sidewalk? If you can get him outside and keep his back turned to his office for just five minutes—probably less—it would give me plenty of time to go through all his pockets."

Angelica looked unconvinced. "Five minutes is a heck of a

long time. If the conversation goes bad and he stomps back to his office while you're still in there, you'd better have a pretty good excuse ready for him. But you know, no matter what you tell him, he's going to see right through you. Bob may be a jerk, but he's not a fool."

"You still care about him, don't you?" Tricia as much as accused.

"Well, of course I do. Sort of. Despite what you think, Bob's a complicated person. He overcame adversity—a terrible early childhood—and then put himself through college, not to mention almost single-handedly saving the entire village of Stoneham."

Angelica sounded like a one-woman Bob Kelly fan club.

"And he cheated on you with a low class bimbo." As soon as she said the words, Tricia regretted it. Angelica didn't need to be reminded of Bob's betrayal. Still, Tricia had never warmed to the idea of the two of them as a couple and was not unhappy when Angelica's feelings toward Bob had cooled to almost arctic temperatures.

Angelica removed a large grocery bag from the fridge and set it on the counter. It moved. "Am I supposed to call him? I really don't want to do that."

"Then the next time the phone rings . . . answer it."

"And say what?"

"I don't know . . . that you're willing to listen to him?"

As if on cue, the phone rang. Angelica glanced at the caller ID. "It's almost as if you'd arranged this."

It rang again.

"So answer it."

Angelica jerked the receiver from the wall. "Hello. Oh. Hello, Bob."

Tricia gave her sister some privacy and wandered over to the window to look across the street. The lights were now off in Amy Schram's apartment. She had a good idea why . . . and she didn't like it. Not one bit.

TWENTY-FOUR

Angelica hung up the phone. "There, happy?" she said, sounding anything but.

"Yes, thank you," Tricia replied. "What did you tell him?"

Angelica checked on the pot of water, which had come to a rolling boil. "That I would speak to him outside his office tomorrow at eleven o'clock. That means you've got to get into position hiding on the north side of his realty office so that when he comes out the door, you can scoot right in."

"How are you going to do that?"

"Once he's outside, I'll start wandering south down the sidewalk toward the Chamber headquarters. You'll have five minutes—no more—to do your dirty work."

"Dirty work? Bob's the guilty party here."

"He's already angry with me—he'll be even more upset when he finds out I tricked him into leaving his office so you

236

could go in to snoop." Angelica took a lobster out of the bag and held it head down over the pot. Tricia turned away.

"You're a good sister. And a good cook." Or at least a brave one. Tricia didn't think she could kill a living thing and then eat it. "When will it be ready to eat?"

Angelica glowered at her. Like Bob, she was no fool, either. "You just want to change the subject."

"You are so right," Tricia agreed. "Let's break open the bubbly and celebrate your good fortune. I'm ready to make a toast." She stepped over to the champagne bucket and withdrew the chilled wine. Angelica had already removed the foil, and Tricia unwound the wire cap while Angelica gathered up the flutes. The cork popped with a hiss and spray of tiny bubbles and Tricia poured. She took a glass and held it up in salute. "To *Easy-Does-It Cooking*. May YouTube have pushed it right onto the *New York Times* best sellers list."

"I'll drink to that," Angelica said. They clinked glasses and drank.

Now all Tricia had to do was play sleuth and not get caught, because if Bob did catch her he could have her arrested for trespassing, malicious mischief, and goodness only knows what else. And what would Grant Baker have to say about that?

Sleep did not want to come that night. Though Miss Marple never even stirred through the entire night, Tricia tossed and turned, worrying about her plan to invade Bob Kelly's office the next day. She turned on the light, read her book, turned off the light. Lather. Rinse. Repeat. Tricia finally drifted off near dawn and then slept right through her alarm.

Feeling exhausted, she couldn't even manage a brisk walk on her treadmill before dragging herself to the shower. Next she fed the cat, grabbed a tub of low-fat yogurt, and descended the stairs to Haven't Got a Clue. Coffee wasn't going to perk her up. She needed high-test caffeine and headed across the street to the Coffee Bean.

Mary Fairchild was standing in line behind two or three other customers when Tricia entered the store. She loved the mingled aromas of fresh ground coffee, chocolate, and cookies and pastries fresh from the Patisserie. If Nikki refused to sell to her she could always make a deal with the Coffee Bean's owner, Alexa Kozlov, and pay her a surcharge to get them.

Dressed in her By Hook or By Book apron and a heavy cardigan, Mary stood there, slouching, her gaze unfocused, staring at nothing.

"Hey there, are you okay?" Tricia asked.

Mary seemed to snap to attention. "Oh, Tricia. Yes. I'm fine. I didn't have a good night. I came in here for an espresso to get me going."

"Bad nights must be contagious. I'm here for the same thing."

"I've been doing a lot of thinking," Mary admitted, "and . . . I've decided to leave the Tuesday Night Book Club."

"Oh, no. Why?" Tricia asked.

Mary shook her head. "I don't think I can read and enjoy a mystery story ever again. Not now that I've actually known a murder victim."

The man in front of Mary, who'd obviously been eavesdropping, turned to give her a curious look, but she seemed oblivious to him.

"I'm so sorry you feel that way. The books we read *are* fiction."

"Yes, but—" She shuddered. "I only knew Pippa Comfort for an hour or so; she seemed like a nice person. For someone to treat her so brutally and leave her lying on the cold damp ground . . ." She closed her eyes and shuddered again.

Tricia rested a comforting hand on Mary's arm. "I understand. We've enjoyed having you as a member."

That meant the group had lost two members in less than a week. If any more jumped ship, it wouldn't be worth holding the meetings. Then again, that would give Tricia more free time to either maintain her website or return to her long-neglected hobby of book repair. Or—and most appealing—give her more time to read! She almost smiled.

"If you have a change of heart, just let me know," Tricia said.

"I'll do that."

It was Mary's turn to step up to the counter and give her order. Tricia waited patiently for her turn when she felt a pair of eyes upon her. She turned to find Harry Tyler standing behind her. "Good morning. We seem to keep bumping into each other a lot lately."

"Yes. You're out bright and early."

"Actually, I should be back at the inn packing. I'm out of a home and need to find a place to live."

"The owners have told you to leave?" Tricia asked, disbelieving.

"Pippa had the hotel management experience. I was the groundskeeper and maintenance man. Without her . . ." He let the sentence trail off.

Forcing him out less than a week after his wife's death was extremely coldhearted of Nigela Ricita Associates. Did Angelica know about that? She'd have to ask. And yet she wasn't quite willing to give him her full sympathy.

"I thought you'd already found a place to stay—at least you did last night."

His expression hardened. "I beg your pardon?"

"I saw you go into Amy Schram's building last night. Then, darned if all the lights didn't go out soon after. Was her electricity cut?"

"I don't think I like what you're implying."

"Do the police know you've been having an affair with Amy?" she whispered.

"Can I help you, Tricia?" Alexa asked from behind the counter.

Tricia turned and stepped up to the counter, giving her order—and asking for a half dozen of Nikki's thumbprint cookies before remembering that Mr. Everett would be working for Ginny that day at the Happy Domestic. Mr. Everett's loss, her customers' gain.

She paid for her order and waited until Harry had given his. They didn't speak again until they'd both left the shop. It was Harry who initiated the conversation.

"What I do or don't do isn't really any of your business, Tricia."

"Of course not. But if you were with Amy the night of the murder, you've got an ironclad alibi. And if you weren't . . . you're still in the running for chief murder suspect. And now so is Amy."

"She had nothing to do with Pippa's death—and neither did I."

"Does Chief Baker know about this?"

"As a matter of fact . . . yes. I didn't kill my wife and I'm damned if I'll get tossed into jail for it."

"How does Amy feel about the situation?"

"She isn't happy. And her parents aren't thrilled with her seeing someone who's almost thirty years older than she is."

"I don't imagine they would be. So, what are you going to do next? Move in with Amy for the duration? Try to find some work locally?"

"Actually I'm heading for New York on Sunday. I've got an appointment on Monday morning with a literary agent, Artemus Hamilton."

"Yes, I know him. He's my sister's agent."

Harry raised an eyebrow. "Do I have you to thank for this meeting?"

She shook her head. "Neither of us mentioned you to him. *He* asked for *your* number."

"He wants to talk about a book deal."

"For your fiction?"

"No, a memoir."

"But the ending is still up in the air. Wouldn't it be better if you could exonerate yourself in Pippa's murder?"

He didn't comment.

"And what happens to Amy? Do you just walk out on her like you walked out on me?"

"The circumstances are much different. I was a different person then. I like to think I've grown up."

"And yet you still date twenty-two-year-old women," she pointed out.

A muscle along his jaw flicked angrily. "I guess the word *forgive* isn't in your lexicon."

"And the word *fidelity* isn't in yours, either."

Harry lifted the plastic lid on his coffee. The steam curled into the brisk morning air. He took a sip and recapped it. "This conversation is going nowhere. I think it's time we said good-bye—and for the final time."

"I'm more than ready," Tricia said, and what's more—she honestly was.

"Good-bye, Tricia."

"Good-bye, Harry."

And they parted. Never to see each other again.

A sheepish-looking Linda arrived precisely one minute before Haven't Got a Clue's scheduled opening. "Sorry I'm late," she said, and hurried to the back of the store to hang up her coat before Tricia could even say hello. She returned to the front of the shop, still tying the strings on one of the store's aprons. Tricia would have to get one made with Linda's name embroidered on the side.

"Was traffic heavy this morning?" Tricia asked.

"Um . . . no," Linda said, and laughed nervously. "My phone's been fixed and the first call I got was from your sister, of all people."

Tricia's face went lax. That was quick. "I see."

"I feel extremely flattered that she wants to go to the trouble of . . ." She paused, as though trying to come up with an explanation that wouldn't make her look eager to explore other employment opportunities only three days after being hired.

No use heading for the embroidering shop this week, Tricia thought.

"I assume you'd much rather work at a nonprofit than in retail," Tricia said, trying to sound nonjudgmental. If she were in the same position, that was what she'd prefer. But she owned the retail establishment in question. And when she'd hired her, Linda had promised she'd stay longer than just a couple of weeks—or even months.

"You took a chance by hiring me, Tricia, when nobody else would. I have to admit, I'm sorely tempted by what your sister offered. The opportunity to work at another nonprofit isn't a dream come true, but it would be familiar work, and, if I say so myself, I was damn good at my job. I just wasn't as young and pretty as one of my less-skilled colleagues."

Tricia could understand that, too. She'd been let go from the nonprofit she'd worked at for more than ten years despite having more experience than her counterpart, who'd been a cousin of the director. But she hadn't needed the job to survive, either. Back then she'd had a stockbroker husband with a six-figure income. And within a year of losing that job, she'd also lost her husband to what she called a midlife crisis.

It still hurt to think about it.

"I wouldn't leave you in the lurch, either," Linda continued, which said to Tricia that Linda had already made up her mind to jump ship the minute she could. Much as she wanted to be angry, she couldn't muster any real resentment toward Linda. Instead, she merely felt depressed.

"It's not entirely up to the two of us. There are two other people involved in this job swap. After the exhibition she put on yesterday, I can't say I'm thrilled with the idea of having

Pixie work for me, and I've made it clear to Angelica the terms she'd have to agree to before I'd hire her. Still, I can't stand in your way if Grace decides you'd be a perfect candidate to work for the Everett Charitable Foundation. I care too much for Grace and Mr. Everett. No one knows how much time the two of them have together. I'll do anything I can to make them happy. Replacing you would be inconvenient, but Haven't Got a Clue will survive yet another transition."

Linda heaved a notably heavy sigh of relief. "Your sister already arranged for me to talk to Mrs. Harris-Everett at one this afternoon. It's over my lunch hour, so it shouldn't be an inconvenience."

"Did Angelica say anything to you about when she would speak to Pixie?"

Linda shook her head. "Although I got the feeling she was hoping she could arrange it for later today. Pixie has to report to her parole officer on Monday. He's not going to be happy if she tells him she quit her job."

Did that mean Pixie might agree to anything to stay employed so as not to violate the terms of her parole? A moody employee could become a detriment to the well-being of Haven't Got a Clue's bottom line. Tricia would not stand for bad behavior directed toward her customers, and if Pixie couldn't live up to that edict, then there was no place for her at Stoneham's only mystery bookstore. Still, Grace had pull. Maybe one of the other booksellers would hire her.

But she was getting ahead of herself again.

"I'm so sorry about all this, Tricia. After so long without a job, and using up all my savings, I'd given up hope that I would again work in a job that I'd trained so hard for."

Tricia held up a hand to forestall any more such talk. "Let's not discuss this anymore right now. Let's just concentrate on our daily routine and serve whatever customers come our way."

Linda nodded with what seemed like relief.

The shop door opened, and an older woman bundled up in a long cloth coat and a bulky scarf tied around her neck entered the store. "Goodness, but it's cold outside," she said, stamping her feet on the bristle welcome mat.

Linda practically leapt into action. "Hi, can I help you find anything?"

"Yes. I'm looking for Sara Paretsky's *Blood Shot*. Do you have any copies?"

"I'm not sure. Why don't the two of us have a look?" Linda suggested, and led the woman to the shelves on the north side of the shop.

Tricia hadn't realized how tense she'd felt during the previous conversation with her (most likely) soon-to-be ex-employee. Her head felt heavy and she wondered if her neck could support it for the next hour, let alone the rest of the day. And she still had that little adventure at Kelly Realty to look forward to.

She rubbed her neck and glanced out the window to see Amy Schram working on the urn she'd placed in front of the store days before. She looked like she'd been crying. Noting that Linda didn't seem to need any help with her customer, Tricia ventured out into the cold.

Amy held a gardening claw in one gloved hand and a bag of knobby flower bulbs in the other. Tricia crossed her arms over her sweater set to stave off the chill and approached her. "Is something wrong?"

Amy sniffed. "Everything." Her mouth trembled and she squeezed her eyes shut, tears leaking to cascade down her cheeks.

Tricia suspected she knew the reason for those tears. "Can I help?"

Amy shook her head and continued to claw at the soil. Tricia watched as she retrieved seven bulbs from the sack and placed them in a circle, then covered them with dirt.

"I know about you and Harry Tyler," Tricia said gently.

"Who?" she asked, but Tricia wasn't fooled. She could tell by Amy's expression that she knew exactly who Tricia was talking about.

"How long have the two of you been sneaking around?"

Amy looked up, a mixture of anger and shock covering her features.

"I live across the street from you, remember. I've seen him coming and going," Tricia explained.

"Have you been spying on me?"

Tricia sighed and shook her head, wishing they were having this conversation in her nice warm store instead of on the freezing pavement. "He's a little old for you, isn't he? How did you meet?"

"I've been taking a night class from him at the high school."

"Oh, yes. He mentioned he was teaching. When did you suspect he was actually Harrison Tyler?"

Amy's chapped cheeks went a darker shade of pink. "I thought he looked familiar the first night of class. I knew I'd seen his picture before. I couldn't place his face at first, but then I came into your store a couple of months ago and saw the portrait on the wall. Mr. Everett told me all about him and sold me a used copy of *Death Beckons*."

"Did you confront him with that information?"

"Not at first. I wanted to see if I could get him interested in me."

"And we both know how that ended up."

"Okay, I admit it. I was sleeping with Jon Comfort—but that doesn't mean I wanted to kill his wife. I wasn't looking for a lifelong commitment or anything. I mean, it was just sex with an interesting man. What's wrong with that?"

What was wrong with young people these days? Casual sex was one thing, but this attitude that intimacy was just an afterthought appalled her. She was terribly out of step with the times, but somehow that didn't make her feel bad. Instead, she felt sorry for Amy. Would she ever experience a true, loving relationship, or would her whole concept of love be just jumping from one lover's bed to another?

"Have you told Chief Baker about your affair?"

Amy cringed. "Affair? It wasn't an 'affair.' I told you, it was just sex. And . . . I figured it would be kinda cool to be involved with someone who was going to be notorious one day."

"What were you planning? A memoir? Your life with Harry Tyler?"

"Some chick got famous sleeping with J. D. Salinger. Why shouldn't I do the same with Jon . . . er, Harry?"

Ah yes, another New Hampshire love story. The distance between Stoneham and Durham, where Salinger had hidden out for most of his adult life, wasn't all that far, after all.

"Too bad it didn't last long enough for me to have anything to interest *People* magazine, let alone get a book contract," Amy groused.

"So, you've got literary aspirations of your own?"

"Do you think I want to spend the rest of my life delivering flowers and watering plants in hick towns like Stoneham and Milford?"

"If nothing else, your tryst can be construed as motive for murder."

"Except I have an ironclad alibi for Sunday night."

"Harry hinted to me that he went to see you on Monday night—and that's where he was when his wife was killed."

"Then he lied. I have no idea where he was, but he wasn't with me. I was visiting my parents. It was my brother's twenty-fifth birthday. I took video with my cell phone and so did everyone else who was there. They're time dated. When Pippa Comfort died I was stuffing my mouth full of birthday cake." She looked down at her hips, which strained against the fabric of her heavy jacket, and struggled to suppress a sob.

"Harry broke up with you this morning, didn't he?"

Amy nodded. "He told me he was leaving town. He wanted to make a fresh start. He told me I should go on a diet and find someone my own age. That I'd be much happier in the long run."

Amy wasn't fat by any means. Whatever assets she had were usually well hidden by her work clothes, which did tend to fall on the bulky side. Had Harry tried to make her feel bad before he left so that she would let go more easily, or did he just have a cruel streak in him? Tricia hadn't noticed that in her dealings with the man, but he'd certainly changed since she'd known him twenty years before.

Amy looked back to her van parked down the street and hefted the claw in her hand. "I've got to get back to work."

And Tricia was eager to get back inside. "For what it's worth, I'm sorry about your situation. Harry once left me, too. That was when he disappeared all those years ago."

"I guess he's good at loving and leaving, then," Amy said. "I'll see you later, Tricia," and she moved down the sidewalk, only to pause in front of the Cookery, where she began to loosen the soil in the urn outside the shop.

Tricia returned to Haven't Got a Clue just in time to help Linda with a sale.

As Tricia bagged the books, adding the store's latest newsletter, she couldn't help but dwell on her conversation with Amy. Where had Harry gone the night of his wife's death? Why had he lied? Was anybody going to mention any of this to Chief Baker?

As the customer departed, she held the door for Angelica, who stepped inside. She was wrapped in a big baggy parka, with a white knit cap covering her head, matching mittens, and sturdy boots. "Good morning," she called.

"What are you dressed up for? A visit to an igloo?" Tricia asked.

"We've got our little rendezvous set up for eleven, or did you forget?"

Tricia looked at the clock. "You're more than half an hour early."

"I couldn't sit around the apartment another minute. What's a person got to do around here to get a cup of coffee?"

"Take off your coat and I'll get you one," Tricia said, and headed for the beverage station. Sadly, she'd never finished her espresso, which was by now stone-cold.

The door rattled once more and another customer arrived. Linda put on her best smile. "Can I help you?"

"Yes, I'm looking for some books by John Dickson Carr."

"If you'll follow me, I'd be glad to show you."

Angelica nodded in admiration as she watched Linda guide the customer to the back shelves.

Tricia handed her a cup of coffee. "I've got lots to tell you, but I don't want to do it here. Come on upstairs." Angelica followed without question. "We'll be back down in a few minutes," Tricia said to Linda as they passed her and went through the door marked PRIVATE.

Once inside Tricia's apartment, Angelica dumped her coat on one of the kitchen island stools, hitched up a hip, and took another. "So what's the dirt?"

"Harry has been having an affair with Amy Schram."

Angelica's jaw dropped. "He's old enough to be her daddy!"

"Exactly. He dumped her this morning and is heading to New York to see Artie. He wants Harry to write a memoir on his missing years."

Angelica scowled. "The rat ought to be horsewhipped, not rewarded for pulling a vanishing act." She sipped her coffee. "Anything else?"

"He told me—and presumably Grant Baker—that he was with Amy, but Amy denies it. The funny thing is, she hasn't spoken with the police. Why would Harry lie to me about it?"

"Maybe he lost more than a career during the years he was among the missing. He could've lost his marbles, too," Angelica said, and took a healthy sip of coffee. "What else has the rat been up to?"

"He told me he was being forced to leave the inn."

Angelica blinked. "He did?"

"You mean he wasn't?"

"Not that I know of. I spoke to Antonio just yesterday, and he made no mention of it. In fact, he's been so busy, he hasn't had time to do anything about replacing Pippa."

"So Harry's lying?"

"Well, he's certainly not telling the truth about that, either."

"That makes me feel better."

"That he's lying?"

"No, that you wouldn't be involved in anything so cold-hearted."

Angelica laughed. "Well, that's a given."

"So there's no talk about selling the inn and giving up on it?"

"Why would we sell it? It's beautiful, Stoneham needs more places for people to stay, and why shouldn't we make the money on it instead of someone else?"

Angelica—logical to a fault.

Tricia bent down and leaned her elbows on the island's granite top.

"I need to talk to Grant about Harry and Amy. Only he'll probably think I'm just calling him because I'm lovesick and miss him."

"Men! Such egos," Angelica agreed and rolled her eyes. "Anything else new?"

Tricia sighed. "Mary Fairchild has quit the Tuesday Night Book Club. She says she can't read mysteries after knowing a murder victim."

Angelica nodded. "I can see someone being shook up over that. But she's a real nut for mysteries. She'll come around. My predictions are seldom wrong." Lately she seemed to be on a roll.

"Linda told me you'd spoken with her this morning," Tricia said.

"Yes, and I've also spoken to Grace and Pixie. We're on for this afternoon after Booked for Lunch closes. Three thirty sharp." She looked down her nose at Tricia. "Be there."

There was no arguing with Angelica when she wore that expression. Just as quickly, her expression changed to keen interest. "Now, we need to talk about the adventure we're about to embark on."

"I figured I'd make a circuitous route to Kelly Realty and wait until you get him outside, and then I'd make my move. You could call or text me to let me know when you're in position."

Angelica indicated her coat. "I decided I'd better dress warmly. Bob can be a bit of a blowhard when he wants to be, and I have no intention of entering his office after your five minutes is up." Angelica looked at the clock and then drained her cup. "You'd better get going if you intend to be in position before I get there."

"Oh, right," Tricia said, and straightened. Suddenly her stomach was full of butterflies.

"I'll use your facilities and leave in ten minutes. Anything else you want to tell me?"

"Whatever you do, just keep Bob looking south. If he sees me, I'm done."

"Yes. The way he feels about you these days, I'm sure he'd have you arrested for trespassing," she said blandly.

Tricia didn't like the sound of that, but she didn't want to back out now. She'd already wasted too much time and energy worrying about it. "I'll grab my coat and go out the back door. Lock up and reset the alarm for me, will you?"

"Will do."

"Don't forget to call me," Tricia called as she headed down the stairs to Haven't Got a Clue.

"I won't!" Angelica answered.

Tricia emerged from the stairwell and closed the door behind her. Linda stood behind the register, holding the latest copy of *Mystery Scene* magazine. "I've got an errand to run," Tricia said, grabbing her coat from the peg on the wall. "I'm going out the rear door. I should be back in about twenty minutes. Will you be okay?"

"Sure," Linda said.

Tricia gave her a quick wave, disarmed the security system, and headed out the door.

She took off down the alley at a brisk pace, heading south. She intended to cross Elm Street and walk along the alley behind the west side of Main Street, hit the cross street, and come up on Kelly Realty from behind.

Everything was going according to plan until she made it to the back of Booked for Lunch when a voice called out behind her. "Where do you think *you're* going?"

TWENTY-FIVE

Tricia stopped dead to face Michele Fowler, who stood next to the Dumpster behind the Dog-Eared Page, holding a black plastic bag full of trash.

"Uh . . . just taking a quick walk."

"In the alley across the street from your own store? Are you lost?" Michele asked in jest.

Tricia laughed nervously and looked at her watch. Angelica would be in front of Kelly Realty in less than five minutes. "No. Just taking a shortcut."

"To where?" Michele asked, and tossed the bag into the Dumpster.

"Um . . . Elm Street."

Clad in wool slacks and a cardigan, Michele crossed her arms and wandered closer. "Wouldn't it have been shorter just to cross Main Street?"

Tricia laughed again. "Exercise."

"Angelica told me you faithfully use your treadmill every morning—four miles, if I'm not mistaken."

"It never hurts to do more," she said, and started backing away.

"Come over later for a drink, why don't you?"

"I'd love to. Must get going. See you later!" She gave Michele a wave, turned, and picked up her pace.

She passed the back of the *Stoneham Weekly News* and halted on the sidewalk at Locust Street as a line of cars snaked its way around the corner from Main Street, headed by a long silver hearse. Whoever had died had a lot of friends. Tricia glanced at her watch. Angelica would be in front of Bob's place in less than four minutes.

By the time the last car had passed, Tricia saw Angelica leave Haven't Got a Clue. That gave her less than two minutes to get into position. She jogged around the back of the village park, past the gazebo still under reconstruction, and crossed Hickory Street to enter the alley behind the Chamber of Commerce. She slowed her pace as she approached the back of Kelly Realty. Was there a window overlooking the alley? She couldn't remember. She tiptoed along the side of the building. Yes, there was a window. She edged up to it and peeked around the window frame. Inside was a small conference room, with a rectangular table and six uncomfortable-looking plastic chairs. Thankfully there was no one inside, and Tricia made her way to the corner of the building, but didn't go any farther. Her phone vibrated in her jacket pocket. She took it out and flipped it open.

"Tricia, I'm in position."

"I'm ready, too."

"Remember—you have five minutes and no more," Angelica cautioned, and ended the call.

Tricia folded her phone again and stashed it back in her pocket. She decided to count to sixty to give Angelica time to lure Bob outside his office. Then she sneaked up on the edge of the building and took a look around the corner of the cement-block building, hoping Bob was looking in the other direction.

Dressed in one of his kelly green sport coats, Bob stood in front of the Chamber of Commerce facing Angelica, his back turned on his office. Angelica looked at him coyly and brushed at her bangs—surreptitiously giving Tricia a wave to make her move.

Tricia dashed around the corner and pulled open the heavy plate glass door, darting into the warmth of Kelly Realty. Sure enough, it was empty. Her luck was holding.

Although she'd been inside Bob's office on many occasions, she didn't remember where he hung his coat and those of his employee and visitors. Her gaze darted around the room and saw a small alcove with a closet on the other side of the large display window.

Five different green Kelly Realty sport jackets were lined up on the rod. Tricia hurried across the room and fumbled to inspect each right sleeve. Aha—the third one was the charm. She stuck her hand in the left-hand pocket and came up with a half-empty matchbook from the Bookshelf Diner and a wrinkled business card from the Full Moon Nudist Camp and Resort, containing Clay Ellington's name, phone numbers, and e-mail address.

In the other pocket were four more business cards, but not from Chamber members who had been awarded the prize of a night's stay at the Sheer Comfort Inn. No doubt about it— Bob, the swine, had dipped his hand into the glass bowl, pulled out four cards, and announced four different winners.

Had he been bribed by everyone he called as winners? She might believe that of Ellington, but not Chauncey and Mary. They were her friends . . . they couldn't have ulterior motives for being at the inn the night Pippa Comfort died . . . could they?

Tricia wasn't sure what to do. If she took the cards, she'd

be removing evidence. But did the cards actually prove anything? Bob could just as easily say he had them for another reason, or that he'd picked them up after a meeting.

She glanced at her watch. Angelica would be getting antsy by now. She had better get out of the office before she was caught.

She crept to the door and looked through the big display glass. Bob still stood with his back to the building.

Tricia eased out the door, her heart pounding. And what was she supposed to do now? Sneak around the back way? That would look suspicious—twice in ten minutes. Instead, she plunged ahead. She would walk right past Bob and rescue Angelica.

She walked right up to the former couple. "Hi, Bob. What are you doing here, Angelica?"

Angelica gave a nervous laugh. "Bob and I were just talking."

"You did remember that we have a meeting with Grace," Tricia said.

"Oh my goodness, is that today?" Angelica said. She turned to Bob. "I'm sorry, but I really must run."

"But we haven't really settled anything," Bob said, not at all pleased.

"I really don't think there's anything to settle," Angelica said.

Tricia tugged on her sister's coat sleeve. "We really need to go." She gave Bob a sympathetic smile. "See you later, Bob." She yanked Angelica's sleeve harder, hauling her along. Angelica tottered on her high-heeled boots and nearly stumbled but quickly righted herself and moved into step.

They paused at the corner and waited for a car to pass. "Thanks for the save," Angelica muttered. "What did you find?"

"Just what I expected. In his right pocket, business cards— but they weren't from any of the raffle winners, including you.

But there was a business card from the Full Moon Nudist Camp and Resort in his other pocket."

They crossed Main Street. As they passed in front of the Patisserie, Tricia looked through the big display window and caught sight of Nikki Brimfield, who glared at her. She didn't like being persona non grata for no good reason.

"What are you going to do next?" Angelica asked.

"I need to talk to Bob. Confront him."

"And say what—you cheated at the raffle?"

"Maybe. I certainly can't go to Grant with my suspicions. I've got no proof."

"It would be your word against Bob's," Angelica agreed. "Maybe you should just forget all this investigation stuff and go back to worrying about your store and employee situation— or almost certain *lack*-of-new-employee situation."

They paused outside the Cookery. Tricia looked down the road. There was no sign of Bob. "What did Bob say to you?"

Angelica sighed dramatically. "I thought he'd berate me for being a partner at the inn, but instead he begged me to take him back. As if *that's* ever going to happen. Thank you for showing up when you did. I was afraid he might try tears next."

Poor Bob. He'd blown his relationship with Angelica and he just didn't understand why.

Angelica glanced at her watch. "I have things to do before we meet Grace and Pixie."

"Ugh. Don't remind me. I'm looking forward to seeing Pixie like I'd look forward to having a tooth pulled."

"Just give her a chance. That's all she really wants," Angelica said.

Somehow Tricia doubted that.

Stoneham in early April was dead, dead, dead. With nothing in the way of an appetite, Tricia had forgone lunch. When Linda returned to Haven't Got a Clue after her midday break,

Tricia felt the need to escape the confines of her shop. She had business to conduct. It took less than three minutes to walk from her store to Kelly Realty. She just hoped Bob would still be there.

She found Stoneham's savior leaning back in his office chair, his feet planted on his desk, staring at the nineteen-inch television bolted to the wall and tuned to ESPN, watching a rerun of some championship golf game. He looked up at Tricia's arrival, grabbed the remote, and hit the power button. The screen went black.

Bob put on his best poker face, sitting straight in his chair. "Hi, Tricia. What can I do for you?"

"I haven't got time to mess around with niceties, Bob. Did you rig the raffle for the night's stay at the Sheer Comfort Inn?"

"Tricia!" Bob scolded, and quickly looked away, suddenly finding it necessary to straighten the papers on his desk.

"You didn't answer my question," she said, and rounded on him.

"Cheating on a Chamber raffle wouldn't be right," he protested.

"That doesn't mean you weren't above doing it."

"I'm hurt by your accusation."

"And you'll be even more upset once I tell Chief Baker about it. There's got to be something illegal about it. And if there isn't, what do you think the Chamber members will say when I tell them?"

Bob said nothing, but Tricia could almost smell his smoldering anger.

"Don't you dare deny it—not after you tried to bribe me not to accompany Angelica to the inn on Sunday."

His mouth curled into a sneer. "It's your word against mine. No one will believe you, Little Miss Village Jinx."

"Maybe not, but they *will* believe Angelica."

Bob's eyes bulged at the threat. "Now wait a minute; there's no reason to get your sister involved in this."

"Everybody's going to find out once I tell the police. And you might even be charged with obstructing justice for not volunteering this information to the Stoneham police." Tricia tapped her left index finger against her chin, gazing up at the ceiling in mock contemplation. "I wonder how you'll look in one of those orange jumpsuits prisoners wear. I hear they chafe."

"Okay," Bob said, looking chagrined. "So I accepted a little honorarium for making sure certain people won the raffle. I was going to give it to charity."

"Which one?"

"The Food Shelf. Libby Hirt can always use the money."

"Have you done so?"

"Uh . . . I haven't had time. I'm a very busy man."

"It's been a week since the raffle; what were you waiting for—Christmas?"

"I'm going to do it. Look, if it'll make you happy I'll write a check out right now." He withdrew a large ledger book of checks, opened it, and took out a pen. "No one has to know about this except us."

Tricia shook her head. "Uh-uh. Pippa Comfort died that night. Someone who was at the inn that night killed her. You might be an accessory to her death."

Bob's mouth dropped open in horror. "But—but I wasn't even there!" he protested.

"You may have given her killer the opportunity to strike."

Bob shook his head, waving his hands in front of him in denial. "You can't pin anything on me. I may have taken their money, but as far as I knew they all just wanted a cheap night in a homelike setting. That's my story and I'm sticking to it. I'll even take a polygraph."

Tricia had no doubt he'd ace such a test. Bob had little to no conscience. She'd never felt such contempt for another human being. "I'm so glad Angelica dumped you. You are lower than a slug." And without another word, Tricia turned and left his office.

As she walked back to Haven't Got a Clue, she contemplated her next move. She had to talk to Baker, but her meeting with Angelica and Pixie was less than an hour away. Bob wasn't likely to volunteer the information, but it would keep for an hour or more.

Still it was disturbing to think she'd spoken with Pippa's murderer and that person—whoever it was—had pretty good acting skills.

She didn't have a clue who'd bludgeoned Pippa Comfort to death.

TWENTY-SIX

 "It's almost three thirty," Linda said, and pointed at her watch. She hadn't told Tricia how her interview with Grace had gone, but the small smile that covered her lips and the gleam in her eyes left no doubt that a job offer had been—or was about to be—made.

Tricia felt sick at the thought of conducting yet more interviews for the job of assistant manager at Haven't Got a Clue. The prospect of working with Pixie was just as nauseating.

"You don't want to be late," Linda encouraged.

A submissive Tricia collected her coat from the peg at the back of the store and exited the shop, feeling like a child being forced to go to the class bully's birthday party.

As usual on a cold April afternoon, traffic on Main Street was less than light. In fact, there wasn't a car in sight, and Tricia jaywalked to get to Booked for Lunch. She noted the lights were still on inside, but the neon OPEN sign had been extinguished. She tried the door handle, found it unlocked, and entered the café as though stepping before a firing squad.

Angelica had changed her clothes since Tricia had seen her at lunch. She now wore a tight black pencil skirt and a tucked-in black-and-white striped shirt with a button-down polka-dot bib. She'd donned a pair of reading glasses on a chain that gave her the look of a high-powered secretary—or worse, the high school principal from Tricia's past. She stood on three-inch heels in the aisle between the booths along the south wall and the counter opposite.

"Right on time. Take off your coat and take a seat," she chimed, directing Tricia toward the first booth, where Pixie already sat. Dressed in a tan-and-brown striped vintage dress from what appeared to be from the 1940s, with her hair once again done in a pompadour, Pixie looked like she'd just stepped out of the pages of an old *Life* magazine.

"Hello, Pixie," Tricia said, her voice barely audible.

"Mmm," Pixie grunted.

Not an auspicious beginning. Angelica didn't seem to have noticed.

"Now, ladies, let's begin. First off, Pixie has something to say."

Pixie glowered, but her anger seemed to melt under Angelica's reproachful glare. "I'm . . . sorry, Ms. Miles. Er, Tricia. I was rude and I apologize." The words sounded rehearsed and not at all sincere. Had Angelica coached her on this?

Tricia sighed. It was only polite to acknowledge Pixie's apology. "I accept," she said, and even managed a wan smile.

Pixie looked . . . frightened? She really *didn't* want to go back to jail, and who could blame her?

Tricia turned up the wattage on her smile, hoping she didn't look demented. "Angelica tells me you know a lot about vintage mysteries."

Pixie's eyes widened with interest at the change of subject. "My dad was a big fan of Erle Stanley Gardner. He used to read to me at bedtime, but instead of fairy tales he read me all the Perry Mason stories. When I got a little older, we used to watch reruns of the old black-and-white TV show. Oh, that Raymond Burr—what a guy! Did you ever see *Ironside?*"

Tricia had only seen the show in reruns, not when it had run on network TV, but she nodded just the same. "I have to admit I liked the latter-day TV movies better than the old Perry Mason show. Let's face it, William Katt as Paul Drake Junior was a lot sexier than William Hopper on the original series."

Pixie grinned. "Oh, you better believe it. Did you know he was actually Barbara Hale's son?"

"I did," Tricia admitted. "I had a crush on him when I was in junior high. You had to love all that curly blond hair."

"Ahem." All eyes turned to Angelica. "Let's stay on topic, ladies," she admonished, and Tricia and Pixie were both suitably cowed once again. "Tricia, did you have any questions you wanted to ask Pixie?"

Tricia fought the urge to squirm. She had a lot of questions, but would the goodwill they'd just shared disappear if she asked them? She decided to tread lightly.

"Have you ever worked in a retail business before?"

"Oh, sure," Pixie said. "Before my last stint in stir, I was a checkout girl at Hannaford's in Nashua. Held the job for almost six months. Then I met this guy in a bar and got arrested again . . ." Her sentence trailed off. "But I've sworn off my old ways," she said, suddenly sitting up straighter. "I mean, at my age there aren't that many men who are interested."

"How are you at getting along with others?" Angelica asked. "Tricia has an elderly part-time employee."

"Yeah, I know. Mrs. Harris-Everett's hubby. She's real fond of the old geezer."

Tricia's eyes widened in indignation. "We call him Mr. Everett. He deserves that kind of respect."

"Oh sure, I could call him that. Unless he tells me to call him something else, that is."

"Are you reliable? Will you show up for work every day?" Tricia asked.

"I've got a car. It's kind of a relic, but it works. Just ask Mrs. H-E, she can tell you I never missed a day and I was on time every day, too."

That wasn't saying much. She'd worked for Grace for only a couple of weeks.

"I know a lot about old mysteries," Pixie continued. "I read every one in the prison library at least three times. I can talk 'em up good for the customers, too. If you'll give me a chance," she added with sincerity.

Tricia glanced at Angelica, whose eyes were encouraging as she nodded like a bobblehead figurine.

Tricia didn't like feeling cornered into making a decision, but if Linda was going to leave anyway, what was the point in fighting it? "Okay. We'll give it a try—on a trial basis. Two weeks, and then if the situation seems to be working out, we'll call it permanent."

"How much are we talking per hour?" Pixie asked, then held up her left hand and rubbed her thumbs against her fingers.

"Two dollars over minimum wage."

Pixie nodded. "I'll take it. You won't regret this, Ms. Miles."

"Call me Tricia," she insisted.

Pixie smiled, and the light glinted off a gold canine tooth. Tricia hadn't noticed that before. It was all she could do not to shudder.

"Can I start tomorrow?" Pixie asked, sounding eager.

"Yes. Ten o'clock. If you've got time now, we can go over to Haven't Got a Clue where you can fill out the paperwork, and then I'll show you around."

"Oh yeah, I've got time. I don't have to see my parole officer until Monday morning. Don't worry, it's at eight o'clock. I'll be done in plenty of time to start work."

"And I've already spoken to Grace. If it's okay with you,

Trish, Linda can start at the foundation first thing Monday morning. Talk about a win-win situation," Angelica said.

Although she should have seen that coming, Tricia was still startled at how fast things had escalated around her.

"Time is money," Angelica said, pointing to the clock, "and I've got work to do now that I've done my good deed for the day."

Good deed indeed, Tricia thought, and pushed her way out of the booth to stand, grabbing her coat. Pixie did likewise.

"I'm a long-lost relative of Edgar Allan Poe, you know," she said as she shrugged into the sleeves of her bulky brown faux fur coat. She struggled to fasten the oversized buttons, which made her look like she was hugging a big old bear.

Tricia doubted her claim. Poe had had no heirs. "Not directly," she said.

"Oh, of course not. The guy died without kids. But my daddy always said we were several cousins once, twice, or maybe even fifteen times removed. I should've paid more attention. He was really proud of that."

Perhaps that was all Pixie had to be proud of after a life spent on the seamy side. Tricia had always thought of herself as broadminded, and to prove it, here she was contemplating hiring an ex- (at least she hoped) prostitute to work for her.

I must be out of my mind, Tricia thought, and trudged behind Pixie to the exit. But when she got there, she found Grant Baker standing outside the door.

"At last," he said, sounding frustrated. "I've been all over the village looking for you. Frannie Armstrong finally told me I could find you here."

"Why didn't my assistant, Linda, tell you where I was?"

"I think it was the uniform that scared her. She probably thought you were in trouble. Which you are."

"What for now?"

"Because you won't stop asking questions and bugging people about the Comfort murder."

"Why should I?"

"For one thing, it could get you killed."

"Oh, please."

"I mean it. There's a lunatic running around out there bludgeoning women."

"Just one so far."

"And I'd like to keep it that way," Baker snapped.

"Uh, I don't think I need to be a part of this conversation," Pixie said. She seemed to be having an allergic reaction to Baker's uniform.

"Why don't you go over to Haven't Got a Clue and I'll meet you there in a few minutes," Tricia said.

"Whatever you say, boss," Pixie said, and headed out the door.

"Boss?" Baker asked.

"It seems I have yet another new employee," Tricia said.

"I've got some work to do in the kitchen," Angelica said, and turned on her heel, leaving the two of them standing in the front of the café.

"I'm actually glad you found me, Grant; I was going to call you, anyway. I've spoken to everyone who was at the inn on Sunday night, and I can tell you that none of them have been completely honest with you about why they were there."

Baker suddenly looked a bit more interested. "What are you saying?"

"At the last Chamber of Commerce meeting, Bob Kelly pulled four business cards out of a fishbowl as winners to stay the night at the Sheer Comfort Inn, but announced four different names."

"What makes you think that?"

"Bob tore his coat sleeve the day of the meeting and hasn't had it repaired. He hung the jacket in his office and I checked the pockets not five hours ago. When I confronted him, he admitted that Clayton Ellington, Chauncey Porter, and Mary Fairchild had bribed him to announce them as the raffle winners."

Now Baker was extremely interested.

"Have you spoken to Bob?" Tricia asked.

He shook his head. "What reason did these people have to want to be at the inn on that particular night?"

"Clayton Ellington was Pippa's former lover. His wife didn't want him visiting an old flame, but she just happened to be out of town on Sunday night."

"And Chauncey Porter?"

"He's a lonely—probably horny—old man who once tipped Pippa heavily back in the day when she was a Playboy bunny at the New York club."

"And Mary Fairchild?"

"She only wanted a no-cost night at an inn with her husband to rekindle their romantic life."

"And what about Angelica? Did she bribe Kelly, too?"

"Heck no. Bob had hoped she'd invite *him* to spend the night with her at the inn, not me."

A creaking noise sounded from behind them, and they turned to look at the back of the café. The top of Angelica's head was visible above the swinging half doors that led into Booked for Lunch's kitchen—just enough for them to see her eyes.

"Can we have some privacy here?" Baker asked sharply.

Angelica's head disappeared from sight, but Tricia could still see her feet below.

Baker turned back to face Tricia. "Just drop it, will you? Let the police handle the investigation. My God, it's only been five days since the murder. These things can take years of careful investigation before they're solved and a suspect arrested."

"I don't sense any urgency on your part. And it seems I've been able to gather more information on the case than you and your men."

He glowered at her. "My department is doing everything humanly possible to solve this crime. And the fact that it doesn't seem apparent to you doesn't mean we aren't following all leads that come in. For instance, cell phone records prove that Clayton Ellington talked to someone, presumably his wife, at her cell phone number on Sunday night for at least twenty minutes before your 911 call and then for ten minutes after. He's in the clear."

"How about Harry Tyler? He told me he was with Amy Schram the night Pippa was killed, but Amy says no. She also said she hasn't spoken to you about it, either."

Baker sighed. "I've already spoken with Mr. Tyler—several times. I'm satisfied with his explanation as to where he was on the night of the crime."

Tricia's eyes widened.

"And no, I'm not going to share that with you," Baker declared.

Tricia was about to argue the point when Baker raised an admonishing finger and wagged it in front of her nose. "I'm not going to tell you again. Stay out of this, Tricia."

And with that, he turned and exited the café, slamming the door behind him, rattling the glass within it.

A squeak issued from the doors to the kitchen and Angelica emerged. "My, my. He was a tad upset."

Tricia sighed. "He's just annoyed that I knew more about the inn's guests than he did."

Angelica moved closer and placed a hand on Tricia's arm. "He's right, though, Trish. Poking around and asking questions could get you killed. Mother and Daddy would never forgive me if I let that happen."

Tricia doubted that. In the recent past, her parents had rarely ventured north from their South American vacation home to spend quality time with either of their offspring, and they couldn't even use the excuse of ill health.

She put those thoughts out of her mind. It did no good to dwell on them.

"I'd better go. Pixie is waiting."

"I have a feeling she's going to work out just fine," Angelica said.

"If she doesn't, I'm holding you to your promise to help me find someone else."

"I stand by my word. Now, go back to work and stop thinking about Pippa Comfort's murderer—at least for the rest of the day."

"With pleasure," Tricia said, and opened the door to leave. But as she crossed the street to return to her store, she was sure that it was a promise she wouldn't be able to keep.

TWENTY-SEVEN

 Pixie hadn't lied. No matter what vintage mystery author Tricia threw at her, she came up with at least one title to go with it. Was there actually a chance Pixie might be an asset to Haven't Got a Clue? Tricia would find out the next morning when Pixie had to interact with real customers.

Tricia also noted how restless Linda had become once all the job-swap arrangements had been finalized. Her gaze kept sliding to the clock on the wall, as though willing it to hurry to closing time so she could be shed of the place once and for all.

"Since you're starting a new job on Monday, you may as well go home," Tricia said.

"I wouldn't feel right about that," Linda said. "I already feel guilty about leaving you like this."

Tricia looked around the store, which was devoid of customers. "I doubt anyone else will come by this late in the day."

"Well, if you're sure," Linda said, already untying the apron she wore.

"You can go, too, Pixie," Tricia said.

"Are you going to stay open until six?" she asked.

Tricia nodded.

"Then I'd just as soon poke around, get to know the place. If you don't mind."

"Be my guest."

Tricia watched as Pixie strolled between the aisles of shelves, reading the spines of the books. Occasionally she ran her fingers over a book and smiled.

Tricia turned her attention to the unopened stack of mail that sat on the counter while Linda collected her coat. Bills, circulars—nothing very interesting.

Linda appeared before her. "I'm sorry things didn't work out as you'd planned, Tricia. But I'll be eternally grateful for the chance you've given me."

Just go! Tricia longed to say. Instead, she said, "Good luck in your new job. Stop by on Monday and I'll have your check ready."

"Thank you." Linda took one last look around the store, smiled, and left it for good.

Tricia went back to opening the mail. The door rattled. Had Linda forgotten something? No.

"I thought you'd left town," she told Harry Tyler.

"I just wanted to say good-bye."

"I thought you'd done that, too."

"Okay, I came in to buy a copy of *Death Beckons*. Would you believe it? I don't even own one."

"Sorry, we're all out. For some reason, we had a run on them. What do you need it for, anyway?"

"I thought I'd give an autographed copy to my new agent."

"Gee, maybe you'll have to pay full price for a new copy. Do you even have eight dollars?"

"Yeah. I do. But if *you* want to give me some money, I wouldn't say no."

"I don't think so. And by the way, I spoke to one of the inn's owners. She told me you were not asked to leave the property. They were willing to let you stay as long as you needed after your tragic loss."

Harry shrugged. "It's time for me to move on."

"That isn't the only lie you told me. Your alibi is unraveling. Amy Schram swears she wasn't with you on Monday night."

"It's really none of your business."

"It is when my sister owns a piece of the Sheer Comfort Inn."

"Ah, now I see why you're trying to mess up my life."

"You did that the day you faked your death and walked away from everything you knew and loved—and especially those who loved you."

He cocked his head to one side and gave her a lascivious grin. "Did you count yourself among them?"

"Don't flatter yourself," she lied.

"What are you going to do now, call your boyfriend and have him come after me?"

"He's probably already after you, Harry. You were just too arrogant to believe it could actually happen."

"I did not kill Pippa."

"Then who did?"

"Maybe it was Clay Ellington. They had a thing for each other all those years ago. Maybe it was that old guy who creeped her out."

"Chauncey Porter?"

He nodded. "For all I know it could've been you or your sister."

"Don't make me laugh. We'd only met her a few minutes before she was killed."

He shrugged. "Go ahead, talk to the cops. They can't touch me because I've got an alibi. And it wasn't Amy."

"I suppose you were having more than one fling." And then

she saw in his face that it was true. "Another one of your students?" she accused.

He laughed. "Hey, it turns out teaching is a very powerful aphrodisiac. Why shouldn't I take advantage of the situation? My wife was as cold a fish as they come."

Or had she been disgusted by her husband to the point of avoiding his touch?

Tricia shook her head. "What did I ever see in the likes of you?"

"The same thing my students do, what many of my readers did. You wanted to be with someone famous. Someone who could do what you couldn't."

"And what was that? Get published?"

Harry nodded.

Tricia had to fight to keep herself from slugging the guy. "Get out of my store."

"I'm hurt. You never even mentioned the little gift I sent."

Tricia's eyes widened.

"I told you we'd meet again."

"That picture was taken years after I was with you."

"I told you, I eventually made it back to the East Coast. You were with some joker eating at a sidewalk bistro in Portland, Maine. I snapped your picture. I mailed it last Saturday when I was in Nashua on an errand for the inn. I'd been carrying it around all these years. I thought maybe we could get together again. I didn't know you'd turned into a bitch."

That was the second time in two days Tricia had been referred to by the *B* word. She didn't like it. Even though he'd been with Amy and some other woman, the rat had still plotted to add her to his stable. She hoped Amy was smart enough to get tested for sexually transmitted diseases. No doubt Pippa had withdrawn her affections once she'd found her husband had no inclination to remain faithful.

"Then why did you disappear when I entered the inn?"

"I'm not stupid. Pippa was my meal ticket. Believe it or not, I didn't go out of my way to make her angry."

Tricia didn't believe it. "And what about the other stuff?"

It was Harry's turn to look puzzled. "What other stuff?"

"The cocktail napkin and the scarf?"

"I don't know what you're talking about." This time, she believed him.

"I gotta go. I'm packed and ready to meet that agent first thing Monday morning. Look for me on the *Times* best sellers list in about eighteen months." He flashed his teeth one last time and sauntered out the door.

"Good riddance," Tricia called after him.

"Gee, you're having a lousy day," Pixie said. Of course she'd been eavesdropping.

"You have no idea," Tricia muttered.

"What was all that talk of murder?"

"It's a long story."

"I've got time to listen," Pixie offered.

Tricia shook her head. "Not tonight. Maybe I'll feel more talkative in the morning."

"Look, the place is dead. Hell, the whole *town* is dead," Pixie said. "Shut the door, go up to your apartment, kick off your shoes, and have a snort. It'll make you feel better."

"That does sound pretty good right now," Tricia admitted.

Pixie bit her lip and looked thoughtful. "I really am sorry about what happened over at the Everett Foundation. The truth is, I was in over my head at that job and I knew it. I thought I was being a good employee, and I screwed up. Mrs. H-E should've just fired me, but she gave me a chance and I blew it. And now you've given me a chance, too. I'll try not to let you down, Tricia."

"Thank you, Pixie. I hope this works out for both of us."

Pixie smiled. "I guess I'd better get going." She grabbed her big brown coat from the chair in the reader's nook where she'd left it, and put it on. "I'll see you tomorrow at ten."

"Have a good night," Tricia said, and walked her to the door.

From her perch behind the register Miss Marple said, "*Yow!*"

"Good night to you, too, Miss Marple," Pixie said, and headed out the door.

Tricia locked it behind her and turned the OPEN sign to CLOSED.

"*Brrrpt?*" Miss Marple inquired. If the store was closing, that meant a kitty snack or even her dinner might be in the offing.

"Not yet," Tricia chided her.

As Tricia closed the blinds, Miss Marple jumped down from her perch. "*Yow!*"

Tricia had intended to go get the vacuum cleaner, but instead she paused to pet her cat. "Who do you think killed Pippa?" she asked.

Miss Marple nuzzled her hand, purring loudly.

"I don't really think it was Harry. He probably *was* with his latest conquest. Apparently he doesn't know that a zipper can stay up as well as go down."

"*Yow!*" Miss Marple agreed, walking back and forth on the counter, letting Tricia pet her from top to tail.

"Clayton Ellington was on the phone—probably having a fight with his wife—for the fifteen or so minutes between the time Ange and I saw Pippa and Sarge and I found her dead."

Miss Marple bristled at Sarge's name.

"And then there's Chauncey. But somebody hit him. Was it to keep him quiet? Do you think he could have seen something and now the killer is out to get him?"

"*Yow!*" Miss Marple agreed.

"That only leaves one person who could have done it."

Mary Fairchild.

But Tricia really couldn't believe Mary was responsible for Pippa's death. What was her motive? Still, what was she doing standing on the landing? She'd held the liqueur glasses, so she might have just been down in the parlor availing herself of the sherry—but she'd been breathless, as though she'd run up the stairs. And she'd been startled when Tricia appeared before her. Had she dumped the candlestick, run back to the inn, grabbed the glasses for her alibi, and hoped someone would see her?

Tricia glanced at the clock. Most of the stores on Main Street closed at six. She still had a few minutes to catch Mary—talk to her about it.

And say what? *Everyone else has been accounted for—did you kill Pippa Comfort?*

"I've got nothing better to do," she told Miss Marple.

"*Yow!*" Miss Marple admonished, but whether it was to ask her to stay or demand an early dinner, Tricia didn't know.

She retrieved her jacket from the back of the shop, grabbed her keys, and headed out the door. "I'll be back in a little while. You're in charge."

"*Yow!*" Miss Marple protested again.

But Tricia didn't listen. One way or another, she was sure she'd learn the truth about Pippa Comfort's death before the day was done.

TWENTY-EIGHT

Like Haven't Got a Clue, By Hook or By Book had no customers this late in the day. Mary sat behind her cash desk, crochet hook and yarn in hand, working on a baby blanket. She looked up as Tricia entered.

"What brings you here?" She looked at the wall clock. "There's still five minutes until your store closes."

"I've given up for the day. I wanted to talk to you about Sunday night at the inn."

Mary cocked her head, looking puzzled. "I don't understand."

"I've been thinking about how strange it was to find you standing on the landing. You looked . . . furtive."

"Furtive?" Mary repeated, and her hands stopped moving.

"Yes, you were also out of breath, as well as being pink-cheeked. Like you'd been outside and had just run up the stairs."

Mary laughed nervously. "I don't know what you're talking about."

"I think you do. And I'm here to encourage you to go talk to Chief Baker."

"About what?" Mary said, growing a little testy.

"I've ruled out everyone else, Mary. It's got to be you who killed Pippa Comfort, although I'm not exactly sure why."

"What are you talking about?" Mary asked, fear entering her eyes.

"You've been very interested in the case. Asking a lot of questions, running around the village looking over your shoulder. And you quit the book club because you said murder made you uneasy. I could understand that, especially if you'd recently committed one and were afraid of getting caught."

Mary shook her head. "You don't know what you're talking about."

"You bribed Bob Kelly to win the raffle for the night's stay at the Sheer Comfort Inn. There's no use denying it; Bob's already admitted you gave him money to announce your name as one of the winners."

Mary's cheeks flushed red, and Tricia thought she might be about to burst into tears.

"I think you should leave right now, Tricia," Mary said, standing. "Please, leave right *now*."

Tricia shook her head. "Not until you tell me everything."

"Why? So you can go to the police?"

"I've already shared everything I know with Chief Baker." Okay, that was a lie. But Mary didn't know that. "It's just a matter of time before he comes to arrest you."

Mary's face crumpled. "Please, Tricia—go home. Now!"

Before Tricia could do more than shake her head, the curtain that covered the doorway to the store's back room parted, and Mary's husband, Luke, stepped into the store. "Is something wrong, dear?" he asked.

Mary shook her head furiously, jumped up from her stool,

and scurried around the cash desk. She grabbed Tricia's arm and began to steer her toward the door. "Tricia was just leaving."

"I don't think so."

Mary stopped dead, and the hairs on the back of Tricia's neck bristled at Luke's tone.

Mary turned to face her husband. "It was just a matter of time, Luke."

A matter of time? Tricia felt confused.

"I will not cover up for you again," Mary declared.

Luke's expression changed from feigned puzzlement to cunning. "A wife can't be made to testify against her husband," he said smugly.

"Who says I'd be coerced?" Mary countered, although her voice wavered.

Luke's eyes widened in anger. "You are my wife and you will do as I tell you . . . or do you want to suffer the consequences?"

Tricia's head was spinning at all this. "What's going on?"

Mary turned to her with anguished eyes. "I can't believe I'm saying this . . . but it could only have been Luke who killed Mrs. Comfort."

"Why?" Tricia asked, stunned.

"He was missing at the time of the murder. I didn't think anything of it when he asked me to lie for him."

"Why did you have to lie?"

"Because I didn't want his children to know."

"Know what?" Tricia demanded.

"That their father had started smoking again."

Confused, Tricia couldn't believe what she'd just heard. "What?"

Tears flooded Mary's eyes. "That's what I thought! When he came back in I smelled cigarettes on his breath. I . . . I never thought. I would never have believed he could have hurt, let alone kill . . ." Her choking words came to a halt.

Luke was silent, his mouth a thin line, his eyes blazing.

Tricia shook her head. "Smoking? Why would he kill Pippa?"

"Oh," Mary cried, frustrated. "It has nothing to do with smoking, and everything to do with who Mrs. Comfort used to be."

"A Playboy bunny?"

"No, the driver who ran my wife down," Luke cried.

Tricia looked from him to Mary, puzzled.

"Not Mary," Luke said testily, "my *first* wife!"

"But I thought you said you and Luke had been married half your lives," Tricia hissed at Mary.

"Yes, but not to each other." She turned back to her husband. "Joanna's death was an accident! She was distraught. She jumped out in front of the car. The police ruled her death a suicide. Even the jury in the civil suit agreed."

Luke kept shaking his head in denial, his expression one of pure hatred. "I never forgot that woman's face."

"But Luke, she didn't mean to hit Joanna. She stepped out in front of the car. It just happened to be poor Pippa who hit her."

"That woman took the best part of my life from me."

Tricia noted Mary's expression change from sympathy to annoyance.

"Haven't I given you at least one minute of pleasure in the fourteen years we've been together?"

Luke turned to her. "I was lonely. I missed my wife. I needed someone to take care of me and my home."

"Is that all I've meant to you?" Mary cried. "A maid and a sexual substitute?"

Luke said nothing, but his expression—lifeless eyes and a slack jaw—said it all.

Tricia wished she were somewhere else. She backed up a step.

Mary's mouth trembled and her voice was shaky when she spoke. "And to think I actually lied to protect you."

"Lied how?" Tricia wondered aloud. "Did you know Pippa was responsible for Joanna's death?"

Mary shook her head. "Not when I first spoke to Chief Baker."

"When did you find out?" Tricia asked in spite of herself.

Mary glared at her husband. "This morning. I found him looking at newspaper clippings. He kept them in a scrapbook. I'd never seen them before today." She shook her head. "That's just sick, Luke. That's really, *really* sick."

"I'm not sick," Luke declared angrily. "It might be sixteen years, but I grieve every day for the loss of my wife—the love of my life."

Mary's anguished expression was painful to witness. "In all the years we've been together—for all the things we've suffered together—didn't it mean *anything* to you?" she tried again.

"When I said 'I do' to Joanna, I meant it forever."

"And when you said it to me—what was that worth?"

Luke wouldn't meet her gaze.

Mary took several gulping breaths, her eyes brimming with tears.

Luke glanced over to Tricia and seemed to realize what her being there—hearing that conversation—meant.

Tricia took another step back.

"You're not going anywhere," Luke said.

"Are you insane? You can't hurt Tricia," Mary said, aghast, and scrambled to step in front of her.

Luke rushed forward, shoving them back and pinning Tricia against the big display window. His arms swung like pistons, aiming for Tricia's face, but Mary did her best to protect her, taking most of the blows herself. Both women were screaming, trying to shield themselves from his furious bashing, when the door burst open.

"What the hell do you think you're doing?" Pixie screamed, and rushed at Luke, who shoved her aside, knocking her into a metal rack filled with knitting patterns. It crashed to the floor, with Pixie following.

"Get out, Pixie, get help!" Tricia hollered, but instead Pixie wriggled out of her big bulky coat and struggled to her feet. She let out a terrible wail and leapt at Luke, her right leg flying high into the air and striking his head with an audible crack, making him stagger into the cash desk.

Pixie was a blur of motion as again and again her legs hit her target—front kicks, side kicks, back kicks—pummeling a quickly punch-drunk Luke, who finally crumpled to the carpet.

"Enough, enough!" Tricia cried, and grabbed Pixie by the arms, hauling her back.

"I was just getting started," Pixie cried, her chest heaving from exertion.

"Do you always attack first and ask questions later?" she tried again.

"Only when I see my boss being beaten. Take that, you bully." Her leg lashed out again but this time missed. She made another lunge, and Tricia had to haul her back to keep her from starting in on Luke once again.

"Whoa—whoa!" Tricia cried.

Mary crouched down to help her husband, taking his bleeding face in her hands. "Luke—are you okay?"

"Better call 911, Tricia," Pixie said, and then seemed to realize that it would mean cops would be arriving. "Holy crap! I think I've just blown my parole."

"No, you haven't. I'm going to make sure the Stoneham police know you saved us from goodness only knows what."

Tricia grabbed the wireless phone on the cash desk and punched in the numbers.

"Aw, crap!" Pixie yelled even louder, looking down at her dress. The old threads on the vintage seams had popped on both sides, leaving her standing in her slip and nylons. "That's the end of this dress."

"I'll buy you a new one," Tricia said.

"But I only wear vintage clothes," Pixie protested.

"Then I'll buy you an old one."

TWENTY-NINE

The Dog-Eared Page wasn't scheduled to open for at least another month, but three of the bar stools were filled and the liquor was flowing on that cold Friday night in early April.

Angelica and Sarge had been first on the scene after the cops showed up at By Hook or By Book, clucking like a mother hen and worrying about her baby sister, when all Tricia wanted to do was to put an ice bag on her eye where one of Luke's punches had connected.

Once all the statements had been given and the suspect had been taken away in handcuffs, Michele Fowler had arrived on the scene, reminding Tricia of her invitation earlier that day to join her at the pub for a drink. She extended the invitation to Angelica and Pixie as well.

It was a regular coffee klatch gathered around the bar, but caffeine wasn't an ingredient in the drinks of choice.

"Can I get you another?" Michele Fowler asked Tricia, who had already finished her second gin and tonic.

"Oh, what the heck," Tricia said, and drained what was primarily ice water from her short, squat glass. She held it against the side of her face, which didn't seem to be swelling too badly.

"And again," said Pixie, and banged her glass down on the old oak bar. She'd already slammed back three drinks. There was no way the woman would be able to drive home that night. Well, Tricia had a pretty comfortable couch. Pixie had saved her from a beating—and possibly worse—so she could crash there. Whether she would be fit to start her first day of work at Haven't Got a Clue the next day was another matter.

"Oh, this is nice and cozy," Angelica said, her gaze taking in the entire tavern, while Sarge snoozed at her feet. He felt completely at ease as well. "I can see we're going to have fun here in the future," she said, and reached for a pretzel from a bowl on the bar.

"I've already got musical entertainment booked through July," Michele said.

The door opened and pink-cheeked Bob Kelly strode through it. "Are you having a dry run tonight?" he asked hopefully, rubbing his hands together presumably to ward off the cold.

His arrival startled Sarge, who jumped to his feet, growling and baring his teeth.

"Down, boy," Angelica gently admonished, and Sarge sat back on his haunches but continued to growl at his quarry. "Sorry, Bob, but this is a private party," Angelica said.

His tone soured. "Yes, I hear Tricia has once again kept Stoneham safe from yet another murderer." He squinted at her in the dim light. "Is that a black eye you're sporting?"

Tricia glared at him. "No."

He returned her glare. "My mistake. Your cop pal came to visit me this afternoon."

"Are you in trouble?" Angelica asked.

"Not now that they've got the killer."

"Too bad," Tricia said.

"I'm sorry, Mr. Kelly, but I can't sell you a drink. I don't yet have a liquor license," Michele said.

"Can't I just sit here at the bar and visit with you ladies?"

"No," Tricia and Angelica chorused.

"Hey, fella—are you dense?" Pixie asked, her words beginning to slur. "Your company is not appre-appre-appreciated."

Bob straightened, taking umbrage at her tone. He looked for help from Angelica and Michele, but the two of them could only shrug.

Michele finished making Tricia another gin and tonic and set it on the bar top.

"You don't want to rile Pixie here. She's a kickboxer," Tricia told Bob.

"Learned it in stir," Pixie said proudly.

"Pixie?" Bob simpered, giving her a once-over with a jaundiced eye.

Pixie staggered a little as she dismounted her stool and rose to her full height—all five foot two or three of it. "Yeah, you got somethin' to shay about it?"

Bob took in Pixie's tattered dress, her torn hose, and her disheveled hair and backed up a step. "You ladies have a nice evening." He left without another word.

No sooner had the door closed when it opened again, admitting Chief Baker, who held a bouquet of pink carnations—the kind sold by the convenience store up by the highway. This time Sarge stood and wagged his tail. "Are you serving liquor without a license?" Baker asked Michele, and reached down to give Sarge's ears a scratch.

She sighed.

Tricia took another sip of her drink. "Oh Grant, give it a rest."

"I'm entertaining a few friends," Michele explained. "I am *not* open for business. And maybe I should just lock that door." She shook her head. "I'd offer you a beer, but someone might say you were on the take. But feel free to help yourself to the pretzels."

"That could still be construed as a bribe," Angelica pointed out.

"Good point. No pretzels for you, either," Michele said, and removed the bowl from the bar.

"These are for you," Baker said, and handed the flowers to Tricia.

"Thank you," she said, and made a show of smelling them—not that they had much of a scent. Had the convenience store been out of roses? And why had he decided to give them to her in front of witnesses—so that she'd feel more forgiving? Should she let him off the hook that easily?

Not a chance.

"To what do I owe the pleasure?"

"A small peace offering."

Tricia glanced askance at Angelica, who frowned.

"You mean now that I've found the killer for you, I'm no longer a suspect and you can be seen speaking with me in public?"

Baker looked startled, like a deer caught in headlights.

"I—I—I . . ."

Tricia sighed, placed the carnations on the bar, and picked up her glass, pressing it to her cheek once more. "So what happened with Luke Fairchild?"

Baker swallowed before answering. "He demanded to see a lawyer and then clammed up. His wife, however, was willing to tell us everything. She's already agreed to testify against him when the time comes."

Tricia shook her head. "He should never have told her he loved his first wife more."

"He told her *that*?" Angelica asked, appalled.

"All men are rats," Pixie slurred, and rattled the ice in her glass, but Michele made no move to make her another drink. Pixie squinted up at Baker. "You're probably a rat, too."

"Shhh! Pixie. Have some respect. He's *supposed to be* Tricia's boyfriend," Angelica grated. She cleared her throat. "There's just one thing I don't understand. Who mugged Chauncey Porter?"

"Angelica," Tricia warned. They had promised they wouldn't say anything about it.

"Luke Fairchild," Baker answered. "Porter closed his shop early and came to see me this afternoon. After your arrival at the inn, he came down to the parlor to have a glass of sherry. He saw Fairchild grab one of the candleholders and slip out of the inn's front door."

"Why didn't he just tell you that from the beginning?" Tricia asked.

"He was angry. He felt humiliated by Mrs. Comfort's disparaging remarks. He might not have said anything if Fairchild hadn't come after him the other night."

"I suspected he was lying when he wouldn't talk about it," Angelica said.

"You knew about the mugging?" Baker asked, annoyed.

Tricia nodded. "But we promised Chauncey we wouldn't say anything."

"Why did Luke come after him?" Angelica asked.

"Fairchild says Porter was trying to blackmail him for money. I've yet to determine if that's true."

"Poor Chauncey," she said.

Considering his dire financial situation, he might have been driven to blackmail, but Tricia didn't want to believe it. If Fairchild could kill without conscience, he could certainly lie, too.

Tricia looked up at Baker.

Tricia stood. "Ladies, I've got a cat who is hours overdue for her dinner." She turned her attention to Pixie. "You're in no condition to drive. You can stay the night on my couch if you like."

Pixie shook her head, then put a hand to her temple—presumably to keep the room from spinning. "You live on the third floor. I can't walk up that many steps when I'm this potted."

"I'll be heading home soon," Michele said. "I'll give her a lift. And I can pick her up tomorrow to go to work at Haven't Got a Clue, too. I have a feeling we're going to become good pals, Pixie." She leaned forward and lowered her voice. "You must tell me where you got that dress. I'm sure it was lovely before you saved the day."

"Yeah, it was a beaut. I can tell you all the best places to get vintage togs."

"I guess I'd better get going, too," Angelica said. She grabbed their coats from the bar stool next to her and passed Tricia's along, then stooped to pick up Sarge. "Thanks for the drinks. Talk to you soon," she told Michele, and headed out the door.

Tricia put on her coat. "I'll second that. Let's do lunch soon," she told Michele, who was already collecting glasses and tidying up the bar.

Tricia picked up her flowers and allowed Baker to walk her across the street to Haven't Got a Clue. She unlocked the door and realized she'd left the lights on hours before. Miss Marple got up from one of the chairs in the reader's nook and scolded her for being away so long, while Baker closed the door behind them.

"Have some cookies. That will hold you while I say good night to Grant," she told the cat, and rounded the beverage station's counter to grab the bowl and bag of snacks she kept for emergency purposes.

"Does Grant *have* to leave?" Baker asked.

Tricia shook out half a bowl of treats and set them on the floor. Miss Marple wasn't kidding about her hunger pangs. She dug in.

"Maybe we should talk about that," Tricia said, resealing the bag of treats and putting them away. "I won't deny it—I was hurt that you could even consider me a suspect in Pippa Comfort's death."

"And I explained more than once that I can't be seen playing favorites. I owe it to the citizens of Stoneham to act above reproach."

"Yeah, yeah, yeah," Tricia muttered, and unfastened her coat. She went to hang it on the peg at the back of the shop, but Baker captured her arm and then drew her into an embrace. "We're finally alone."

Tricia wrapped her arms around him, looking squarely into his eyes. She *had* missed him. And despite what Pixie had said, she didn't think of him as a rat. Well, not a big one, anyway. "Yes, we are."

Baker cocked his head to one side. "Now, please tell me there are no other men in your past likely to surface any time soon."

"Harry was definitely a thing of the past. But the funny thing is, he only took credit for one of the objects that came in the mail."

Baker frowned. "What came in the mail?"

"Oh, trinkets. A picture. A cocktail napkin. A scarf. Harry took credit for only one of them."

"Why don't you tell me all about this over a drink?"

"I think I've reached my limit for the night."

"Then how about a cup of coffee?" he countered.

"I can make coffee. I can make a damn *fine* cup of coffee," she said, and leaned forward to kiss him.

She wrinkled her nose and smiled at him, resting her forehead against his.

The door to Haven't Got a Clue opened and a sandy-haired man stepped into the shop. "Tricia, where have you been?" he asked. "I've been parked on the street for hours waiting for you."

Tricia's heart began to pound as she recognized the man who stood in her doorway. Someone she hadn't seen in more than three years—her ex-husband.

"Christopher?"

ANGELICA'S RECIPES

SAUSAGE AND VEGETABLE STRUDEL

(Makes 2)

3 tablespoons melted butter
3 tablespoons olive oil
10 sheets phyllo pastry
1 cup chopped red or green bell pepper
1 cup sliced mushrooms
1 cup chopped onion
1 pound bulk sausage, browned
½ teaspoon oregano
Sea salt and freshly ground black pepper
1 cup shredded mozzarella cheese
1 egg, beaten

Preheat the oven to 375°F.

Mix the melted butter and olive oil. Brush one side of five of the phyllo pastry sheets with the mixture and stack them on top of each other.

Sauté the bell pepper, mushrooms, and onion with the sausage until the onion is clear, but not browned. Drain the fat and discard. Add oregano, salt, and pepper to taste.

Spread half of the mixture over the surface of the stacked pastry, leaving a 2-inch margin all around. Sprinkle with half of the cheese. Fold the short edges in and roll up from the long side like a jelly roll. Brush the surface with beaten egg and place on a well-greased baking sheet. Repeat the process with the other half of the ingredients to make a second strudel.

Bake 30–40 minutes or until golden brown and crisp. Let stand for a few minutes before slicing.

Serves 4–6

SIMPLY CRACKERS CANDY

> *1 sleeve of saltine crackers (about 35)*
> *2 sticks butter (1 cup)*
> *1 cup packed brown sugar*
> *1 11.5–ounce package chocolate chips**
> *¾ cup chopped walnuts (optional)*

Preheat the oven to 400°F.

Line a baking tray with foil and cover with the saltine crackers. Boil the butter and brown sugar for 3 minutes, until frothy. Pour over the crackers.

Bake 5 minutes. The butter/sugar mixture will bubble. Remove from the oven and sprinkle with the chocolate chips. Let set for 5 minutes. Spread the chocolate with a spatula and sprinkle with nuts, if using. (Gently press the nuts into the chocolate.) Refrigerate at least 1 hour; break into pieces. Refrigerate the leftovers . . . if there are any.

I use milk chocolate chips, but you can vary the recipe with semisweet chocolate and even peanut butter–flavored chips.

CREPES FLAMBÉ À L'ORANGE

1½ cups sifted all-purpose flour
3 eggs
2 cups milk
2 tablespoons melted butter
¼ teaspoon salt
½ teaspoon vanilla extract
2 tablespoons plus 2 teaspoons granulated sugar
½ cup water
½ cup orange marmalade
1 medium orange, cut into thin slices
½ cup Grand Marnier (or any orange liqueur)

Put the sifted flour in a large bowl and make a well at the center. Place the eggs in the center, then beat and mix with the flour.

Slowly add the milk. Mix very well. Add the butter, salt, vanilla, and 2 tablespoons of the sugar. Mix until well blended. The batter will be thin. Set aside and let rest for 30 minutes.

Cook the crepes like pancakes in a flat nonstick pan. Pour ¼ cup of the batter into the pan at a time. Allow each crepe to cook for 1–2 minutes on one side, then use a nonstick spatula to flip the crepe. When the crepes are cooked, roll them into tubes and transfer to a serving dish.

In a small saucepan, mix the water, marmalade, and remaining 2 teaspoons sugar over low heat. Simmer and reduce until you have a thin syrup.

Drizzle the crepes with the syrup. Garnish with orange slices.

In another saucepan, bring the orange liqueur to a quick boil, then light (using a match or butane lighter) to make a flambé. Carefully pour over the crepes while the flames are still active. Allow the flames to burn out before eating.

Serves 4–6

THUMBPRINT COOKIES

1 egg
½ cup butter, softened
¼ cup packed brown sugar
½ teaspoon vanilla extract (almond extract tastes good, too)

1 cup all-purpose flour
¼ cup finely chopped walnuts
⅔ cup any flavor fruit jam (Mr. Everett likes
    raspberry!)
¼ teaspoon salt

Preheat the oven to 300°F. Grease foil-lined baking trays.

Separate the egg, reserving the egg white. Cream the butter, sugar, and egg yolk. Add the vanilla, flour, and salt, mixing well. Shape the dough into 24 1-inch balls. Roll them in the egg white, and then in the walnuts. Place on baking trays about 2 inches apart. Bake 5 minutes.

Remove the cookies from oven. With your thumb, dent each cookie. Put jam in each thumbprint. Bake another 8 minutes.

Makes 24 cookies.

Turn the page for a preview
of Lorna Barrett's
next Booktown Mystery . . .

NOT THE
KILLING TYPE

Available in hardcover
from Berkley Prime Crime!

"Can I freshen up your coffee?" Darlene Boyle, one of the Brookview Inn's waitresses, eagerly asked, brandishing the polished chrome pot over the linen-clad table.

Tricia Miles looked up from her crumb-scattered place setting. "No, thank you," she said and put a hand over her cup, just in case Darlene decided to pour anyway. The truth was she'd had more than enough coffee, but she didn't think she could make a discreet exit for the ladies' room—not with her eagle-eyed sister, Angelica, sitting next to her. But Angelica's attention was focused on the front of the dining room—as it had been during the entire Stoneham Chamber of Commerce breakfast.

Tricia had other company at the table for six—her former assistant, Ginny Wilson; and Michele Fowler, the manager of Stoneham's newest enterprise, the Dog-Eared Page, a cozy pub on Stoneham's Main Street. Still, they'd all run out of polite chitchat, and boredom now reigned. Darlene represented a new conversational victim.

"How's that son of yours?" Tricia asked.

Darlene positively glowed. "Now that he's been nominated by our local congressman, he's just put in the paperwork for the Naval Academy. He refuses to even consider any other college. I don't know what he'll do if he's not accepted."

That seemed unlikely. Mark Boyle was Stoneham High's pride and joy. He'd won every scholastic prize he'd gone after, and scholarship opportunities abounded, much to his single mom's relief. But all seventeen-year-old Mark could ever talk about was the Naval Academy. The kid was motivated to earn what he could toward his schooling. Summers he was employed at the Brookview, lifting, carrying, hauling garbage—whatever needed doing—and Tricia had never seen such a hardworking young man.

"Anybody else want coffee?" Darlene asked, but the others shook their heads and fidgeted in their seats. Smiling, she moved on to the next table, was likewise rebuffed, and retreated to the coffee station at the side of the room to set down the pot and join her colleagues, who were also waiting for the meeting to begin. Or rather, they waited for the meeting to finish so they could ready the room for the inn's lunch crowd. Chubby and cheerful Henry Dawson—a fixture at the Brookview Inn, and nearly as old as Tricia's part-time employee, Mr. Everett—greeted her with a smile, as did Ginny's fiancé, Antonio Barbero, who managed the inn for Nigela Ricita Associates.

The noise level in the room was as high as Tricia had ever heard. The November meeting was always well attended, and this one was no different. She didn't even recognize half the members, many of whom owned businesses that contributed nothing to Stoneham's reputation as a book town. Doctors, dentists, day care centers, a pizza parlor, and more.

Tricia turned back to her tablemates. Angelica sighed, both bored and agitated. "When is he going to make the announcement?" she grated under her breath. The who was Angelica's former beau, Bob Kelly, president of the Stoneham Chamber of Commerce. The what was the annual Chamber election.

"Who knows?" Tricia made to get up, but Angelica's arm swung out to grab her, holding her firmly in her seat.

"You can't miss this."

"You've been saying that for half an hour. Nature is calling, and I must listen," Tricia said, but Angelica didn't let go. Meanwhile, Bob was too busy gabbing, laughing, and generally enjoying himself to move the monthly breakfast meeting along.

"It looks like I'm going to have to make a real show of leadership and take matters into my own hands." Angelica grabbed her water glass and a spoon, stood, and tapped on the glass. It took more than a minute for the noisy room to quiet down, but soon enough every eye was fixed on her. She wasn't hard to look at. Dressed in a black blazer and slacks, white turtleneck, with a necklace of jet beads, she looked authoritative but approachable. Angelica took great care of her skin and applied only as much makeup as was necessary. She'd also recently gone back to a shorter hairstyle and, with freshened highlights, looked younger than her forty-seven years.

Bob Kelly also stood and moved to the lectern, sudden annoyance creasing his brow. "Was there something you wanted to ask?" he inquired tersely. A year before he wouldn't have been so brusque. A year before his relationship with Angelica had been of a romantic nature. That was before he cheated on her. The phrase "hell hath no fury like a woman scorned" certainly applied to Angelica, who'd previously been cheated on by four husbands. And she was about to drop yet another bomb on Bob.

"This is November," Angelica reminded him. "Time for the annual election for Chamber of Commerce president."

All eyes turned toward Bob. He waved her comment aside. "Yes, and I'm very pleased to serve the Chamber for—what is it? The eleventh year now?" He laughed, but nobody in the audience joined him. "Now, did anyone else have a concern?"

"Excuse me, Mr. Kelly," Angelica said, and there was ire in her gaze. The members turned their heads toward her. "But you can't be elected for a twelfth term if we haven't had an opportunity to vote."

Bob laughed. "Yes, of course you're right. Now since I'm running unopposed—"

The heads turned back to Bob. Tricia began to feel like a spectator at a tennis match.

"How do you know you're running unopposed if you haven't opened the floor for nominations?" Angelica asked. Everyone looked back to Bob, who appeared positively shocked at the idea that someone would actually run against him for the job. He had a poor—or was it a selective?—memory. Angelica had told him she intended to do just that some three months before.

"Well, as a formality," he said, backpedaling. "I open the floor for nominations."

Tricia knew her cue when it came. "I nominate Angelica Miles," she said. There was a gasp from those assembled, as all eyes turned to take in the sisters.

"But-but," Bob stammered.

Angelica's smile was positively evil. "Talk about gob-smacked," she muttered.

"I'll second that," Ginny called out. Good old Ginny. Of course, she'd been in on the plan, as well. She'd been Tricia's assistant at her mystery bookstore, Haven't Got a Clue, for over two years until several months before when Ginny had been offered the manager's job at the Happy Domestic, a charming little shop filled with home décor accessories and books pertaining to that same subject.

Out of the corner of her eye, Tricia saw another figure stand. "I'd like to nominate myself, if that's all right."

Tricia, Angelica, and Ginny turned in unison to take in the man. Stan Berry was known around the village as "the sign man." He had a shop in his garage over on Oak Street. He always wore flannel shirts and jeans, and as he rarely ever spoke at Chamber meetings, nominating himself for Chamber president took everyone by surprise.

"I'll second that," said John Marcella, owner of the convenience store up on the highway.

It was Angelica's turn to look gobsmacked. She had figured she could easily defeat Bob, who was not universally loved by the booksellers. He owned most of the real estate on Main Street and, during the past few years, had inflated the price of the leases to the point of forcing some of the merchants out of business.

"Well-well," Bob stammered. If he'd been shocked by one person challenging his iron-fisted control of the Chamber, two absolutely blew him away. He stood there, mouth open — speechless.

"What's the protocol in situations like this?" asked Nikki Brimfield, owner of Stoneham's bakery, the Patisserie.

Everyone looked back at Bob. "Uh . . . we've never had a situation like this," he admitted. "I'll have to consult the Chamber's charter and get back to . . ."

"According to the charter," Angelica said, and all eyes turned back to look at her once again, "the nominees must be given time to state their qualifications for the job before the voting commences."

Tricia clenched her teeth and rubbed her aching neck, hoping the speechmaking wasn't going to turn into long-winded harangues. When he got going, Bob was difficult to silence, and Angelica was just as fond of singing her own praises. Stan was the wild card. Tricia crossed her legs and raised her hand. "Perhaps we could take a short recess before that happens."

"No, let's get it over with," said Alexa Koslov, one half of the married couple who owned the Coffee Bean, the only place in town to get piping-hot espresso and other gourmet coffees. "I've *got* to get back to my shop."

"I'll second that," said Glenn Baker, owner of Baker Funeral Home. "I've got two showings this afternoon."

Bob seemed seized by indecision. Apparently he'd never even given a moment's thought to the idea that he could be replaced as Chamber president before the meeting's end. "Well . . . I guess so. Let's hear from you, Stan."

"Whatever happened to ladies first?" Angelica groused.

Again the audience turned as one as Stan stood once more, this time looking a lot more formidable. "The current leadership of the Chamber of Commerce has been serving our community for more than a decade. In that time it has vastly favored the booksellers, a minority of its members, over the rest of the organization. It's about time that changed. If you vote for me, I'll see that each and every business member has equal representation."

Enthusiastic applause followed. Angelica gave Tricia a worried look. "He still hasn't told us his qualifications," she muttered, channeling some great ventriloquist. She never even moved her lips.

Once the noise had died down, Nikki Brimfield raised her hand. Berry called on her. "That's a great platform, Stan. But have you ever held any kind of leadership role before?"

Stan nodded. "I own my own business. Isn't that leadership enough?"

Nikki frowned, but others in the audience again applauded. Tricia wasn't sure if she could count on Nikki to vote for Angelica. Since she became engaged to Tricia's former lover, Russ Smith, Nikki seemed threatened by Tricia's presence. And although Tricia had been seeing someone else off and on for more than a year, Nikki's jealousy hadn't abated.

Stan hadn't answered Nikki's question. His was a one-man business. Had he ever managed a workforce—or even one employee?

Michele Fowler, manager of Stoneham's newly opened pub, the Dog-Eared Page, raised her hand, but Stan ignored her and instead acknowledged John Marcella.

"What can we hope to see once you're our Chamber president?"

Stan seemed to stand a little taller. "The first thing I'll do is reduce the membership dues—and the mandatory participation in stupid ideas like planting flowers and hanging banners around town."

Tricia's mouth dropped. The tourists— the very people who came to Stoneham, spent money, and had not only revived the near-dying town's economy, but made it possible for businesses like Berry's to flourish—were not only attracted to the pretty village because of the booksellers, but thanks to the very things Berry wanted to eliminate.

His suggestions received a lukewarm response as a number of those in attendance—especially those whose businesses flanked Main Street—looked dubiously at each other. Both Berry's and Marcella's businesses were located off the beaten tourist track, and admittedly, they weren't on the receiving end of such attention-getting devices.

"Do you have anything else to add?" Bob asked gravely.

Again the members' heads swiveled to look at Stan. "Yeah. We'd also stop promoting moronic events like Founders Day. I'm sure everyone can agree that it was a major fiasco!"

Several people gasped at the reference. Back in August, a small plane had crashed into the village's picturesque gazebo, killing the pilot and one of the Chamber members. Naturally, the rest of the planned festivities had immediately been canceled—at great expense to those who'd been participating in the event.

Michele was now frantically waving her hand, trying to gain Berry's attention, but he refused to look in her direction.

"I believe Ms. Fowler has something to say," said Antonio Barbero at the back of the room. Not only was the handsome young man with the lilting Italian accent the manager of the Brookview Inn, but he was a Chamber member *and* Ginny's fiancé.

Stan sat down, but Bob gave Michele the nod to speak. She stood.

"Mr. Berry, what other plans do you have for the Chamber, especially with a slashed budget to work from?" Her pleasant English accent always seemed to encourage people to listen to what she had to say.

Berry didn't bother to stand. "I'll cut the newsletter down to once or twice a year, and make these breakfast meetings quarterly instead of monthly—and in a much cheaper venue," he added with a sidelong glare at Antonio, whose expression darkened. Darlene and Henry turned their gazes to their boss and looked worried.

"But how can we make progress with so little communication?" Michele asked, perturbed.

"You can always call me at my shop. And that's another thing. We can get rid of the Chamber office, which would save us thousands of dollars in rent every year."

"Excuse me, Stan," a testy Bob interrupted. "But I *own* the building the Chamber office is housed in and the yearly rent is exactly twelve dollars. That's one dollar a month."

"Well, then we'll get rid of the utility costs *and* that secretary you hired. She won't have much to do after we downscale the newsletter and cut these meetings by seventy-five percent."

No one commented on these last suggestions, and Michele sat down, looking absolutely horrified.

A slashed budget. Quarterly meetings? A curtailed newsletter? No secretary to take care of the day-to-day operations of the Chamber? Tricia felt as shaken as Michele looked.

"But most of all, it would be clear that there'd be no conflict of interest with some members getting preferential treatment as there is today." At this, Stan turned to stare at Bob.

"I beg your pardon?" Bob demanded.

"Mr. Kelly, you own most of the storefronts on Main Street. Most of the Chamber's resources have been funneled into bolstering the businesses located there. You collect the rents and, I might add, raise them on a frequent basis, which makes it harder for the rest of us to compete."

As far as Tricia knew, Barry wasn't competing for business with anyone else in Stoneham. To whom did he refer?

Before she could ask, Angelica stood and cleared her throat. "If I may speak now, Mr. Kelly," she said, and the look she gave Bob was enough to sear the hair off the top of his head with laser-like precision.

Bob seemed shaken by Berry's accusation and muttered, "Go ahead, Ms. Miles," and he sat down once again.

Angelica stood to her full five-foot-six-inch height—plus two inches for heels—poised and confident. "Ladies and gentlemen of the Stoneham Chamber of Commerce, it's my heartfelt ambition to serve you as your next president. Not only would I build on the work by my erstwhile predecessor, but I'd expand upon it." She leveled her gaze at Berry. "Not only would I increase the floral offerings during the spring, summer, and fall seasons, but I would encourage those businesses not directly on Main Street to do the same."

She took in the group at large. "As I'm sure some of you might remember, Stoneham was in the running for the prettiest village in New England and made the list of finalists. The publicity brought in quite a lot of people to our fair village."

"That was my idea," Bob said, raising a hand to claim ownership.

Angelica ignored the outburst. "Thanks to the opening of several new businesses—the Paige Dialysis Center, the Sheer Comfort Inn, and the Dog-Eared Page, and investment here at the Brookview Inn—we've also seen quite a jump in visitors."

"All done on my watch!" Bob called out.

Angelica frowned and leveled an annoyed glare at Bob. "I believe it's *my* turn to speak, Mr. Kelly."

"Here, here," Michele said, and Tricia and Ginny dutifully applauded.

Bob glowered.

Angelica continued. "Not only would I promote our Chamber and its members, but I would seek out and encourage new development to take place here in Stoneham."

"And just how would you do that?" Marcella asked with a sneer.

"Networking. Both online and in person."

He turned away with a snort of derisive laughter.

Russ Smith, the editor of the *Stoneham Weekly News*, stood. "It doesn't sound like you'd be offering the Chamber any more than its current president is already doing."

Bob beamed with approval at this comment, while Angelica somehow managed to keep her face impassive. Russ had never much cared for Angelica, even during the year or so Tricia had dated him. The feeling was mutual.

"In closing, I want it known that, as Mr. Berry has pointed out, with me in charge, there'd be no conflict of interest. I don't own any real estate on Main Street." With that, she sat down. Polite applause followed.

Russ turned back to face the front of the room, his steno pad and ballpoint pen at the ready. "And what have you got to say for yourself, Bob?"

Bob returned to the lectern, his chest puffed out so that it was straining against his Kelly Realty sports coat. "This conflict of interest accusation is totally baseless. I have no financial interest in any of the businesses on Main Street."

"I beg your pardon, but isn't your real estate office located on Main Street?" Marcella accused.

"Yes, but that has no bearing on the improvements the Chamber has made for the businesses located there."

A rumble of mumbling circled the room. Russ waited until it subsided to speak again. "Do you have anything else to add?"

"I believe my record speaks for itself," Bob asserted, his head held high. "I brought the booksellers to Stoneham. I made this village a destination spot. I deserve the continued respect of my colleagues, and I deserve to remain the head of the Stoneham Chamber of Commerce."

Modestly was not one of Bob's strengths.

Everyone looked at each other in the hushed silence that followed.

An uncomfortable Tricia grabbed the edge of the table and stood. Her bladder was about to burst. "May I make a suggestion? Why don't we recess ten minutes to allow us all to think over all the candidates' platforms, and then we can vote."

"Splendid idea," Michele agreed.

"Ten minutes it is," Bob agreed and banged his gavel against the top of the lectern.

It seemed that quite a few of the Chamber members were in the same predicament as Tricia. Half of those present got up from their seats and made a beeline for the inn's washrooms, which were located just outside the dining room. Tricia moved to join the crowd, but a tap on her shoulder made her turn. It was Ginny.

They moved out of the line of stampeding Chamber members. Ginny leaned in closer to speak. "Stan Berry jumping into the race was sure unexpected."

"You're telling me," Tricia agreed.

"Still, I think Angelica's got a good shot. Bob's long overdue to retire from the job. I know I'm not the only member who'd like to see a breath of fresh air when it comes to leadership. I'm just surprised that the only other viable candidate seems more intent on dismantling rather than enhancing the Chamber's activities."

Tricia tried not to squirm and nodded. "I'm in complete agreement, although I do think Ange could be taking on far too much work. She's already got her café, her bookstore, and her cookbook-writing career. That's already more than I could handle."

Ginny nodded. "Me, too, and I don't even own the store I manage."

Tricia smiled. "You have more important things to worry about right now. Like your wedding next Saturday."

Ginny frowned. "Yeah."

"What's the matter?" Tricia asked, concerned.

Ginny waved a hand in dismissal. "I'll have to tell you later. This isn't the right time."

"You're still planning on marrying Antonio, aren't you?" Tricia asked, a bit panicked. She'd already bought her bridesmaid dress, shoes, and a matching bag, plus a lovely gift for the lucky couple.

"Of course. But things just aren't going the way I'd like. It's Joelle," she said and frowned. The wedding planner hired to take care of the upcoming nuptials. "I saw her outside in the lobby a little while ago. I swear, that woman harasses us more than she helps us. If she's not calling or arriving unannounced to bug me, she's doing the same to Antonio." She glanced at her watch and sighed. "I sure hope we get out of here soon. Brittney's never opened the store by herself before." Brittney Sanders had been working at the Happy Domestic for a little over two months. Ginny had once complained that Tricia hadn't given her enough responsibility—or the keys to Haven't Got a Clue—but now she seemed to feel the same way about her own store. To make matters worse, Brittney would be on her own for the entire weekend of wedding festivities. Ginny and Antonio had decided to delay their honeymoon until after the holidays and had planned a Caribbean cruise for early January.

Ginny peered around Tricia. She turned to see Antonio by the table with the coffee urns, beckoning his bride to be to join him. "Talk to you later," Ginny said and scooted away.

Tricia resumed her course for the ladies' room. There was sure to be a line. Would Bob hold the election before she could return? It might be one way for him to cheat Angelica out of at least one vote.

By the time Tricia made it to the lobby, the line for the restroom was indeed long. She wandered over to the inn's check-in desk where Eleanor McCorvey, the inn's sixty-something receptionist, seemed to be shuffling all the papers around her workstation.

"Lose something?" Tricia asked.

Eleanor didn't look up. "My letter opener. It was here last time I looked."

"When was that?"

"Ten–fifteen minutes ago," Eleanor said and sniffed as she shuffled through a pile of file folders. "I can't have lost it. I've had it for years. It's an antique—brass with a lovely heart on the top. My sister gave it to me for my birthday when I got my first part-time office job at sixteen. She's gone now, so it's kind of precious to me."

Tricia eyed the line to the ladies' room, which was definitely not moving, although no one else had joined the queue.

Eleanor grabbed a tissue from the box on her workspace and blew her nose.

"Are you okay?" Tricia asked, noting Eleanor's red eyes.

"Allergies; someone wearing a lot of perfume walked by earlier."

Could that have been Angelica? She was known to splash on a little too much of the stuff.

Tricia glanced at the line to the restroom, which still wasn't moving. "How're things going with you and Chauncey?"

Eleanor's romance with the owner of the Armchair Tourist had been the big story around Stoneham during the summer months. Chauncey Porter had undergone quite a transformation since he'd lost more than fifty pounds through a new diet and exercise regimen. Since they started dating, Eleanor, too, had lost weight. Tricia often saw the couple walking hand in hand through the village at night.

Eleanor set the files aside and finally turned her full attention to Tricia, smiling shyly, although her eyes looked puffy and her nose was rather red. Was she coming down with a cold? Tricia took a step back, just in case.

"Things are *wonderful*. I'm having the time of my life. We've even talked about going on a cruise next spring, that is if Chauncey can find someone to look after the store for a few days or a week."

"Sounds lovely," Tricia said, biting her lip. Her own situation was getting dire.

"Are you okay, Tricia? You look rather panicked."

"I really, really need to use the ladies' room, but as you can see, there's a line out the door. Is there another bathroom nearby I could use?"

Eleanor looked beyond her to the line of impatient women and then nodded toward the hall in the opposite direction from the restaurant. "There's a unisex handicapped washroom at the end of the corridor."

"Bless you," Tricia said and hurried off. She passed a small meeting room, complete with a table, computer, and a fax machine, set up for business guests to use. Next to it was a door with the universal sign of a wheelchair-bound figure. To be safe, Tricia knocked on the door. "Anyone in there?" She waited several seconds before she tried the door's lever handle. It obligingly moved. "Yes!"

She yanked the door open and, to her horror, found Stan Berry sitting on the toilet. It looked like he'd found Eleanor's letter opener.

It was sticking out of his bloodied chest.